SERENADE WAY

and Other Stories

AMATA ROSE

Wasteland Press
www.wastelandpresss.net
Shelbyville, KY USA

Serenade Way and Other Stories
by Amata Rose

First Printing – April 2011
ISBN: 978-1-60047-564-1

Printed in the U.S.A.

0   1

TABLE OF CONTENTS

SERENADE WAY......3

A MELODY FOR TWO.....97

LUKE........157

Acknowledgments

I owe great gratitude to the following people, without whom these novels would never have reached their current state: Dani Zahoran for her keen insight and belief in me, Karlyn Thayer for her character critiques, Joseph Talamo for psychological perspective and mythological analysis, and Aaron McKee for being a good friend and story-teller.

SERENADE WAY

For Dani

The friend who told me to never let anyone put me in boxes

"In the beginning when the world was young there were a great many thoughts but no such thing as a truth. Man made the truths himself and each truth was a composite of a great many vague thoughts.

Hundreds and hundreds were the truths and they were all beautiful.

And then the people came along. Each as he appeared snatched up one of the truths and some who were quite strong snatched up a dozen of them.

It was the truths that made the people grotesques. The moment one of the people took one of the truths to himself, called it his truth, and tried to live his life by it, he became a grotesque and the truth he embraced became a falsehood."

From *Winesburg, Ohio*
Sherwood Anderson

GALATEA WILLIAMS

Her fists pummeled him, black nails raking flesh. His features contorted and blurred before her wild eyes, and the only thing that mattered was that she KILL him…

She felt hands on her shoulders, shoving her away. As she stumbled backwards she saw Skeeter move in. The light from the hallway haloed the shaggy mess of his dark hair, and the intensity in his eyes sent daggers of energy through her. She had time to think only, *No Skeeter, don't do it…*

Too late. She watched the face erupt in a fountain of blood as their classmate fell back onto the school's linoleum floor. One hit was all it took. The jerk did not get back up.

Skeeter turned and looked at her. Their eyes locked. "You okay, Tea?" he asked.

"What the hell are you trying to do?" She crossed her arms. "Get yourself expelled?"

"He shouldn't have called you that."

A bell rang distantly, and the crowd of students that had gathered for the fight dispersed as heavy adult footsteps thudded down the corridor. Their principal stepped into the ring. She watched the rank energy coiled in Skeeter's muscles relax, his shoulders slouch, his head drop.

"All right, I'm going," he mumbled.

She watched Skeeter progress down the hall with the principal until she could no longer see him. Her hands balled into fists in the pockets of his leather jacket. *She could have taken care of the jerk herself; she hadn't asked Skeeter to be her hero.*

But Skeeter was her protector, and she knew he would never relinquish that role for as long as they both lived. And she didn't want him to. Skeeter was the only hope, the only person she would ever trust, the only thing keeping her from going over the edge…

As far as she was concerned, everyone else could go to hell.

SKEETER DELUCA

He saw Galatea as soon as he stepped out of the school.

"Hey, Skeeter," she called.

Flipping up the gray hood of his sweatshirt, he walked across the rain-drenched parking lot towards her. "You're soaked."

She shrugged and snubbed her cigarette on the wet black asphalt, then hurried to keep pace with him.

"Couldn't you have picked a nicer day to get in a fight?" he asked.

She frowned. "I was doing fine by myself. Why'd you take over?"

"I saw the look in your eyes. You wouldn't have stopped." He didn't slow down for her, though he knew she was struggling to keep up. "That would have been jail time, Tea. Not just expulsion."

Her jaw set. She looked at the ground. "Did he expel you?"

"No. Just a pep talk, to get my act together. And I'm suspended."

She risked a glance at him. "How long?"

"Three days."

She relaxed. "You didn't have to hit him that hard to have knocked him out."

1

"You know the rules of the street," he reminded her. "Your first punch always has to be your best." Then, without transition, "How are things now?"

"Come on, I don't want to talk about it."

"Are you with your mom now?" he pressed.

"Yeah," she said, moving slightly away from him. "You want a smoke?"

"No." He stopped walking. "When are you going to face what happened?"

"I've already--"

"No, you haven't. You haven't been the same since—"

"Fuck, you don't get it!" She exploded. "I can't just forget what he did. I can't just move on. It's not that simple."

"I'm not saying it's simple." He wouldn't be intimidated by her anger. "But you have to at least *try* to get a grip--"

"Why the hell do you think I go to the tunnels at night?"

"The tunnels?" He snorted. "That's how you're choosing to fight this?"

She lit up. Her voice was as steady as she could make it. "At least I'm doing something. What about you? Is trying to get yourself expelled getting you any closer to going to college?"

"I'm not going to college," he said. "I'm going to the Marines. That's what I want to do."

"Bullshit."

He grabbed her arm. "Don't swear at me."

"Don't lie to me." She shook herself free. "And don't act like I'm fading away or something. I'm still creating—"

"Spray painting abandoned tunnels. Yeah, Tea, like that will make an impact on anyone."

"Who said I'm trying to make an impact?" She stuck her hands in the pocket of her hoodie and strode away from him. "You're way off base. Why the hell would I want to be seen in a world that condemns people like you and alienates people like me? No way. I'll keep to the shadows, thank you."

"Like a ghost," he said. "You'd rather be a ghost than a person."

She spun around. "Just because I like the cemetery--"

"That's not what I mean," he said. "Think about it. Ghosts can't reach out and touch anyone. Ghosts can't make any difference in the lives of the living. Ghosts can't even let themselves feel—"

"You want to talk about ghosts?" Her eyes narrowed; her voice was deathly quiet. "Let's go back to the days before the trial—"

"Tea—"

"Do you remember what I was like then? Do you remember what an empty shell I was?" Her voice rose, then broke. "Do you want to know how close I came to becoming a *real* ghost--"

"No," he said. "No. You've come a long way since then. I'm sorry I brought it up."

She took a deep breath. "I am trying."

"Okay. Don't get upset."

"I'm all right." She tossed the cigarette away. "Just don't call me a ghost, okay?"

"Okay."

2

She fell back into step with him. He watched as she tried to get her emotions back under control. Finally, she said, "Thanks for beating the shit out of him for me."

His hood fell back, and he let the rain sting his face. He had disturbed her more than he had meant to; he hadn't expected her pain to still be so raw. She had been so strong; he couldn't stand how she was letting herself be so shackled. But now, apparently, was not the time to challenge her. "You know what I don't understand?"

"What?" She waited, watching him.

"I could tell he was proud of me for what I did." He sensed her relax with the change of subject. "Even while he was preaching about not letting guys like Kruger get to me, I could tell he was proud that I had fought him for saying that to you."

She scowled. "Why do you care if he's proud of you?"

"I didn't say I cared. It's just that sometimes… sometimes it's hard to know if I'm doing the right thing."

"It probably doesn't help that I was the one you were defending."

"Don't say that."

"Even if he hates me, he's probably rooting for you, same as everyone else," she continued. "Given what he knows about your family—"

"My family has nothing to do with the choices I make."

"I know that," she said.

He knew she was trying to make eye contact with him. She was always telling him how much she loved his eyes—how they were like black velvet. He purposefully avoided her searching stare. "Where were you going now?"

"Scavenger hunting. For my new place."

He glanced at her just long enough to see the mischievous smile that flickered over her full lips. "I thought you'd given up that idea."

"I never give up on an idea," she replied. "Besides, I found the perfect room. Dry, rat free." She glanced at him. "You should come over for a while."

"Sorry," he said. "Can't."

"Why?"

"Have to see Fink."

She frowned. "Can't you see him later?"

"No."

She crossed her arms, shielding herself from the cold. "Is this because you missed rugby practice?"

He nodded.

"Well," she said. "Have fun."

"I'll walk you to the warehouse first," he said.

"You don't have to."

"I want to."

They walked in silence. He loved that that silence wasn't awkward, and how when he was with her nothing else seemed to matter. He didn't even mind the numbing rain or how the needle-like droplets stung his face raw. And as always, she seemed lost in her own thoughts.

Shadows slithered through the dusk as they crossed the set of railroad tracks and moved to the abandoned factory buildings adjacent to the trailer park. She turned to a low-lying box of a building, its sheath-like metal walls scarred with graffiti.

"This?" he asked, trying not to appear concerned.

"All the windows are cemented in place, and you can't hear the wind or feel the rain." She arched her eyebrows. "Inside."

He ignored her blatant invitation. "How do you get in?"

"I had to scale the roof. Just once," she added, watching him crane his neck. "I installed a padlock. We can get in through the front."

He followed her-- memorizing the combination her quick fingers revealed-- then stepped inside the building. He glanced around. "It's going to get cold in here in winter, Tea."

"I'll think about that later," she said. "It's only October."

He ducked out of the building. "Well, I have to get going."

"Skeeter." She paused, lingering in the doorway. "I found another tunnel."

He tensed. "Where?"

"At the end of the tracks," she said. "Not too far from here."

She was challenging him, daring him to bring up their previous conversation. But not because she wanted to talk about it; she just wanted drama. He didn't have time for drama today. After a pause, he said, "Spray paint can be a weapon. If you aim for the eyes--"

"Nothing's going to happen." Her voice was flat.

He dug his hands into the pockets of his windbreaker. "I don't like you coming out here. Not by yourself."

"I always head through Cemetery Lane," she said softly. "No one has ever followed me."

"That doesn't mean someone won't, some day."

"What are you thinking right now?" she asked. "I mean, what are you really thinking about?"

"You won't like it."

"Tell me."

"I'm thinking…" He paused. "I'm thinking your personal demons are too powerful for you to find happiness in life. And I'm wondering what will help you. Because I really can't stand how much you hate yourself."

She started to say something, then bit her lip. She started walking away from him, down the tracks, without a word.

He caught up with her, stopped her. "If you insist on going—"

She turned to face him. "I'm going.

He willed himself to stay patient. "Do you remember what I showed you? With the—"

She pulled the knife from her pocket and flicked the blade open. *Flick of the wrist, drive upward, a wrenching turn to inflict maximum pain.* Exactly like he had showed her. She sheathed the blade and shrugged. "I'll do whatever I have to do."

"I'd prefer for you to be careful," he said.

"Thanks for walking me here." She tried to move past him. He continued to block her exit.

"The dump's a half mile away from here," he said. "Can't you go scavenger hunting some other time?"

4

Her lips curled. "Plenty of daylight left. The sooner you let me go, the sooner I'll be able to get back." She laughed. "Don't look so serious. I'm not asking you to come with me, and I'll be back before dark. Promise."

He let her go. "I'll come by later tonight to make sure you're all right."

"You don't have to," she said, but he heard the happiness in her voice that she tried to mask. "Get going."

Now he lingered. "Don't let anything happen to yourself."

Her features went slack. "I won't."

He turned. The sinking sun showed him more time had passed than he had thought—but that happened frequently when he was alone with her. He pulled up his hood and started out into the rain.

DEAN FINK

Dean Fink stood inside his warm, brightly lit house, staring out into the rain-bleared street. He frowned, arms crossed. "Where were you today, Skeet?"

"Detention."

"Why?" he asked, then gave him a knowing look. "What's her name?"

"Fink—"

He shook his head and stepped aside. "Never mind. Come on in."

He led the way into the living room and sank onto the sofa near the cheerfully crackling fire. He glanced at his six-foot-three friend, standing awkwardly by the fireplace grating. "She must be something, if standing up for her was more important than coming to rugby practice."

Skeeter stared at the flames. "Sorry."

"We need you on the team, Skeet." He sighed, dropped his feet. "You can sit."

"Wouldn't want to ruin your mother's cushions."

He glanced over his soaked clothes, then shrugged. "It's just water. Besides, Mother wouldn't mind. You know she loves you."

"You know I always train on my own, Fink. When I can't—"

He decided to make Skeeter uncomfortable, for just a little longer, with the hope that discomfort would help him make better choices in the future. "That's not the point. The point is that if you continue to perpetuate this behavior, you will most likely get yourself expelled. And then where will the team be?"

"It's my temper," he said. "I can't control it."

"It's not like you to lose your head over a girl." He frowned. "Really, Skeet, why can't you just play by the rules until the season ends?"

"I never broke a rule."

"I contest that," he protested. "I can count at least five incidences from the start of last month..."

Skeeter looked over his shoulder, cocked an eyebrow. "That's not what I meant."

"What do you mean?" he asked testily. "You can't follow some rules and bypass others."

"I don't mean to break society's rules, Fink. They're just in conflict with my own most of the time."

He snorted. "That's wonderful. If everyone followed their own rules, we'd have massive anarchy. That must be convenient for you, though."

5

"It's not."

He started to reply, but a knock sounded on the door of the living room. Fink jerked; Skeeter turned.

"Hi, Mrs. Fink," Skeeter said.

Mrs. Fink beamed. "Why, Skeeter, how lovely to see you." She was a pretty, petite woman, middle aged, her strawberry blond hair always curled to perfection. She smiled timidly at them. "Dean, I'm so sorry to interrupt, but your father just called and said he won't be home until later tonight…"

As if on cue, he turned. "Skeet? You want to stay for dinner?"

"Thanks, but I should go home."

"You know we hate wasting food, Skeeter," Mrs. Fink said gently. "And I've already set a third place."

"Thanks, Mrs. Fink, but I should go." He paused. "I just want to apologize again for missing rugby practice. I'll be there tomorrow."

"Don't worry about it, Skeet," Fink said, grudgingly.

"Can we at least give you a ride home?" Mrs. Fink asked.

"Thanks, I appreciate the offer, but I'll walk."

Fink reclined on the living room sofa, listening to the front door close. He heard his mother sigh and felt a flash of irritation.

"That boy," Mrs. Fink said. "He reminds me of your father in so many ways."

"Skeeter?" Fink asked. "You don't know Skeet very well, Mom."

"Well, let's go eat dinner," she said abruptly. "I don't want it to get cold."

He ate hurriedly, and only realized halfway through the meal that she had not eaten anything. He put his fork down. "You don't need to worry about Dad."

"I'm not worried about your father." She smiled, but the corners of her mouth sagged. "I'm very proud of how dedicated your father is to his practice."

"But?" he prompted.

"But…" She hesitated. "Sometimes I'm afraid that dedication comes at the expense of being a good father for you."

He glared. "Dad's a wonderful father. You know I want to be just like him."

"You want to be a lawyer, Dean?"

He nodded curtly.

She began to push around some of the food on her plate. "Has Skeeter decided what he wants to do after high school?"

"I don't know," he said, annoyed. "I suppose he'll join the military."

"The military?"

"Skeeter would never be able to hold down a nine to five job."

"I thought he worked as a line cook after school."

He shrugged. "On the days he doesn't have detention."

"What about college?" his mother pressed, concerned.

"Skeet's not much of an intellectual, Mom. Besides, he'll enjoy the military."

"I still can't imagine Skeeter killing anyone. He has too much heart to--"

"Skeeter will do what he has to do." He pushed away his plate. "And if you didn't know, Skeeter has been in more fights than probably the rest of our school—combined."

She sighed. "I just wonder where Skeeter would be now if he had been born to a different family—"

"Skeeter wants to join the military," he said, growing increasingly irritated.

"Does he know he's always welcome here?" she asked. "If he ever wants a warm meal, or a place to—"

"He knows." He stood, pushed his chair away from the table.

She looked startled. "Are you finished already, Dean?"

"I have homework to do. And I don't understand my English homework, so I have to call someone."

"That reminds me," she said. "Nikki Dietrich called today."

He turned. "She did?"

"She asked if you had picked up her school work."

"Right," he said, fighting his disappointment. "I told her I would do that."

"It's not like Nikki to miss school, is it?" She asked. She folded her napkin in half.

"No, it's not. Can I borrow the car?"

"You have to be home by eleven," she reminded.

"I know." Receiving permission, he grabbed the keys to the Mitsubishi and headed out. He had to pass through Cemetery Lane to get to Serenade Way, where Nikki lived, and he cringed as he angled the car into the narrow, cracked entrance of the old cemetery. Late September in Pennsylvania inflamed the tall oaks lining the rows of graves, leaving only a few of the leaves a mottled green. Despite the autumn beauty, Fink hated the old cemetery. He would have driven faster had he not feared the damage that speed on the uneven roads would do to his car. Every time the Mitsubishi shuddered over one of the brick swells or potholes in the pathway, he felt a flash of fear that the car would die, and that he would have to get out and walk through the cemetery. But he passed onto Serenade Way without incident, and felt only relief to leave the cemetery behind.

NIKKI DIETRICH

Her mother had given her the phone half an hour ago. That meant that Dean should be at her house any moment. She sat in the foyer—the room closest to the door—and pretended to read the novel she was supposed to read for their history class: *The Great Gatsby*. It was supposed to be a classic and a very powerful book, but she found herself increasingly distracted as the minutes ticked by.

Four minutes later, she opened the door on his first knock. "Hello, Dean."

"Hi, Nikki." He smiled at her, his eyes appraising. "I like your hair that way."

She tugged on the chestnut curl that fell in a loose ringlet over her shoulder. She usually straightened her hair, but she hadn't gone to school and she hadn't exactly expected him to show up like he said he would.

"Thank you," she said. "It's good to see you."

He started to reply when a shadow moved towards them across the threshold. She watched Dean tense as he found himself confronted by the bulk of her father. Her heart sank.

"Hello, Mr. Dietrich," Dean said politely.

She turned immediately, and tried not to smile as she saw her father cross his arms over his chest in typical Daddy protection posture. "Daddy, you remember Dean, don't you? He gave that lovely speech for the new inductees of the honors society last year."

Her father said nothing.

"He's come to give me the work I missed from today," she explained. "So he has to come inside. Come on inside, Dean. Daddy, be civil."

Her father fixed an icy stare on Dean Fink before he walked away without saying a single word. Feeling bold—maybe because he seemed so uncertain—she put her hand on his arm and pulled him into the foyer. He came willingly, and she sensed that he was relieved when they were alone together.

"Are you getting ready for the holidays already?" he asked.

She followed his gaze to the red and green garlands weaving up the stairs' banister. She forced a smile. "We thought we'd decorate early this year. Come on into the living room where it's more comfortable."

He followed her into the next room, then sat down across from her. "Your father doesn't seem to like me much."

She smiled and tried not to seem too desperate to convince him otherwise. Dean was smart; he was always thinking, that's what she loved about him, and he would be able to see through a lie in a second. Still, she was glad her father had left them alone; her father had scared off everyone who was interested in her, and she hadn't cared because none of those boys had been Dean. But now, with him sitting across from her—everything was different. "It's nothing personal. Daddy just doesn't want me to get hurt." She frowned. "Even though he believes, like I do, that life involves necessary pain, and that sometimes getting hurt can teach people the most meaningful lessons of their lives."

"That's one of the things I like about you," he said. "I like that we can have a conversation like this."

She looked at him. "Like what?"

He smiled. "About something other than the weather, or shopping, or... how beautiful you look tonight."

"Thank you." Embarrassed, she looked away and felt him watch the blush creep into her cheeks. She said, as more of a distraction than anything else, "Can you explain what I missed in science? I should be able to handle the rest of the work, but science was always difficult for me."

"Sure." As intended, he dropped his beautiful blue eyes and sorted through the neat pile of papers in his backpack. "So why did you miss school? Is everything okay?"

"No," she said.

The nonchalance of his manner dropped away instantly. His eyes, startled, flew to meet hers. "What's going on?"

She took a random paper from him. "I don't want to talk about it."

"But—"

"Science," she said.

He took the paper from her and substituted the correct worksheet. "We're going over oxidation reactions. McCafferty did a demonstration today, which she expects us to replicate tomorrow. I could try to explain the experiment to you, but the process would make more sense if you could observe the products." He moved closer to her. "The lab report isn't due until next week, and I have all the necessary materials at my house. If you wanted to come over some time—"

"That's a very kind offer," she said. "That would be a nice change of pace for me."

"Maybe I could give you a call sometime this weekend?" he said. "So we can set something up?"

She smiled. "That would be nice. Do you have my phone number?"

He was quiet for a minute, watching her with an intensity that made her heart quiver, his eyes keen and bright like he was thinking about something, and then he said, "No."

She picked up a pen from the table before them. She picked up his hand and forced the palm open. She scarred the numbers into his palm with ink, then closed his fist. "Don't forget it, okay?"

"I won't."

He was so close to her. So, so close to her, and so warm. She felt a moment of indecision, then she smiled and stood. "Thanks for coming over tonight. I'll see in you in school tomorrow, okay?"

He was still watching her. "Okay. Let me know if you need anything else. Feel free to call me tonight, any time."

Her father was waiting in the hallway. She cleared her throat as she led Dean to the door and said a quick good night. She closed the door and turned.

"That boy is trying to get in your pants, Nikki," her father mumbled.

She blushed. "Oh, Daddy. Dean isn't like that. You think everyone is--" She broke off and said pointedly. "I'm going to go do my homework. The homework Dean brought over for me."

But when she got to the living room, she went and watched from the window. As soon as his car pulled away, she let the heavy drapes fall back into place. She wished she could tell him—everything—but she wasn't sure that he would understand.

Though Dean Fink would be the first person she would want to tell. He was always so kind to her, always asked how she was doing and seemed genuinely interested in her answers—and they had grown up together. She had grown up with her mother's constant hints that she and Dean would make the perfect couple. Dean was going places, her mother said, and it was important that Nikki find a real man...

She felt herself blushing, and suddenly she was angry with herself. She shouldn't be having these thoughts, not when her father was dying.

But the thought of that—the thought of her father dying—was what had directed her thoughts in the first place. She felt so weak and helpless, when she had always felt so sure of herself and strong—and maybe she sensed that Dean Fink would be willing to help her pick up the pieces of her life. After. But she wasn't able to talk to him—or anyone—about it. Not yet.

She had to wait, and hopefully Dean Fink would still be there when the time came.

DEAN FINK

He had her number memorized as soon as she wrote the digits on his hand, but felt it burned into his palm where the pen had scratched it. He had been after Nikki for years, and this was the first opening she had given him...

Yet she had seemed distracted.

Fear replaced his contemplations as he headed back through Cemetery Lane. He disliked the old cemetery even worse at dusk. The sliver of moon in the darkening sky cast flickering shadows over the cracked gravestones. The movement made him feel like ghosts were roaming through the desolate aisles.

"Goddamn creepy place," he muttered, risking a glance down one of the lanes. Then he saw her.

She was sitting on the old well in the middle of the cemetery. She sat carelessly, one leg draped over the well's edge, the other tucked under her. She was barefoot, and she was sketching.

He could see the tendrils of her cigarette smoke near her, but he could not see her face. Her features were obscured by the wildness of her dark hair—streaked neon blue—that trailed past her waist in thick, tangled waves. He glanced at the darkening sky, then against his better judgment guided the car down the aisle and rolled down his window.

"Hey," he called to the strange young woman. "Do you need a ride somewhere?"

She jerked her head up, and the hatred in her eyes made him go numb. Without a word she snapped her sketchbook shut and hopped off the well. A moment later she had disappeared into the shadows, leaving only the smoking ember of her cigarette glowing dimly in the grass.

The way she had looked at him made him doubt his own intentions in offering her a ride, and he felt a wave of guilt. The intensity of the feeling disturbed him; he hadn't meant any harm. Darkness was falling, and the cemetery wasn't an extremely safe place...

Then anger fused through him. She had no right to make him feel that way—dirty—when he had sincerely offered to help her. He felt tempted to drive through the aisles until he found her and could confront her...

The car hit a pothole and jarred him from his thoughts. He could almost feel the damage to his car.

"Jesus," he muttered, and veered back onto the smoother part of the ill-paved road. He glanced in the direction the young woman had retreated, then tried to dismiss her from his thoughts. He willed himself to think instead about Nikki Dietrich—Nikki, the promise at the other end of Cemetery Lane.

SKEETER DELUCA

He crossed the railroad tracks and scanned the abandoned buildings before he sidled over to the warehouse she had chosen. He tapped out a quick succession of beats on the metal door, then waited. The door scraped open, and she ushered him inside.

"Damn cold day," he said, his breath visible in front of him, even though he was inside the metal walls. "Not much warmer in here, either."

"Wait until you see my room," she responded.

"Did you finish it?"

She nodded. He followed her to a ladder inside the warehouse and climbed into a loft. She held open the thick blanket she had hung over the doorframe.

"Don't you think that makes it a little obvious that you're staying in this room?" he asked.

"Please, Skeeter. You can't see the blanket from the outside. And no one but you is even aware that I'm here." She paused, finished. "But you can come any time you want."

"I don't like that I've come two days in a row," he said. "If someone was watching—"

"You worry too much," she said, ducking past him. "Come see what I've done."

He walked around the tiny concrete enclosure, examining the Spartan additions she had made: a scratched up desk in one corner, a beat up mattress with a patchwork quilt in the other corner. But what caught his attention were the candles—and the glass bottles that caught the candlelight and danced splintered rainbow fragments around the walls.

"How long did it take?" he asked.

She shrugged.

"It looks great."

"Thanks, Skeeter."

"I brought something for you." He hesitated, then handed her a round wad of newspaper. "Happy house-warming."

She unwrapped the paper gently. Surprise flashed across her features. "Are you serious?" She laughed. "Where on earth did you get this?"

He looked at the tiny crimson Buddha nestled in her hands. "I kind of collect them."

"You collect Buddhas." She placed the figurine on the palm of her hand and turned it, so that the glass Buddha looked lit from within. "That doesn't surprise me."

"Do you like it?" he asked, feeling stupid.

"I love him. And I know exactly where to put him." She crossed the room and cached the Buddha in front of a red taper candle and a shrine of multi-colored glass, then sat back on her heels and observed the effect. Her eyes glistened. "Thank you."

He met her eyes and felt something happen. He couldn't tell what it was, but the next moment he saw her frown and cross her arms over her chest.

"I wasn't expecting you tonight," she said. "I'm surprised you'd come see me after visiting your precious Fink."

"What do you have against Fink?" he asked. "He doesn't even know you exist."

She looked away from him, but not before he had seen her sneer. "Let's talk about something else, Skeeter."

"You brought it up," he said. "But I have to go."

She turned quickly. "Where are you going?"

"The school."

She stared at him. "You're going back to the school when you don't have to be there?"

He shrugged. "There's a concert tonight. I want to check it out."

"You're going to a concert." Her eyes searched his face. "Do you want me to come with you?"

"No."

"Well, be careful." Her voice was rough. "Don't get into any more trouble. And thanks for stopping by."

He hesitated. She wasn't looking at him, so he looked away. "Goodnight, Tea."

She didn't respond. Silently, he turned and went down the loft's ladder. He didn't feel right leaving her there alone—but the place was her choice. He respected her, so he would have to respect her decision. And he knew, very well, that she could take care of herself.

But he still didn't like leaving her alone. And he wondered if she really liked the Buddha.

NIKKI DIETRICH

From her vantage point on the top riser of the stage, she could see all the people in front of her. She scanned the faces quickly—once, twice. She bit her lip to hide her disappointment that he wasn't there.

She hadn't expected Dean Fink to come to her concert; after all, she hadn't told him she was performing. But a part of her had wanted him to find out on his own and come. She glanced down at the music score in front of her, then back at the audience. Her heart stopped.

Was that Skeeter DeLuca? She stared, then dropped her attention back to the score before sneaking another look in his direction. He was standing in the shadows of the auditorium, and he was staring at her. At least, she thought he was—but she was confused by his expression. He was looking at her—and listening to the music—with a look of rapture on his face. She didn't look in his direction again, but she found that dismissing him from her thoughts was nearly impossible.

As soon as the last bars of the encore faded away, she left the risers and started threading her way through the crowd. She smiled at the people who congratulated her on her performance—but all she wanted to do was get away. In her distraction and hurry to avoid him, she bumped directly into Skeeter DeLuca.

"Oh, hi, Skeeter." She stumbled back and knew she was blushing horribly.

"Hey, Nikki." His hands buried in the pockets of his slate gray hoodie, he kept his distance from her. "You did a really great job up there."

"Thanks," she said. "Wow, it's really great that you could come out."

He smiled, and she felt herself blush harder. He was just so big, and so-- much of a man. And he had such a reputation...

"I have to go," she apologized. "I have a lot of homework tonight that's going to take a while. Especially that poetry assignment. Poems are just so hard to write."

His eyes remained on her face. "Do you have any leads?"

"Leads? Oh, I have no idea yet," she stuttered. "I guess we'll find out tomorrow?"

"Good luck," he said. "See you."

She felt him watch her as she sped to her mother. Maybe there was something about Skeeter that she just wasn't seeing. He was Dean Fink's best friend, and that meant he had to have some redeeming quality...

And he had come to her concert.

She would try not to judge him so harshly.

DEAN FINK

He looked up at Nikki, surprised that she had come directly to his desk when she was already late for class. She should know he wouldn't be able to talk to her right then. But their teacher was still bustling around, and the desperate gleam in Nikki's eyes concerned him.

"Can I talk to you after school today?" She whispered.

He calculated quickly; it was Friday, and the rugby team never practiced on Friday. "Sure," he said, trying not to sound surprised. "What did you have in mind?"

"Well, I was actually wondering…" She glanced over her shoulder at their teacher. "I was wondering if you wanted to come to my youth group with me. At the church? We could walk there right after school today."

"Isn't that at least a couple of miles?" he asked. "Won't you get tired?"

She shook her head. "I run six miles a day, Dean."

"I'll see you after school then," he said, processing this information.

Their teacher called for attention. Nikki slipped into her seat, then dutifully raised her hand when their teacher asked for a volunteer to read the week's poetry assignment.

Dean watched her walk to the front of the room, taking in every small gesture: the way she brushed away a strand of silky hair that fell across the delicate arch of her eyebrow, the way her lips rounded around her words as she read, the way she stood tall and still while she read. He spent most of her poem wondering what she wanted to talk to him about, and caught only the last couple of lines.

"…when I was younger, I believed I could do anything and the world would follow me. Now I am older, I'm certain my life is meant for great things."

The students clapped as Nikki made her way to her seat, and then the door opened. As all eyes turned to the door, a young woman slouched in.

"Hey," she said into the sudden silence, her backpack slung off one shoulder. "I got transferred from Dorman's class."

The teacher looked over her green-rimmed glasses. "Mr. Dorman's class?"

"Yeah. Sexual harassment problem with one of the other students. He wouldn't stop—"

"Thank you, I'm sure we don't need the details," the teacher said sharply. "We are all aware of last week's disruption, Miss Williams."

The young woman shrugged. Her nails were painted black and matched the grungy miniskirt she wore over ripped black tights and bulky combat boots. Her long brown hair –streaked blue-- was knotted on top of her head and held in place with pencils. A large amulet shaped like the world dangled from a hemp cord around her neck.

Fink sat like a statue, his heart beating unnaturally fast. He recognized her instantly as the young woman he had seen at the cemetery at night. He felt another wave of rancor curdle through him. Just looking at her, raking his eyes over her, was like hurtling himself into a void…

"Take a seat, Galatea," the teacher said.

The young woman surveyed the room. Their eyes locked. She flicked her hair over her shoulder, and he smiled tensely. The hate burned more darkly in his heart as she slinked to the seat in front of him and dropped her backpack with a thud.

"We're in the middle of a poetry unit," the teacher said. "You'll have to make up—"

"I already did the assignment," Galatea said. "Skeeter told me the guidelines, so I--"

The classroom became unnaturally quiet. Galatea became aware of the changed atmosphere and trailed off. Fink glanced at Skeeter, but he was looking down at his desk with intense focus.

"Joseph told you the guidelines? " the teacher said into the sudden silence. "How convenient. Now I know he knew about the assignment. So no excuses, Joseph. You're up next."

Skeeter, his face bright red, slouched his way to the front of the room. Once there, he stared at his feet and straightened his paper, then mumbled indistinctly.

"If I can't hear you the first time around," the teacher interrupted, "I'll make you read the poem again."

Skeeter stood straighter. The class waited.

Fink hadn't expected to see her again—but here she was, a part of his school. She reeked of cigarette smoke and incense and outdoor air, a scent that clung to her like a thick, exotic perfume. And her hair-- he wondered if she ever brushed the tangled mane. He wanted to wrap his hands through that hair…

"I'm sorry," Skeeter said. "I can't do this."

Fink noticed the subtle shift in her back—the tensing of shoulders, the slight dip of her head. He glanced up as Skeeter walked back to his seat and realized he had been completely unaware of what had been going on in the class. The bell rang, jarring him further from his thoughts.

"Joseph, please wait for a moment after class," the teacher said. "Otherwise, class dismissed."

As the other students filed out of the room, Fink continued to watch Galatea. The way her body curved to the left indicated that she wanted to talk to Skeeter. But Skeeter was walking slowly to the front of the room. Fink followed the shifting movement of her head, the direction of her gaze, and he realized that she had decided, instead, to talk to Nikki. He stuffed his books into his backpack and cut a direct path to Nikki Dietrich.

He noticed Galatea glanced at them once before she slung her backpack over her shoulder and left. He turned to see if Nikki had realized the dynamic that had passed between them, and found her lost in a reverie. She smiled at him, but her thoughts seemed elsewhere; her books and papers remained scattered on her desk, though the final bell had sounded over a minute ago.

"Ready to go?" he asked.

She looked confused for a moment, then nodded and started to pack up her books. "Don't forget your paper, Dean."

He turned and noticed a single piece of folded paper under his desk. He left Nikki and retrieved the note, then stuffed the paper hastily into his backpack. He walked with her out of the classroom, scanning the halls for a sight of the wild hair, the dark and grungy clothing. No trace of Galatea. He felt a stab of relief—and disappointment.

"Dean?"

He turned to see Nikki looking at him strangely. He fell back into step with her. "What is it?"

"Why did you want to leave class so quickly?"

He couldn't imagine putting his irrational suspicions about Galatea into words; he wouldn't be able to explain to Nikki.

"I didn't want us to be late for our next class," he said.

She cocked her head. "English is our last class of the day."

"Late for the buses," he amended.

Her eyes widened. "Did something happen to your car?"

"No," he said, realizing the mistake. "But sometimes if I hurry, I can get out of the parking lot before the buses go."

"I thought all cars were supposed to wait until the buses had left," she said, hurrying to keep up with him.

"Only—sometimes," he said, grasping for anything he could say to distract her from her train of thoughts. "Besides, I wanted to start out for the youth group as quickly as possible, to make sure we get there in plenty of time."

"That's sweet of you. But I thought we were going to walk there?"

"Sure," he said.

She hesitated. "Unless you don't think your car will be okay in the student parking lot for an hour more--"

"Sure. If not, I'll deal with it then." He picked up the pace. "Let's go."

He glanced at her as they walked away from the school. With her auburn-chestnut ringlets and the matching brown scarf and beret, she could have been a model in a fall catalogue. He struggled to keep his thoughts clear—to start a conversation, so he wouldn't be distracted. "I'm not really religious, Nikki. Maybe I should have told you that before--"

"That's okay." She slipped her arm through his. "My youth group is open to all beliefs. And we won't try to evangelize you." She held up one gloved hand. "Promise."

He felt her closeness to him like fire. "So how is everything going?"

"I'm really glad you're coming today, Dean," she continued. "It will be wonderful to hear a different perspective." She paused. "I like the catechisms, but sometimes I think it's better to think for yourself."

"I just hope I don't make anyone uncomfortable." He didn't like how quickly she had changed the subject.

"I hope you do." She kicked at a stone. "Sometimes people need to be questioned—"

He stopped walking. He grabbed her arm, bring her to a halt. "What's bothering you?"

She dropped her eyes. "Nothing. I'm fine."

"Nikki," he prompted gently, "you've been missing a lot of school. And you're never… really here, anymore. So something is bothering you. Whatever it is, you can tell me."

Her voice came out flat. "My father is dying."

He stared at her, shocked. "What--"

"Cancer." She smiled, tightly. "We're afraid he might not make it to Christmas."

The memory of her house—the red and green garlands in early October—flashed through his mind. "I'm sorry, Nikki."

"So am I," she said, quickening her pace. "But at least we have advance warning, so we can spend time with him, and make sense of this before—" She looked away from him. "Dean, I'm just so confused."

He tried to quell his sudden uneasiness. "Confused about what?"

She looked away. "There's just so much I've taken for granted. It makes me wonder if I shouldn't... try to experience a little more pain." She looked past him, straight ahead at the road. "I've been so sheltered."

"There's a big difference between traumatizing yourself and dealing the best you can with something traumatizing that happens to you. I don't think you should ever *choose* to traumatize yourself." He wondered if he should follow the philosophical thread she had spun for him, or try to take the conversation back to her personal pain. From the fragile set of Nikki's features, he decided the first option was safer, and said, "The premise isn't so ridiculous."

She missed a step. "The premise of what?"

"The premise that usually people learn more from bad experiences--" He stopped speaking as she put her hand on his arm and halted.

"I don't want to talk about this anymore," she said. "But thank you for listening to me. I'm so glad I've finally told someone. I've felt so alone."

He put his arms around her, felt her sudden resistance, and released her quickly. He started down the road again, content to be silent. Then he realized she was not following him. He turned to find her staring intently into the tangle of woods bordering the road.

"What?" he asked.

"I saw a kitten," she said. "It looked like a stray. We can't leave her, Dean."

She actually sounded... glad for the distraction. His hands clenched in the pockets of his winter jacket as he watched her start towards the woods. "What about the youth group meeting?"

She stepped over the guard rail. "What's more important?"

"Come on, Nikki. It's just a stray cat."

"No, it's not." She strode over to him; her eyes flashed with intense anger. "This is about something much more than that. This is about society's fucking expectations and rules. I am so tired of playing by the rules. We are *going to make the time to go off the path and do the right thing.*" She gritted her teeth. "I am not leaving here until I've found that cat."

He stared at her, stunned. "Okay."

She stepped over the guard rail and disappeared.

"I'll... I'll wait for you here!" he called.

He heard the crack of a twig—then silence. He waited by the side of the road, his hands in his pockets, his shoulders hunched against the biting wind. He wondered how long she would insist on looking for the kitten; he wondered if he could persuade her that it really was *just a stray cat.* But the fire he had seen in Nikki's eyes had been intense; if he hadn't seen it for himself, he would not have believed that she was capable of that kind of anger. Or that kind of faith. Even if he had noticed the kitten himself, he would not have given it a second thought. But Nikki was treating the kitten like a test, like something God had put in her path to see what she was made out of...

Probably something to do with her father, he thought. *His illness is probably making her question everything she thought she knew. She's probably grasping for any thread of guidance she can find...*

The idea intrigued him—that every moment in life represented a choice, a link to a higher power, a stepping stone to follow...

If that's true, he mused, *there are a lot of tests I've failed, a lot of moments I've missed...*

16

A gust of wind blew by him, and he shivered. He scanned the woods. Potential lesson or not, he was cold, they were late for the youth group, and she was acting crazy…

"Nikki?" he called softly. Silence.

He shifted, uncomfortable. *Since when had he been uncomfortable with silence?* He checked his watch. Two minutes had passed. He shifted again and glanced over his shoulder. *How was he going to explain why he was standing by the side of the road if someone came along? What if someone thought he was trying to hitchhike? How much longer was he going to have to wait?*

He turned around and jerked. She was there, standing right in front of him, the a ball of gray fur hanging immobilized from her hand—and he hadn't heard anything, so lost in his thoughts had he been.

"You found it," he said, to mask the new source of his discomfort. "Is it… is it okay to hold it like that?"

She nodded. "Mother cats carry their kittens by the scruffs of their necks when they're little. It doesn't hurt them."

He looked at the kitten uneasily. "Was it hard to find?"

"No, she wasn't hard to find. The poor thing was crying with hunger."

"I didn't hear anything."

Nikki cradled the kitten to her, keeping the paws locked in tight so she wouldn't be scratched. "That's because you weren't listening."

He wondered why he still felt so uncomfortable. "I'm surprised she didn't run away."

"I can be very patient. I waited until I was sure I could catch her." She tucked her jacket around the kitten's prostrate form. "And I've had practice. I've worked at humane shelters and animal sanctuaries since I was a little girl. I let the kitten know I wasn't going to hurt her."

"And that made her hold still?"

"You'd be surprised by how animals respond to respect."

He watched her step lithely over the guard rail. He fell in step with her as she started walking—away from the church. "Where are you going?"

"She needs to go to a vet. Right away."

He stumbled. "Do you want me to drive?"

"I think that would be a good idea, especially if you want a healthy pet."

He stopped. "Wait a minute, Nikki. You want *me* to keep the kitten?"

Nikki kept walking. "I can't keep her. My mom is allergic."

"She probably has fleas," he said. "Look at her fur--"

"Mange," she corrected. "That's not a hard problem to fix. The worms won't be hard to get rid of, either."

"I'll drive," he said, feeling queasy. "I'll even help pay for whatever medication she needs. But I think it would be a better idea to leave her at a shelter. I'm sure she'll find a good home quickly--"

"Of course she would. But you need to keep her."

He wondered if this one of her 'faith' things. "How can you be so sure? Just because I was there when you found her?"

"Maybe. But I think it's more than that. I think she's going to be a great teacher for you." She reached over and fit her free hand into his; she gave his hand a gentle squeeze. "She's already starting to change your heart. Two minutes ago you were calling her 'it.' Now you're calling 'it' a 'her.' In a few more minutes, you'll have given her a name."

He felt his defenses weakening—not because of the cat, but because Nikki was asking him to do something, and Nikki was holding his hand. "You name her. I'm not good at naming things."

She shook her head. "I'm not accepting that answer. You have to name things in biology all the time."

"That's classification," he countered. "That's different, based on predetermined factors..."

"Precisely." She handed him the cat. "You name her."

He looked down at the tiny form that had somehow ended up in his arms. There was no doubt in his mind that the kitten was very sick; she didn't fight, she didn't even move in his arms. *What if he agreed to take care of her and she died on him? What would Nikki think of him then?* He swallowed. "She was near witch hazel. I guess I could call her Hazel."

"Perfect." Nikki smiled. "The name matches her eyes. You can't see them now, because they're closed, but she has the most beautiful hazel eyes."

Great, he thought. *I go after Nikki and I end up with... a goddam cat...* He felt squirmy holding her, and held her out to Nikki as they approached the student parking lot. "You hold her. I have to drive."

Nikki took the kitten without protest. He snuck a sidelong look at them as he slid into the driver's seat and turned on the engine. He wracked his mind for some way to make something good out of an incredibly awkward situation. He latched onto a possibility.

"You know, Nikki..." His hands tightened around the steering wheel. "I don't know the first thing about the medications it's... she's... going to need. I don't know that I can take care of her."

"It's not overly complicated. But if you're willing to try," she said, "I'll help you. I can come over every day after school until she's well."

He could accept that—a sick cat in exchange for seeing Nikki every day, at his house, in his room... "Okay." He paused. "How exactly do we get to the clinic?"

She directed him, and the vet confirmed Nikki's assumptions. They left the clinic loaded with medications to treat mites, mange, tapeworms, and allergies. He hadn't liked the way the vet's eyes had roamed over Nikki—but at least the vet had also given them a cardboard box to contain the animal. He could hear the thing clawing around inside as Nikki placed the box in the backseat of his car.

"I'm really sorry about what I said before," she said, "about my father. I shouldn't have just sprung that on you."

"I'm glad you did." He hoped she wasn't going to get upset. "I want to know what's going on in your life."

"I'm grateful to you for that," she said. "For letting me be real with you. I just wish..."

"What?"

She hesitated. "I've wanted to get to know you better for a long time. And now, when I finally have the chance... you must think I'm so weak."

He flicked on the turn signal and slid into the fast lane, passing a car that was inching its way down the highway. "I don't think you're weak. You're under a lot of stress. No one can be strong all the time. Besides..." He glanced at her. "That's not what friendships should be about. I have a lot of respect for you, hands down. I'd rather see the vulnerable side of you, since that's the side you never show."

She looked over at him, clearly startled. "What about you? Is there a side of you I haven't seen yet?"

He winced. "I'm not ready to share my deep, dark secrets with you yet."

She laughed. "There's my answer. I never knew you could be so *funny*, Dean. Here, turn down this street. It takes you right to Serenade Way."

He turned as she had indicated. She looked back at him as she got out of the car. "I'll be over tomorrow, after school. Call me any time, if you have any questions or concerns about her."

"If you still think that would be best," he said.

"I do. I think you're going to be a great match for each other." She opened the back door and moved the cardboard box to the front seat. She latched the passenger seatbelt around the box, then gave him a little wave. "See you tomorrow."

The kitten started yowling as soon as she left the car, as if it knew she had gone.

"You had better shut up," he said, watching as Nikki opened the door, waved again, and went inside. "You're alone with me now, you little beast."

He hesitated, then reached over and adjusted the passenger's seatbelt more tightly around the box. He knew Nikki wouldn't want anything to happen to the kitten—and he supposed he didn't want anything to happen to it—her-- either.

He backed slowly out of the driveway, keeping his eye on the box to make sure it didn't shift out of place.

SKEETER DELUCA

He waited by the teacher's desk, his shoulders slumped, his hands buried in his pockets. "You wanted to see me, Miss Zydek?"

"Yes, Joseph," the teacher said. "Thank you for waiting."

He was silent.

"Joseph, will you please take your hood off when you're in school? You know the rules."

He obeyed, moving slowly because he knew she was afraid of him.

"You know you'll fail if you refuse to do the poetry assignment," she said.

"I'm not…" he started, then cleared his throat and lowered his voice. "I'm not refusing to do the assignment, Miss Zydek. I just don't like talking in front of people."

"You'll have to get over that, Joseph."

"I'll try," he said.

"I don't understand. You did the assignment." She nodded at the piece of paper he still had clasped in his hand. "All you had to do was read your poem. Why didn't you?"

"I decided it wouldn't be a good idea to read the poem out loud," he said.

She frowned. "Can you tell me why?"

"No," he said.

"I want you to understand," she said, drumming her fingers against the desktop. "If you refuse to complete this assignment, you will fail my class for this quarter. Is that understood?"

"Yes," he said.

"You are dismissed," she said.

"Thanks." He started towards the door.

"Joseph."

He turned. "What?"

The teacher was watching him cautiously. "I'm not your enemy, Joseph. Or at least, I'm not trying to be."

"Okay," he said.

She didn't say anything else, so he turned and left.

GALATEA WILLIAMS

She wondered about her poem as she walked home through Cemetery Lane. Twice she had stopped amidst the graves and rifled through the books and crumpled papers in her backpack in hopes that she had overlooked the folded piece of paper. Despite the nagging sense of unease, she realized she was lucky to have lost the poem. Her feelings for Skeeter would have been obvious had she read the poem out loud to the class...

And she didn't want him to know what she felt. Not when he was in love with someone else. Knowing he didn't love her didn't stop her from thinking about him, though-- especially since he wasn't afraid to challenge her. In searching for the poem, her fingers brushed up against a folded worksheet, on the back of which was the newest design that had come while her thoughts idled through U.S. History class.

She thought about the design. She thought about the tunnels—and what Skeeter had said.

Ghosts can't reach out and touch anyone. Ghosts can't make any difference in the lives of the living. Ghosts can't even let themselves feel—

Skeeter's words had haunted her, lingering because of the truth she sensed in them. He was right; she was fading away. For all her efforts to move on, to get past her feelings of self-loathing and degradation, she was in a static situation, and she wasn't doing enough to change herself or her circumstances. There was nothing that she wanted more than to change, to let the past go and move forward with her life. She knew some women could get past it; she knew some women found the courage to go on to lead productive lives. She didn't want to be a ghost; she didn't want to be a shell. She didn't want to fade away. But she felt so helpless...

She stopped and lit a cigarette. Her nerves still jangling, she started walking. *Keep moving*, she thought, gritting her teeth. *Get home, get away, keep moving...*

As she walked up to the house, she saw her mother's newest boyfriend crouched by the back of the blue Elantra parked in the driveway.

"Hi, Bob," she said.

"Hey, kiddo," he said, without looking up.

He was the only person she would ever let get away with calling her that. The balding, slightly overweight man had been hanging around the house for the past six months, and in that time he had only treated her with kindness. She stood with her backpack slung over one shoulder and watched what he was doing.

"How was school?" he asked. When she didn't answer, he glanced up at her. "Did you go to school today?"

"For a while."

He dipped the tiny brush into the bottle of touch up paint. "Did you back into something last night when you were out?"

"I might have backed into a building."

"Galatea."

"Tight turn-around space," she said.

He capped the bottle. "Were you going to tell me or your mother?"

She studied the back of the car. "I'll pay you for the damage."

"Don't worry about it, kiddo. Just let me know if this stuff happens, okay?" He paused. "If I can catch it fresh and get the paint on it, then the rust don't spread."

"Okay, I'm sorry," she said.

"No big deal, okay?"

"Okay. Thanks."

"Just gotta get it before the rust sets in is all." He wiped his hands on his jeans. "I'm glad you didn't get hurt."

She nodded. She knew Bob wouldn't yell at her for making a mistake—but there was still that internalized reaction, to cringe, to fear a beating…

"Are you going to be around tonight?" he asked.

She shook her head. "I'll make dinner before I take off, though."

"Where do you go?" he asked her.

She shrugged.

He turned his attention back to the shimmering paint. "Be careful from now on, you hear?"

She nodded, then watched him drive the car back into the garage. Maybe Bob was a nice guy. Or maybe he was nice because of what he knew about her. She felt the instant wave of revulsion for herself, of shame for what had happened--

But Skeeter had helped her realize… that it hadn't been her fault. Skeeter had been the only one who hadn't looked at her differently after he found out—not after he had found out about the rape, not after he had found out that she had left him bleeding on the sofa for it…

Skeeter had been the only one who had stood by her.

The first time—after-- that Skeeter had touched her—and looked directly into her eyes—she had cried. He had held her in his arms then, the first time, the only time, and while she cried he told her she was beautiful, repeated it over and over until she broke down completely in his arms…

Skeeter had held her while she vomited, had hid her until he could explain to the cops, to her mother, to the court, what she had done in delayed self-defense…

Skeeter had been strong enough to deal with all the shit that happened afterwards: the gang violence, the threats from his own family, the taunts from the kids at school. But those consequences of his actions had left a toll on him. Since the court case, he had refused to speak in front of groups of people. He had told her he didn't have any thoughts worth sharing, but she sensed that his silence was really a fear—a fear that stemmed from his speaking out and seeing the repercussions.

He had never stopped being there for her when she needed him. And she had needed him—a lot— in the days and months following her trial. Her fear had decreased slightly after her mother had divorced the bastard and they had moved

21

away. But even then, there was still the deadness she felt during the day, and the nightmares at night...

She clamped her hands over her head, trying to tear out her thoughts. *Calm down,* she told herself. *It's over. You're safe...*

She looked at the house and saw that Bob had left the garage door open for her. She had sworn to hate men—all men-- except for Skeeter. And so she had kept her distance from Bob, especially because she liked him. Still, she would not let herself trust him. She went inside and dropped her backpack by the stove. She would leave as soon as she had finished cooking and stashed some of the food to take with her to the warehouse.

Skeeter might laugh at her efforts to make the warehouse habitable, but the thought of going to her asylum gave her the strength to get through the rest of the day. In her mind she saw the glass bottles and her tiny red Buddha, glowing as if lit from an inner fire. She pictured a similar flame burning in the center of her chest, in her heart.

That had been the only goal, after, since... to keep her spirit alive and burning strong.

No matter what.

Or else he won. And she became a ghost. She went to her room and dumped her schoolwork on the floor. She packed the cans of spray paint from under her bed into the empty pack. She went downstairs and drained the pasta and broccoli, added sauce and spices, put the pots back on the stove. She heard the reassuring clink of the cans as she slung her backpack over her shoulder, and she left the house by way of the garage. Before she left she inspected the car and could barely see Bob's handiwork covering the damage she had caused. For a moment she was blinded by tears.

Rust.

Damn liar.

He had covered up the scratches because he hadn't wanted her mother to notice the damage, and he had done so in the freezing air outside instead of in the garage because he hadn't wanted her mother to smell the metallic residue of the touch up paint. Bob acted as peacekeeper between them too much; he didn't realize that they didn't care to try to repair what had been broken. She would never forgive her mother, and her mother would never stop hating her...

She closed the garage door and shivered in the cold. She wished she had thought to change out of her skirt and leggings into something warmer, but her mother would be coming back soon and she didn't want to chance an encounter. Besides, she had already started down the driveway, and once she started walking she never turned back. The walk to the warehouse would warm her anyway.

Half an hour later, the sight of the sagging warehouse buildings filled her with relief. She used the warehouse's wall to shield herself from the wind as she fumbled with numb fingers at the lock, then entered the building gratefully. Her heart stopped.

"Hey, Tea."

She found her voice. "Skeeter. How'd you get in?"

"This building isn't as secure as you think it is."

"Well, it's good to see you," she said; his frown indicated she had a lecture coming.

"Tea—" he started.

"Come on up to my room," she said, shivering. "It's warmer there."

She felt his eyes on her as she climbed up into the loft—felt the brute power of him behind her. She tried to compose her thoughts, knew she had to seem as nonchalant and disinterested as she always tried to appear. She brushed by the blanket and sank onto the mattress in the middle of the room. She patted the empty space beside her. "Have a seat, Skeeter."

As he sat beside her, as her feelings for him intensified, she forced her attention onto making conversation. "What did Zydek do to you for not reciting your poem in class today?"

"She said I have to recite it tomorrow."

"Did you tell her you don't like speaking in front of people?"

"It doesn't matter. She's a teacher. She can't make exceptions for people." He paused. "I just wish Fink didn't have to be there."

"Forget about Fink," she said. "Pretend he's not there."

"I can't. I feel like the stakes are higher for me when he's around."

"Do you want me to help you practice?" she asked. "Maybe it would be easier if—"

He shook his head. "I'll be okay for tomorrow. I wrote a different poem."

"What was wrong with the first one?"

"It was for you," he said, and she felt her heart flare. "But it was stupid."

She forced herself to seem indifferent. "Maybe you should write a poem for Nikki. I'm sure that one wouldn't be stupid."

He stood and walked away from her.

She forced scorn into her voice, to cover the sudden pain she felt. "How long have you liked Nikki, Skeeter?"

"Drop it."

She had to appear like his reaction meant nothing to her. She had to make it seem like the tone of his voice—he had never used that voice with her—hadn't hurt her. Because something about the way he was standing let her know he was upset about something else. Something more important.

"Skeeter?" she asked. "What's going on?"

"Nothing."

She racked her mind. If Skeeter was upset, one of two things were involved: Fink or his family. And he had made it very clear they were not to discuss Fink. So family. "Is it something about Kenny coming back to town?"

"I didn't know you knew Kenny was back in town."

She had startled him, so much that he wasn't even able to hide his surprise. Something serious, then. "How long is he on parole?"

"The less you know the better."

She thought about dropping the subject, then decided she wasn't going to—even if she made him angry. "If I can help—"

He turned. "I'll handle it on my own. I don't want you getting messed up with Kenny."

"Why do you have to be so goddam strong all the time?" she asked him. "What if one of these days you need someone's help?"

He shook his head. "I'll always be strong enough to do what I need to do. So don't worry."

"Just…" She paused, accepting defeat, knowing he wouldn't budge. "Just know that I'm willing to help, Skeeter. If I can. Ever."

"I know that," he said.

"We promised not to have secrets from each other," she said. "I don't want you to hide parts of your life from me—"

"You don't need to know about the fucked up side of my life, Tea."

"Why?" she asked. "You know about mine."

He looked at her—too intense, too long.

"Promise me you'll let me know if I can help," she said.

He took a step towards her. "I promise."

She looked at him directly, her heart in her eyes, and felt—through their locked gaze—that he was on the verge of telling her something. Then he stepped back.

"What poem are you going to read tomorrow?" he asked.

His words cut through the intensity of the moment like a jagged piece of glass. She thought again about the poem she had written for him; she shrugged. "I don't know. Whatever I write in the first five minutes of class."

"I thought you said you had already done the assignment."

"I had," she said. "But the poem I wrote was for you. And it was stupid." She smiled when he glared, then shrugged. "Besides, I lost it."

He shook his head.

Okay, she thought. *The playing ground has been leveled.* She knew exactly where they stood. Goddam friends.

"Why are you so concerned with Nikki?" he asked suddenly, shattering the illusion that she could predict—anything—with him.

"You're in love with her," she said, and she hated herself for the way her voice cracked and her eyes blurred before she got herself back under control. She said firmly, "As your friend, I'm worried about you. I don't want you getting involved with a girl like Nikki."

His dark eyes were suddenly too intense. "What do you mean, a girl like Nikki?"

"She's a coward," she said—not because the words were true, but because she wanted to make him angry.

"She's not a coward."

He was not angry at all. He was perfectly calm. She didn't even try to fight her frustration. "Damn it, Skeeter, why do you even care if I like her or not?"

"I don't," he said. "But I know how you can be when you don't like someone."

She felt like he had slapped her. "Are you afraid I'm going to try to hurt her?"

He did not answer.

"Don't worry, Skeeter," she said, beyond boiling point angry. "I'm not going to do anything to Nikki. I know how much she means to you. And you should know I'd never do anything to hurt someone you love."

"Thank you," he said.

"Even though," she said, "I don't like her."

"You don't have to," he said, standing. "As long as you leave her alone."

She watched him walk to the front of the room. "I don't want you to be angry with me."

"I'm not," he said, lifting the blanket so he could pass through the door. "I'll see you tomorrow."

She crossed her arms over her chest. "You still didn't tell me how you got in."

"Basement window." He came back through the doorway-- briefly. "Broken pane. I boarded it up for you."

"Thanks."

"No problem." He disappeared through the doorway, let the blanket fall back into place.

She listened to see if she could hear him leave. No. No sound, except for the scraping of the warehouse door opening and closing. *Damn him*, she thought, but she was really frustrated with herself—frustrated with boundaries and limitations and her own bitterness. Skeeter was the only person she still trusted completely...

Skeeter, she realized, was also the only person who could still make her cry.

DEAN FINK

Fink crossed to where his bulging backpack waited in the corner of his room. He had just wasted an hour in his laboratory, making sure he knew exactly how to do the lab for when Nikki came over the next day. The thought of being alone with Nikki in his room—and the proven success of his version of the lab—excited him; he wanted to show her the experiment right away.

Well why not, he thought, rooting through the backpack for his phone. Even though he had seen her barely an hour ago, he could still call and ask if she had time to come over. Maybe she had changed her mind.

A piece of paper fell out of his backpack. He looked at it blankly for a moment, then unfolded the paper.

Remembrance shot through him, sudden and wild as fire. *The folded piece of paper by his desk...*

It was a poem. From her.

½ a heartG. W.
Love ItselfDrives People
To Greater Heights   To Sacred Places
Rejection-- conversely-- Destroys, Makes wild.
Doubt becomes Lethal. Insanity looms LARGE.
Never the same b/c you didn't l o v e   me.
Storm: empty and afraid to face the day
But I will; until I can see the sun
Till I can hear the trees' song
And delight in the night w/
fireflies. Not long.
Now   the   story
Has played out
Still   look
Anyway.

The poem was formatted as a full heart, not half a heart—and the grammar was horrible. But as he read the poem, he wondered if she had meant for him to find it. The paper had been so close to his desk—and it had been the only piece of paper that had fallen out of her binder…

A knock on his open door made him jerk. He involuntarily crumpled the poem in his fist.

"What?" he snapped, turning around.

His mother looked at him calmly, unfazed by his outburst. "Your father called. He won't be home until later tonight. How does dinner in an hour sound?"

He had successfully hidden the paper from her sight. He said, calmer, "That would be fine."

"How was your day at school, Dean?"

"Fine." He shot her an impatient look. "I'm in the middle of some work."

"You and your father both." She managed a smile. "I'll call you when supper is ready."

As soon as his mother left, he cast Galatea's poem on his desk. He was appalled by the strong emotion it had raised in him, by how guilty he had felt on being caught with it in his possession. He was wrong to have thought about her— to have taken the poem in the first place—and the only thing he should do was destroy the contaminated thing…

He glanced around the room, feeling like he was being watched, then crossed his room and closed the door to prevent the smell from drifting. He went to his miniature laboratory and lit the Bunsen burner, then watched satisfactorily as the blue flame ate through the corner of the notebook paper. The paper writhed in charcoal coils until nothing remained but a blackened pile of ash on his desk. He felt a moment of triumph—and then a sudden, numbing emptiness.

What was it about her? he asked himself, disturbed by his actions. *What was it about her that made him act so crazy?*

Then he thought back to the afternoon with Nikki—and he wished he was back by the guard rail, freezing in the violent wind and looking for the stupid cat. There had been something about that moment he had missed…

The pile of blackened ash stared at him accusingly, and he decided it would be better to stop thinking for a while.

NIKKI DIETRICH

She watched as Skeeter slumped against the blackboard. It should have been humorous to see him standing like that—Skeeter, who had such a rough reputation around the school—but she felt bad for him. She would have to tell him, at some point, that public speaking was the number one fear in the United States…

She glanced at Galatea Williams, intrigued by how Galatea's eyes followed Skeeter's every movement. She understood that; she had noticed the strange, strong connection the two of them seemed to share. More surprising, however, was that in watching, she became aware that Dean Fink was also watching Galatea closely— watching her with the same intensity that she was watching Skeeter. Except the way Galatea was looking at Skeeter filled her with warmth, and the look in Dean's eyes, and the way he was watching Galatea, made her uneasy. She would have to ask him later what was bothering him.

Skeeter cleared his throat. "Some memories are happy, some sad." He paused. He cleared his throat again. "Either way you'll go mad."

"Go on, Joseph," the teacher prompted.

Nikki smiled sympathetically as Skeeter looked at her. His hands clenched into fists around the paper, and he looked away quickly. "Teetering on the brink of insanity. Compromise a cold, hard reality." He paused, then exhaled. "When I was younger I believed in magic. Now that I'm older, I'm certain I can't fly."

Nikki glanced again at Galatea and was startled to see her staring back through narrowed eyes. Nikki looked away, blushing, as if she hadn't already been aware that Skeeter hadn't taken his eyes away from her once since going to the front of the room. She hadn't even seen him blink…

"Galatea, would you honor us with your poem?" the teacher asked.

Galatea pushed herself out of her chair. Nikki was glad her attention had been diverted; Galatea was too intense. She watched her stalk to the front of the classroom. She wondered how a walk could contain so much blatant attitude and defiance, but somehow Galatea accomplished it.

"You need your poem," the teacher reminded her, looking at Galatea's empty hands.

"It's in my head." She leaned against the board, her arms crossed over her chest. She raised her dark, delicate eyebrows. "Shall I begin?"

Receiving permission, she turned and faced the class. "I don't understand why people don't see what is right in front of them," she started. "But what I understand most is why some things can't be understood."

She walked back to her desk and sat down.

The teacher stared, taken aback. "Was that your entire poem?"

"That was it."

"You must have put a lot of effort into that poem," the teacher said.

"Poems can be simple, can't they?"

"Yes, they can. But that sounds like an excuse." The teacher paused. "And that wasn't even a poem. That was more prose than anything."

"Whatever. That was all I wanted to say."

"I won't accept this from you, Galatea," the teacher said softly. "You're much more creative than that."

Galatea tensed, then grabbed her backpack and started for the door.

Nikki didn't blame her. The class wasn't exactly a friendly place to begin with, and the pointed, predatory way Fink's eyes were trained on her back—Galatea must have felt the heat of that stare…

"Where are you going?" the teacher asked.

"Home."

"Galatea—" But the door had slammed shut. The teacher turned, looking helpless. "Please excuse me, class. I have to call the office and let them know--"

"Don't bother," Skeeter said. "She's long gone already."

"I'm going to call anyway, Joseph. That girl needs to learn to control her emotions, just like everyone else--"

"No." Skeeter's voice was packed with heat. "That's exactly what she doesn't need. And she doesn't need people telling her that--"

"Do you want to join her?" the teacher snapped. "The door's right there."

Skeeter's chair scraped the floor as he stood and picked up his backpack. Nikki was startled by the fierce feeling on his face as he walked towards the door.

"Joseph—" the teacher started.

The door slammed again. Looks were exchanged, followed by cautious snickers.

"All right, class," the teacher said, struggling to regain control. "That will be all the poetry we'll hear today…"

Nikki's eyes remained on the closed door. For some reason, Galatea and Skeeter seemed to have taken the life in the class out with them. She wished she had followed them out of the room. She fell into a daze, and didn't realize the rest of the period had passed until she saw Dean Fink standing next to her desk.

"Hey, Nikki," Fink said, some indeterminate amount of time later. "Can you come over today? I think I finally have everything to help you make up that lab you missed…"

She looked up. "Sure. I can come over right now."

"Oh," he said. "Well, I have practice right now--"

"Whenever, then," she said.

"Great." He looked relieved. "I can come pick you up later tonight."

"That would be very kind of you, Dean," she said.

His answering smile made her feel better, but she remained distracted and disturbed by the dynamic she had seen playing over his face in class. She decided to ask Dean about her observation later that night.

SKEETER DELUCA

He knew exactly which back streets she would take, and he caught up to her a mile away from the school. He knew she heard him coming, but she didn't stop after she realized it was him. Though she didn't speed up her walking, either.

He closed the distance between them, grabbed her arm, turned her around. "What the hell was that all about?"

"Hello, Skeeter," she responded calmly.

"You can't just walk out of class like that. Zydek already has it out for you. What are you trying to do? Fail? Or get yourself suspended?"

"Expulsion would be better."

"Tea—"

She shook off his arm. "I don't care, Skeeter. Stop trying to make me."

"You have to care."

"Why?" she spat. "You don't."

"I'm not going anywhere in life, except to the Marines, if I'm lucky." He paused. "If I'm not in jail before then—"

"Shut up, Skeeter." Her eyes blazed. "And stop trying to make me live your dreams. When are you going to start believing in yourself?"

He had never seen her so angry. He stared back at her, at a loss for words. "What's with you?"

She turned and continued walking. "I'm tired of hearing you put yourself down. I'm tired of hearing how you're going to throw your life away--"

"I'm being realistic."

"You're being an idiot." She kicked at a stone. Missed. "You're just as stuck as I am. But at least I'm not hiding from that truth."

He waited, but she frowned and turned away from him. He fell into step with her. For the first time in a long time, he didn't know what she was thinking.

"I think you're trying to distract me," he said finally, "into side-stepping the real issue. What made you leave English class?"

The air filled with stony silence.

"Are you going to tell me what's going on?" he asked.

"Are you?" she challenged.

He took a moment to process her words. "I told you I have to deal with it on my own."

"Then so do I." Her lips curled. "We'll each fight our uphill battles on our own, I guess. I hope your ghosts aren't gaining on you as fast as mine are."

"Don't be like that, Tea."

She snorted. He stopped walking. She continued on for a few paces, then turned. "Are you coming?"

He shrugged. "Not if you aren't going to talk to me."

She turned—dismissing him. "If you figure out how to beat the odds and come out a winner, let me know. Until then... well, I guess I'll see you later."

He watched her stalk off and wished he could tell her... what? He didn't know. Even if he knew what he needed to say, she had already walked away from him. Galatea liked drama, and he wasn't about to feed the flames. He'd give her a day to cool off, then he'd stop by the warehouse and make sure she was really okay.

He turned and started walking back to the school.

DEAN FINK

"You promised you wouldn't miss practice again, Skeet." Fink stuffed his practice clothes into his duffel bag.

"Sorry. I got here as soon as I could."

"What were you thinking, leaving class today?" he raged.

"I didn't think."

"Well, you need to start thinking." He slung the duffel bag over his shoulder. "If you get yourself expelled, you can't play on our team. And we need you."

"Good to know you care, Fink."

He frowned. "You don't want to talk about her, do you?"

"No."

"Fine." He turned. "I have to go pick up Nikki anyway."

"Finally," Skeeter said.

"I'm helping her make up a science lab, Skeet."

"Still an opening. Use it for what it's worth."

"What would that be?" he asked.

"An entry. Into something larger."

He paused, feeling a stab of... something. "That was profound."

Skeeter shrugged.

Fink tried to control his thoughts as he drove to Serenade Way, but all he could see in his mind was her image: tangled dark hair, wild eyes burning with hate. He didn't understand why she hated him—or why her antipathy made him so violently angry. He told himself to forget her, but found himself checking the cracked aisles as his car crawled through Cemetery Lane. Disheartened when she didn't appear, he turned his thoughts with renewed vigor to Nikki, and felt an instant lightening in his mood.

She opened the door on his first knock. Her face was pale, and she looked like she had been crying.

"Hi, Dean," she said.

"Hi, Nikki," he said, and stumbled over his next words. "I came to pick you up for—"

"I remember," she said.

"Is this a bad time? We can always—"

"Please take me away from here," she whispered.

"Okay." He held onto her arm and walked her to his car. He opened the door for her, then quickly crossed to the driver's side and started the engine.

"I'm sorry," she said. "It's just that—"

He looked at her hesitantly, but when she started to cry he pulled her into a hug. She let him hold her for a minute, her head buried in his shoulder, then she moved away from him. He put out his hand; she linked her fingers through his. He agonized over what he should say, but she didn't give him a chance to speak right away.

"I'm sorry," she said, holding his hand tightly. "I really didn't want to break down. It's just that I love him so very much, and when I think of losing him…"

"Here," he said, processing as he handed her a tissue.

She dabbed at her eyes. "I guess I need to focus on the fact that I'm not alone, that so many others have lost people they love…" She paused. *"Seek not to be understood, but to understand--"*

"Bullshit," he said, squeezing her hand. "Life dealt you a crappy hand, Nikki, and you don't have to be nice about it."

"Thank you for saying that. That's exactly how I feel, but I've tried to stay optimistic. For Mama." She tucked the used tissue into a pocket. "It's ironic. Daddy is the one who's dying and Mama and I are the ones who are breaking down." She looked at him, contrite. "I didn't mean to cry all over you."

"I don't care," he said.

She unlinked her hand from his and leaned back in her seat. "I know you've noticed how protective Daddy is, but I want you to know that it's not because he doesn't like you. He just wants to know that I'm going to be taken care of, that I'm not going to be hurt…"

"Let's talk about something else," he said.

She nodded quickly.

"I'm willing to talk about your father," he amended. "But you always seem so sad when—"

"I understand, Dean." She closed her eyes. "How was practice today?"

"It was great. Skeet can really pack some power."

She opened her eyes. "It surprises me that the two of you are friends."

"Why? Everyone loves Skeeter."

"He intimidates me," she said.

He laughed. "Why?"

She frowned. "His reputation—"

"Skeet likes practical jokes. That's all."

"The two of you just seem so different." She paused, sensing a stalemate. "Talk about something else?"

"Sure," he said.

"Back in tenth grade." She was quiet for a moment, then she glanced at him. "Do you remember when all the fire alarms went off at the same time and hard rock music started blaring from the cafeteria?"

"Of course I remember," he said, not liking where the conversation was going.

"Everyone knows Skeeter did it, Dean," she chided. "Why did you take the blame for him?"

"They were going to expel him."

"But why did that matter to you? Everyone knew how much Skeeter hated you."

"I don't know." He had forgotten that there had been a time... but that was in the past. "I guess I just liked the guy."

"But why?" she persisted.

"First off, he was one hell of a forward." He remembered how the two of them had first met—on the rugby field, when Skeeter had sacked him hard enough to give him a minor concussion. "He knew how to take risks. He knew how to make people laugh, and he didn't care at all about the rules that govern every single moment of my life." He thought, scowled, then forced a smile. "It was kind of liberating, taking the heat for him. Though my father..." He paused. "Though my father has never forgiven me for the call he got from our principal. Talk about something else?"

"Sure." She watched him keenly. "Wasn't it strange in English class today how Galatea left so quickly?" When he didn't answer, she continued thinking out loud. "I thought her poem was lovely, and I think she was right. Sometimes a simple poem can be much more beautiful than anything purposefully profound or complicated. Do you think she came up with it off the top of her head, like Miss Zydek thinks?"

In his mind he saw her other poem, burning and blackening on his desk.

"I don't know," he said.

She paused. "Talk about something else?"

"Yes," he said.

But they didn't talk. She looked out the window as he drove to his house, and he left her alone with her thoughts. He realized he was jealous that she was sitting beside him, thinking about something else.

But she surprised him. As he pulled into his driveway, she turned to him and said, almost timidly, "Let's not rush this, okay, Dean?"

"What do you mean?" he asked, startled.

She slipped her hand onto his leg. Her touch was gentle, timid. "I really like you. And I... I think you like me..."

"I'm crazy about you," he affirmed.

She blushed. "But let's not--"

"No," he said, quickly. "We won't."

Her eyes teared up. "Thank you."

Her tears irritated him, but as he got out of the car he saw that she had composed herself and was smiling at him. And she was beautiful when she smiled.

"You're going to like this lab," he said, to distract himself as much as to distract her.

"I'm sure I will."

He led her to his room. He went directly to his lab, waiting to hear her admiration. But when he turned, he saw her looking at the corner of his room.

"Is that Hazel?" she asked. "In that box?"

He glanced at the corner. "I didn't want her to make a mess out of my room."

Nikki crossed the room quickly and bent down by the cardboard box. "Cats are very clean, Dean. You don't mind if I let her out?"

"Sure," he said. "I mean, I only kept her in there because she was sleeping..."

The gray kitten streaked out of the box and ran to hide under his desk. Nikki stood up. He looked at her uncertainly. "I'm doing my best."

The kitten looked at him accusingly from under his desk—two glowing green eyes amidst a storm cloud of wild fur. He was surprised to find he felt guilty.

"I'm sure you're doing fine," Nikki said, unconvinced. "You really need to let her run around, though. I'll pay for any damage she might do."

"I would never ask you to do that," he said, still feeling the kitten's glare.

"Wow, is this your lab, Dean?" Finally, she had noticed the odd assortment in the corner of his room—but she was using it as a distraction. "This is really cool."

He moved towards her, still relieved that his purpose was clearly before him once more. "I usually just do simple chemical reactions," he said humbly. "Should we get started with the experiment?"

"I'd love to," she said.

He looked at her, undecided about the entendre of her words—then remembered she couldn't read his mind. He turned on the burner, listened to the gas coil through the rubber tube. He handed Nikki a pair of safety goggles as the flame sprang to life. "Better put these on."

"Do you have a pair?" When he shook his head, she handed the goggles back to him. "You wear them. I'll stand behind you."

He slipped the goggles over his head, then picked up a number of tiny glass vials from the bookshelf by his lab. "You'll pick up these concepts really quickly. They're just simple reactions to show that when heat interacts with certain metallic salts..." He added a fine powder to a thin metal rod, then placed the rod above the flame. A streak of red shot towards the ceiling.

"Lithium chloride," he said—then, on sudden inspiration, "Hey, Nikki, what's your favorite color?"

"Orange," she said.

He looked over the vials on his shelves, then with the precision of a surgeon extracted a tiny tube. He added a pinch of the chemical to a different rod, then held the rod over the flame. An orange flame—a spark of warmth.

"What kind is that, Dean?" she asked, awed.

"Calcium chloride," he responded. "Did you like that?"

She nodded. He opened a different vial, repeated the process; the flames turned blue.

"I know that one," she said. "Cupric chloride."

He turned. She smiled at him. He felt slightly irritated. She did not seem to notice.

"You really like science, don't you, Dean?" she asked.

He turned back to the burner, let his eyes play over the flames. "I'd like to find a cure for something."

"I see," she said. "Are you going to be one of those people who tries to find a way to make us live forever?"

He wondered at the disapproval he heard in her voice. "Think about it, Nikki. A cure for cancer. And then your dad—"

"My dad's not afraid to die. And while it's horrible that he's going to…" She paused. "I wouldn't want him to live forever. Immortality would come at too high a price."

"Scientists aren't aiming for immortality," he remonstrated. "Usually they aim to improve the quality of life, not the quantity of life."

She cocked her head. "I thought you wanted to be a lawyer, Dean."

He paused. "I suppose I could be both," he said, wondering why he suddenly felt sad. "Lead a double life."

"Like Jekyll and Hyde," she said.

"I hope… not quite like that."

"Repression does interesting things to people," she said. She took the rod from him, added a chemical, placed it over the flame. His attention was momentarily diverted by the streak of green flame.

"Potassium chloride?" she asked.

He shook his head. "No, potassium chloride burns purple. That was copper sulfate."

After that they ceased talking. She watched the reactions with increasing interest, and at one point she put her hand on his shoulder and leaned closer. He thought about how much he enjoyed having her there, about how beautiful it was to be alone with her.

Eventually he put the caps back on the little glass vials and returned the chemicals to their places on the shelf. He turned off the burner and caught her smiling at him. He smiled back. "I enjoyed having you here, Nikki."

"I love your lab," she said. "And I don't think you want to be a lawyer at all."

He shrugged.

"I had a great time," she started uncertainly. "Thank you for having me over."

He glanced at the clock. "It's still early. We could talk for a while if you have time—"

"I should probably get home."

"Right," he said, wondering if he had misread her or if she had intentionally misled him.

"But maybe…" She paused. "Maybe you can come to my house sometime, when things have--"

"Sure," he said, as he walked her to the door. At least he still had the car ride back with her, when he could flesh out what he thought he had been feeling from her…

But there was a strange car parked in his driveway. He glanced at her as she waved to the driver. "Boyfriend?"

She shook her head. "I called my mom to come pick me up."

"When did you do that?" he asked. "And why? I could have driven you home."

"You already went out of your way enough for me today," she said. "And, besides, sometimes… sometimes Daddy likes to be alone in the house."

He watched her walk away from him, and he wondered if he was a fool for wanting her the way he did.

NIKKI DIETRICH

She waited until her parents went to bed before she left the house. She jogged in place for a few minutes to warm up her body, then she started to run. Her parents wouldn't stop her from running if they knew, but they would worry. She didn't want them to worry, and she needed her night runs to escape from the memories…

Some good, some bad, either way you'll go mad…

She wondered what had happened to Skeeter to make him understand.

She pushed herself to run harder. She wanted to be surrounded by total darkness, and knew she had to leave the cheerful lights of Serenade Way behind. She ran down the uneven aisles of Cemetery Lane to the gravel bike trail that stretched for miles in each direction. She kept to the shadows of the weed-choked trail as she passed the hulks of the warehouses. She was afraid of those deserted buildings and the crimes that she heard took place by the railroad tracks. The potential danger elevated her heartbeat to a painful thudding—but there was a certain appeal for her in the broken railroad, the dilapidated buildings, the graffiti scrawled on the fading walls. Her fear monopolized her other feelings, and she felt relief in the release of thought…

Her favorite spot on the trail was on a wall near a fenced-in building. A single yellow bulb spotlighted the spray-painted silhouette of a woman with a dove flying away from her outstretched palm. Though the spot was three miles away from Serenade Way, Nikki made sure she ran to the silhouettes on every run.

That night, looking at the chalky lines of spray paint, she realized she was not ready to stop running. Her pain was still too raw. She had to run to the tunnel; she felt its shivering walls calling to her like a siren's song. She had found it soon after her father's fatal diagnosis: a concrete corridor, twenty feet tall, with glowing graffiti that stretched over the formerly unforgiving slabs. She had gotten lost amidst the colorful bursts of flowers, giant painted mushrooms, shimmering rainbow fish with beaded scales—and the tunnel had become, for her, a place of solace, where she occasionally caught sight of something new. Maybe that was why the tunnel called to her; like her, it was in a constant state of transformation.

Though she sucked in serenity from the cold walls and their colorful pictures, she had never been to the tunnel at night. She fought the excessive fear by focusing on her father—and how the doctor was increasingly sure that he would not live to see Christmas. She thought about how her father had given so much of his life to protecting and ensuring the happiness of others. He deserved to live longer, especially since Christmas was his favorite holiday…

Her tears froze on her cheeks. She kept running.

She almost ran inside the tunnel without noticing the sound coming from within—a faint hiss that clouded the air in metallic vapor. As soon as she sensed the sound, she became aware of movement in the tunnel. Terrified, she veered off the bike trail and crouched down in the shadows. She prayed that the person in the tunnel hadn't seen her.

The hissing sound inside the tunnel stopped. Nikki held her breath as a person in a bulky leather jacket stepped into the moonlight.

"Who's there?"

Nikki recognized the voice, but she could not move. She watched Galatea Williams walk farther out of the tunnel, spray paint can in hand.

"Don't fuck with me!" Galatea yelled. She waited, arms crossed, then backed into the tunnel. The hissing sound resumed defiantly. Nikki's instant reaction was to run away, but she felt an obligation to reveal herself. She stood numbly and started walking towards the tunnel.

"Galatea?" Her voice sounded tiny, shaken, as she stepped outside of the tunnel's entrance. "It's just me, Nikki Dietrich…"

The sound stopped, and Galatea turned towards her. "We go to school together, remember?" she stuttered, as Galatea walked towards her menacingly. "We have cl-class together. English."

Galatea stopped in front of her. "Are you alone?"

"Yes."

She cocked her head. "Why the hell are you alone?"

"I…"

"You need to go home. Now." Galatea crossed her arms over her chest. "You're on the wrong side of the tracks."

"I was going for a run."

Galatea arched a dark eyebrow. "A run? Right now? Why the hell would you go for a run right now?"

Nikki started to explain—how sick her dad was, how she would go insane if she stayed in the house and heard her mother's quiet sobbing for one more minute-- then decided to stay silent.

"Huh," Galatea said, and turned back to the tunnel.

Nikki followed her. "What are you doing out here?"

"Decorating." Her voice was smooth, neutral—blank.

"You're the graffiti artist?"

Galatea's eyes glinted. "I wouldn't try calling the police on me. I'll be out of here before you finish the call--"

"They're beautiful," Nikki said. "The paintings. I mean, I can't see them right now, but I've been here during the day, and... and if I had painted them I would be proud of myself."

Galatea stared at her. Then she shook the spray paint can in her hand and turned back to her work.

Nikki watched her. "Why do you do it? Paint these walls?"

The hissing stopped momentarily. "It's my way of fighting."

"Fighting what?"

"You don't need to know."

Nikki grasped for something to say. "I liked your poem. The poem you recited today, in English class."

Galatea glanced over her shoulder. "You're crazy."

"I hardly think you have the right to call me crazy," she said.

Suddenly Galatea was standing beside her again. Nikki swallowed, but looked back at her. In the dim light she saw something flicker through Galatea's eyes, and then Galatea looked away.

"I hardly think you have the right to call that bullshit I said off the top of my head poetry. Poetry should come from the heart, it should mean something…"

"Didn't those words come from your heart? Didn't they mean something?"

Galatea was silent for a minute. "Come on," she said, finally. "I'm walking you back to wherever you came from."

"Don't be silly," Nikki said. "I can run back."

Galatea stopped walking. "You're a long way from home, Nikki. You shouldn't be out here alone."

"You're out here by yourself," she countered. Her teeth chattered with cold.

"You have more to lose than I do." She tossed the can into her backpack. "I'm done for the night anyway."

"Really, I—"

"Nikki." Her voice was cold. "You're acting like a five-year-old throwing a tantrum. You can be really immature, you know that?"

She felt a flash of anger. "We aren't going to be any safer in a pair than we'd be by ourselves. I hardly think that's a childish—"

"Stop whining and follow me. I'm walking you past the warehouses, then I can give Skeeter a call to walk you home if you want."

Nikki started to protest, then bit back her words. She felt a temporary sense of relief; the desolate area of abandoned buildings was the part of the trail she feared most. She fell in step as Galatea started out of the tunnel. "Fine. But you don't need to call Skeeter."

"I'm sure he'd enjoy the time with you."

"That won't be necessary." She felt her face burning. "I'd get home a lot quicker if you'd just let me run."

"Probably. But I'd blow a lung if I tried to keep up with you."

Nikki waited while Galatea lit up. "Did you paint the woman with the dove? A couple of miles from here?"

Galatea blew out smoke. "I'm not admitting to anything."

"Well." Nikki paused. "I really enjoy that painting when I run. So thank you."

"I don't know what you're talking about."

Nikki remained silent as they approached the warehouses. Galatea walked her past the last dilapidated building, then stopped under the dim lights. "You sure you don't want me to call Skeet? He could be here in a couple of minutes."

"Thank you, but I really don't think I'll encounter anyone."

Galatea reached into a pocket of the leather jacket, held out her hand. "Just in case."

Nikki stepped back. "I don't think I'll need that."

"Have you ever used a knife before?"

"No. And I'd never use it. So you can just put it away."

Galatea paused. "It would make me feel better if you took it."

"Why?"

"Because it's more important for you to be safe than it is for me to be."

Nikki stared. "Why would you say that?"

She sneered. "Because it's true."

"Just because I have more money—"

"Money has nothing to do with it." Galatea's voice cut like the cold. She paused, then said more quietly, "You said you liked my poem, Nikki?"

"Yes. But I don't see what that has to do with—"

"Right. You don't see what's right in front of your eyes."

Nikki paused. "Promise me you'll come to school tomorrow. So at least I'll know that you made it home okay…"

"I am home, sweetheart," she said, veering off the trail and heading back towards the warehouses. Before Nikki had a chance to say anything else, Galatea had disappeared into the shadows.

DEAN FINK

He dimmed the light so his parents would think he was asleep, then stared at the pile of dusty books stacked on his desk. His mind battled with him as he reached for the first yearbook, but he knew he would feed his obsession.

He looked around his room. His feelings were ridiculous. It was not a crime to look through a yearbook—or several of them. He shouldn't feel like a criminal when he was doing nothing wrong.

His gaze fell on his lab equipment, and he remembered the afternoon date with Nikki. She had put her hand on his shoulder at the end. She had smiled at him on her way out, and she had invited him to her house when everything had calmed down...

The day had been perfect.

Yet there he was in his room, the glossy pages of the yearbook he had already opened glaring at him in the dim light. His hands clenched into fists as he tried to clear his thoughts. They were just yearbooks, just goddam yearbooks…

He found her quickly. Such a strange name…

He started at a sudden sound in his room, then looked over his shoulder and relaxed. The kitten had knocked over a CD he had left on the nightstand. Nothing more than that. At least Hazel had the sense to stay away from his lab and experiments. He supposed he didn't mind if the creature stayed permanently; she helped him feel less alone, at times.

He turned back to the rows of frozen faces in front of him. Some of her features had remained the same—the intense dark eyes, the strong forehead, the arched eyebrows and the ridges of her cheekbones. But her overall appearance changed drastically. In her fifth grade photo her hair had hung in thick ringlets, bangs cut perfectly straight across her forehead. She was wearing tacky jewelry and her smile was huge. She looked beautiful-- perfect.

No one is perfect, he thought angrily. *No one, and especially not her.*

He jerked when the kitten landed silently on his desk. She wrapped her tail around her legs and looked down at the book with unblinking eyes.

"Hello, Hazel," he said. He knew the habit was silly, but he felt the need to address the kitten by its name every so often.

Her keen green eyes seemed to ask what he was doing. The unblinking stare made him uncomfortable. He picked the kitten up and put her on the floor, then turned back to the books and rifled through the remaining years.

By her ninth-grade portrait, Galatea had stopped smiling. Tenth grade brought the heavy eyeliner and garish eye shadow, and the same unsmiling expression. Her eleventh grade portrait brought the wild dark hair, streaked blue, the defiant spark in her eyes, the strange pallor of her complexion.

The kitten mewed, startling him again. He didn't understand why the feline gaze seemed to affirm he was doing something wrong. He glanced down at Galatea's photos; he wanted to burn them all. But his parents would notice the damage to the yearbooks, and he didn't want to indulge the irrational impulse anyway. Resigned, he closed the books and carried them back to the living room.

He crept back to his room and felt better, knowing the yearbooks were undamaged and where they belonged. He searched for Hazel and found her curled up in the cardboard box in the corner. He went back to his desk and pulled his chemistry book in front of him. Five minutes proved he could not concentrate. He cursed her for the distraction and wondered why she could turn his thoughts into dark, ugly things.

Nothing short of a direct confrontation would bring him any peace. He resolved to talk to her the next day at any cost.

NIKKI DIETRICH

Even after mother's sobs quieted, Nikki could not sleep. She lay in bed and stared blankly out her window, watching the healing darkness of the night fade into a bruised dawn. She silenced her alarm before it went off, then threw on some clothes and snuck out of the house long before her mother would be up to make coffee. She walked the snow-covered streets aimlessly until she heard her school bus chugging up the hill, and she reached the bus stop just as the ancient bus's doors creaked open. She was a mess; she hadn't brushed her teeth, she didn't have her school books, and her mother would worry that she hadn't been home to say good morning.

She didn't care.

The ride to school was uneventful. She dragged herself through the school day, telling herself that if she could get to her last class she would be all right. In English she would see Dean Fink, who always seemed strong enough for both of them…

But something seems very wrong with Dean, she thought, as she watched him stare blearily around the room from tired eyes. Then she noticed how she had her own head propped up on her hand, to keep from falling asleep. Too many late nights studying for midterms had her sleep deprived, and he was much more driven than she was. She shook her head and tried to clear her mind. There was nothing wrong with Dean Fink's zoning off during that time of year; her own fatigue had her imagining things.

Yet she could not shake the malevolent feeling she was picking up; she could almost see the negative energy, hovering around him like a dark cloud. *I'll ask him about it later*, she thought. *I'm too tired to think right now…*

She tried to focus on Miss Zydek's lesson: something about the major Victorian poets. Her favorite time period. Still, she found herself distracted—not only by Dean, but by Skeeter DeLuca, of all people.

He had been moved, moments before, to the far side of the classroom by the window because he was not participating in the class discussion. Nikki felt bad for him; Skeeter wasn't trying to be disrespectful. He always listened intently to every word Miss Zydek said; he just wasn't willing to speak in class.

The few words of remonstrance their teacher had directed towards him seemed to have taken something out of him. The light from the window accentuated his profile, and Nikki kept sneaking glances at him—the dark hair that spiked across his forehead and shagged around his ears, the sharp line of his nose and the expressive arch of his eyebrows, the silver glinting of the chain around his neck. She wondered, briefly, why he wore the chain every day under his hoodie.

Then he looked over and saw her looking at him. She dropped her eyes, already feeling the blush creep across her cheeks. But he wasn't going to let her off easily. A streak of rainbow light played across her desk. She followed the light subtly with her eyes; the prism had been what had diverted her attention to him in the first place. After he had moved seats he had pulled out the tiny crystal and had channeled the light from the windows through it, dancing streaks of rainbow light around the room when Miss Zydek's back was turned.

The light was beautiful, and she couldn't help but look over and meet his eyes. He smiled. She offered him a guarded smile in return, before they both became aware that Miss Zydek was observing their silent conversation.

"Joseph DeLuca," she said, striding across the room and stopping before his desk. "Can you explain to me what that is?"

He hid the crystal in his palm. "Nothing, Miss Zydek."

The teacher held out her hand for the crystal. Skeeter opened his hand and displayed an empty palm. A look of indignation crossed the teacher's face.

"Maybe you should look in the bottom right hand drawer of your desk," he said, lowering his head. "I thought that's where you stored all contraband items."

The classroom remained silent as she walked across the room then opened the drawer, from which she extracted the offensive crystal. Nikki couldn't hide her smile; Skeeter was known for his magic tricks as well as for his reputation. The teacher looked at Skeeter, a reprimand etched into her face.

"Put this in its proper place," she said, marching over and placing the crystal on Skeeter's desk. "Which is your pocket, and not in my desk. And never again in my classroom."

"Sorry," Skeeter said. He didn't sound very sincere.

Miss Zydek clicked back to the front of the room and launched once more into Victorian verse.

"Excuse me, Miss Zydek." Dean Fink's precise voice cut through Nikki's thoughts; she glanced over to see him looking at the huge black watch he wore perpetually. "We have exactly one minute and thirteen seconds of class time left."

"Thank you, Dean, I am quite aware of that. We never seem to have enough time." She sighed. "But to take a tangent and visit the Modernists—as T.S. Eliot said, 'There will be time'…"

Skeeter looked up suddenly. "Time for visions and revisions."

"Very good, Skeeter." Miss Zydek looked stunned.

"Only my friends call me Skeeter," he said. "Please don't call me that."

The bell rang. Miss Zydek sighed and slapped the chalk down, then turned to face the sea of students perched on the edges of their seats. "Class dismissed," she said. "Joseph, please see me after class."

Nikki knew Fink wanted to walk her out of school and that he didn't like waiting. She watched Skeeter from the corner of her eye as she reluctantly packed her books. With no excuse to linger, she turned to meet Dean Fink.

Odd, she thought, the fake smile fading from her lips. *Where did he go?*

She stepped out of the classroom and scanned the halls, but he was gone. She dismissed her sudden misgivings. She could talk to Dean later.

Galatea brushed by her, disorienting her thoughts. Nikki glanced into the classroom one last time and saw Skeeter standing by the teacher's desk—his shoulders hunched, his head bowed. She followed Galatea's lead and quickly started out of the school, realizing as she walked that Galatea had disappeared as suddenly, and completely, as Dean Fink.

SKEETER DELUCA

"Are you familiar with the poem I mentioned in class?" Miss Zydek asked, when the classroom was emptied of other students.

"Yes," he said. *The Love Song of Alfred J. Prufrock*, right?"

"Yes." Miss Zydek looked at him. "Which class made you read T.S. Eliot?"

"I read it on my own," he said, not looking at her.

"That's quite a challenge."

He shrugged. "I like poems."

She paused. "Do you have a favorite poem by Eliot?"

"The Waste Land."

She smiled. "Let me guess. *Do I dare disturb the universe?*"

He shifted. "Look, Miss Zydek, I don't mean any disrespect, but I have to go to rugby practice."

She looked at him sharply. "You're failing my class. You shouldn't be playing on the rugby team."

"It's an unofficial team," he said.

She glanced down at the papers in front of her. "You never turned in your 'Most Important Thing About Me' poem."

"I'll do it now," he said. "The Most Important Thing About Me is that I read."

She looked at him. "Joseph, I want to talk to you for a minute. Please sit down. I'll explain to your coach."

"It's an unofficial team. We don't have a coach." He sat down and buried his hands in the pockets of his hoodie. "What do we need to talk about anyway?"

"You have very low standards for yourself." She folded her hands in front of her. "And you underestimate yourself. You know that, don't you?"

He didn't say anything.

"I expect much more from you," she said. "I know you're capable of doing great things."

"Those are nice words," he said. "But you can't save me from the life that's been placed before me. No one can. Things take their place in a natural order, okay?" He paused. "The universe disturbs me, Miss Zydek. Not the other way around."

"The path you choose is your own," she said firmly. "Especially when you are strong enough to disturb the universe. What do you think about that?"

He paused. "Just give me a zero or a day's worth of detention, okay? That's what all my other teachers do."

"No, I'm not going to give you that option," she said. "You're obviously smart enough to handle the class work…"

He shook his head.

"I don't want you to fail my class. There's no reason why you—" She sighed when she saw him looking impatiently at the clock. "All right, Skeeter. You may go to practice."

"Thank you," he said. "But please don't call me Skeeter."

"Okay," she said quietly.

Something in her tone made him pause and turn back. "Miss Zydek?"

She looked up.

"Thanks for not confiscating my crystal." He hesitated. He felt uncomfortable, but that didn't matter. He would say what he had to say. "It was my granddad's. He gave it to me before he passed on." He paused. "He got me started in magic and I admired him a lot and… just thanks for not taking it."

"If I see it in my class again I'll have to take it," she said sternly. "Do you understand that?"

"Sure," he said. "And thanks for the new seat. I like being in the sun."

"Do you need a pass? To walk the halls this late after the bell rang?"

"Yes, that would be good." Then he had nothing more to say, so he took the pass and left the classroom. He was disturbed by the teacher's words—or by something else. A heavy uneasiness settled over him, making him feel physically ill. He couldn't shake the feeling… but rugby would make him feel better. Rugby always made him feel better.

He passed through the gym-- but the locker room was deserted. He dropped his duffel bag and waited, hoping someone would show up. Five minutes later, Marcus Wilson—Fink's co-captain—walked into the room.

"What's going on?" Skeeter asked him.

"Fink called off," Marcus said. "Said something came up. You didn't get the message?"

Skeeter shook his head.

"I'm thinking a lot of the other fellas didn't either," Marcus said. "It was very last minute on Fink's part. So I say we stick around for a while, see who shows up."

"And practice anyway?"

Marcus smiled. "That's the game plan."

Good, Skeeter thought. He needed to hit something.

GALATEA WILLIAMS

She knew he was following her, knew he had been following her since she had left the school. She cut through Cemetery Lane, hoping to discourage him—but he continued after her doggedly, hanging back a few hundred yards, still unaware that she knew he was there.

Fine, she thought, stopping in the middle of the cemetery. *If he wants a show down, he can have one.*

"What do you want, Fink?" she asked, not turning around.

He must have been fewer than fifty feet behind her at that point, because she felt him beside her in seconds. She turned and saw him studying her; she recognized the way his eyes raked over her. She bent her head over a cigarette and lit up—nonchalantly, to show she was not afraid of him.

Even with her head lowered, she saw his eyes lingering over every part of her: the jeans she had cut holes in and enhanced with poetry in permanent marker, the oversized gray sweatshirt, the multi-colored scarf she used to tie back her hair. She raised her head; met his cold blue eyes.

"Either you're a creep," she said, "or you have something to say to me."

"What makes you think that?" His voice was dangerously quiet, low.

She crossed her arms over her chest before she realized it was a gesture of vulnerability. She straightened and tossed her head. "I saw you staring at me today."

"I wasn't the only one staring," he said. "You dress like a freak. I hardly have to explain that."

"Then start by explaining why you're following me," she prompted.

She waited while he remained silent, burying her hands in the pockets of Skeeter's leather jacket. She straightened, realizing her shoulders had hunched in to shield her body from the cold.

"I need to talk to you," he said finally.

She kept the edge in her voice, the defiance in the arch of her eyebrows. "Why didn't you talk to me at school?"

"I wanted us to be alone."

His words made her distinctly uncomfortable, and she laughed to unbalance him. "But we're not alone. Not here." She exhaled, a stream of acrid gray smoke. "We're surrounded by spirits. You can feel them, if you tune in." She paused. "I'm surprised you followed me here. I'd think you would have the world to fear from a place like this."

"I don't know what you mean," he said.

"I mean that right now— you look like you already feel the shadows slithering over these tombstones like creatures crawling under your skin." She smiled—a dangerous smile. "So why don't you just tell me what's on your mind."

He stared at her. He remained silent.

"All right, then." She dropped the cigarette, crushed it into the uneven, cracked pavement stones with the toe of her leather boot. "I don't know what the hell your problem with me is, but it's damn creepy the way you stare at me, the way I turn around and you're always there. I want you to stop stalking me."

His eyes sparked. "That's a horrendous accusation."

"Horrendous?" She cocked her head. "Because it's true?"

"At least I'm not like you," he said.

She noticed he was shaking. "And what am I like?"

"A criminal. A vandal. It takes no courage to live like you do."

A warning went off in her mind, but he had angered her and she ignored the sudden flash of intuition. She brushed her hair away from her face, glared at him. "Well, it certainly doesn't take any courage to live like a fink. Not when you have the whole world on your side."

"Don't walk away from me," he said.

She ignored him. He strode after her and grabbed her arm. He jerked her around.

She froze, feeling the grip of his fingers bite into her skin. "Let go of my arm."

Instead he grabbed her other arm and stepped closer. She pulled the knife out in a flash and flicked it open. The appearance of the weapon was enough to make him let her go. She kept her eyes narrowed as he stepped away from her.

"Is that a—"

"Big surprise," she said. "Under that pretty boy exterior you're just like every other guy. So I'm warning you, Fink; don't fuck with me."

He stood still, his eyes on the blade.

"And don't come here again." She flicked the blade closed and pocketed it—to show him he wasn't a threat. "This place is my sanctuary. And remember what I said: we're not alone here. Everything you do here gets watched."

"Then maybe you should watch yourself as well."

His voice wasn't shaky enough to make her feel safe; the gleam in his cold eyes continued to scare her. She smiled. "I don't care who watches what I do."

A moment of silence passed between them, tension building like a gathering storm. He stepped by her, keeping a wide berth. She watched him continue down Cemetery Lane. She started walking in the opposite direction.

He was strong, she thought. *Stronger than he looked.* She could still feel his hand on her arm, and she was certain that when she took the hoodie off later that night she would find a bruise. His parting look had also unsettled her; he didn't compromise with what he wanted. She had underestimated him; she would make sure she was never alone with him again.

She wished she had waited for Skeeter after class. If she had let him walk her to the warehouses after school, she would have avoided the encounter with Fink. But a confrontation had been inevitable—she had felt something brewing inside Fink for weeks—and she was glad, on reflection, that she had been alone when it had come. Skeeter wouldn't always be there for her…

And she didn't want Skeeter to know. Making him choose between her and Fink was not a risk she could afford to take. But she would make sure she was prepared. She pulled out her cell phone and called Skeeter.

SKEETER DELUCA

He watched her in the concrete room, tracing the flickering candlelight over her delicate features. "I can't do it, Tea."

Her eyes flared, like he knew they would, but he had to convince her that her latest idea was a very bad one. "I need you to, Skeeter."

"I won't hit you."

"Skeeter." He didn't like the way her voice was perfectly calm; he wasn't facing the dramatic, emotional Galatea he thought he knew. This woman was cold and calculating. Unshakable. "You told me once that you would never deny me anything I wanted. Do you remember that promise?"

"I didn't think this would come into it."

"I don't see how this is any different," she said, and now he sensed the faintest hint of frustration and anger in her voice. "You've been teaching me how to fight for over six months."

"So you're ready. You don't need me to actually—"

"I need to know that I can defend myself, if I ever had to."

His eyes scanned her features, the way she was hunched into herself on the threadbare mattress. He leaned against the wall. "Did something happen? Something you haven't told me about?"

"No," she said, too quickly.

"If someone is giving you—'"

She stood and moved towards him, and he felt himself flinching back into the wall. She stepped closer, until there was no distance between them. She put her hands on his chest, where they burned like fire, and when he looked down at her he saw her dark eyes were glistening with tears.

"Skeeter." She gritted her teeth. "I *need you to do this for me.*"

He pushed her backward. For a moment she looked like he had slapped her, and then her eyes narrowed in understanding. He circled her, hating himself more with every second for the contact he knew he was going to make with her. *But she had asked him.* Still, that didn't make it right…

Her uppercut caught him off guard, and he blinked. She backed away from him, and he caught the emotion in her eyes. The pain. The fear. The doubt. He knew—as long as she felt like that—she would never be ready. She cared about him, he knew, but what he saw in her eyes was not a fear of hurting him—but of hurting anyone. If she were in an actual fight, that emotion would get her killed.

He closed in. Tackling her to the ground was easy, because she wasn't expecting it. He felt the softness of her body under his. Her eyes, so close, were startling. He could feel her heart beating, could hear the whisper of her breath and the sharp intake of his. And then…

No, Tea, he thought. *Don't…*

But she did. She closed her eyes, and her whole body relaxed.

He swore at himself, and hit her.

Her body jerked, and then, like he knew it would, her instinct kicked in. The sudden knee jerk to his groin blind-sided him with pain, and he felt himself tumble head first over her as she used the move he had showed her to overthrow an opponent. The punches came in fast and hard, and he raised his hands to shield himself until he could gain ground. He never thought he would dance with her like this, see that venom in her eyes directed at him. He punched up, heard the crack of bone as her nose broke. He backed away, horrified.

Snorting blood, she came after him.

He picked up the mattress and used it to block her. If that wasn't enough to snap her out of it, he didn't know what he would do. He couldn't hit her again.

She shoved the mattress out of his hands and he found himself in front of a wildcat. He caught her by the shoulders. The gentleness in his touch seemed to catch her off guard and bring her back to reality. She stiffened, and the vulnerability in her eyes burned him. He couldn't meet her eyes for the first time that he could remember; he didn't know what he was feeling, but he didn't want her to see it.

"You're ready," he said, looking at the ground. "Sit down."

She sank onto the mattress. She started to wipe the blood away from her nose, but he caught her hand. Gently.

"Let me set it."

She barely flinched. He scanned her face, but he couldn't tell anything because she wasn't looking at him. He wanted… to say so much to her. But he couldn't think of what to say. He leaned back on his heels, and she took that moment to look up.

His hands found hers. There was a moment, when he held her hands and looked into her eyes, that the words built up inside him almost came out. Then he let go of her hands and backed away from her.

"It'll heal straight," he said. *He had to get out of there.*

The blanket flapped closed behind him and he jumped from the loft to the ground level. As the door scraped shut behind him, he listened—to see if she had tried coming after him.

She had not.

As the cold rain stung him back to feeling, he remembered the fight she had been in at school. There had never been any question of whether or not she was ready... *so why had he fought her?*

The only thing he knew was that hurting her had hurt him worse... worse than he thought anything could. He saw her wildcat eyes, saw the tears leaking down her bloodied cheeks as she avoided eye contact with him, and before he had consciously made the decision, he was heading towards the trailer park and the fight he knew he could find there.

DEAN FINK

"This is very unexpected, Dean," Nikki said after she had opened the door. "But I'm glad you stopped by. I wanted to talk to you."

It's here again, he thought, looking into Nikki's eyes. *That feeling of warmth, of release, of freedom...*

He felt the burden he hadn't known he was carrying slip away. He started to speak, but Nikki cut him off.

"Dean." Her hand propped open the door though the frigid air outside made her shiver. Her voice was low and solemn. "This isn't a good time."

A female voice called from somewhere in the house.

"Just Dean, Mama!" Nikki looked over her shoulder. Her body still barred his entrance as she turned back to him. "I'm sorry, Dean, but this really isn't--"

Mrs. Dietrich appeared behind Nikki in the doorway. She was a short, thin woman, and he supposed she could have been pretty if she hadn't looked so pale and sad. He had never seen anyone look as sad as Nikki's mother.

"Have you come to take Nikki away for a while, Dean?" she asked, in a soft, kind voice.

"Mama, I've just explained to him that—"

Mrs. Dietrich put a hand on her shoulder. "I think it might be good for you to get out of the house, Nicole. I won't expect you back for at least an hour."

Nikki looked ready to cry. "I don't want to be away from Daddy right—"

"You kids go for a bike ride," Mrs. Dietrich continued. "Enjoy this last bit of nice weather before winter really hits. Dean, you can ride her brother's old bike..."

Nikki turned to him. "Dean, will you wait for me outside? I want to talk to Mama for a minute."

He nodded, then waited on the front stoop of the house with his jacket pulled close to cut the wind chill. The garage door opened and he watched as Nikki -- dressed in a yellow rainslicker and rubber boots—wheeled out two bikes.

"Mama said it might rain," she said, looking at the darkening sky without amusement. "Isn't this crazy weather we're having? First it snows, now it's been nice but they're calling for hail--"

"I know this isn't a good time," he started. "I understand that you want to be with your dad. I can always—"

She handed him a red rainslicker. "You should probably put this on. Daddy thinks you should take it."

"The bike ride was your dad's idea?"

"This is all very strange," she said quietly.

He glanced at the sky again, at the dark storm clouds threatening the horizon. *Well, why not?* He pulled the red rainslicker over his head. "Nikki, if we hurry we might even be able to get caught right in the middle of the storm."

She stared at him for a moment, then giggled, then tried to stop, which only made her giggle harder. He didn't understand her reaction, but he was glad to see her smile.

"Is your dad much worse?" he asked carefully, as they started down the asphalt driveway.

"No. He seems better."

"Then why—"

"He's going to die, Dean. Today."

He didn't know what to say. He let her know by the pressure of his hand on hers that he was there for her and willing to talk—but that he didn't know how to begin.

"So this is your brother's bike?" he asked awkwardly, when he felt that the silence had stretched on for too long between them. "I didn't know you had a brother."

"He's in college. We don't see him much." She glanced down the street. "Did you walk here?"

He remembered suddenly why he had left his car at the school. *There she was again, like a dark cloud, spoiling even his time with Nikki...*

"I'd rather go for a bike ride anyway," Nikki said, reading the changing emotion on his face. "I have something really special I want to show you."

"What?"

"You'll see when we get there." She kicked up the kickstand and mounted her bike in one fluid motion, then went streaking down Serenade Way—a flash of yellow rubber.

He glanced over the beat up bike in front of him, then pedaled furiously until he caught up to her. "What did you want to talk to me about?"

"Oh," she said, "forget I said anything about that."

"What?" He waited with increasing alarm at her preoccupation.

"I don't know, Dean," she said, after a long hesitation. "You seemed distracted in English class today, and I was wondering if everything were okay."

"Everything's fine," he said.

"Just wanted to check." She looked ahead of her. "We should ride single file until we get through Cemetery Lane, because the aisles are narrow and uneven..."

"Lead the way."

She set a fast pace. His thighs were burning by the time they reached the bike trail. Once there Nikki pedaled harder. He felt his muscles brace like steel, ready for the challenge. He pushed himself to keep pace with her, and she responded by pushing herself harder. He passed her, increasing the distance between them, concentrating only on getting there first, until he reached an intersection in the trail and realized he didn't know where he was going.

He glanced over his shoulder and stopped abruptly; he hadn't realized how far behind Nikki was. He waited until she pulled up to him and thought about asking if she wanted to call the race a tie, but her eyes focused straight ahead. One look at the determined set of her features and he knew not to ask. He pulled ahead, but no longer had to hold back— he was biking his hardest, and this time she was only a few feet behind him.

Rain started to fall in large, splattering drops. He could tell by the steady crunching of gravel behind him that she would not let up until he did. His muscles began to burn from the intense effort, but as he heard her panting behind him, he felt the heat building up inside his body. He vamped his speed.

"Dean... stop."

He barely heard her, breathless, behind him. He slowed and turned. She had gotten off her bike and was limping slowly towards him. He quickly dismounted and started walking back towards her.

"What's wrong?" he asked. "Are you hurt?"

She shook her head. "No. But I had no idea that you were so fast."

He wheeled his bike beside hers, retaining the amiable silence. She stopped and leaned her bike against the fence bordering the trail.

"We're here," she said, still sounding winded.

He saw that they were standing a short distance away from a tunnel. "Where are we?"

"Near the park," she said.

"I like the park," he said. "But I've been there before. Never from this direction, but—"

"I wanted to show you the tunnel." She held out her hand and he took it. Her palm was sticky with sweat and rain, and she was trembling with exhaustion. The heat in his body became almost painful as he walked with her towards the tunnel.

"See the walls?" she said, holding his hand tight. "Aren't they beautiful?"

He didn't care about the walls, didn't even see them. "Nikki."

She turned. Her eyes widened, and she took a step towards the wall of the tunnel. "What is it, Dean?"

"What do I get for winning the race?" he asked.

She swallowed. "What race?"

He stepped closer to her, put a hand up on the wall behind her. "The race here."

"Is that why you were going so fast?" she asked. "I tried to stay in the lead to show you the way here..."

He put his other hand on the wall, boxing her in.

"When you took off I thought I wasn't going fast enough," she stammered. "And then I couldn't tell you to slow down because you were so far ahead and—"

He cut off the flow of her words by pressing his mouth against hers. The inside of her mouth was sweet and moist, but it took him only a minute to realize the full force of his desire before he realized she was not kissing him back. Then he could feel only the cold, wet slime of the wall against his hand. *For a minute he didn't care...* then he stepped away from her abruptly.

"I'm sorry," he mumbled.

"I... I just wasn't expecting for you to kiss me." She sounded like she was trying to explain to herself what had happened.

"I'm sorry if I made you uncomfortable, Nikki."

She blushed. "It's all right. Girlfriends do these things with—"

"Do you want to be my girlfriend?"

She blushed a shade deeper. "It's just that so much is happening right now--"

"You don't have to answer me now." He glanced at her face and saw that she was still embarrassed. In looking away from her, he saw the walls of the tunnel for the first time-- noticed that a delinquent had sprayed graffiti over about half of the available space.

"What were you saying about these walls?" he asked, suddenly—and keenly-- interested.

She rushed to answer him. "Oh. I just think these paintings are lovely, and I wanted to show someone else, because, even though this tunnel is so close to the park, I don't know how many people actually come through here, or even know this place exists--"

The tunnel seemed to have been abandoned. A few lights lined one edge of the ceiling but gave no real light, and the ceiling leaked in several places. The walls of the tunnel spotted jagged cracks, where the rain and chill had collided and made the walls look like they were bleeding ice. He felt Nikki twine her fingers through his again, and though that was a good sign, he noticed that her hand was freezing and that she was shaking.

"And to think that we know the artist," she said. "It's really incredible."

He wondered why she sounded nervous. "We do?"

"Galatea did this. At night." Nikki glanced around the tunnel. "Can you imagine? I had no idea she was so talented."

Her name sent a shiver through him. Also—a flash of understanding. He remembered the confrontation in the cemetery—how she had seemed shaken only when he had called her a vandal.

Now he knew why. He turned to Nikki and tried to control his voice. "Are you sure it was Galatea?"

She nodded. "I saw her when I was running."

"You run here at night?"

"Not so much anymore..." She trailed off. "You won't tell on her, will you, Dean?"

"I have no evidence that this is her work." His mind was racing. "Besides, what could I possibly gain from telling someone about this?"

"I don't know. I'm sure it was a silly question. I don't know why I asked you, except that I felt guilty--"

That annoyed him. "You didn't spray-paint the walls, did you?"

"No. But I still feel guilty. Maybe for bringing you here and--"

"You can't always trust your feelings. In fact, you never should. Especially not over your reason."

"She didn't tell me not to tell anyone." Nikki looked around the tunnel. "I'm sure she wouldn't even care if you knew. So, in conclusion, I shouldn't worry?"

"Right," he said. "Anyway, we should go."

"You don't like it here, Dean?"

"You're shivering," he said. "And the worst of the storm hasn't even hit yet."

"I'm sorry that you don't like the paintings," she said, following him out of the tunnel. "I didn't think you would, but for some reason I wanted to show you."

"I'm glad you showed me."

"You're not angry?"

"I'm not angry that you showed me." He paused. "I am angry that you ran here at night, by yourself. That wasn't safe. Promise me you won't come back here again, Nikki."

"I can't promise that I won't come back here," she said, walking resolutely to her bike. "I don't like making promises I know I won't keep. But I won't come here again at night."

His bike had fallen against hers, and he started to disentangle them. He propped her bike up. She looked at him thoughtfully. "Can we go slower?"

He nodded. He let her set the pace and rode leisurely by her side through the rain. Back in her garage, he stripped out of her father's rain poncho and helped her dry off the bikes. There was a moment of awkward silence between them.

"I can drive you home," she offered.

"I want to walk," he said. "I need some time to think."

"At least let me walk you to the end of the driveway."

"Stay here where it's dry."

She shook her head. "I'm already soaked."

They walked to the end of the driveway. He kissed her chastely on the cheek, and was glad to see a smile flit over her lips.

"Bye," she said.

"Bye." He started down Serenade Way. He turned back to find her watching him and waved. She waved back. The image of her—in her bright yellow rain jacket and boots, her hair spilling over her shoulders in damp chestnut-colored curls—remained with him as he walked into the gathering dusk. But the image of the tunnel remained burned as indelibly in his memory. And when he thought of the tunnel, he thought of Galatea...

Galatea and the feel of her body under those bulky clothes, the smoke and the incense and her wild, tangled hair...

He shielded his eyes from the stinging rain and glanced down the remainder of Serenade Way. He was not looking forward to the walk through Cemetery Lane, but it was the quickest route to get him home.

NIKKI DIETRICH

She tried to compose her thoughts before going inside. She had to appear normal; her mother could not know that something wrong had happened. She watched her breath form a cloud of vapor in the empty garage as she tried to untangle her thoughts. She liked Dean Fink. She looked forward to seeing him in school and she dreamed about him almost every night; she wasn't disturbed by the fact that he had kissed her. It was the violent way he had kissed her...

But she liked him. She would stand by him. He had seemed understanding enough in the tunnel, so she wouldn't waste her time worrying over silly things. She checked to make sure the bikes were stacked neatly in their places, then she walked into the house. The sudden heat and light made her dizzy, and she paused to orient herself.

Her mother stood in the kitchen, leaning against the stove. The washed out quality of her face and the stoop in her usually square shoulders instantly let Nikki know that something was wrong.

"How is he?" she asked, anxiously.

Her mother looked up and smiled. Nikki left her rain gear in a sopping heap by the door. "What happened?"

Her mother looked away. "He's asking for you."

She hurried down the dim hallway to her parents' darkened room. She paused in front of the closed door and told herself it was impossible to smell sickness, to smell death-- that her mind was creating things to prepare her to face her worst possible fear.

She knocked, then opened the door. Her father lay still, looking too small in the king-sized bed; she couldn't believe how much the disease had changed him. She blinked back her tears as she walked into the room.

"Hi, Daddy," she said, trying to keep her voice steady. "Mamma said you wanted to see me."

"You're all wet, Nicole." His voice—a voice whose volume and strength had once made hardened criminals cringe—had become weak, raspy with fatigue.

"I was out riding."

"With Dean Fink?"

She nodded. He looked at her for a long time, and when he held out his hand, she went quickly to him.

"At least the sun is still out," he said, and she leaned in to hear his whispered, painful words. "And you weren't by yourself. You think we don't know about your runs, Nicole, but parents always know…"

"I don't usually run at night," she said, her voice catching. "Only sometimes, whenever-"

"Promise me you'll be careful."

"I'm always careful, Daddy."

"That boy," he said, and frowned. "He makes you happy?"

She thought about Dean Fink, and nodded.

"Just don't believe everything he tells you, Nicole."

"Okay."

"It wouldn't be the first time a boy put on a good face to try to get into your pants."

"Oh, Daddy," she said, embarrassed.

"Let me speak, Nicole." He coughed. "Don't make him into something he's not. Your mother made that mistake, and look at how that turned out."

Her parents had been happily married for over twenty years. She could not check the tears that her father's attempted humor brought to her eyes.

"Please don't go," she said, her voice wavering—breaking. "You can't leave us yet. We need you."

He looked at her, his eyes clear and serious. "I need you to be strong for your mother, Nikki."

She could not be strong—not even though he needed her to be. She choked back a sob and pressed his hand to her lips.

"Nicole," he said sternly. "Promise me."

She wiped away her tears. She nodded. She didn't want to leave him, but she could see that even their brief exchange of words had exhausted him.

"Let me see a smile before you go."

She smiled. "I love you, Daddy. I'll let you rest."

"There's my girl." His eyes followed her as she stood. "Tell your mother I want to see her."

Nikki nodded and left the room quickly. She closed the door behind her. She passed into the kitchen.

"Mom," she said, keeping her face lowered to avoid a confrontation. "He wants to see you."

Her mother remained standing still. When Nikki raised her eyes, she found her mother's gaze fixed unwaveringly on her own, a look of strong yet quiet resolution there. Suddenly, her mother was hugging her tightly.

"I love you, Nikki," she said.

"I love you too, Mom."

"You're a beautiful child. A precious blessing." She pulled away, and her eyes were serene, though glistening with tears. "I can see so much of your father in your face, in your personality…" She squeezed Nikki's shoulder gently. "He'll be with us, here in this house, even when he's gone. You know that, don't you?"

She didn't answer. Her mother passed by her quickly, and Nikki understood. She went quietly to her room and sat down on her bed. She knew she would feel better if she cried, but she didn't feel like crying. She couldn't cry when she felt so numb.

The uncertainty of death, she knew, was the worst. That was the stage that accumulated the most intense pain and fear and suffering for him—for them. Death itself would be easier to confront. She remembered the look in her father's eyes as he had given her his last words of advice—how wise and calm he had seemed. She wondered how they could ever properly grieve for him, when he had been so at peace with himself in the end.

She knew the exact instant when he passed away, not because of her mother's sudden scream or the echoes of her mother's sobs through the walls of her room, but because a great calm settled over her soul. Though she didn't know the details, she knew the outcome-- that he was all right.

The pain, the sorrow, the disbelief would come later, but in that moment she only realized that he was gone, and that he was all right.

DEAN FINK

He could barely see as he drove through the cemetery, the uneven aisles teeming with the dusk's shadows. The full moon in the curdled sky sent slivers of jagged light across the tombstones.

A guy like you would have everything to fear from a place like this

He listened to her voice, without wondering how she had intruded into his thoughts.

A flash of anger tore through him, and he stopped the car. He was tired of being afraid.

He parked by the side of a cracked aisle and got out of his car. He started walking towards the well where he had first seen Galatea. The night air chilled him, but he took his hands out of his pockets and let the wind rattle against him. He thought he sensed movement– but it was only a slithering shadow, inching its way across the tombstone beside the well.

His mind was playing tricks on him– the mind he used to have under such good control.

His mind was trying to convince him to stay away from the well, riddling his reason with fear. He thought he heard a whispering voice; he thought he sensed the shadows move; he ignored everything until he reached the well. He looked down into the water and saw his own reflection.

The faint light from the moon obfuscated his features, made the lines of his face bleed into dark ripples. He stared into the empty sockets of his eyes and wondered what he had become. But he continued to stare, unwaveringly, at his reflection.

A small spark went through him, and for a moment he felt free. Then came thoughts that started in the base of his body, crept through him like magma, superseded the impression of epiphany.

Thoughts of Galatea.

Damn Galatea for distracting him.

If he had not heard her voice in his head, he would not be in the lonely cemetery at the late hour, staring like a madman down into a scummy well.

He backed away from the stagnant water, suddenly feeling the darkness and the spirits and the dead around him like a suffocating envelope. He could not continue to live with the unfaced demons; they would kill him. He would do whatever he needed to do to rid himself of their ambiguity—even if it meant giving into them. He could not ignore the promptings of his mind; doing so would be a form of suicide.

The dark prompting that occurred to him as he stood by the solitary well in the cemetery seemed more reasonable as time passed, reframed by this new perspective. He would think no more of implications or consequences, of previous insights and doubts. He simply had to do what needed to be done.

GALATEA WILLIAMS

"Suppose you tell me the truth," the guidance counselor had said.

She had fought to keep her hands unclenched. "Nothing."

"Who beat you up?"

The guidance counselor was well-meaning, she knew, but she wasn't going to tell the prim, middle-aged lady with the pencil skirt and nicotine-stained nails anything. "I told you it was nothing." Just the slightest edge to her voice, to let the woman know she wasn't going to budge.

The woman had taken off her glasses and propped her head on her hand. "This doesn't have anything to do with the fight Skeeter got into, does it?"

Her heart had quickened. "I don't know what you're talking about."

"Well, since we're clearly not talking about you..." The counselor's eyes had pierced hers. "Do you have any background information about what happened in the trailer park last night? Because Skeeter is another one of my students, and since he's not here to tell me—"

"Skeeter never misses school."

"He's not here today. But I suppose you knew that?"

She had dropped all defenses. "Is he okay?"

"I don't know, Galatea. I was hoping you could tell me that."

"I have to go."

Now she watched as he packed a last wad of putty into the crack in the ceiling. He had a black eye she hadn't given him, and the left side of his face was completely swollen. From the difficulty he was having breathing, she thought something was probably also wrong with his ribs.

He craned his neck to see his handiwork. "I think that should do it. Let me know if it starts leaking again."

She took the wad of remaining putty from him. "You look like shit."

"Thanks for noticing. You sure you still want to live here?" he asked. "Come summer time, there are going to be rats…"

"Friends," she corrected, wondering when exactly they had stopped telling each other the truth.

"Flea-ridden friends."

"Yes, Skeeter, I'm sure I still want to live here. Having a sanctuary is worth any number of little inconveniences. As long as you don't mind helping me out once in awhile."

"Sure," he said.

They were not to talk about it. He had made that clear to her. What he hadn't made so clear was why. She glanced at him as he came to sit beside her on the mattress. *She at least had to try.* "Something seems like it's bothering you."

"Fink called off practice today."

She was afraid he would see the sudden flash of anger darken her eyes. Then she realized-- he was using Dean Fink as a distraction. "Come on, Skeeter. I know you better than that."

He arched his dark eyebrows, and the bruises made his eyes that much more intense. "I heard you skipped out on half your classes today."

She shrugged. "When I heard you weren't in school, I freaked."

He shifted. "How's your nose?"

"Don't worry about it." *Was that what was really bothering him—that he had hurt her? Or was there something else?* "We always—" She caught herself and broke off abruptly.

"What?"

We always hurt the ones we love. But she couldn't say that to him. She couldn't put that word—*love*—on the table between them. He might not realize it, but she did; they were so similar that he had hurt her to hurt himself. *It was fucked up,* she thought. *But what isn't right now?* "Nothing."

"Tea," he said, after a minute. "I have to ask you something."

He was still being serious. She felt herself tense. "What?"

"Is something going on? Between you and Fink?"

She felt so stunned she could barely speak. "Your ridiculousness has reached epic proportions, Skeeter."

"I asked you a question."

She couldn't believe it. *Was he angry? Jealous?* For so long she had wanted to draw some kind of emotion from him—but she didn't like this. She didn't want him to even think along those lines. "Nothing," she said. "Nothing is going on."

He stood. "Well. That putty should hold."

"Thanks," she said, unsettled.

"Anything else?"

"Yes." She looked away. "I learned something about Nikki Dietrich that might interest you."

"What?"

"Nikki's tougher than you think she is," she said. "You might make a good match after all."

"Nikki and Fink are perfect for each other."

"Is that why you won't move in on Nikki?" She crossed her arms. "Because Fink likes--"

"Nikki is out of my league."

"I disagree." She clasped her hands together. "And I don't think Fink is a good match for anyone. All he has to offer people is death."

"Tea, that's absurd. And Nikki can handle him. But humor me. Why did you say that?"

She scowled. "He doesn't seem to have much of a heart."

"I don't see that as a flaw."

"You don't?"

"You think it's better to be like us?"

She frowned. "What do you mean by that?"

"To feel too much."

She shifted closer to him. "I think it's better to feel too much than to not feel anything at all."

"Well, I don't. I hate everything about our lives. I hate not having money. I hate that people will always think we're low and dishonest, no matter what we do." His hands clenched. "But what I hate most is that there's no way for us to get out."

"You're wrong, Skeeter," she said. "There are a lot of ways to get out. Art, music, writing--"

"Those are temporary escapes. When you come back from those highs, you're still here."

"Here's not such a bad place to be," she said. "If you surround yourself with beautiful things, you can almost forget."

"I can't," he said.

She let silence fall over the room. She had never been able to help when Skeeter fell into one of his rare moods. She had never been able to convince him that making the best of what they had was all they could do. She knew he wanted more. She admired him for it, but she knew his standards made life harder for him.

"If there's anything I can do..." she started.

"I'll work through it on my own."

The answer she had come to expect.

"Galatea," he said, startling her. "There's a broken window in the basement. It leads to a shaft which angles up to the roof of the building. I can see everything above and below me, and all I had to do was find your location, then let myself off at the appropriate floor. That's how I got in today."

"I can't believe I didn't hear any of that," she said, disappointed that he had shifted back into the role of her practical protector. "I doubt anyone would go to that much trouble to get in."

"He would if he wanted to find you in here." He glanced at her, started to say something more-- didn't. She wondered if it would have made a difference.

"He'd have to find this place first." She sighed. "Though sometimes I wish this place were even more remote. I can still hear sirens and traffic..."

He sat down, turned her to face him. "Why are you doing this? I thought you felt safe at home now."

"I do," she said, trying not to respond to his touch and failing. "I also feel unwanted. And that's a sucky feeling, Skeeter. To feel unwanted."

He let go of her shoulders, folded his hands in his lap. He waited silently for her to continue.

"Though maybe I deserve that." She paused. "After what happened—"

"I've already told you what I thought about that."

She felt the old anger destroying her. "Up to that point, I had tried to live my life as best I could. But what did it matter in the end?"

"The 'end' isn't here yet. And you can't judge yourself by what others do to you." He paused. "Only by what you choose for yourself."

"That's a nice thought." Her voice was devoid of emotion. "But the fact remains that the thing was done."

"It didn't blacken your soul, Tea," he said. "No one can do that except for you. And that's what you're doing, living in constant hate and fear."

"What's the point in fighting?" she cried out suddenly. "I lived as best as I could and he took everything away from me in—"

"Tea."

She clamped her cry short and looked at him. He took hold of her shoulders, drew her gently but firmly closer to him.

"If you don't fight, he wins. The world wins." He looked directly into her eyes, frowned. "You know that."

"The world has already won. I don't even want to fight anymore." She looked away. "It doesn't matter anymore."

"It matters more now than it ever did before." He tipped her chin up so she had to look at him. "What triggered this?"

She put her hand over his, removed his touch from her face. "I don't know why I should keep fighting. Nothing is ever going to change."

"You fight," he said. "So that in the end, no matter what happens, you know you didn't compromise."

She paused. "Have you ever lost something, Skeeter? Something as precious as—"

"I've never had anything to lose." He paused. "You mind if I stay here tonight? Kenny's on probation."

That was all it took for her to understand. "No."

"It probably doesn't matter," he said. "They're going to get me involved some day, somehow…"

"You can stay here as long as you like," she said.

"I know it's going to happen eventually." His eyes flashed. "I'm going to end up running from something I didn't do—"

"You could always turn them in," she said.

"Brothers don't incriminate brothers."

"What would Kenny be doing if he—"

"He'd be saving his own skin. Surviving."

"And that's perfectly acceptable?"

He turned slightly towards her. "Not everyone is as stupid as I am."

"Doing what you think is right doesn't make you stupid."

Skeeter paused. "He's building up the money so I can go to college, so I don't have to deal to get by."

"Is that what he told you?"

"Why would he lie to me?"

"Oh, I don't know, Skeeter," she said angrily. "Probably because he's an addict and a pusher and a—"

"He knows he wouldn't have to lie to me about what he does," he said. "Or why he does it."

"Let's be real." She sensed him stiffen, but continued anyway. "The only way you're going to get money for college is on a scholarship."

"Fine, let's be real," he said. "I'm not going to college. I'm going to the Marines, if I make it that far."

Her face crumpled. "I'd be so worried, every day, that you'd get shot. And I don't know what I'd do without you."

"You'd be fine," he said. "Besides, everyone has to die sometime. I'd rather die honorably."

"Let's talk about something else."

But she had let him get too far with the idea. "That's the only thing I want. To die honorably."

"Live honorably instead. Like you're already doing." She looked at her hands. "I'm sure you could get a scholarship, maybe even several, for academics and athletics—"

"My academic record is shot," he said. "You know I don't care about anything but English. And rugby is unofficial."

"What do you mean it's unofficial? You practice more than any other sports team at our school does, and you play harder than--"

He shrugged. "We practice because we want to. We want the challenge, not the recognition. It's not important that anyone else knows what we do."

Her lips curled. "I refuse to believe that Dean Fink would put any effort into something that wouldn't gain him some kind of recognition," she said.

"What do you mean by that?"

She glanced at him. "Why can't I say one word against Dean Fink without having you get defensive?"

"You don't know him." Skeeter's voice remained hard. "Don't ask me to pick between the two of you."

"Don't worry, I know who you'd choose," she said, and there was the ugly thing out in the open between them. "I would never ask you to choose. But I'm allowed an opinion. And I'm surprised that Dean Fink plays on an unofficial rugby team. Even because of his size--"

"He's stronger than he looks," Skeeter said. "He plays hard, and he can take a hit. And he's fast, which makes him perfect to be a back." He stretched. "Though that's part of the thrill of rugby. Not getting hit, and not getting hurt."

"So that's the thrill of it for you." She crossed her arms over her chest. "What's the thrill of it for Fink?"

"It's a game that tests your strength, your intelligence, your stamina," he said. "And it takes discipline and determination. I'm sure that's what Fink loves about it."

She resolved herself to never say another word to him about Dean Fink. No matter what happened, she would never mention Dean Fink to him again.

"I'm going to sleep," she said, finally. She looked at him, keeping her features blank.

"There's only one mattress, and it gets damn cold here at night. So are you okay with that?"

He hesitated. "You sure?"

Keep it natural. Once the lights were out it wouldn't matter. She shrugged. "There's nowhere else for you to sleep."

She blew out the candles, then slipped out of her street clothes. She sensed him take off his rain-soaked clothing before he sat on the edge of the mattress, looking down at her in the darkness.

"Would you get in, Skeeter?" she asked, teeth chattering. "It's freezing."

He eased onto the mattress, careful not to touch her, and pulled the quilt around them. She shifted, slightly, so that her head lay on his chest—testing, waiting for his reaction. Slowly, he slipped an arm under her shoulders.

"Hear the rain on the roof?" she asked softly. "That's one of my favorite things about this place."

He listened to the metallic patter above them. "I might have to come here more often at night."

"Any time you want," she said. "Even if Kenny isn't in town."

"I might not come around for a while after this, though," he said.

She was instantly alert, propping herself up to look at him, her hand on his chest. "Why?"

"Kenny's people might follow me," he said. "I don't want to lead them to you."

She leaned back on the mattress, turned away from him.

"Tea?"

She turned back to him. "I'm just going to pretend that I didn't hear what you said."

And then she pretended to fall asleep in the silence that ensued, though she was really intensely alert—of the rhythm of his breathing, the heat and strength of his arm around her, the drumbeat of the rain on the roof and the quiet hum of his heart. She knew she did not want to sleep—not with him so near her—but it had been awhile since she felt so safe, and awhile since she had slept, and eventually she dozed off.

NIKKI DIETRICH

Halfway through the night she gave up trying to sleep and retreated to her desk. She drank the words in her Bible until the tiny print made her eyes burn, and then she cried. At first crying was a relief, a release—but she could not seem to stop as the full weight of her loss hit.

She drove to school the next day half-blinded by tears, and spent half an hour crying in the student parking lot before she got out of her car. She stumbled to the front office to check in. The secretary was not there, but Skeeter DeLuca was—sitting silently in front of the principal's office, reading a book. He looked up when she entered. She tried to clear her thoughts; his smile made her feel dizzy.

"Is anyone here?" she asked him. Her voice sounded strange to her—rusty.

"The secretary just went in the back." His smile faltered, and his dark eyes searched her face. "If you need to talk to the principal, you might want to come back in a while. I'm next on the list, and that always takes a while."

"Did you get in trouble again?"

"Par for the course. What happened to you, Nikki?"

She wasn't sure she would be able to say the words, and then she wasn't sure she'd be able to say them without reawakening the sluice of tears. "My father died last night."

"Get out of here."

She took a deep breath. "He did."

"No, I mean go home," he said quietly. "I'll tell Fink to bring over your homework tonight and then--"

"No. Please don't."

His voice was firm. "I'll tell the secretary why you're not in school when she gets back."

He had made the decision for her. She turned from him, relieved. "Thank you." She paused. "What are you reading?"

He looked up. "Faulkner."

"Really?" she said. "Which novel?"

He held up the book: <u>As I Lay Dying</u>. She took an involuntary step backwards. He looked at her blankly, then he quickly lowered the book.

"Sorry," he mumbled.

"Skeeter." She didn't know what broke the words from her, but suddenly his envelope was in her hand, and she was holding it out to him like a peace offering. "Here, this is for you."

"What is it?" he asked, guardedly.

"An invitation. To the funeral." Her voice sounded more steady. She paused, then continued. "I know it will be awkward, and I understand if you don't want to—"

"I'll be there," he said.

She smiled, a certain dark feeling ebbing out of her—like chains being broken. "Thank you."

He nodded quickly, then looked down at his book and distinctly turned a page. She was relieved to escape from the stuffy building into the biting winter air. She felt light-headed and dizzy and sick, and she didn't know how she would get home without crashing. But she did, and her mother asked for no explanation as she tore up the stairs and cried herself into a comatose sleep.

Later, as the day of the viewing approached, she realized that Skeeter was the only person she really wanted there. After having cried herself sick on the night her father died, she had started writing out the invitations—and Skeeter's was the first one she had labeled. She didn't know why—but she wanted him there.

He came early to the funeral. He came directly to her; she recognized him, and her world clicked back into place. The suit, though it fit his angular frame well, looked unnatural on him, and he seemed uncomfortable in it.

"Hello, Skeeter," she said, as soon as he was in speaking distance. "You look nice. I like your suit."

"It's Dean's." He paused. "He's coming. He wanted to go home after practice and get cleaned up, but he'll be here."

"You're here now," she said.

"I skipped practice. So I could tell you why Dean would be late." He paused. "I like your dress."

"He loved yellow." She blushed. "It's a color of life and hope—"

"You don't have to explain," he said. "I just like your dress."

People started to file into the room. Nikki moved closer to him, shielding herself from the rows of black-clad mourners. "This isn't what he would have wanted."

Her eyes swept over the crowd before she looked at him. Their eyes connected. She knew instantly that he understood, and she quickly dropped her gaze.

"I'm not going to stay long," he said. "I don't really like these kinds of things, but I wanted to come--"

"You can leave whenever you want," she said. "We won't be offended. And thank you for coming."

He followed her gaze to the sea of black that continued to file in. "He must have been a great man."

"He was." Her eyes teared up. "And he was a great father."

He touched her lightly, hesitantly, on the shoulder. "I'm sorry. I didn't want to upset you."

She shook her head. "I'm glad you're here, Skeeter. Please don't apologize."

"Well, there's Fink." He sounded relieved. "I'll leave you two alone and go sign the guestbook or something."

She couldn't help but smile as he walked away, but she was also relieved that Fink had arrived. He looked very handsome to her, even though he was dressed in a somber black suit and wore an equally serious expression. He kissed her lightly on the cheek and tucked a strand of her hair behind her ear.

"Here," he said, handing her a single yellow rose. "I wanted you to have something beautiful in the midst of…" He broke off, smiled. "I didn't know at the time it would match. In remembrance of how he lived?"

She nodded, glad she didn't have to explain. "I'm glad you could come. Thank you."

His hand was warm, strong, comforting around hers. "I wanted to be here for you."

She looked into his eyes to make sure he was all right; on the few times they had driven down Cemetery Lane together, he had seemed uneasy being around the dead.

But his voice was steady, and he seemed different. She didn't know exactly what had changed about him—but something had changed.

"How are you doing?" he asked.

She managed a genuine smile for him. "I'm fine for now. But I don't know how I'll be once the service starts. Dean, if I… if I leave… please don't come after me. Let me be alone."

"I'll respect that," he said quietly.

"Thank you."

"We'll sit at the end of an aisle." He guided her towards the back of the funeral home. "Then, if you need to leave---"

"You think of everything. You always have a plan." She sat down.

He sat beside her. They didn't talk. Nikki watched the proceedings numbly, reassured by his presence and his arm clandestinely encircling her waist, keeping her close to him. She concentrated on her breathing; she was relatively sure she would be able to make it through the service without making a scene.

She watched her mother break down halfway through the eulogy, and suddenly she couldn't take it. The black suits of the people suffocated her with their darkness, the tears in the eyes of people who couldn't possibly understand, the corpse that looked like a wax dummy—a wax dummy masquerading as her father...

She was out of her seat and down the aisle and out the door. In the cool air outside her pain expulsed in one loud sob of sorrow. She sat down on the steps and put her head on her knees and cried until her sides were sore, until her tears plastered her face, until she had to stop so she could breathe. She took a shaky breath and looked up. She saw Skeeter leaning against the wall near her. She froze, then tried her voice.

"I didn't know you were here," she said.

He nodded, determinedly not looking at her.

She unwound the yellow handkerchief from her hair, wiped her face. "I hope you didn't come out here after me."

"I didn't." He paused. "I couldn't watch the speeches. Then when you came out, I couldn't go by you to get back inside." He paused. "I didn't want to disturb you."

"I keep running into you when I'm completely out of control." She dabbed her eyes. "You must think I'm trying to make you uncomfortable."

"I wasn't thinking that at all."

"No?"

"I was thinking of something my friend said. That sometimes we..." He paused. "I mean, people like my friend and me, that we feel too much."

"And people like Fink and me don't," she expanded.

He looked away. "I see she was wrong."

"Well, I hardly feel in the mood for a discussion." She blew her nose. "But I assure you that Dean would say I'm being overly sentimental about this. And I agree with him."

He sat down beside her on the steps. "You're not. There's nothing more important than family."

She looked down at her hands, and he looked out in front of him.

"You lost someone you loved," she said.

He hesitated. "My grandfather. Years ago."

"I'm sorry."

"He lived a long life, and he used it well." He reached into the pocket of his suit, pulled out the tiny crystal on its piece of twine. She watched as he absently started making rainbows dance across the sidewalk.

"Tell me about him," she said.

"He was different than the rest of my family. He was concerned with doing what he thought was right." He paused. "He gave me this before he died."

"You must have loved him a lot."

"I did." He paused. "I want you to have this."

"Skeeter, I could never--"

"You have to hang onto things that make you smile. I have other things of his." He took her hand in his, only long enough to uncurl her fingers. He dropped the crystal in her open palm. "Besides, Miss Z will end up confiscating it if I keep it."

"Thank you, Skeeter." She felt her hand close around the tiny crystal, felt the smooth, glass ridges of the prism. "Will you show me how to make the light dance?"

"Just give it a try."

She held the tiny crystal up to the light. The sun filtered through the clear facets, dancing over the salted sidewalk in rainbow beams. She glanced up, saw a small smile on his face. She looked at him, trying to understand. "You really don't mind if I keep it?"

He reached under his shirt. The sunlight glinted off the silver chain.

"This was his, too," he said.

She reached over and took hold of the tiny gold cross, aware of how close the gesture brought them. "You wear this all the time."

"Every day," he said.

"So you can keep him near." She paused. "Was your grandfather religious?"

"In his own way." He paused. "The cross reminded him to have faith."

"To have faith in God?"

"No. Just to have faith in something." He paused. "Nikki, if you ever need anything, please let me know."

"Thank you, Skeeter."

"I'm serious," he said. "Anything at all—"

She started to respond, and then a duct of warm air let them know that someone had exited the funeral home. Skeeter slipped the cross back under his shirt. The expression on his face didn't change.

"Nikki."

She recognized Fink's voice, and her hand closed protectively around the crystal. She glanced at Skeeter. She wanted to address his insistent words, but not in Dean Fink's presence.

"I know you told me not to come out after you," Fink continued apologetically. "But the service is finished, and your mother is looking for you..."

"It's all right, Dean," she said, using Skeeter's shoulder as a prop to help her stand. "I was just coming in."

Fink put his arm around her shoulders. "Are you okay?""

She managed a small smile. "I'm a mess, but Skeeter helped cheer me up."

"Thanks, Skeet," Fink said.

She stepped closer to Fink, thankful for his arm, supporting her-- for his body, strong and stable, against hers.

"I'm going to go now," Skeeter said, standing. "I'll get your suit back to you as soon as-"

"Sure. Don't worry about it."

She saw Skeeter glance at her, and she managed a small smile. He attempted a smile, then turned and walked into the parking lot, his broad shoulders sharp under the suit. She turned to Dean Fink, who was watching her with a concerned expression on his face.

"Can we go inside?" she said, before he could speak. "It's cold."

He paused, then held out the yellow rose he had brought her. "You left this inside. I didn't want it to get crushed in the shuffle of everyone moving."

She held the flower delicately against her chest. "Thank you."

He held the door open for her, and she smiled at him as she passed through. But one moment in the funeral home zapped her energy. She turned to him quickly.

"Dean, can you take me to your house? I can't... I can't go home right now."

He seemed surprised, but nodded.

"Let me tell my mom," she said, ducking out from under his arm.

"I'll meet you by my car. I parked in the front lot."

She walked through the crowds to her mother, but on the way out she paused in front of the guestbook. Her father had hundreds of associates, but her mother had only invited those she knew he had respected. Those considerations had greatly reduced the number in attendance—but there were still over a hundred names in that book. Nikki glanced over the sea of signatures without reading the comments. A second glance through the pages showed her that Skeeter had not signed the guestbook. He had come and gone without leaving a trace—as if he hadn't wanted anyone to know he had been there. As if he had wanted to be invisible.

She knew that waiting made Fink impatient, and she hurried back to meet him. As she strapped herself into the passenger seat, she wished she hadn't asked him to take her to his house; she would have to talk to him, and she didn't want to talk to anyone.

DEAN FINK

"Dean, just take me home, okay?" she said, after they had driven in silence for ten minutes.

He glanced at her. Her face looked puffy, like she had cried acid instead of tears. He nodded and changed direction. Twenty minutes later, he parked in front of her house. He turned off the ignition. "If I can do anything—"

She looked at him, and the light in her eyes went out. "Come inside with me."

His brow knit, but he followed her through the cold air into the warmth of the house. He followed her to her room, then stood staring at her in silence. He realized—for all his brains and accomplishments and work ethic—he did not know how to communicate with others. He did not know what she was trying to tell him.

"How can I help?" he asked, moving closer to her with stiff steps. "Can I help?"

She grabbed the collar of his shirt, pulled him towards her. "Kiss me."

He stared at her.

She sank onto her bed. "Kiss me like you did that one day."

She was still holding his collar; he had to move with her. He propped himself above her on his elbows and looked at her. "Nikki, this isn't a good idea. I'm worried that the emotional imbalance you are currently experiencing is interfering with your rational--"

She pulled him down. Her body beneath his felt frail, like he would break her. He was so close to her now—close enough to make him forget everything else.

"Don't you want me to be happy?" she accused.

"I want you to be happy."

"Then I want you to kiss me," she said. "Right now."

His emotions were driving him crazy; he needed time to think. He took her hands and removed them from his shirt. He stood up and left the bed. He took off his coat, placed it neatly on the chair by her desk. Then, slowly, he walked back to the bed and sat down. He prepared to tell her he wouldn't do this, not when she wasn't thinking clearly—but she chose that moment to close her eyes, to lean back into the pillows on her bed, to open herself completely to him…

He moved gently onto the bed beside her and pressed his lips against hers. The gesture was meant to be comforting and gentle. But when her arms twined around his neck, when she bit him, he lost control and kissed her harder. His tongue forced open her lips, and he felt warmth flow through him as he listened to her moan softly.

Her eyes stayed closed as his lips moved down her neck, down to the smooth skin visible above the scoop neck of her dress. He felt her hands twine through his hair and press his face against her chest. He turned his head and lay still.

"I can hear your heart beat," he said.

She kept her eyes closed, and he knew she wanted him to continue. Soon he wouldn't be able to stop. He needed to make a decision about what he was doing. He had to break the chain of power his lust had over him; he forced himself to shift slightly. Then he was helping her sit up, his hand against the small of her back. He leaned in and kissed her gently. When she opened her eyes, he smiled uncertainly.

She seemed to understand.

He stood and walked to her desk. He absently picked up one of the papers he saw lying there. Then his focus sharpened, and his eyes narrowed as he realized that he was reading a poem she had written… about Skeeter.

He turned quickly. He noticed the emotion flitting over her face, before she stood and moved to the desk. She took the paper from him. She turned it face down.

"Nikki?" he asked her. When she didn't answer him he hesitated. Then he picked up his coat. "Fine. If you don't want to talk, I'll go home."

"Nothing is going on between us." Her voice sounded hard to him.

He felt the slightest flash of redemption. *Nikki and Skeeter? He must be going crazy.* "Then why are you writing about him?"

"My emotions are still so jumbled. It's going to take a while to be able to—"

"To continue on like nothing happened." He would give her the benefit of the doubt. *Innocent until proven guilty.*

Her brow furrowed. "What?"

"If I lost my father, it would take me awhile to be able to act like nothing had happened." He paused, not quite comfortable with the look she was giving him. "I know that's what my father would want, anyway. He doesn't believe in excuses. He's told me to never let anything stand in my way."

"Thank you, Dean," she said. "I'll remember that."

She thought he was an asshole. He paused. "You can call me if you ever need anything, Nikki."

"Thank you."

"I usually go to bed by midnight, but you could even call me after that."

There was a blank, vacant look in her eyes that he didn't like. "Thank you, Dean."

There was nothing left for him to do but leave. He kissed her awkwardly on the cheek; she did not walk him to the door. When he looked back at the house, he saw she had already turned off her light, even though it was early evening. He guessed she must have gone to sleep; there was nowhere else she could go, since darkness had fallen.

He could only give her the time and space she needed. People as strong as Nikki didn't break; she would be fine.

But he was not. Facing his own mortality at the funeral, his frustration of his recent lack of control in his life, and the knowledge that Nikki would be okay, while he was getting farther and farther off track, filled him with a strange, strong energy.

He had to find an outlet. Before he turned out of Cemetery Lane, he saw the bike trail that cut by the old abandoned warehouses. Without much thought he angled the car into the lane that would take him to the tunnel.

GALATEA WILLIAMS

She added a touch of detail in the darkness, listening to the hiss of the paint and the rattle of the near-empty can. Then she froze, every sense straining. She knew instantly she was not alone. She turned, saw the dark hulking form blocking the tunnel's entrance.

The can of spray paint dropped from her hand, landed with a metallic clatter against the tunnel's wet floor, and rolled into a half frozen puddle. She started running. She heard his footsteps behind her, pounding the concrete, echoing off the shivering walls. Her body tensed for the force of contact, while her mind spun through every self-defense tactic she had learned…

The force of his tackle knocked the breath out of her before the impact of concrete. The stiff heel of her boot connected with his side but didn't hurt him. His body was like stone and crushed her into the ground. He grabbed her wrists in one of his hands, pinned her arms over her head. His tongue filled her mouth, suffocating her scream. She bit down. He spit his blood back into her face, blinding her.

She knew what he was going to do; she closed her eyes and tried to take herself away. But the world that rose to meet her was swarming with demons, poisonous memories of the past— *and she could not let it happen again.* She opened her eyes, awakened by the pulsing of his groin grinding against her.

She heard a voice in her head. *You're ready.*

But she wasn't ready. She wasn't ready to kill someone…

Then she felt his knees forcing her legs open, his hands pawing at the hem of her skirt, and *she wouldn't let it happen again.* Panic and fear drained out of her, replaced by a cold buzzing in her mind. She drove her knee upward into his stomach, used the leverage to flip him over her. She reached out and found the spray can she had dropped; she lashed out and felt the cold metal tear into his face. She pulled out the knife and plunged the blade into his side, jerking up to split the wound open. As his blood spilled over her hands she felt something in her recoiling, even as her pent-up hatred and anger reared up and demanded that she inflict maximum pain…

She yanked the blade out, brought her heel into his groin and twisted. His sudden cry of pain let her know she had incapacitated him—temporarily. She had two choices and little time to decide: she could kill him, or she could try to get away. His blood slick between her fingers, sticky on the unsheathed blade, she stood in the unlit tunnel and stared down at him, her breath fogging out in vapor before her. *Run away*, a delayed voice whispered through the haze of red blinding her.

If she ran, and he got back up…

Already he was starting to straighten on the floor. She grabbed the can she had dropped and did the only thing she could think to do. She watched as he howled in pain, hands clenched over his eyes, the metallic heaviness of the spray hanging like poison in the air.

Then she ran.

She didn't perceive anything as she pushed herself out into the night as fast as her bruised body allowed her. Demons, darkness, pain—they didn't matter. They vanished, in a mirage of dancing candles and broken glass and a beautiful red Buddha…

Get there, she thought, pushing herself on. *Don't think. Get there and you'll be okay.*

Bleeding, stumbling, she made it to the warehouse and padlocked the door behind her, then collapsed into a merciful blackness in the midst of her sanctuary.

NIKKI DIETRICH

She had been staring at the blank walls in her room for over an hour when the urge to run—to run away—hit her. She could think of no place of sanctuary besides the tunnel. Knowing her mother was asleep in her room, passed out from Nyquil, she laced her running shoes and let herself quietly out the door.

Now she sat stunned in the shadows, the tears frozen on her face. Her horror had driven all feeling from her body; she felt as senseless as one of the unseeing stones of the tunnel. Through her numbness, she heard a distant prompting telling her that if she did not act, Dean Fink would die. The knowledge of what he had tried to do crushed her-- but he needed help. And she could not walk away from anyone who needed her help.

Her every step into the tunnel destroyed the last remaining strength she had— but she kept walking mechanically, fighting nausea and the desire to leave him there, to leave him there to die…

She knelt beside him and slipped her hand under his head. "Dean?"

His face—so deathly pale, so like wax—scared all other thoughts from her mind. Her touch brought only the slightest reaction from him. His head turned towards her, and she had to fight a wave of nausea as she saw the jagged flaps of his cheek, slit open from can, and the bloody pulp of the flesh opened by his temple. And his eyes…

She strained to count his pulse-- barely there. She raised his shirt, and almost passed out at the sight of the gash—the blood. She forced her panicked thoughts to something she knew she could handle; he was a wounded animal, that was all. Exhaling shakily, she re-examined the side wound—long, ugly, jagged… and shallow. He was not losing as much blood as she had feared. If he was conscious, she could move him. She bent closer, but could not bring herself to say his name. "Can you walk?"

He groaned. Conscious. But something was wrong. His eyes were hazy, unfocused. She fought the dizziness and revulsion that wrapped around her like dark wings; she forced herself to speak calmly.

"Can you walk?" she repeated.

"Jumped," he groaned. "There must have been—"

"You can explain later." Her eyes fell on the spray paint can lying frozen to the concrete in a puddle near his head, flicked to the red paint that ringed his unseeing eyes. She fought the urge to vomit as she pieced together what she had heard in the tunnel, after she had ducked into the shadows where she sat paralyzed with terror. "Come on. We have to move."

She stood with him, not caring if she hurt him. Slumped under his weight, she realized she could support him if she used her hip to take the brunt of his weight off her. She didn't want him near her, but she had no choice. She had to help him.

"Did you drive?" she asked, hoping he was conscious enough to understand her... but he was barely there. Wracking her mind, she remembered seeing the glint of a fender as she ran to the tunnel. After seeing the car was deserted, she hadn't given it a second thought...

Her heart sank when they reached the car and she saw that all four tires had been slashed. She didn't bother to tell him what she saw.

"Keys?" she whispered, teeth chattering.

He did not answer her. His sudden weight against her made her stumble, and in panic she realized he had passed out. She leaned heavily against the side of the car, knowing that if he fell away from her, she would never be able to pick him up again. She searched his pockets; his keys were there. Still propping up his limp body, she opened the door, let him tumble in. She prayed as she slid the key in the ignition, then started crying when the car roared to life. She turned on the heat, could not look him.

He had left his cell phone in the cup holder.

She looked through his contact list, and when she saw Skeeter's number, she felt as if her heart had stopped.

If you ever need anything, he had said.

She couldn't call him. She couldn't do it.

Anything at all

Her heart pounded painfully. Skeeter was the only one who could help her— who could help them. He was the only person she knew who understood this side of life and would know what to do-- the only one she knew strong enough to handle the dark side of the world. He was the only one who would help her without asking questions...

If you ever need anything. Anything at all...

She gritted her teeth and made herself call him.

"Fink." Skeeter's voice was calm, confident. "Hey, buddy, isn't it past your bedtime?"

"Skeeter," she said.

"Nikki?" he said, instantly concerned.

Her sobs choked the words. "Skeeter, I need help."

"What?" he said. "What can I do?"

She could barely breathe. She shut her eyes, willed herself to latch onto something—anything-- that would give her the strength to speak. "Do you have a car?"

He sounded uncertain. "Fink has a car, Nikki. I'm sure he'll--"

"Dean's dying," she babbled. "He was jumped…"

"Shit," Skeeter said. "Where are you? Are you okay?"

She told him. She hung up. She put the phone back in the cup holder. She looked at the body beside her, felt her breath catch in her throat. She turned the heat on full blast, then she was out of the car, her feet pounding the gravel as she raced the three miles back to Serenade Way. Her heart thudded as she stumbled up the asphalt driveway, up the stairs, into her room. She leaned against the door and listened to the rushing in her head.

No one had seen her; no one had witnessed what she had done.

Her clothes were streaked with his blood. She stripped, shivering, and stuffed the bloody things in a bag she stashed in the back of her closet. She stole to the bathroom. The tears she cried seemed never to end, but though she could feel for Galatea, she could cry for Galatea… she could not help her. No matter how hot she made the water, no matter how long she stood and let herself be scalded, she knew she would never feel clean again.

SKEETER DELUCA

"Shit," he said. "Shit, shit, shit…"

The car—except for the unconscious form of his best friend slumped against the front seat—was abandoned, and the interior was burning up with heat. Skeeter leaned over the prostrate form, slapped Dean Fink's waxy cheek.

"Fink? Buddy?"

His hand hovered near Fink's mouth: breath. Relieved, he bent down to examine the car's slashed tires. His thumb traced the gashes, linked the width of the blade to the red spray-paint scarring Fink's face. He turned in the direction of the warehouses, his eyes darkening, then spun around at the sound of footsteps behind him. A flashlight caught him square in the face.

"Don't move."

He put his hands up and blinked into the light as the police officer reached into the holster by his belt, pulled out a gun, trained it on him.

"You alone?" the police officer asked.

Hands still raised, he nodded.

The police officer's eyes fell to Fink's leg—dangling motionless out of the passenger side's door. "All right, buddy. Up against the car. Nice and easy."

Skeeter obeyed. Rough hands at his wrists, then the bite of handcuffs as his arms were locked behind him.

"What the hell happened here?" the officer muttered under his breath, poking his head into the passenger seat.

"I don't know," Skeeter said, and received a blow from behind. He gritted his teeth and attempted to control his temper as the bright light blinded him again.

"Got a call about screams in the tunnel," the officer said.

"Screams in the tunnel?" he repeated.

"Lucky for this guy the tunnel isn't as remote as people think," the officer said. "Nice little ridge of neighborhoods right through the woods."

"I didn't do this." He sensed it was too late to try to defend himself.

The officer was smiling—a hard, knowing smile. "You're a DeLuca, aren't you?"

"Joseph DeLuca," he said.

"We're going to get in my car," the officer said. "We're going to take this guy to the hospital, then you and me are going to take a ride down to the station."

"You don't understand. He's my best friend."

"Anything you say will be used against you." The officer spat on the ground. "Owing that you're a DeLuca, the odds are stacked against you."

Skeeter moved slowly towards the cop car and got in. The door clanged shut after him.

"Don't try anything now," the officer said, climbing into the front seat and starting the ignition.

Skeeter pressed his forehead against the cool glass of the window. *Was it Nikki?* He thought. *Nikki who had called him, then called the cops? Why would she do that—set him up?*

He was somehow certain she hadn't. And even if she had, it didn't matter. What mattered were the three clues pounding through his mind…

Knife wounds and slashed tires

Spray Paint

Tunnel

Wake up soon, Fink, he thought, his hands clenching in the cuffs. *Wake up soon and straighten this out so I can find Galatea and figure out what the hell is going on.*

DEAN FINK

He lay in the white-washed walls of his hospital room. Night had fallen, and he was alone with his thoughts.

Skeeter. They thought Skeeter had done it.

The thought made him laugh—a hoarse, rattling sound that started in his chest and brought an ungodly amount of pain to the rest of his body. He winced, concerned once again for his sanity.

He thought back to the police interview—the baited questions, the repeated questions-- and how disappointed the officers had seemed when he swore fervently that Skeeter DeLuca was not responsible for what had happened to him. He had told the police that he had called Skeeter to come help him after he had gotten jumped. He had kept the truth chained inside him; he had not even mentioned her name. And now he was left alone in the empty hospital with the slithering ghosts of his lies-- reduced to a quivering bundle of nerves and fear.

He jerked at every shadow, at every headlight beam that bled in through the blinds. He was afraid of the sound of the rain falling outside, of the reflection of light off the hospital window pane—a creeping, cowering fear that made him despise himself. Nothing was clear either; he had been partially blinded by her attack.

He could not battle the skewed reality and the hallucinations with his weapon of choice—his reason. He had lost all faith in reason; *where had reason been in that tunnel?* The details congealed in his mind; his memory was a hazy blur. He remembered only that he had seen her and had been filled with hatred and darkness… and the sense of being possessed by something that was not himself.

The rest was a blank.

Maybe she would tell them—tell them what had really happened. It would be better if everyone knew, and he had to accept the consequences of his actions. But the thought and consequences of people knowing filled him with horror: years spent in jail, the disapproval that would follow him for the rest of his life, the condemning looks that would never again let him live a free and independent life. ..

There was no witness to what he was thinking, and there had been no witness to what he had done—but that did not make the demons go away. Even if she didn't tell—he would never be free again.

What had made him try it? He had set out only intending to spray paint over the walls. To destroy that part of Galatea Williams—to appease the blackness in his soul without actually hurting her. But then he had lost control. And he didn't know why.

If he could go back in time, he would have begged Galatea to kill him, rather than leave him there in the hospital with no respite from the inquisition of his soul and the thoughts that were eating him alive.

GALATEA WILLIAMS

Galatea sat in the warehouse room. It was bare, stripped of the mattress and the candles and quilts. She had wanted to be in a center of desolation, surrounded by blank concrete walls—somewhere she could feel empty. But she had brought the little red Buddha because it gave her courage. She kept the tiny figurine in front of her, where she could see the smooth glass and the contented little face.

She had never known that Skeeter collected Buddhas—but when she thought about him, it made sense. He always tried to enjoy life; he was always in constant denial that they were both trapped by their circumstances. She knew how frustrated he was with her; he didn't realize that she was also frustrated with herself. What she had read from sources on overcoming rape had told her—that sometimes getting over the trauma would take time. Skeeter didn't want to give her time; she didn't want to give herself time. She believed him when he told her she would have to find something inside herself to overcome her feelings of worthlessness and degradation. That was why she felt helpless; she had to find strength in a self she had dismissed…

How do I do it? She turned the Buddha in her palm, watching the reflections of the candle flames through the crimson glass. *How do I face the world alone when I don't feel like I'm strong enough?*

Skeeter had said—that she had to try. He had told her she had to make a change, even if it was a small one…

Maybe she could start with her beliefs about herself. Maybe she could tell herself, over and over and over again until she believed it—that the rape hadn't been her fault. Maybe she could tell herself, over and over and over again until she believed it—that she was beautiful…

She tested the idea in her mind. *It wasn't my fault. I'm beautiful. It wasn't my fault*— and she felt a flash of… something. A flash of strength, a flash of anger. She realized she was angry that she had condemned herself, that she loathed herself for something that had been out of her control. Stronger than that was her hatred of her father—that he had done something to make her feel unworthy of being alive. She had been a creative and joyful child; she had dreams of being an artist or designer, and of forging her own path. And because of him—because of what he had done—she was afraid of her own light. She was afraid to do anything that would get herself noticed, because she had seen what had happened...

Rage pounded through her: black, consuming. *What had happened to her was not normal; how could she have expected herself to keep living her life like nothing was wrong?* Maybe that had been her first, and worst, mistake: not standing by herself, not being gentle with herself, when she hadn't been able to *just move on.* Her second mistake would have been from letting the act destroy the most beautiful thing about her: her vision for life, her beautiful dreams. Not only had she given up on herself, but she had let other people direct her actions and dictate her destiny. *Even Skeeter...*

The metallic door of the warehouse scraped open. Jerked from her thoughts, she hid the tiny Buddha protectively between her palms. She heard footsteps come up the ladder, thought dully that it didn't matter who had found her. But she was wrong.

"Hello, Tea," Skeeter said.

Her heart started pounding painfully, reminding her that she was still alive—that there was someone in the world she still cared about. "Hello, Skeeter."

He stood in the doorway, his hands crossed over his chest, evaluating her with a look that made her blood run cold. "Where have you been?"

"Don't start on me about school." She turned her attention to the Buddha. "What are you doing here?"

"Looking for you," he said. "Have you been avoiding me?"

She shrugged, not looking at him.

He crossed the room, sat down in front of her. She drew her knees into her chest, buried her head. Then his hands were on each side of her face, forcing her to look at him. His dark eyes scanned her features; she knew he was taking stock of each new bruise.

"I thought we didn't have any secrets from each other," he said softly.

She looked directly at him, felt the magnetism between them on an entirely different level. "I didn't start the tradition."

"You know why I don't tell you everything," he said.

"No. I don't." She felt a bite of anger—a desperate desire to tell him everything. "But I'm sure it's for a reason you think is valid. And I trust you on that. So you... you have to trust me on this one."

"What happened?"

She shook her head.

With a gentleness that sent heat racing through her body, he bent closer and moved his lips over her face, kissing each bruise. She closed her eyes and thought about how beautiful it felt, to be kissed by him—that each kiss erased a memory of pain, of hurt, of abuse. After a moment she realized that he had stopped kissing her, though she could still feel the soft heat of his breath on her skin. She opened her eyes.

"You finally have the chance you want," he said, and though he was breathing hard the tone of his voice worried her. "All you have to do is take it, Galatea."

The use of her full name was a second warning. "I don't know what you're talking about, Skeeter."

He shook her, slightly. "What happened to Dean Fink?"

"I don't know," she said, shaking off his hands. "What happened to Dean Fink?"

"He's in the hospital." His dark eyes evaluated her. "Bloody, bruised, blind. And you don't seem much better off."

She did not look at him as she processed that Dean Fink was still alive—that he had not died in the tunnel. She should not have been surprised; Dean Fink had always had something looking out for him. "That's unfortunate," she said. "I suppose now he can't play rugby. I hope that won't hurt your team."

He paused. "You know I'd kill any bastard who hurt you."

"I can take care of myself," she said, hoping a false show of anger would get his thoughts off track. "I can't keep hiding behind you."

"I'm here for you," he said.

She turned away. "You're going to be gone some day. Gone to be blown up by bullets in some fucking foreign country, fighting and dying for something you don't believe in because you think that's all you're good for."

"What happened?" he repeated.

"I don't know. Why don't you ask him?" She paused. "You haven't been to see him yet? That surprises me. He is your best friend, isn't he?"

"I saw him the night he got attacked," he said. "He had some pretty bad knife wounds…"

She shrugged. "Anyone who jumped him could have had a knife."

"That's true. But I taught you how to stab someone. To stab so you would wound without killing. And I also taught you how to slash tires." He paused. "And there was also the spray paint on his face."

She remained silent.

"Look at me, Galatea." His touch, now, was not gentle. "I want to know why you attacked Dean Fink."

For a moment she felt a wild, mangled hope—that he already knew. She looked into his eyes. "Skeeter."

His hands moved to her shoulders. He leaned closer to her. "What?"

Her voice was barely audible; she didn't know if she could tell him. "Why don't you ask Fink?"

His eyes burned into hers. "I'm asking you."

"I wanted to hurt you." She swallowed. "So I told him to meet me in the tunnel. We were just… going to have some fun. But things got out of hand, and I—"

"Tell me the truth, Tea."

She remained motionless. *He didn't believe her. Thank God he didn't believe her. She had been right to trust him, to believe that he knew her better than that.* Still—she didn't trust herself to tell him. "You don't want to know the truth, Skeeter. If I told you the truth, I'd lose you."

"I don't believe you," he said. "You know how much honesty matters to me."

She shook her head. She remained silent.

"You think it's okay to lie to me? Don't you know that's the surest way to lose me?"

She felt his hands tighten on her shoulders. "I can't lose you, Skeeter. You're in love with Nikki."

He reached out and picked the crimson Buddha out of her palm. He hurled the tiny figurine against the wall. She didn't turn, but she heard the glass shatter and ricochet off her back. He crouched down by her, and one last time they were close, face to face.

"You're a fool," he said, his eyes hard. "I don't love Nikki. I could never love a coward."

"Nikki's not a coward," she said. A fierce trembling took hold of her. She could not stop it, could not control it—even though she knew he would never be able to respect her again when he realized she was afraid of him. And he realized her reaction all too soon.

"Lock the door after me." He stood. "I won't be back."

Forever. He meant forever. She heard the door close behind him. She sat with her back pressed against the concrete wall among the littered slivers of red glass, and there was nothing in the room to give her strength. She thought back to the hour she had spent in the warehouse before he had come. For once she had felt strong. She could have built off that brief glimpse into strength, had she not realized that her hope had not come from within her. She had always been banking on him. Now the moment had come and gone, without that final stand from him; there was nothing left in the world for her to fight for.

The intensity of the emptiness inside left her so barren that she could not even cry.

SKEETER DELUCA

He couldn't believe she had lied to him.

He couldn't believe she thought he would just let go—that he wouldn't search for truth.

Until he discovered the secret, uncovered the mystery, found out who had hurt her.

So he was going to the hospital—for peace of mind, for information—but he couldn't let Fink see any of that. Especially his suspicion—and his anger. He lied at the front desk and said he was Fink's brother, then followed an orderly up to the stark hospital room. He sat down in the chair beside the hospital bed.

"Overachiever," he said.

Fink looked in his direction.

"I thought fucking up my shoulder in rugby was something," he said, trying not to stare at Fink's unseeing, translucent eyes. "But you went and got yourself in the hospital. Always have to be the best at everything, Fink?"

Fink managed a smile that was not a smile. His tongue darted out, slid across dry lips. His voice was raspy. "How's the team?"

"We miss our captain." Skeeter forced himself to sound nonchalant. "So what did you say to Nikki to make her beat the shit out of you?"

Fink's smile vanished. "Nikki?"

"Who do you think called me to come get you?"

"I don't know." His voice was barely audible. "I don't remember anything."

"Let me refresh your memory, then, with what I know." He felt the intensity of his anger, barely kept at bay. "I got a phone call from Nikki. I went to the tracks. I found you, bleeding in your car…" He paused. "I need you to tell me what happened before that."

"I don't remember any of that. I passed out, Skeeter."

Skeeter made an effort to control his voice. "Do you remember anything that happened before you passed out?"

Fink did not say anything.

"Tell you what, Fink." He reached into his pocket. "I'm going to flip this coin, and you're going to call it. Call it wrong, you tell me the truth. Call it right, and I'll give you the choice."

There was a long pause. "Okay."

"Call it."

"Heads," Fink said.

The penny went spiraling through the air, then landed on the white bed sheet. Skeeter glanced at Fink, realized that he couldn't see the result. "Heads."

"Heads? What does that mean again?"

"I have to believe what you tell me." He paused. "Fink?"

The silence stretched on between them. A further moment of silence, then, "I must have gotten jumped, Skeeter."

His hands clenched into fists. "You don't know the guys who fucked you up?"

"Sit down, Skeeter."

He sat, wondering how Fink knew he had slipped into fighter mode. Fink's blank eyes followed him as he pulled his chair closer to the hospital bed. "Give me names, Fink."

"Let it go, Skeeter."

He frowned. "If you answer one question for me."

"What?"

His eyes narrowed. "What happened to your eyes?"

"I don't know what happened. I passed out, and when I woke up I was here. I don't remember anything that happened before--"

"All right. I'm going to go now." He stood. "Concentrate on getting better, buddy."

He felt Fink's hazy eyes following him as he left the room, and he knew that something had happened in that room, in that moment, that was darker than anything that had happened up to that point.

NIKKI DIETRICH

She watched with growing alarm as Galatea's uninterrupted string of absences stretched on. She found out, eventually, why Galatea wasn't returning to school— through an unexpected eavesdropping on her teachers' conversation one day when she was late for lunch.

She had remained in a state of indecision; she wanted to help, but she was no close friend of Galatea's, and she was as guilty as Dean Fink. She had not stopped him, and then she had not stopped him. She had shut down her feelings and listened to the part of her mind that confirmed she was too cowardly to do what was right-- even if she could determine now what that was.

Every day she watched Skeeter DeLuca stare at the empty seat in their English class, a sad confusion etched into his face. But he looked at her frequently, too-- his eyes gaping question marks. She avoided Skeeter and found this prevention worked; he never approached her, never spoke to her, never did more than send her, at random intervals, that piercing, brooding stare.

Dean Fink was an entirely different problem. He returned to school two weeks after the night in the tunnel. She had not visited him in the hospital, and she could not look at him without feeling distinct horror. He did not talk to her, nor did he seem to notice the distance she kept from him. He kept up with his work and drove himself in the same relentlessly ambitious way-- but she sensed he had changed. She noticed how the corner of his mouth spasmed occasionally , how he never smiled, how he never participated in class and stammered when he was called on to answer. Worst were his eyes—translucent, empty, skittering around the room ceaselessly. Every day she watched as he grew more anguished, more nervous.

Confrontations with both of them, she knew, were imminent.

Skeeter approached her first. He cornered her in an upstairs hallway, and she found herself alone in the janitor's closet with him, his huge body blocking her only exit.

"I have to get to class," she said half-heartedly.

"Have a seat, Nikki." There was none of the former gentleness in his manner.

The interior of the closet was dusty and dark, and she could barely see. She sat down on an overturned bucket as Skeeter flipped on the light.

"Are you going to tell me what's going on?" he demanded.

"I'm not the one you need to talk to," she said.

"You're the one I'm talking to now," he said. "You were there the night this shit went down."

"I'm not denying that," she said. "But I'm not the person you need to talk to."

"Who do you think I should talk to?"

"Galatea."

"I tried. I tried to talk to her, but she wouldn't tell me the truth." He glanced at her. "And now I don't know where she is."

"Have you tried looking for her?"

"It doesn't matter. Right now she doesn't want me to find her--"

She felt a flash of anger. "If you cared about her, that wouldn't stop you from trying--"

"I need to know what's going on, Nikki," he said flatly. "First Galatea disappears, and now all Fink does is sit through class like a damn zombie. And you've been avoiding me the night since that call." He started pacing in the enclosed space. "No one is telling me a damn thing--"

"Maybe you should go see Galatea again," she interrupted. "She'd probably appreciate a visit."

He stopped. "What are you talking about? Do you know where she is?"

"I heard some teachers talking." She clenched her hands tightly in her lap. "Galatea checked herself into St. Lucia's."

He stopped pacing. "The place for crazies?"

"For troubled young women," she corrected.

Concern—unmistakable—flashed over his face, and then his eyes became like hardened steel. "Then maybe that's where she needs to be."

She remained silent, staring at him. Then she stood. "She was a fool to care about you. You're ready to write her off, and you *don't even know anything*. If you won't visit her, I will."

He pushed her back onto the bucket. "Do something better. Tell me what happened."

The anger continued to course through her, and she was no longer afraid of him. "No, Skeeter, you tell me what happened. Because what I saw didn't break her. Nothing could break her, unless it was something that you did. So what did you do?"

He grabbed her; he hurt her. "What did you see?"

She lowered her eyes, her voice failing her once again.

He let her go and stepped back. He cleared his throat. "I'm sorry."

"Not as sorry as I am—that you gave up on her." She watched him pace back and forth, thought like a storm cloud on his forehead. Then she shifted uncomfortably on her bucket, her moment of courage passed. "Can I go?"

He looked at her—like he had forgotten her. Without a word he stepped aside, and she walked by him. Once in the bright, empty hallway, she felt like the closet confrontation had been part of a particularly bad nightmare—but she left awakened, knowing the next move was hers.

He was too full of anger, she thought. She could never trust him to visit Galatea at St. Lucia's. She would have to get there first.

SKEETER DELUCA

He sat on an outcropping of elevated rock, looking out at the horizon of hazy hills in the distance. The wooded trails were five miles from the trailer park, and he went there less often than he would have liked. But when he really needed to think, he went.

December had brought snow. He was half frozen, but he remained seated amidst the ice-coated trees. There was something purifying about freezing.

But Galatea kept intruding on his thoughts. Despite his attempts to think rationally and dismiss those other thoughts and feelings—they would not die or fade. And it would be all too easy for him to give into his feelings, to let anger, and not integrity, drive his decisions.

He had few facts to guide his actions. The truth he sensed contradicted Galatea's words. But the alternative-- that she was in all ways innocent—by necessity incriminated Dean Fink. And if she had really checked herself into that god-awful place, then something horrible must have happened…

He leaned back, felt supported by the strong trunk of the tree. He could believe what he felt, but that would mean that Galatea had lied to him, and that Fink…

Time to move. Staying in one spot for any longer would result in frostbite. He stood and he walked and he realized that they were all rotten: him, Fink, Galatea. Galatea had too much consideration for him, and he had too much consideration for Fink, and Fink… Fink's only consideration was for himself. Truth would never surface with such an inveigled web of conflicting motives amongst the three of them.

The bleak, frozen landscape in front of him reminded him that periods of hibernation were necessary for change. After the death of winter there was the thaw of spring. He would wait, and later he would use what remained to determine his next move.

NIKKI DIETRICH

The house-- a quaint, stylish brown and white stucco, with a golden door knocker shaped like a lion's head—was not what Nikki had expected. She listened to the loud, hollow sound of metal against wood, then stepped back as the door was opened by a tall, stately woman with coal black eyes and dark hair streaked with gray. The woman's face was pale and haggard, the circle under her eyes dark like bruises.

"Hi." She was determined to speak though she had no confidence. "My name is Nikki Dietrich. I go to Wesleyan High with Galatea. We have English class together."

The woman's somber face went slack, and then she looked over her shoulder. Finding no one there, the woman turned her attention back to Nikki. She remained silent.

Nikki looked at her uncertainly. "I noticed that Galatea's been missing a lot of class lately. And I'm worried about her. I would have called, but I don't have her number and—"

"Bless your heart." A storm of emotion crossed the woman's face as she stepped aside and opened the door wider. "Come in, dear. I'll get Bob."

Nikki watched as the woman went up the carpeted staircase to a darker second landing, then scanned the house's interior. On the wall to the side of her was a full length mirror, the edges gilded. She barely recognized her own reflection. The girl in the mirror was slight and frail, her pale face mousey and afraid. Self-consciously she smoothed back her hair and tried to make herself look more presentable. She glanced up in time to see a heavyset man coming down slowly.

"Myra says you're a friend of Galatea's," he said.

Nikki nodded.

"Best come in out of the rain," he said. "I think Myra just put some water on for tea."

He walked past the mirror, down the hall. Nikki followed him into a sea-green room bordered by pictures and names of herbs. The man seemed lost in the cheerful kitchen. His hands shook as he offered her a mug of steaming tea.

"Best have a seat," he said.

She sat down. He sat opposite her, his hands folded around the mug in front of him.

"You want to know about Galatea," he said.

Nikki nodded.

"All she ever wanted to do was make her part of the world a beautiful place," he said. "It's a shame, the way she burns her way through life instead." He paused. "I suppose you know she's at St. Lucia's."

Nikki unglued her lips. "What happened?"

"She came home one day…" He paused, cleared his throat. "You have to understand, that's strange for Gal. Avoids this house like the plague. Bad blood between her and Myra. It's a shame, but I'm not going to be the first one to throw stones at either of them. Both been through hell, they have. But Gal came home one day, about two weeks ago." He paused, not looking at her. "Fifteen days to be exact. January 12 at 3:05 exact. She asked me…and she never asks me for anything…."

"What did she ask you?" she prompted.

"She asked if I could... drive her to Saint Lucia's." He bit off the last words. "That home for the crazies."

She looked at him, her eyes full of compassion. "Saint Lucia's is a temporary placement for troubled young women who need a brief break from life...."

"You seem to know a lot about it," he said tonelessly.

"I volunteered there for awhile." She paused. "Very few of those young women are hopeless cases."

"But Gal... in a place like that." He paused, cleared his throat again. "I wouldn't have taken her. But she said she would take herself... and she was scared." He frowned. "Myra and me decided to go along with it, but we had hoped she'd check out by now..."

Two weeks, Nikki thought. But two weeks wouldn't take her back to the night she had witnessed in the tunnel. She recalled her closet conversation with Skeeter, and was even more certain that something else had to have happened between them.

"Do you know what—" she started.

"I asked her, you can be sure." It was the first time he had talked to anyone about it; she could tell because of the raw pain behind his words and his hesitation. "It was the only question I asked her. Why? Why?"

The emotion crumpling his face kept her from prompting him further. After a moment, he looked up once more. "What she said... hell, I didn't understand any of it."

She found her voice again. "What did she say?"

"She said... that the world had lost its sole spark of beauty." He paused. "Myra said you're in English with her. What the hell is that supposed to mean?"

"I don't know," she said. "What was Galatea's sole spark of beauty?"

He shook his head. She looked at him uneasily, not wanting to plunge him into deeper pain. "Would I be able to visit her?"

"Would you want to?"

She nodded.

Some of the tension left his strained face. He stood. "I'm sure Gal would appreciate the visit. Let me get you directions."

He took a long time coming back. But when he returned to the room, she understood why; he had been crying. She pretended not to notice his red-rimmed eyes as he handed her the brochure and a paper with a phone number on it.

"Thank you," she said.

"Nikki," he said, and she glanced up, startled. "Nikki... you're the first one to come and ask about her. Thank you."

Tears came into her eyes. She nodded. He looked away and stood, and she left her tea on the table as she followed him into the hallway.

"There was a boy," he said. "He stopped by here a coupla times after Myra and Gal moved in. He told me that if I ever hurt Gal..." He smiled suddenly. "Well, I won't repeat it. He was a stripling then. I could have crushed him with my finger. But there was a fire in his eyes when he spoke about her. I suppose he's grown up now, too." He paused. "You might want to talk to that boy. If he's still around."

"I'll do that," she said, knowing she had already told Skeeter everything she was going to. She waited as he opened the door for her, then stepped outside. "Thank you, Bob."

She walked to her car, the warmth of the house leaving her as the wind whipped by. She knew her next step, but she had no idea what she would say when she got to St. Lucia's. She knew only that she had to get Galatea to listen to her. She had to have faith that if she could get herself there, the right words would come...

Twice she had to pull over to the side of the road to retch up the tiny bit of food she had been able to force down for breakfast. She arrived at Saint Lucia's pale and trembling, and half wondering if she should commit herself.

The inside of the home was warm and muted. An aquarium of brightly colored fish sat on a table by the front window. Seeing no one at the desk to help her, Nikki went to watch the tiny, frolicking fish. But she wished she hadn't. Several tiny golden fish were stuck on the filter-- most dead, though some convulsed feebly in death throes against the current. She recoiled, nauseated, as a woman in light blue scrubs walked to the front desk.

"Should the fish..." she said finally, to break the unnerving silence. "Should the fish up front be stuck to the filter like that?"

"Oh, are some of them dead?" The woman said cheerfully. "Honey, we just got them little ones shipped in yesterday, and a lot of 'em get damaged in transport and get too weak to stand the current."

"I think some of them are still alive," Nikki said uncomfortably.

"I'll have to talk to Jeannie about lowering the filter pressure." The woman smiled. "So who are you?"

Somehow she told the woman who she was, and somehow her feet carried her down the eerily quiet hallway. The nurse stopped in front of a white door. "This one right here is Miss Gal's room. One of our best behaved young women. Sane and never violent, so we give her visitors the option of an orderly." The woman shrugged. "Not necessary, but if it would make you feel more safe..."

Nikki forced a smile. "I'd prefer to go in alone."

"Her father came several times," the nurse said. "At least I think it was her father. But anyways, he brought her sketchbooks, though it don't seem she takes any interest in them..." The nurse paused. "Try to get a smile out of her, will you, honey?"

Nikki nodded and waited while the woman retraced her steps down the hall. Then she looked at the absurdly white door. Uncertainly, she knocked. She waited, then knocked again. Receiving no response, she opened the door.

The blinds were drawn, but enough sunlight filtered through the slats to reveal the interior of the room. Nikki saw her sitting on the bed, dressed in a formless white shift. She felt a flash of fear go through her at the blank expression on Galatea's face—a fear that vanished the next moment, when an incredulous smile replaced the vacancy on Galatea's face.

"Hello, Nikki," she said.

Reassured by the control in Galatea's voice, she stepped farther into the room. Galatea watched her approach, then smiled when she stopped halfway into the room. "You can come closer, Nikki. I'm not crazy."

Nikki sat down on the bed. "I know you're not."

"You'll have to excuse my rudeness." Her eyes were sad, and she smiled vacantly. "I'm not quite sure why you're here."

Nikki hugged her, and when she felt Galatea's arms around her waist, she held her tighter. Galatea felt thin and fragile in her arms, and Nikki felt pain flare up in her heart.

"I'm here to visit you," she said. "How are you doing?"

"The days aren't so bad," she said, letting go of Nikki. "I like the sunlight. But the nights… the nights are cold. Then the emptiness gets inside and freezes me--"

"Can I see your sketches, Galatea?" she asked, to distract her from her haunted thoughts.

Galatea blinked. "I suppose so. Let me get them for you."

Nikki watched her amble to the nightstand in the far corner of the room and come back holding a plastic bag full of sketchbooks. She selected one at random and flipped through the pages. Halfway through she looked up.

"You must really like sunflowers," she said. "You painted so many."

"Vincent Van Gogh painted sunflowers," she said. "To him, they symbolized happiness and hope."

"Is that what they symbolize for you?"

"No. I draw them because…"

"Why?"

She blinked, shrugged. "Because Skeeter likes them."

"These other ones," she said. "They're sketches for the tunnel, aren't they?"

Galatea looked at her with studied calm. "I don't know what you're talking about."

She reopened the book to where she had left off. "You're stronger than this, Galatea. You shouldn't be here."

"There's nothing out there for me."

She closed the sketchpad. "I'm surprised you'd let a guy do this to you."

Galatea looked up sharply. "What?"

"I'm surprised you would let a guy do this to you." She was on dangerous ground and she knew it, but she had to say try. "Even if that guy was Skeeter."

Galatea's eyes darkened. "What are you talking about?"

"I know you love him. But to let go of any sense of possibility for your own life because he might not love you back—" She fought to keep the fear out of her voice; Galatea's eyes were like daggers. "I thought you were stronger than that."

Galatea shrugged. "It doesn't matter."

"Galatea. You have so much to offer the world…" Nikki sensed the battle was lost, but she lingered. She closed her eyes and prayed that whatever words she needed to say would come to her. "For you to choose to rot away here--"

"I won't rot away here," she said placidly. "Don't you see how perfect this place is for me, Nikki? No one will bother me here. I don't even have to acknowledge reality. I can surround myself with art and imagination and—"

"I didn't know you were a coward."

The room became, suddenly, too quiet. Galatea looked like she had been slapped. "I'm not a coward."

"What do you think running away from life makes you?"

"You don't understand—" she cried.

"I don't," Nikki affirmed. "Because I've never lived through anything like you've been through, Galatea. You feel more deeply every single day than I've ever felt in my entire life." She paused. "You're stronger than I am. Maybe than I'll ever be."

"You're wrong, Nikki."

"Not about this," she said. "Galatea—I can't stand to see you here. You don't belong here."

Galatea looked away. "Get out of here."

"I will." Nikki backed away. "But I had to talk to you. I'm sorry if I bothered you."

"You didn't bother me. But I'd like you to leave me alone now, please."

Nikki went, feeling shaken.

She did not know that after she left Galatea untucked one leg out from under her, then pushed herself off the bed. She crossed to the wooden nightstand where Nikki had left her sketchpad, and she opened it thoughtfully. She glanced through the sketches ... and that same night, she checked herself out of St. Lucia's.

SKEETER DELUCA

He rapped on the warehouse door once, sagging with pain, his breath visible in front of him, praying that she would be there. He hadn't spoken to her since she had come back to school; he still couldn't believe that what Nikki had told him was true, and that Galatea had spent the past two weeks in St. Lucia's. She was too strong for that. He knocked again, then sagged with relief when the door grinded open.

"Skeeter?"

She was there, of course she was there. "Can you let us in?"

She shoved the door open. "Oh, shit. Are you hurt?"

"No, but he is." He grunted. "Can you help me?"

She slipped out of the warehouse and used her shoulder to prop up the bulk of the body he had brought with him. He kicked the door shut behind them and then stood, examining her in the dim light. Her every muscle was tensed, her dark eyes bleeding questions. He turned away and pressed his face against the cold metal door as he listened for something other than the steady dripping of the rain inside the building.

"I didn't do it," he said, gritting his teeth. "There was a fight--"

"You don't have to explain." She looked down at the bloodied body. "I know who he is."

"You do?" *Damn, the warehouse was freezing...*

"Kenny DeLuca tried flirting with me far too many times for me not to recognize him." She paused. "We've got to move him. The concrete is going to zap whatever body heat he has left. And we don't want him to go into shock. Assuming he's still alive?"

He nodded, glad he didn't have to explain anything—that she wasn't asking him any questions. "Get his feet."

"Will he be okay if we move him?" she whispered.

"He'll be fine."

His words were the only assurance she needed. She grabbed the legs as he heaved the body up under the armpits.

"Corner," she whispered, breathing hard. "There's a dry room there."

He remained stooped by the body after they moved to the room. He tore off his hoodie and pulled out his knife. The dim light glared off his muscles, the blood-streaked white undershirt.

"What can I do?" she asked.

He tossed the sweatshirt at her, handed her the knife. "Cut this up." His hands glistened with blood as he started bandaging the wounds with the frayed strips of fabric she handed him.

"He'll only need a few days here to recuperate," he said.

"You can't leave him here," she said, kneeling beside him. "He needs a doctor."

"He needs to be somewhere safe. This is the only place I know." Skeeter turned, gripped her shoulders. "No one can know about this. If anyone found out he was dealing again--"

She shrugged off his hands. "Tell anyone who asks that he got jumped by dealers who thought he was still dealing."

He realized that his intrusion was the first time he had talked to her, really looked at her—since. She looked like shit: dark circles under hungry eyes, pale skin, dark hair a rat's nest around her delicate features. *He couldn't worry about that now.* He suffocated his sudden concern for her. "That won't fly."

She crossed her arms. "What do you want me to do?"

The hatred burning in her eyes stung him, but he wouldn't let her see that. He couldn't afford a second of weakness; he would straighten things out with her later. "Look after him."

"I'll do anything I can, Skeeter," she said tonelessly. "But if he dies or if someone finds this place—"

"He won't die. And I'm sure no one followed us here."

"You dragged him here?"

"No one I trust has a car."

"Dean Fink has a car," she said. "Why didn't you—"

"Fink can't ever know anything about this," he said, eyes flashing. "Can't ever be involved in the least way. Do you hear me?"

"He's no better than you are," she said. "He has no more right to be free from this than you—"

"Shut up, Galatea."

"How the hell do you get off talking to me like that?"

He exhaled. *Patience. She was right.* "I'm sorry. I'm stressed out, okay?"

She shook her head. "So it's okay to incriminate me, but—"

He didn't understand her anger, couldn't believe that she didn't understand. "You're the only person I can trust with him."

Something flickered over her face, then her expression became blank. "I promise I'll look after him. But if he dies—"

"DeLucas don't die easy." He paused. "If I thought he was in any real danger I'd take the chance of putting him in the hospital. Hell, I'd tell the doctor I had stabbed him myself. But he's been through worse."

She paused. "How badly are you hurt?"

"I'm fine."

"You're bleeding. Where?"

He glanced down. "My arm. It's nothing. I have to go. I'll be back with—"

"Sit the fuck down."

He sat on the concrete floor. She tore a strip from the hem of her miniskirt and knelt. She placed a tourniquet around the gash in his arm, then sat back on her heels. "Too tight?"

He watched her. "No. Thank you."

She scowled and crossed her arms over her chest. "If you're going to play the renegade hero, you have to take care of yourself."

The next moment he was kissing her, his hands forcing her face into his, his tongue unlocking her lips and stealing her breath. He felt the track of warm tears on her cheeks, and he pulled away.

"I'll be back," he said, unsettled.

When he returned to the warehouse, he saw that she had dragged the mattress into the room and thrown the patchwork quilt over the body. She looked up when he entered, but made no movement towards him. He dressed Kenny's wound in silence, wondering why she didn't say anything-- wondering if she felt awkward around him. He could not bear that thought.

"What are you going to do?" she asked, finally.

"I'm going to do what I have to do."

"You're not going back to clean up after him, are you?" She felt like crying when his face went slack. "Skeeter?"

He didn't look at her. "Can he stay here tonight?"

"Only if you stay here, too."

"I can't do that."

"Then he can't stay." Her teeth were chattering; she was trying to hide it. "If he wakes up and tries to—"

"I'll stay tonight." He hadn't planned to tell her like this—but the words were coming out before he could stop them. "Then I'm clearing out, Tea."

She looked at him blankly. "What did you say?"

"I'm clearing out." He watched the meaning of the words dawn on her face. "I can't stay in this town anymore. Not after this."

"At least graduate from high—"

"That's too long to wait." He looked down at the bleeding body on the mattress. "We'll leave in the morning, before the cops pick up on what happened."

"Why?" she asked. "Why do you have to go?"

"Every day," he said, "I feel the walls coming closer. Every day is a greater risk, just by being here."

Her eyes glinted. "Where are you going to go?"

"Who the hell knows?" He stood, kicked the mattress. "I'll get by until I'm eighteen. Then the military won't turn me away."

She didn't respond. He looked at her as she scrunched up against the concrete wall, her dark eyes trained on Kenny. Maybe the thought that he would be leaving her soon intensified the depth of his feelings—or maybe it made him realize for the first time that feelings were there. Or maybe he just wanted to talk to her, to work out some of the confusion whirling around inside him…

She put her hand on the ground beside her, as if she had understood his thoughts. "Come join me?"

"I don't want to keep you up."

She shook her head. "I'll stay here tonight. Keep you company."

He moved towards her. Slowly. He had finally placed the gleam in her eyes. Distrust. She didn't trust him anymore, and that recognition stripped him of the unthinking courage that had gotten him to the warehouse. Still he slipped an arm around her--and felt her stiffen. She moved away from him quickly.

"Look, Tea," he started. "I know I've been an asshole, but I had to think things through--"

"It's not what you think," she said.

He started to wrap the extra blanket he had brought with him around them both, but she moved away from him once more and sat, her chin grinding into her knees, her eyes stonily focused ahead. He hesitated. "Do you want to talk?"

She shook her head.

"Well, I have a lot of questions. I want to know why you were at St. Lucia's. I want to know why you aren't asking me any questions when I haven't talked to you for over two weeks and then brought—"

"Shut up," she said.

"Not this time." He felt like his heart lurched in his chest, but he wouldn't let her back out of the conversation. "You don't have to do this for me. Not when I've—"

"I love you, Skeeter." Her voice was cold, but her eyes were sparking. "I'd do anything for you. I thought that was obvious."

He couldn't speak. He couldn't believe the words he had heard. He could think of nothing to do except move closer to her.

She tossed the blanket in his face, effectively separating them. "Go to sleep. I'll keep first watch."

He had never seen her—so coldly controlled. He tried to keep the emotion out of his voice. "I missed you, Tea."

"I'd like to believe it. But I don't. I think your emotions are out of whack, and that you're being irrational. Sleep it off," she advised. "Everything will seem better in the morning."

"You think so?"

She looked at him, without a smile. "For you? Yeah, I think everything will work out fine. "

He hesitated. "What about for you?"

She snorted. "Don't pretend like you care."

He reached out, caught her arm, forced her to look at him. He saw anger— vulnerability—love—hate-- battling in the dark depths of her eyes. Hate won. She wrenched herself away from him.

"I changed my mind," she said, picking up the blanket. "I'm sleeping upstairs."

"You don't even want to be in the same room with me?"

"Wake me if you need anything."

"Why are you being like this?"

"Why?" She looked over her shoulder at him. "I can't help how I feel about you. But I am so fucking sick and tired of how you treat me—"

"I've always been there for you," he accused.

She shrugged. "It's not enough. I hate to say that. I hate to judge you. But I can't deny that what I feel is—that it's not enough for me."

She left the room. She didn't look back.

He listened to the steady dripping of a leak somewhere in the building, to the soft sound of her steps up the rungs of the ladder. He wished he could follow her...

If it hadn't been for Kenny—would he have gone to her? He had accused her of being a coward, but he was the coward for avoiding her... for avoiding his own feelings. He realized he loved her—but the realization came too late. He had betrayed her trust, and he would never be able to earn it back.

He stared down at the concrete floor, knowing he had lost her.

GALATEA WILLIAMS

She sat in the warehouse room listening to the hissing of the candle wax and the steady dripping of a leak—somewhere in the building—as she stared at the shattered shards of the Buddha that remained like sprays of blood on the concrete floor. She felt a strong sense of déjà vu; she had sat in this same space weeks before, thinking about the same things...

She had changed her thoughts. She had gone to St. Lucia's. She had come out of that place. So much had changed—and she was still in the same goddam place...

She was still thinking about Skeeter. But rather than fading away because she thought he had abandoned her, now she was in deep pain that she had betrayed him, by believing that he didn't care...

She did not want to think about Skeeter now. She couldn't dismiss him from her thoughts so easily now because he had come back for her, with his dark eyes and kisses and pretty words...*and bleeding brother.*

She gritted her teeth as the tears started down her cheeks. She realized that Skeeter was using her—maybe that he had always used her. She had thought that the connection between them was real, but he had played her into thinking he cared: the same way he had played the principal into siding with him, the same way he had played Dean Fink into believing he was an unthinking powerhouse, the same way he had played--

She cut off her thoughts. Anger was no use. She had always loved Skeeter DeLuca, and she always would. And even though it was clear to her now that he was using her-- she still loved him. She still had to fight herself from going to him, knowing it was her last night with him...

She felt lost. There had never been a time when he hadn't been there for her. He had never betrayed her trust... until she had gone to St. Lucia's. *And he hadn't cared.*

She looked at the shards of the Buddha. She remembered how he had smiled when he saw she liked it. She remembered the times he had come to the warehouse to check in on her. She remembered the trial, when he had helped her explain she had acted in delayed self-defense. She remembered being beside him on the mattress, falling asleep with the drumbeat of the rain against the tin roof, his arm warm around her. She wondered if any of it had been real. He either cared about her—or he didn't.

He had abandoned her; he wouldn't have come to her if it hadn't been for Kenny. Her heart screamed against that evidence, but she wouldn't let herself believe the lies she wanted to tell herself. She wouldn't run from the truth—that now there was nothing between them except an unbreachable silence and the promise that tomorrow Skeeter would disappear from her life forever.

Nothing matched up. The strange look in his steel gray eyes, the hardened lines of his face as he scowled, the distance between them— and then his words. That he cared about her. And his kiss. The way he had kissed her…

"I don't care," she said, softly, to the shattered Buddha, to the scarred walls, to the cold air. She had let Skeeter reduce her to nothing once, but something had happened to her at St. Lucia's. And that something would not ever let that happen again.

She didn't believe in him anymore. She would have to find faith in something else.

She sat alone in the warehouse room for hours— not numb. Thinking, violently awake, she watched the sun paint the sky with dawn brushstrokes. She stood and descended from the loft. She found him awake and cleaning up the remnants from last night's catastrophe.

"Where is he?" she asked.

Skeeter turned and looked at her. "He left five minutes ago."

She kept her voice controlled. "DeLucas don't lose any time, do they?"

"You know how it is," he said. "A wound heals and you move on."

She turned and walked to the door.

"I'm sorry for the inconvenience," he said.

She shook her head, crossed her arms over her chest, leaned against the side of the building for support. She knew he was impatient to be gone; though it would be the last time—maybe forever—that she would be alone with him.

Not trusting herself to speak, she asked him anyway, "Will I see you again?"

"Not in school," he said. "I need to keep a low profile. But I'm not taking off right away." He paused. "I don't have enough money saved up."

"How much do you need?"

"Enough to make a start."

"How much is that?"

"About seven hundred dollars." He looked away from her, distracted. "But I'm not taking anything from--"

She smiled, wryly. "I don't have that kind of money anyway, Skeeter."

"Right." He glanced over his shoulder. "Well—"

"Have you told your family you're leaving yet?" she asked. "Leaving for good?"

"I'm not going to tell them until I'm long gone. It'd make them a little crazy if they knew. And that could complicate things. I'm not worried." He offered her a cocky smile. "I just wish I had a plan."

"When have you ever had a plan, Skeeter?"

"You're right." He shook his head. "Thanks for looking after Kenny."

That was how he was going to say goodbye, she thought, watching his hooded figure move away from the warehouse. She watched until he had disappeared down the cracked railroad tracks, then she turned and went to the room he had just left. She dragged the bulk of the bloody mattress to the back of the building.

Torched it.

Seven hundred dollars. She watched the thick black smoke curl to the sky. It would kill her to have him leave, but she would get the money.

DEAN FINK

He jerked when he heard her say his name, could almost feel her hatred as he turned in the direction of her voice. He couldn't make out her features—most objects were still barely distinguishable blurs for him—but he could picture how Galatea would be looking at him. Her dark eyes would be flashing impudently, challenging him, daring him—even after what had happened.

He felt no hatred for her now; whatever force had compelled him was gone. All he wanted to do was atone for what he had done. He had waited for her to blackmail him, but she hadn't been in school. Then, she had avoided him.

Now, he thought. *Justice. Thank God.*

"Where are you?" he asked.

Her hand closed around his arm, nails biting into his flesh. He could sense her nearness by her smell: the exotic perfume of smoke, incense, leather…

"Take a walk with me, Dean," she said.

He wanted to tell her that her guidance was unnecessary, that he had walked the uneven aisles of Cemetery Lane almost ceaselessly since that night—that he knew the way and could walk without stumbling. "What do you want?" he asked, without preamble.

"Seven hundred dollars."

"Is that all?" he asked.

She was silent for a long time. "By Friday."

"Anything."

"You're a bastard. You deserve to burn in Hell." The bite of her nails was gone. "But I'm not going to blackmail you. I want to forget about it, as much as you do." A moment of silence. "If you get me the seven hundred dollars by Friday, Fink, we're done. I won't say a word to anyone, and you can wash your hands of me with a clean conscience…"

He did not answer immediately. Then he said, "If it means anything at all, Galatea, I'm sorry for what I did. I know it can't possibly mean—"

He heard the sharp intake of her breath. "It means something."

He hated himself for being so weak—for needing to explain to her. He would rather the ambiguity of his actions weigh more heavily on his soul, than burden her with his guilt, but he couldn't stop himself from saying the words. "I don't know what happened. I don't know why--"

"It makes sense." He could have sworn he felt her shiver. "You weren't in the tunnel."

"What do you mean?"

"Did you feel like you were there?" she asked, with difficulty. "That night in the tunnel… were you really there?"

When he processed what she was asking him, he found he could not respond. His body shuddered with convulsions.

"I didn't think so," she said, in a voice he had to strain to hear.

He looked at the blurred outline of her face with intense concentration. "You fucked me over pretty good."

"I can't say it was an honor."

Her voice chilled him, reminded him that she hated him. He looked at the ground. "Where should I leave the money? Are you going to be in school?"

A pause. "Leave it in the tunnel. There's a loose stone in the side wall, when you come in." She paused again. "It won't hurt you to look around for it for awhile."

He was silent, analyzing the complications, problem shooting the demand, before he realized that wasn't what mattered. At all. He glanced in her direction. "If there's anything else I can do—"

"Just get the seven hundred dollars in the stone. By Friday."

He felt her glide by him. He felt her absence, as much as he had felt her presence. He started to retrace the path out of the cemetery. The temperature was dropping quickly; he could feel the snowflakes melting on his skin like stings from the demons in Pandora's box. He would get home too late that night to arrange anything, but he would get her money by Friday.

Kenny DeLuca, he remembered, was still in town.

SKEETER DELUCA

He cut through Cemetery Lane, staying hidden in the darkness. He needed to keep his mind clear for the imminent encounter, but his thoughts shifted like the shadows. He couldn't forget how she had looked when he had told her he was leaving-- how crushed and desolate she had seemed. He felt a flash of anger and reasoned that he couldn't stay for her, especially when she wasn't even telling him the truth about what was going on...

He leaned against one of the silent oaks lining an aisle of graves; his eyes scanned the cracked roads spreading out like dark rivers in front of him. Kenny had promised that his days of dealing were over, but Skeeter did not believe him. The police had been watching every member of the DeLuca family ever since Kenny returned to town, and Kenny was still too weak to fend off an attack— police or otherwise-- should another exchange go bad. He would try to protect his brother—his family—awhile longer. But then, like he had told her, he was clearing out.

And then he would be done with them. They had to accept—and he had to accept-- that he had to make his own way.

The cemetery was one of Kenny's favorite places for transactions: right at the corner, where the street and the rotting lane merged. Skeeter settled into the shadows and waited. The church bells—distant—chimed the quarter hour as a dark figure sulked into view on the corner. Surprise stole his caution as he identified the person's build and the uncertain, stumbling lurch of the walk. He stepped forward, incredulous.

"Fink?"

Dean Fink turned with the suddenness of a wishbone cracking. "Hello, Skeeter."

He was glad Fink recognized him; at least he wouldn't lie. "What are you doing here?"

"I'm waiting for someone."

"You shouldn't be here," he said.

"Don't worry, it's not—"

"I know exactly what it is," he snapped. "I don't know why the hell you're involved, but—"

"Back off, Skeeter." His voice was deadly quiet.

He would have backed away from the edge in Fink's voice—if Fink hadn't been his friend. And if he didn't know how ugly the transaction could get. "Fink, listen to me. Get the hell out of here."

"I can't."

"I have a bad feeling about tonight."

Dean Fink's lips curled into a smile. "I'm sorry you feel that way. But I can't back out now. I gave my word I would be here tonight, and here I will remain."

"Trust me. You don't know what you're getting into."

Fink laughed—and that was when Skeeter realized he was already too late to stop what had been set in place. He turned to see Kenny step out of the shadows; he watched the lightning quick exchange as helplessly as a fly trapped in a spider web.

"You promised me, Kenny," he said.

But Kenny was already disappearing into the darkness.

"Just leave it be, Skeeter," Dean Fink said. He sounded tired. "It's a one shot deal. Paying off a debt, then back to—"

"There's never a one shot deal," he said angrily. "Not with this. You start, then it's never over…"

"I appreciate your loyalty, Skeeter." Fink turned to leave. "But this is my choice."

"And this is mine." He stepped in front of him. "You're not leaving here with that. I don't care if I have to kill you."

Fink frowned. "You know what happens to people who try to stand in my way."

Skeeter stepped forward, blade out. "This is too important."

The next moments were a blur. A sudden spotlight blinded him; a voice blared at them to stop. Instinctively he shoved Fink to the ground and ripped the bag out of his hands; then he was on the ground, his arms pinned behind him, Fink standing over him, blinking into the spotlight, *going for a walk I don't know what's going on* **you're a Deluca? DeLuca? DeLuca?** As rough hands shoved him to a police car…

It took him a moment to realize Fink was beside him in the police car—silent, serene. The smile on Fink's face unsettled him, but it proved to him that Fink already knew how it would all play out. He would be framed, picking up charges of assault and trafficking, while Fink —confident, carefree, protected— would come out unscathed, and continue with the life he was destined to lead.

He saw Fink's lips forming the same word, over and over, while his blank eyes stared ahead vacantly. He leaned forward, caught the whispered word.

No, he thought, settling back in the cruiser, wanting to say the words out loud to Fink but knowing Fink wasn't there to hear them. *There is no justice. There is only the way things are…*

And everything is playing out, he thought, resigned. *Exactly as it's meant to.*

DEAN FINK

He stumbled into the night, oblivious to the heated bite of the cold. His thoughts were on the brink, his entire world collapsing within him. His buzzing mind could not process what his father had just told him, could not understand that the corruption of the world had somehow infiltrated the impervious boundaries of his own family...

His father had gotten him out of jail within hours. *Of course he had.* The bail money was less consequential than a mosquito bite to his father. He had always known they were well off, but he had never questioned where that money had come from. His father was a lawyer; there had never been any reason to question if his father was coming by the money honestly. He had never even thought to ask his parents how they had first made their start...

Everything he knew—everything he was—was built on a rotten foundation. He was no different—no better—than anyone else.

He had expected a lecture; he had gotten a confession. Then silence, punctured by the stealthily ticking clock, as he stared at the man he had idolized since childhood—and saw him for what he was.

Haven't you ever wondered why your mother likes Skeeter DeLuca so much, Dean? She sees him as a younger version of me: faced with the same odds, the same temptations, the same ways to escape. Same intelligence...

He could still hear the harsh staccato of the clock ticking in the night's oppressive silence, in the throbbing of his headache...

...the difference is that Skeeter is too much of a fool to accept the avenues open to him. Too wrapped up in his notions of honor and integrity to understand the only truth that exists.

That you can never—never—let anything stand in your way, Dean.

Meaningless, empty words. They pounded through his head as he stumbled towards the only place that still made sense...

So you see, Dean, this is justice. Your life is meant for great things. You have the potential to change the course of humanity, and you have a responsibility-- a duty--to lead others, to use the power and recognition of your reputation and talents to raise the quality of life for everyone else...

Serenade Way. If he could get to Serenade Way, he could think through what had happened. Nikki would help him...

Skeeter will take the fall for you. The same way someone took the fall for me, when I got caught.

He wanted to scream.

Felt his father's hand on his arm. Fingers like lead. Great men are still men, Dean. They make mistakes. If you look closely enough at any great man, you'll see that he made a mistake, and that someone else—for legitimate reasons-- took the fall for him.

He lurched through the darkness, not knowing the exact path, trusting that something would show him the way.

Don't do anything stupid now. You've already compromised your integrity. You'll have to make the best of it.

He ran. He ran through Cemetery Lane, up the driveway to her house, and he felt it again, like a cascading waterfall-- the relief, the release. How many times had he felt like that around her—and what would have happened, had he recognized and followed those feelings?

It didn't matter. Nothing mattered anymore... except that she open the door. He knocked.

The door opened.

"Hello, Dean." Her voice was very quiet. He heard the desperation beneath her carefully controlled tone. He realized he hadn't seen her outside of class in a very long time. "Would you like to come in?"

He remained standing outside. Working to unglue his lips. "I've done something terrible, Nikki."

"I know." She paused. "Would you like to come in?"

It wasn't important how she knew. *She knew—and she wasn't turning him away.* He didn't know what to say; he didn't know what to do. He followed her inside.

"We're in my living room, Dean," she said, after she had guided him to a seat. "We're alone. You can tell me whatever you need to. I'm as guilty as you are; maybe together we can figure out what's the right thing to do. Now that the right time has passed…"

"What are you talking about?" he asked, confused.

A pause told him that she was thinking… something. "Why did you come here?"

He was confused about something, but he couldn't think of that right now. "I don't know what to do."

"I don't know either, Dean." She sounded—of all things—indifferent. "I suppose you'll have to let things run their course."

"Run their course?" Her quiet words made him even angrier. "I can't do that. I have to do something--" He started pacing. "I told the cops the truth. About the drugs. No one believed me. And Skeeter's going to be in jail for up to three years while--"

"Skeeter? What does Skeeter have to do with this?" A pause. "And what… what do you mean…. drugs…."

He stopped pacing. He realized she didn't know what he was talking about. That somehow… his father… must have gotten the police to keep the incident quiet. Nikki didn't know what had happened in the cemetery; no one would know what had happened in the cemetery; Skeeter would never see justice…

"You came to talk to me about…that night in the tunnel." Nikki's voice was shaky. "Didn't you?"

"No," he said. "No, I took care of that--"

"*You took care of it?*" Venom laced her voice. "What you did to her… nothing could pay for the damage you've done…"

He stared in her direction, at a loss for words. "I didn't rape her. Nikki. She's the one who attacked me…" His voice took on the edge of urgency. "But that doesn't matter. What matters is that Skeeter is in jail for something I did, and there's no way to get him out--"

"There's always a way," she said. She did not blame him; she did not remonstrate him; *did she even understand him?* "You're the scientist, Dean. Give them irrefutable evidence of what you did." She paused. "Whatever that was."

He felt a glimmer of hope. "Evidence."

"Don't let Skeeter know," she said, quietly. "He'll never let you take his place. You know that." She paused. "Are you… are you okay?"

He thought about his house-- a mausoleum. He could still smell his father's cigar smoke, lingering in the air, and all around—darkness. Suffocating. He shook his head. "I can't go home."

"You can't stay here," she said, concern softening the cold in her voice. "But I can give you a ride to the police station. If you think that's what you need to do."

The clock in the hall chimed the hour, and the gongs carried all the weight of her sentence. If he went to jail…

"Hazel," he said.

"What?" she asked, clearly startled.

Nights after the attack in the tunnel. Home from the hospital, alone in his room. Lying on the floor. Tears streaking his face. Not wanting to live. Not wanting to open his eyes again. And a warmth on his face, a scratchy, wet warmth on his cheek...

Turning his face to the side. The kitten's hazel green eyes on him; her tail flicking around her feet as she licked his tear-streaked face. A sudden, insane explosion of hope rocketing through his body...

"Will you look after Hazel for me?" he asked, his voice ragged. "While I'm in jail, will you..."

"Yes," she said.

The memory of the kitten was a judgment, a second judgment. The possibility of redemption cut through his tired, frenzied mind, as he sat in the passenger seat and Nikki started up her car. *His life must still be good for something. Maybe, after he got out of jail...*

That was it, then. He would have to rework his entire foundation around the only conviction he still held—that he must live.

SKEETER DELUCA

Echoes of memories splintered like shards of glass in his mind as he sat in the waiting room, his hands cuffed and his head lowered. He didn't know how he'd be able to face Dean Fink, suspecting what he did about Galatea, knowing what he did about the thwarted cemetery exchange—

When the door opened and Dean Fink walked in, he barely believed what he was feeling: that this scene was meant to play out. Fink—the clear-cut features of his face hardened into harsh lines, a look like murder in his sightless eyes—looked the epitome of a prisoner. Like he belonged with guards on either side of him...

"Hello, Skeeter," he said.

Skeeter didn't acknowledge the greeting, and the guards looked at him for a long time before they buzzed the door shut behind them. The strange, animal look in Fink's eyes unsettled him.

"Why are you here, Fink?" he asked, finally.

"I need to tell you something." Fink smiled nervously. "About Galatea."

He could hear the lights buzzing like flies in the ensuing silence. "I don't want to know, Fink."

"But I have to--"

His eyes glittered like dark glass. "I asked Galatea what happened. She lied to me. But if she doesn't want me to know, then I—"

"I have to tell you the truth—"

He shut his eyes. "I don't want to hear it. I don't care what you did to her. It can't be worse than what I did."

"What do you mean?"

He remained quiet, trying to put his thoughts in order. When he finally spoke, his words were the careful result of examining his feelings—and giving voice to personal truths. "I betrayed her. And I abandoned her."

Fink spoke too quickly. "Skeeter. You don't understand--"

"I want you to understand something." He heard the anger in his voice; he didn't try to control it. "I hurt her. I broke her trust in me."

"She'll forgive you," he said. "She loves you. She'd forgive you anything."

"It's not that simple, Fink." He clenched his hands together, unclenched them. "There was only one thing keeping her together—"

"What?"

"Love. And I destroyed that. It would have been kinder if I had killed her."

"That's not—"

"Shut up, Fink. That's the truth—and there's nothing I can do about it now." He paused. "But when you leave here, tell her that—"

"I can't tell her anything. I don't know where she is."

He looked up suddenly. "What do you mean?"

"No one knows where she is," he explained. "She took off after she found out you were in jail."

"Damn it." His chair crashed to the floor. "That wasn't supposed to happen."

"That's why you have to find her," Fink said. "You have to tell the police the truth, about what happened in the cemetery, and then you have to—"

"No." He looked at the security cameras, then made a concerted effort to sit back down and appear calm. "I can't ask you to take my place in here. I belong here, Fink."

"No, you don't." Fink paused. "If you love her, Skeeter, you'll go to her. You won't stay here."

"She lied to me," he said. His chair shattered against the far wall, and he overturned the table in front of them. He heard the warning buzz of the alarm on the wall and knew that he had just betrayed Galatea a second time, because the guards would never let him walk after this...

The guards came. They grabbed him. They started to drag him out of the room.

"Stop!" Fink screamed.

He watched blankly as Fink walked towards them. A single memory flashed through his mind: the night he had spent with Galatea. For a moment he was transported back to the warehouse: hearing the rain on the tin roof, smelling the smoke and wax from the candles, feeling her shiver against him under the sheets, knowing he wouldn't sleep and she wouldn't either but neither of them would acknowledge it the next morning...

It was one of the most precious memories of his life.

Galatea and her damn ideas. *And he had let her slip away.*

He came back to realize that Dean Fink had told the guards the truth about the exchange, that they were trying to get him out of the room—and that he wasn't leaving.

"Fink," he said quietly. "What the hell do you think you're doing?"

"They have to know!" Dean screamed, then rounded on the guards like a wounded animal. "The truth! Won't you idiots listen to the truth?"

Skeeter watched as—unbelievably—the guards grabbed hold of Dean Fink's arms and dragged him out of the room. The security door banged back into place, and he was left.

Alone.

NIKKI DIETRICH

The other line crackled with a heavy silence, and then the angry sound of the dial tone deadened her ear. Nikki replaced the receiver. She would keep trying, because there was nothing else she could do...

"Who were you calling?" her mother asked from behind her.

Nikki jerked. She was startled every time she saw her mother's haggard face and frenzied, lost eyes. "I was just trying to get hold of the police."

"Nikki—"

She started walking towards the door. "I don't want to hear it."

"Nikki!"

She let the door slam behind her. The house was stifling; she had to get away. Though she knew she would never be able to escape from her thoughts—and they were what was truly bothering her...

Galatea was still missing and no one seemed to care. Skeeter was still in jail, and that wasn't right, either.

She didn't know what had happened to Dean Fink since that night she had taken him to the station. She didn't particularly care.

She slipped on the ice beneath the snow and fell. She welcomed the pain. She got back up and continued walking down the bike trail, keeping to the shadows until she reached the tunnel.

Dagger-like icicles hung suspended from the concrete ceiling. She felt a presence as she stood motionless, staring at the faded paintings in the empty space. She could not grasp the feeling exactly, but it was like the foreboding of coming to the last pages of a book. A knowledge that a certain end was coming.

Questions flew through her mind like machine gun fire. Had any factor been even slightly altered—had she not stumbled into Galatea in the tunnel, had she not told Dean, had she not gone running on that night—the outcome might have been different. But it didn't do any good to think about that. Not now.

She moved to the first bare space of concrete and arranged the cans she had brought in a triangle on the ground. Only the primary colors: red, yellow, blue. Only the purest, most fundamental colors...

She felt empty, dazed, as she listened to the hiss of the spray and watched the colors—thick, wet, beautiful—cover the ugliness of the wall. She had never spray-painted before, but the thing developing before her eyes was clearly a sunflower. *Galatea's symbol of happiness and hope.* She felt she had not painted it; she felt like something else had used her body. She felt, suddenly, as if she were being watched, and turned from the concrete slab of wall with a distinct sense of horror.

But there was no one there. She was alone, except for the wind whispering through the empty tunnel and the sound of her own breathing.

She turned back to the concrete canvas, shaking the can of red paint, listening to the ball inside clink against the metal. Without thinking about what she was doing, she picked up the can of blue, and around the sunflower she drew the outlines of a simple cross. *Skeeter's symbol of faith.* She filled the cross in with red, then looped their initials—*GWSDL*—in gold at the top. She looked at the painting, and it seemed ugly to her—raw and crude and ugly. The cold froze the tears that crept down her cheeks.

She felt, in that moment, that Dean Fink was supposed to be there, to help her finish the story. She felt a shudder, like a charge, go through her. *But he was not there.*

She was alone. She had done the best job she could. She knew—somehow—that Galatea would understand.

She stooped to gather the cans. She zipped them into her bag and slung the bag over her shoulder. She thought about all the paintings Galatea had envisioned, how they carried the sparks of beauty and spirit of their creator. She looked at what she had done, what she had meant to be a tribute to them...

I look into my heart and I see evil, she thought. *I see darkness. I feel cowardice running through my veins, feeding off fear...*

The wind froze her as it screamed by, filling her head with a vague pounding. Her hand had clenched around the straps of the pack; she consciously loosened her grip, exhaled.

"I'm sorry, Galatea," she said—praying that in speaking the words out loud they would somehow get to her. "I can't change what happened. But I can give my life in service to others. And hope that I might still be able to do some good."

She paused. There was nothing.

She had not expected a final answer; she would rather be her own judge. Her footsteps echoed through the empty tunnel. She did not look back. Her mind groped for a thread to follow—some thread to tell her what to do next...

There was nothing.

GALATEA WILLIAMS

Exhausted, she leaned against an ancient oak in Cemetery Lane. *Skeeter had been the only person she cared about—the only thing she had to lose—*

And she had lost him.

He was in jail, for a crime she knew he hadn't committed. And she was invisible, unable to help him in any way-- the distance and separation between them now made concrete and real.

Her own Armageddon had already come—the day she realized Skeeter was leaving her. Nothing she could offer was enough for him—nothing between them was enough to make him stay. Her hand shook as she clicked open her lighter, lit a cigarette. The flame flicked out in the wind. She cupped her hand around the lighter, but her hand was shaking too badly to protect the tiny flame.

Disgusted, she threw the cigarette away. She needed the nicotine too much; she was done with smoking. She was done with anything and everything she thought she needed...

She leaned her head back against the tree's trunk, let the wind freeze her face. She would not think about Dean Fink anymore; she would not think about Skeeter DeLuca. *It didn't matter.* Some were entitled, some were doomed, and in the end it made no difference how you had lived your life.

Isn't that the truth? she thought. *And if that's the case...*

She would rather be invisible, than a part of that world. She would rather be a ghost, than have an impact on someone who could hurt her so much. She would rather fade away...

No. I will not walk around dead inside.

The voice inside her that spoke was sudden, unexpected, and harsh. It felt like melted steel lacing its way through her veins, forcing her to stand tall where before she had been weak. The shock to her mind was like a lightning bolt, a powerful surge of energy and electricity that burned away everything that had been distracting her from the truth. Her hands clenched into fists, she pushed herself away from the tree. The cold wind stung her face raw and fanned the fire that had burst open in her heart.

The problem with how she had lived—in shadows, in fear—was that she couldn't see that she *had never wanted to be invisible.* She had always wanted to exist in the world— but on her own terms. Staying quiet, staying asleep, had let her run away from herself, had let the world crush and oppress her without her being aware of it. She had told herself—*if you give up, the world wins.* But she had never believed it until that moment.

Her own actions made sense to her, now. Destroyed, degraded, she had turned to the one person who had never let her down. *Skeeter.* He had told her to stay in school—to go to college—to make something of herself. *But that wasn't what she wanted.* She had slipped from one non-existence, the result of the trauma, to another non-existence—letting someone else tell her how she should live her life.

The pounding of her heart—the quivering in her limbs—let her know that *this was the moment.* This was the moment—the only moment of her life—that mattered. She was being called to make a choice—*and she didn't know what to do.*

She couldn't stay. She couldn't let anyone—or anything—hold her back, and staying in her hometown would not let her break the chains that shackled her. She had no plan and barely any money... but that didn't matter. She had found faith: if not in herself, then in her own life's journey. She had never even thought to do something as extreme as that which she was now considering—to leave, to simply leave and see what happened…

But that was exactly what she was going to do.

NIKKI DIETRICH

She exhaled and closed her eyes, praying with every fiber of her being, her hands clenched into tight fists and tears dripping down her face. *Please, Skeeter. You're the last hope for any of this to turn out right…*

"Nikki," he said, and his voice broke.

Hope ripped through her. He had said her name. She didn't want to risk saying the wrong words, but she was out of time. "Skeeter, please don't hang up…"

"I won't."

She exhaled. "Skeeter, what happened? What—"

"Fink turned himself in. I don't want to waste time going into the details." A pause. "Nikki, listen to me. I have to find Galatea."

She inhaled sharply, and was relieved when he continued without giving her a chance to speak.

"I need to know where the last place you saw her was."

She wracked her memory. "I…. I don't remember. School, I think?"

'That's too long ago. What about the tunnel? I stopped by the tunnel and there was a new—"

She blushed. "No, that was me."

"You?"

"I… I don't want to explain."

A pause. "Do you have any idea where else she might have gone?"

"You knew her better than anyone. I'm sorry, Skeeter, that I can't be of any more help." She tried to think of something helpful to say. "Was there some place that was special for the two of you? Someplace she might have--"

The dial tone buzzed in her ear. She put the phone back in the cradle, realizing the call had been finished anyway. She went to stand in her driveway and looked up at the stars, which never failed to shine.

Good luck, Skeeter, she thought. *If anyone could find her—it would be you. But she knows, and I know—that she has to find herself first.*

SKEETER DELUCA

Was there some place that was special for the two of you? Someplace she might have—

Suddenly, he knew. The memory had come to him at the police station and he had dismissed it, but now he realized it was a thread he needed to follow, to lead him to her...

He ducked into the archway of the warehouse entrance, his heart pounding. He climbed to the loft.

The place was empty. The air was stale, and the mouse droppings in the half-used candles let him know she hadn't been there in weeks. He leaned over and lit a candle, and in the dim light he saw a single piece of torn notebook paper taped to the floor. He picked it up. The ink had smeared and faded and the paper was splattered with water stains, but he could still make out what she had written.

My messed up heart
G. Williams

Love Itself   Drives People
   To Greater Heights   To Sacred Places
   And I   wonder. .   .Do you know?
Do you know I have always Loved you?
   T h a t   I   a l w a y s   w i l l?
      Storm; I'm EMPTY and a f r a I d
I'll never be the same because
      YOU LOVE ME
   But—I still have ½ a heart
      And Until I can see the sun.
         Hear the song of the trees
         And delight in the night--
Without you
I must wander
Until I am
   Free

"Tea?" he said to the empty air—hoping, somehow, that she could hear him. "*Why?*"

Water dripped somewhere in the warehouse; a draft sent the candlelight flickering. He folded the sheet and glanced around the empty room. There was nothing there for him. But somewhere in the world—she was there.

He would find her. He tucked the poem carefully in his pocket. Only time would tell him how, and when, to look for her. But he would find her.

A MELODY FOR TWO

For Leo

In you I have found ultimate strength.

From the midst of the nether world I cried for help.

The waters swirled about me, threatening
my life:
the abyss enveloped me:
seaweed clung about my head.
Down I went to the roots of the mountains;
the bars of the nether world
were closing behind me forever,

When my soul fainted within me,

My prayer reached you

What I have vowed I will pay.

Psalm of Thanksgiving   **The Book of Jonah**

1.

That first day in the theater, I heard my name called as if in a dream.

I had wanted this chance to sing all my life, and now I could only stare at the large, open stage, the rows of empty red seats, the high arch of the ceiling. I forced myself to walk towards the glossy grand piano on the right of the stage. The next five minutes would determine the course of my life.

The woman who had called my name– a tall woman with piled up hair and smeared red lipstick– had escaped my notice to that point. I held my head high and tried to appear confident as I walked to center stage, realizing too late that my black V-neck dress would accentuate the paleness of my skin and the translucent blue of my eyes.

"What will you be singing this evening?" She looked bored.

"Think of Me."

"Speak up." The woman motioned at the rows of empty seats and the looming balcony boxes. "If you want this part, you must fill this space."

My voice sounded hoarse to my trained ears. "Think of me."

She did not smile. "Give your music to the accompanist."

My heels– to make me appear taller than my 5' 3"– clattered against the wooden boards of the stage. My eyes lighted on the accompanist. He was not handsome, but his presence made my heart hurt. Pale and full of sharp angles, his shaggy dark hair falling just past his ears, he sat hunched at the piano with his eyes on the keys and his hands clasped tightly in his lap. He accepted my music score without looking at me, and then a gentle smile stole across his lips as he read the title.

My life hung on this performance. I closed my eyes and focused myself.

"Begin the song," the woman ordered.

He played beautifully, and each ivory note resonated hauntingly across the stage and echoed in my heart...

"Think of me, think of me fondly," I sang, "when we've said goodbye..."

The piano's music crashed to a halt. I turned, terrified, and saw the accompanist looking down at the keys and clutching his hands as if the piano had scorched him.

"Jonah, what's the matter now?" the woman asked him sharply.

He mumbled something incoherent.

"Speak up!" she barked.

"The note." His voice was rough, like a piano that has lost its tune from disuse. "That last note wasn't sung correctly."

"Ms. Hartman was perfectly on pitch. Stop this nonsense," the woman argued. She turned to me. "Please begin again."

I listened to the opening overture. "Think of me, think of me fondly..."

The piano crashed to a halt. The accompanist was shaking his head violently from side to side. "I can't," he croaked.

The woman stood and started towards the stage. "I have half a mind to come and haul your sorry ass out of the--"

"Maybe if we give him a moment alone..." I interjected.

Her eyes flicked to the accompanist. She gave a curt nod of her head. "You have five minutes."

Without another word, she marched down the center aisle. I started to follow her but felt a tightening in my stomach. I approached the piano and the skeletal figure seated there.

"You must play this song," I implored. "I need this chance."

"I do not care about your needs," he said indifferently. "I cannot play this particular song."

His eyes were so dark that the pupils nearly disappeared, and the single opera light cut deep shadows into his features. I caught my breath. "This opera is special to me."

He met my eyes, unaffected in any way by my presence. "It is... not just music. It cannot be played like a regular song, and it cannot be sung like a regular song." He frowned. "Do you understand this?"

I nodded. He kept his eyes on my face. Unable to stand the intensity in his glare, I dropped my gaze to his hands. He had beautiful hands: long, slender fingers and prominent bones and muscles. "You won't play the song because you don't think I can sing it the way it should be sung."

"You can sing it." He did not look up. "But that note must be hit precisely."

"You can help me?"

He nodded. "Sing."

He cut me off--once, twice, three times, four—always at the end of the sixth measure. With each interruption I felt the music building inside me, until the pressure became unbearable. I looked at Jonah and found him staring back—his eyes wide, his body relaxed. Something inside me snapped.

At that moment the theater doors opened.

"I've given you five minutes." The woman strode down the center aisle. "Now play her damn song."

I looked out at the broad sea of empty seats. My heart lurched into my throat, and I concentrated on the soulful depth of Jonah's eyes when they had met mine...

Still in that haze from the repetitions of the haunting overture, I sang. The theater disappeared in the heartbeat of the music. I was alone with magic...

"No." Jonah's distressed voice arrested my song.

Half-dazed, I turned to see him shaking his head.

"That note was flat." His dark eyes burned as his skeletal hands struck a chord. "Sing the note a pitch higher--"

The woman's voice prevented me from obeying his command. "That will do."

During my performance I had drifted towards the piano– towards Jonah. I cringed at the thought of leaving him, knowing I would never see him again, and he wouldn't even look at me. Impulsively, I reached out to take his hand. He drew back from my touch, leaving the music score abandoned on the grand piano's ledge. I backed away as he stood; sitting hunched as he had been I had misjudged his staggering and skeletal height. Without a look in my direction, he disappeared into the shadows behind the stage.

The woman's voice cut into my thoughts. "I'm glad you got the part, Melody, as Jonah appears to have decided he won't play anymore today." She smiled tightly. "Welcome to the troupe."

At some point I realized that she, Gloria Fenstein– my manager– was detailing the times the troupe rehearsed, the standards she expected, the salary I could expect, but I didn't process half her words. My mind was still hazy. For a moment I could still picture him there, his long form bent over the keys, his sharp shoulders hunched, his passionate and intense eyes. I heard the music– living, haunting, powerful. Then the vision faded, and I hurried from the theater.

2.

We had practice for *The Phantom of the Opera* the day after I was accepted. I looked forward to the practice even though Micah, the regular accompanist, had replaced Jonah after a quick recovery from the flu. I think I was the only one who noticed how flat the music he played sounded.

Before vocal warm ups I met Juan Hernando, who welcomed me with a rich baritone voice. He had been chosen to play the Phantom, and his wife, Julia, would play La Carlotta. I also met Vanessa Lithstrom, a beautiful girl of nineteen. Gloria, the manager, hadn't yet decided which one of us would play Christine Daaé, the female *ingenue*. The other would be Meg Giry, a minor role.

As soon as rehearsal was over I asked Don Juan about Jonah. He declared I should forget about 'the skeleton' and bat my eyes at the young actors. I said the actors were all married or attached. He laughed heartily and patted my cheek, then put his arm around Donna Julia and led her grandly off the stage.

I also asked Gloria about Jonah. My inquiries irritated her, and she knew little about him.

Jonah haunted my thoughts. How could I forget the fever I saw burning fiercely in his eyes? The disconsolate sob of the piano when he played?

Two weeks passed before I saw Jonah again. One day I woke and rushed to the theater, thinking I was late. Yet when I walked into the lobby I could not hear the usual buzz of conversations and laughter; the only sound I could hear was the melody issuing from within the theater. I knew Jonah was playing by the sweet sadness in the notes, the lingering and perfect harmony of the piano's sob. I moved quietly into the theater and he was there, sitting hunched at the bench with his back towards me. I floated closer to him, unable to stay away.

He tensed when he sensed me, but he did not stop playing. Then, without so much as looking at me he nodded-- and I started to sing. When the song ended, I knew I had to speak.

"I'm Melody." I did not offer him an ordinary greeting; I knew he would not shake my hand. "You play beautifully."

He cleared his throat. "Will you sing?"

"I'd like to talk to you."

He struck a chord. The music tugged at my heart, but worry nagged me.

"Where are the other actors and actresses?" I asked. "Where did everyone go?"

He struck another chord. "You're an hour early."

Already, my speaking voice sounded harsh and out of place. "Then why are you here?"

He removed his hands impatiently from the ivory keys. "I have no other place to play."

I felt, suddenly, like an intruder. "Do you want me to leave?"

"I want you to sing."

As he started playing, I was filled with a fear greater than I had ever known– a fear that I would disappoint him. I closed my eyes and then... I heard many voices.

My father's, describing what a melody was; my mother's, explaining the importance of my name; Jonah's-- through the repeated melody-- telling me I had missed my cue. All the voices told me to sing.

Tears burned my eyes as the song was ripped out of me. I had never felt such fierceness, such passion. This was the point of no return—and as I realized this, my voice trembled and broke.

His hands crashed into the keys.

"I'm sorry." I bit my lip, feeling like I had betrayed him. "I'm--"

"Again."

"Again?" The word sounded like salvation.

He moved his hands back to the keys. "Sing."

The doors to the theater opened. Jonah shrank from the sudden shaft of light, and my heart sank as I realized the others were coming. Their voices grated on my ears, destroyed the atmosphere of harmony and stillness. I watched Jonah stalk off the stage, then stood awakened to reality as the theater filled with the regular din of noise. I was sure I was the only one who had seen Jonah and was left with the distinct impression that he had been only a shadow.

A beautiful shadow.

I tried to remember the music, but I heard only noise. When I opened my eyes I saw Vanessa standing beside me on the stage, watching me. I smiled at her, and she looked away.

3.

I started going to the theaters early in the morning, even though Jonah did not reappear. To fight my disappointment I turned to the empty seats and closed my eyes, and I tried to bring the theater to life. My voice started becoming hoarse from the double practice, but I couldn't stop myself from going to the theater. I couldn't tear myself away from the empty stage, where possibility hung like a presence in the air.

I wasn't prepared to see Jonah in the theater on the sixth morning-- nor was he prepared to see me. I entered through the side door, which put me directly across from the piano where Jonah was practicing. He looked up, startled, and I stood there frozen.

"What are you doing here?" he asked.

He was thinner and paler than I had remembered, and his dark features were severe in the half light of the theater. His eyes were the same– dark, passionate, intense– but they burned now with some extreme emotion that had not been there before.

Seeing him– when I had thought he was lost to me forever– emboldened me. "I wanted to see you."

He looked at me blankly. I had enough time to feel foolish and regret coming before the theater doors opened, and Link Barclay sauntered towards the stage. He had already been chosen by Gloria to play the *Vicomte de Chagny*, and the ingenue role that I was competing with Vanessa for was the Vicomte's lover. I understood now why Vanessa wanted the role so badly; though engaged to her, Link has made several advances already on me. Though I didn't want the complications, I still wanted that role. Though I had tried—in vain—to communicate clearly with Link that I would not participate in an affair.

"Miss Melody," Link announced, coming towards me on the stage. "Singing your heart out like the little bird you are."

"Good morning," I said, grateful for Jonah's presence by my side.

Link came to stand beside me-- far too close for my comfort. "So this is why you've started to lose your voice. Yet still, you sound divine. May I join you?"

"The theater doesn't belong to me."

"You would never know it, seeing you on stage. What a presence."

A sudden awareness arrested my attention; Jonah had left the piano and moved stealthily out of the theater without my notice. I moved closer to the empty piano, desperate not to be alone with Link.

Link moved as if I had cued him. He strode to the piano and sat down, then looked at me, smiling. "What shall we sing?"

I took a step away. "I wasn't aware that you could play."

"I'm told I play quite well." He arched his hands over the keys. "In fact, I've been told I do several things quite well." He stood abruptly and grabbed my arm. "Where are you going?"

His motion cut off my exit. I kept my eyes lowered, doing my best to ignore the grip of his fingers. "I'm going to leave now, thank you."

He made no move to let me pass. "There's still an hour until our rehearsal begins. And we're all alone."

"I'm well aware of that, thank you." I pulled my arm free and moved towards the stairs. Link started coming towards me. Leaving behind politeness-- I fled. I heard him calling my name, but I did not turn to look back.

I struggled through practice; the notes of the melody cut my sandpaper throat like shards of broken glass. I felt feverish with frustration; that day's rehearsal would decide the *ingenue* role. At the end of practice Gloria pulled me aside. She looked at me, hard. "Take tomorrow off."

I walked quickly out of the theater, and ran directly into Link. I hoped he was waiting for Vanessa, but on seeing me, he stepped forward and grabbed my wrist so I could not pass by.

"I want to talk to you," he said.

"Please let me go."

Instead he slid his arm around my waist and drew me closer. "Why do you keep trying to run away from me?"

I kept my eyes lowered. "Vanessa will be out in a minute."

"Surely you can't be so naive. Vanessa knows about my fascination with you." He laughed and let me go. "She's used to it by now. She won't leave me—and I won't leave you alone, not until I discover what you're hiding from me."

"I'm not hiding anything from you," I said firmly.

He grinned. "No one is as innocent as you're—"

"Let me go. I don't feel well. I need to get home."

He raised a pale eyebrow, then had the audacity to press his lips to the back of my hand. "I'll let you go in a minute. First you are going to hear what I have to say." His hazel-blue eyes narrowed to slits as he took my face between his hands. "I've been watching you in the mornings. You haven't seen me, but he has. *That's* why he hasn't come." Link paused. "You might as well save your voice, Melody. He won't come as long as I'm there, and I have no intention of missing an opportunity to be alone with you."

Anger flared within me. "I'll stop coming early."

"You'll keep at it," he said, caressing my cheek. "You can't keep yourself away."

I tried to wrench myself free but did not succeed. "Jonah has nowhere else to go--"

"Then meet me somewhere else." He gripped my arms painfully. "And don't refuse me. I can be fatal when I don't get what I want."

He let me go. I turned and walked away from him. Cool air breezed by my face. I glanced over my shoulder once and saw Vanessa had exited the theater and was standing in Link's arms, her back towards me. Link looked in my direction as he kissed her.

4.

I was often sick as a child, and on days when I was confined to my bed Papa would let me look through his picture books. Sometimes he would sit with me and explain the paintings, and sometimes we would sit together and make up our own stories.

Once I became so ill that Papa and Mama both thought I was going to die. Mama had prayed for me constantly during that time and had gone on a three day fast as a sacrifice because they couldn't afford to take me to the doctor. Mama told me, later, that when my papa was not sitting quietly with me, he was playing his violin and singing for me. On the day my fever finally broke, Papa gave me *the book*– a pocket-sized tome with a brown leather cover and gold-tipped pages. The inside pages were covered with the works of Frida Kahlo.

She was like you– Papa had written on the inside cover– *Strong in spirit but her health not so much. Keep your spirit strong always, little Melody.*

I realize now they must have sacrificed something dear in order to buy that precious book-- but I know they did so because they loved me.

I learned so much from my papa. I used to be afraid of storms when I was younger. I would scream and cower behind the overstuffed chair in the corner of the living room at the first flash of lightning. Papa worked erratic hours at his art studio; he saw only one such escapade, when he came home one night during a particularly severe storm. He stood in front of the chair, arms crossed.

"Melody," he said. "Come here."

My terror of the storm outweighed my faith in Papa that night. He had to pull me out and tuck me in his arms until we were both settled in the big chair. The horrible storm raged outside. A thunder clap rent the sky; I shrieked.

"This will not do." Papa shook his head. "I did not believe your Mama when she told me." He tipped my chin up. "How can my big girl be afraid of something as beautiful as a rainstorm?"

I cried.

"Listen. Can you hear it?" Papa's tired face expressed strained concentration as he cupped a hand around his ears. "The music. Can't you hear the music, angel?"

Thunder and lightning crackled outside.

"Each tiny raindrop. *Pat, pat, pat.*" He tapped the beats on my leg. "Each clap of thunder, beat of a drum. *BOOM!*" He picked up my hands, clapped them together, and drew them apart. "Every flash of lightning..." He slid my hands over each other– one towards the sky, one towards the ground. "*Zing!* Together," he directed. "*Pat-a-pat-zing, zing-BOOM! Pat-a-pat- zing, zing-BOOM!*"

I listened to the sounds of the storm for my cues. Papa watched me, wiping tears of laughter from his twinkling blue eyes.

"Remember," he said. "Every storm a symphony."

I was not afraid of storms after that, even when a storm claimed my father's life five years later. He had been painting in an open field, and he was struck by lightning. The damage should have left him alive but paralyzed, and I think he made the choice to die.

For a time it was just Mama and me, then Mama became sick. Then I was alone.

5.

The night I went home from the final audition at the theater, I became violently ill. The next morning my throat felt filled with drying cement, and a knifelike pain cut through my head. Yet the air wafting through my window was warm, and when I looked outside the world was shrouded with mist. A familiar fear—the one that surged through me every time I felt deathly ill—compelled me to change into a pearl-gray wool dress, and then I drove to the shore.

A hazy fog crept along the sand and blended the blue of the ocean into the gray slate of the sky. Sea gulls shrieked overhead, sharp as the waves crashing against the shore. I fell once, my balance sucked away by a violent and hungry wave. The wet wool weighed me down to the shifting sand until I was thoroughly soaked. I crawled towards higher ground, then waited until the dizziness passed. Black spots danced across the sand like water beetles, and the salty air burned my jagged throat. A needle-sharp drizzle drilled the seascape, and I forced myself to stand and continue on. The salty breeze and sea spray stung my face raw and left me fiercely alive.

The shore stretched empty before me as I came to an outcropping of dark rocks. I watched the waves cascade through the crevices in thick, foamy jets and I crept closer. I sat down on the dry rock closest to the breakers-- and then I saw him.

I was afraid I had hallucinated him into existence, but he was there. Bared to the elements, Jonah sat up to his waist in water, unmoving as the rock where he sat pounded by waves. He stared out at the horizon over the seemingly endless sea. I wanted to ask him what his eyes saw, but I also felt like an intruder. Yet I could not make myself move.

A wave finally knocked him off the rock. He emerged from the water and started back up the outcropping. He saw me. He stared at me as if frozen, then he stood and started walking away from me over the slippery surfaces of the jagged rocks. I heard the pounding of the waves like the thudding of a single heartbeat as I watched him go.

When he passed me I saw the scars– long, ugly scars that twisted across his back like tangled barbed wire. I tried to follow him, but I slipped and fell. I struggled as the water immersed me—but I had no strength. I could not even call out for health.

From the town I heard the bells chime the hour: ten heavy tolls barely audible over the waves and rain. Through salt blurred vision, I saw Jonah walking away, a vague figure in the distance whose long, thin footprints were erased by the swirling waters.

I held the air in my burning lungs until I passed out.

6.

Someone found me and took me to the hospital.

I was diagnosed with pneumonia and hypothermia. I know I should have been glad to be alive—but I had lost my chance at the theater. I found it difficult to keep the flame inside alive in the weeks that followed.

I took a barista job at Lucy Green's café to pay rent. Lucy was a retired librarian, and her café teemed with bookshelves replete with everything from *Robinson Crusoe* to Nietzsche's *Genealogy of Morals*. The grinding of the espresso machine, the rich smell of dark roast coffee, and the cinnamon sweet smell of streusel blended with the chattering of the customers' discussions. The welcoming atmosphere helped soothe the loneliness I felt, and Lucy let me sit down and read on my breaks.

I always headed straight to the overstuffed chair that reminded me of the old chair I used to hide behind during thunderstorms. The memories of Papa and the stories he read to me would flash into my mind like so many pinpoints of light when I was at Lucy Green's.

Today, my chair in the alcove was not empty.

Someone had left me flowers when I was in the hospital—and the only person who knew what had happened was Jonah. But I knew Jonah hadn't left the flowers for me—why would he, when he left me to die? I felt a flash of anger that he could sit so nonchalantly, immersed in his book.

"What are you reading?" I asked.

He looked up and his eyes were dark with thought– as if I had awakened him from a dream. Maybe that was why he didn't run away from me.

"The Old Testament." His eyes scanned the pages. "God may relent and forgive, and withhold his blazing wrath, so that we shall not perish..."

"What part of the Old Testament is that?"

"The Book of Jonah." He frowned. "The sign of Jonah..." He broke off and lowered his head.

I had never thought to hear his deep, quiet voice again. "What about the sign of Jonah?"

His eyes darkened momentarily; his lips curled in a half-smile. "Irony. To be named after a person whose story personified faith."

"You don't believe in faith?"

"I know there is a God," he said. "He does not interest me."

"Why?"

He sneered. "What hope can there be for us—if our world is the result of a superiorly intelligent being?" His voice became sharp. "What are you thinking?"

I sensed his unhappiness, almost as if we shared one mind. "I wish you weren't so sad."

He looked at me, startled. He stood, placing the book under his arm. "I don't want you to think of me."

Fear hit me as I stood there, alone among the stacks of books. Every book was a world—and I knew my experience with the theater was only supposed to be a chapter. Jonah was probably supposed to be a footnote. I could leave it all behind, and start a new chapter-- but where could I go now, when the only thing I could do was sing? I was surrounded by possibilities and should have felt excited and hopeful... but I only felt afraid.

7.

I knew meeting Jonah in Lucy Green's Café had been random, and I did not expect to see him again. I was singing a few times each week at clubs to make extra money, but my heart wasn't in that singing. In this between-time I felt like my life had been swept away– but I tried to keep busy.

I went to the first performance of Fenstein's *Phantom of the Opera*. Vanessa Lithstrom made a fantastic Christine Daaé, though her performance left me feeling hollow inside. I went to the theater the next day to congratulate everyone. Gloria was full of smiles for me and kind inquiries about my health and prospects. How I wished I could tell her good news, any news! Instead I could only ask about the theater's next production, without any hope of trying for a role. The illness still lingered in me; I still felt frail and very weak each morning.

Don Juan gave me a hearty hug and I received a curt nod from Julia, and then I saw Vanessa. I went to congratulate her on her performance, and she told me she was pregnant. Link had stepped beside her during the course of our conversation, and the uneasy expression on his face confirmed the truth of Vanessa's words. My interest in the child was not lost on him, but neither he nor Vanessa would answer my questions. After a few seconds of silence, Vanessa looked pointedly at Link and disappeared back stage.

Link lingered. "Did you like the flowers?"

My heart dropped. "They were very beautiful, thank you."

"Orange gerberas. They reminded me of you." He reached out and locked a strand of my hair around his finger.

In moving away from him I realized-- Jonah was in the theater. The slightest movement of his body– his fingers smoothing down the pages of the open manuscript on the piano– alerted me of his presence. My wayward glance was not lost on Link, who grabbed my arm and pulled me away from the piano.

"Step aside with me for a moment, Melody."

I could feel his fingers digging into my arm. "You haven't given me much choice."

"Don't underestimate me." Link snarled, and then he smirked. "I think you'll be interested to know, Melody, that I have figured you out. I know what you want more than anything else."

"I doubt that."

He pulled me closer. "I saw how you played with the troupe's children in between sets. How you would sing to them and tell them stories..." His voice dropped a pitch lower and he sneered. "You think that *he* would be a good father?"

"I don't think you understand," I said.

"There's something wrong with him," Link continued. "Don't tell me you haven't noticed– "

"I do not appreciate this conversation." I tried to move away, but he tightened his grip on my arm.

"Have you been with him?" he demanded.

I frowned. "You have no right to talk to me this way. Shouldn't you be focused on the little one coming your way?"

Link let go of my arm. "Vanessa doesn't want the kid. She says a brat will ruin her career." He looked down. "And Vanessa will never let anything ruin her career."

I stared at him. "You have to stop her."

"What am I supposed to do?" Bitterness crept into his voice. "She has the law on her side. It doesn't matter that the child is my son."

"Motherhood is a sacred duty," I pressed. "If I could be a mother..."

Vanessa's voice cut through the air like a chill. "What a charming conversation the two of you are having."

Link started beside me, but I would not be intimidated. I turned, and my voice held an edge I didn't recognize. "I was telling Link how much I wanted to be a mother some day."

"And Link, undoubtedly, was offering to help you." Her lips turned down in a fine scowl.

"Your child will be a blessing," I said.

"A blessing," she said flatly, and then her eyes lit up. "It's really too bad you probably won't ever have a child, Melody. You're too tiny, and too sick." She laughed. "And whatever are you doing with yourself now, now that you're no longer a part of the troupe?"

Link stepped towards her and touched her hesitantly on the shoulder. She dismissed him with a small shake of her head. I struggled to keep my composure. "I'm still singing one or two nights a week--"

"Gloria will be calling us together any minute now." She smiled. "But I really was horrified to hear of your illness, Melody. I know how important this chance was and how hard you worked to get here--"

"Vanessa," Link said.

She ignored him. "I know how much you *wanted* this opportunity. And Gloria told us that the illness could come back at any time? So you can never get rid of the horrid uncertainty?" Her hazel eyes became slits. "At any time, your illness could destroy anything you've built, no matter how much time or effort you've invested--"

"Vanessa," Link said.

"What happened was unfortunate," I interrupted. "And it's true that I might fall ill at any time. But I will always sing."

Vanessa smiled. "I can't say I understand your indifference, Melody. You worked so hard, and then have it all go to absolutely nothing--"

"I can't understand, either," I said quietly. "I don't understand how something can mean so much to you – the whole world, really– and then mean nothing to you at all. But that's how life is."

Vanessa frowned. "If this really means nothing to you at all..." Then she smiled. "But who will play for you? It's so hard to sing without music..."

"I can hear the music in my head,"

"How very poetic. How very..."

Link put an arm around her waist and turned her away from me.

"Remember what I told you," he said to me. "I can give you what you want, Melody—if you give me what I want."

Vanessa looked at Link. She looked at me. The frenzy burning in her eyes was a banshee's.

"Always so good to see you, Melody," she purred. "Come another time."

"I don't think I will," I said.

Vanessa smiled tightly. "I'll let you know when our child is born."

I turned and walked quickly out of the theater. The sky was too blue for the autumn day, the patches of fleecy clouds grazing their way across the sky too purely white. *Maybe, someday...*

But I knew it could never be. I could never have a child, for fear that my health would fail and the child would be left an orphan, as I had been.

My thoughts wandered to unpleasant things. I feared I *had* underestimated Link. The hunter's look in his eyes and his lack of censure around Vanessa did not reassure me– nor did the strength with which he had gripped my arm. A sudden wave of dizziness overtook me, and for a moment my sight was eclipsed by darkness. I closed my eyes and waited, and then continued to my car.

I drove to the cemetery and parked at the bottom of the hill. Leaves spiraled around me as I walked to the indent in the evergreens where my parents were buried. I knelt by the two small graves, and I listened to the wind and tried to connect to the stillness in this place.

Yet I found no solace as I knelt. A single thought infested the possibility of peace: *Would Link continue to watch me as a predator does its prey?*

8.

The next morning the flame of my spirit was barely flickering.

I fell out of bed, the covers tangled around my legs. The sunlight hurt my eyes, and I was covered in clammy sweat. Vanessa's words came back to me... *the horrid uncertainty...to have worked so hard and then have it go to absolutely nothing...*

But these were not my thoughts! I matched my father's past advice for me against Vanessa's words and felt comforted. As long as my pulse still beat, I would fight to keep my song and the flame of my spirit alive.

My wave of panic passed. I shuddered and threw on a sweater. I drove to Lucy Green's without letting myself think. I entered through the back exit but, plagued by fever and dizziness once more, I paused to catch my breath. When I opened my eyes, Jonah was standing before me. His sharp face had become even paler. He passed close by me; he pressed something into my hand. I looked down and saw a small, irregularly shaped envelope. On the front, he had written:

For Melody

I turned and looked at his retreating form. I didn't say anything, but he stopped and turned slowly to face me. We stared at each other for several minutes without speaking.

"I didn't know where else to find you," he said finally.

I watched him leave. I pocketed the envelope until I got back to my apartment, when I slit the seal and found a silver CD inside. As the hauntingly familiar chords cut through the barren silence, I looked at the envelope again and saw I had misread the tiny script: *For a Melody*. The CD consisted of the music from *The Phantom of the Opera*– the haunting chords without the lyrics.

He had been so quiet the previous day during my encounter with Vanessa and Link– but he must have heard her words. *It's so hard to sing without music.*

I did not sing the first time I listened to the CD. I was shaking too badly. I could hear Jonah's soul in the music, and my heart throbbed. *How could I make him realize...*

And here my thoughts stopped.

I knew I was becoming distracted by Jonah when I should be concentrating fully on my music. But without Jonah my heart suffered, and without heart I could not sing.

But Jonah was not willing to see me– and spirit has to be nourished from within. If I could rely on myself and put more faith in my music– then I would find the strength to pull through the uncertainty of my life.

9.

Sometimes the choice to follow intuition sets a series of events into motion, and it's impossible to stop the momentum.

Not two days after he had given me the *Phantom* melodies, Jonah strode into the café. His eyes burned in his face pale, and his entire body was shaking.

He targeted me and moved forward without hesitation. "You need to come with me."

"Now?"

He nodded, impatient. "I need to show you something."

"I'm working." I tried to divert his attention. "Thank you for the CD. I've been singing along with--"

"Will you come?" he demanded.

I could not tell him I would be fired for walking out in the middle of my shift. A refusal to his invitation be a betrayal of my own heart. Still I hesitated. "Where?"

"Follow me."

The wind outside the café cut through my windbreaker as I hurried after Jonah. "Where are we going?"

He cut through the dark woods bordering the highway without answering. I felt thorns tear into my skin and hair as I followed. When I emerged into the clearing after him, my cheeks stung and bleeding from cold and cuts, he was standing with perfect composure in front of a small, dilapidated house before us.

"Jonah." The throb of my heart had become a searing pain. "I need to..." I sank down against a tree, unable to follow as he continued purposefully toward the house. I closed my eyes and waited for the pressure in my temples to fade. Then I made my way to the house.

He had left the door ajar. The space beyond the threshold was cold and bare.

"Jonah?"

There was no answer. Shivering, I went through the kitchen– bare– and the living room, where I paused to look at the music scores scattered. The starkness of the house with its skeleton rooms attested his poverty, and I was saddened that he had nothing to assuage the ugliness– not even a piano.

At the end of the hall I noticed for the first time that there were no doors on any of the rooms. I stood at the top of a set of peeling stairs, where a single naked bulb at the bottom showed me the emptiness beyond was the basement.

The temperature dropped as I started down the steps. There was a worn, cracked work bench near the light—and there was Jonah. His head was lowered; he sat absolutely still.

"Come here," he said.

I looked at the workbench. It was bare except for an overturned glass bowl.

"Will you take him outside?" He seemed, somehow, much younger.

I moved slightly closer. "Take who outside, Jonah?"

Jonah pointed to the glass bowl, a deep frown on his pale, tight lips. I started. A brown cockroach skittered under the glass dome.

My heart sunk. "You want me to take him outside."

"I will make the others leave, but you must take him outside."

I looked at the glass bowl. "They won't hurt you."

"But they'll hurt them."

I felt a chill run through me. "Who?"

"Dorian. And Isabella. And the others."

I needed to leave the house, with its unanswered questions. "I'll take him outside." I cupped the insect in my hands, then turned and retraced my steps. I found Jonah in the basement where I had left him, in much the same attitude as before, except the worry lines in his face had smoothed out.

"Thank you," he said. Something seemed strange about his voice, and he seemed like he was watching me and searching... for something.

"I know that was hard for you," he said in that strange voice. "You don't like insects, do you, Melody?"

I shook my head. Since my childhood insects had terrified me.

"But you took that thing outside, because Jonah asked you to."

I looked up, alarmed. Jonah had never talked about himself in the third person before, and he would never refer to any living creature... even a roach... as a *thing*. Then his head jerked, and his dark eyes glowed with a kindness and warm gratitude I could feel through the distance between us.

"Thank you," he whispered again.

I relaxed. Slightly. "Who are Dorian and Isabella?" I felt very still in his presence now. So different from that previous sense of foreboding...

He hesitated, then shook his head. "You need to take Dorian away from here. Follow me."

I followed Jonah up the stairs, through the kitchen. As we approached a tiny room, I saw a quiet determination steal into Jonah's features– a subtle shift in the lines of his face, a clenching of his jaw, a darkening of his eyes. He was steeling himself to let me into this room.

At first I did not understand. The room was bare, except for a cot covered by a white sheet and a tiny ivy pant in a terra cotta pot on the windowsill. Then I noticed the shelf on the far wall– lined with puppets.

Jonah crossed the room and picked up one of the dark-haired dolls. "This is Dorian."

I looked at the tiny form cradled in his arms. "He looks like he's alive."

Jonah smiled. "You should see him when he moves."

"Will you show me?"

Perhaps it was the look of tenderness on Jonah's awakened face as the puppet looked back at him– or rather, Jonah *made* the puppet look back– but something about the atmosphere in the room changed. The puppet's limbs and expressions moved and changed, surprisingly like a live child. When Jonah stopped working the puppet and put him back on the shelf, I felt like a presence had left the room.

"Where did you get him?" I asked.

"I made him."

"You made him?"

He shrugged.

"You make puppets," I said. "That's what you do?"

Jonah looked at Dorian, the same small smile on his face, but did not acknowledge my question.

"Do you get attached to them?" I asked, instead.

"I do not mind when they leave," he said quietly. "They aren't made to sit on a shelf." He looked directly into my eyes. "Did you know the Japanese believe that puppets have souls, Melody?"

"I didn't." I paused. "You don't keep any of them?"

"Dorian will always stay with me. Except for now-- he needs to go with you until they leave." He paused. "I know you will take care of him."

He held out the puppet to me, but something about the puppet frightened me. "Will you show me how he works?" I asked, stalling.

A smile flashed across his face. "Sit down."

I moved to the cot in the corner and sat down. He came to the cot and stood near me. The light in Jonah's eyes changed. He yanked the white sheet from the cot and turned his back to me. When he turned, I saw that he had wrapped the sheet carefully around Dorian, so that only the painted eyes and rectangular face around them were visible.

"It's raining," he explained. "And it's cold."

Jonah was asking me to leave and I understood. I didn't ask about the sudden change of plans. I took the bundle as gently as I could, fighting my apprehension. "I'll take good care of him," I repeated, tucking the sheet around the puppet more tightly.

"You have a good soul."

I started. "What makes you say that?"

"Your eyes aren't dead, like so many people's are."

I felt slightly uneasy and once again compelled to leave the house. "Do you want me to take Isabella, too?"

"She's not finished."

A silence settled between us.

"I'll call the exterminators for you," I said. "They'll be able to get rid of ... them... in a day."

"One day." He nodded.

I felt completely awkward but pressed on. "You're not going to be able to come back here right after the house is... after the men come. Do you have somewhere else you can go?"

"I'm not leaving the house."

"Could you stay with a friend?" I asked. "Or maybe a..."

"I'm not leaving the house." His stone was expressionless, his voice cold and not so childish now.

"It won't take long--"

"We lived here, before he died."

I paused. "Who?"

"This house holds many memories." No emotion warmed the severe cut of his face. He was absolutely still.

I cradled the puppet to my chest, rocking it. "Jonah. If you need a place to stay—"

"I can't leave this house. I have to remember." He lowered his head and ceased looking at me.

I put out my hand, into his line of vision. Jonah looked at it; then, slowly, he reached out and twined his fingers through mine. His hand was warm; mine felt small and frail inside it. I felt tears start into my eyes; when Jonah saw them, he dropped my hand and turned away quickly.

"Thank you," he said, but his voice had grown cold.

I started up the stairs silently, my heart beating against the bundle pressed to my chest. I left Jonah alone in the empty, cold house with his thoughts, and was unwilling that night to confront my own.

10.

Jonah started coming to the café when he knew I was working. He always sat at a table near the front of the café, tucked into a corner away from the others where he could read without being noticed or disturbed. I was glad to see him.

I was not so glad to see Link. The first day he walked into the café, I felt as if all the air had been sucked out of the room.

"I heard you were working here," he sneered as he came up to the counter. "Moving up in the world, little bird?"

"I'm lucky to still be here." I did not like the gleam in Link's eyes. I felt like something monstrous and oppressive had come into the café with him.

He smiled. "The pretty little bird can't fly away from me here, can she?"

I tried to move away, but he reached out and pinned my arm to the counter.

"I'm a paying customer," he snarled.

I steeled myself. "What do you want?"

"Coffee. Black. 16 ounce."

I went to the coffee pots behind me and pumped caffeine into a Styrofoam cup. I set the cup on the counter. "Anything else."

"I want you." Any tolerance in his face was gone. "Did you hear me?"

I took a step back. "That will be one dollar and fifty cents."

He slammed a fistful of change onto the counter. "I'll be back."

The coins rolled between us. I didn't let my eyes leave his until he backed away, and still I waited to move until I heard the door close behind him. I was trembling as I bent to scoop up the change that had fallen to the floor, and when I stood up, Jonah was there. He had overheard the conversation; the light in his eyes was riddled with... so much pain.

"Melody," he said.

I waited, surprised; we rarely spoke when he came to the café. There was an unreadable edge in his look as he handed me another oddly shaped envelope.

"Is this more music?" I asked.

"Yes."

"Jonah, wait." I opened the package. I looked at the silver disc inside, on which he had written in his neat hand, Dmitri Schostakowitsch. Sinfonie No. 9.

"I needed to share it with you." He was glowering, like he hated himself for giving me a gift.

"Thank you." I wondered if he was trying to communicate with me again through music. "Can I sing with you again sometime?"

The request caught him off guard, but my nervous question had sent a flash through his dark eyes– and ignited a hunger.

"Can you come tonight?"

"Where?" We were whispering, though no one in the café was paying any attention.

"To the theater."

"When?"

"When it gets dark."

My heart started beating faster. "The theater will be closed."

"I'll let you in."

There was no real question. I had to go.

The sprawling theater was transformed by night– Mr. Hyde to the day's Dr. Jekyll. A full moon sent the shadows scattering, but the clear disk was soon concealed by thick gray clouds that coiled like uneasy serpents across the black sky. The high arch of the iron gates and the grandeur of the theater's facade struck into my heart a sublime fear. I was small enough to slip through the gates and stood transfixed by the entrance for a moment; then I knocked, producing a faint, muffled sound which I knew would not carry through the thick oak door. I tried the horse-shoe shaped metal handle; the door opened with a protesting groan.

I had no justification for my presence at the theater. But if Jonah had access to the theater, he might also have left the door open for me...

I stepped into the lobby. Without the chattering of spectators and the clerks and ticket takers, the large hall should have felt empty– but I sensed a presence there. I did not linger; I made my way into the theater's auditorium.

A single bulb spotlighted the piano. A single music score lay open on the shining black ledge, but the theater was dark... and empty. I went to the piano and sat down. For a moment, all I dared do was look at the keys– and then I struck two notes. The sound echoed through the vaults of the theater. I glanced quickly around the theater.

"Melody."

Jonah's voice startled me, and my heart leapt as I turned to him. Tall and ghastly pale, his dark eyes shining, he seemed a specter who clutched the lifeless body of a child in his arms.

"Is that Isabella?" I asked.

He nodded and stepped closer to the piano. "You played a harmonic fifth. A triumphant strain..."

"Did I?" I tried to see the puppet, shrouded in her white sheet. Her painted eyes were darkened by thick, full lashes, and her cheeks and lips held a cherry blush.

"She's beautiful," I said, holding out my hands for her.

He relinquished the puppet to me and watched as I took her tenderly. His eyes were sad.

"You want a child so badly."

I kept my eyes on the puppet. "What makes you say that?"

"I see it."

I looked up at him. "Don't you want to have children?"

He nodded at the puppet. "I have *them*."

"But they aren't real, Jonah." I looked down at Isabella– at her painted eyes and fixed expression.

He took Isabella from me and repositioned the sheet carefully around her. He said nothing.

I hesitated. "I know you overheard the conversation in the café."

"You would have beautiful children with him."

I stared at him, aghast. "Jonah, I don't want anything to do with Link. I..." His sudden attention made me stutter to a stop, and I struggled to compose myself. "Link is going to marry Vanessa. She's already months pregnant with their first child, and she's ecstatic--"

"Vanessa never intended to have the child."

An earlier– unwanted– conversation came back to me. "What would make you say something like that?"

Jonah looked up from the puppet. "It is surprising what you hear when you are invisible to other people."

His words sent chills running through me. "If Vanessa meant to abort the child, she would have had to do so by now. Doctors can only--"

Jonah shook his head. "She wants the child, now, because of you. Because she knows you want one."

"How can you..." I stared at him. "Why would you want to remain invisible when you hear such horrible things?"

"It will affect me." He paused. "And it will affect you. So I listened."

"What do you mean?" When he didn't answer, I prompted further. "What did Vanessa say? If this involves me I need to know..."

He sat down at the piano. "Will you sing? Then... I have something to ask you."

My heart fluttered. "Can you ask me now?"

"No. Will you sing now?"

I looked away. "I don't think so."

"Because..." His long, thin hands were already poised over the keys.

"Because I'm sad."

"Why?"

I hesitated to tell him my thoughts. But he listened.

"I'm afraid she might hurt the child," I said. "Even now. As revenge, for what Link has done to her in the past..."

"Vanessa will not hurt the child before she is born," he said. "She wants the child now. What else is weighing on your mind?"

Once again I hesitated, but finally I said, "I'm afraid I'm going to sacrifice the gift I've been given. I've never felt worthy."

"It is part of you," he said. "You can *never leave it*, no matter how much you want to. Don't you feel it possess you when you sing?"

"What?"

"Passion." His eyes locked on mine. "It can save you or it can drive you insane. As is written in the Book of Thomas... *what you bring forth will save you, and what you do not bring forth will destroy you.*" His eyes flicked to the piano.

My voice was barely a whisper. "Do you think passion can drive a person insane?"

"I know it can." He looked down at the keys. "But do not run from it. You have been marked, as I have been, and it is best not to resist." He paused. "You cannot escape, and you'll be hurt less if you surrender."

I stared at him. "I don't understand this talk of being marked. But you're not afraid... of this passion which possesses you?"

"Are you?"

"I've always believed music was a gift," I answered. "Didn't... didn't the ancient peoples believe that music was a form of divine possession? At least Papa..." I broke off.

Jonah's eyes held a silent question, then he grimaced. "Thankfully you are strong enough to be in control of its power. Some are not so lucky." He fell silent, then added, "You don't need to be afraid. Even I am not afraid, and I am not half as good as you. I know both sides, and they serve their purposes."

"You know both sides," I repeated.

"My father taught me how to make puppets," he said. "When he died he left me his house. I will never leave it. So I can remember."

"Remember... making puppets." I struggled to connect the conversation. "Was it from your father that you learned about the darker side... of..."

"My father liked to destroy." His eyes took on a faraway look. "There are memories. He would take me into his studio when he had finished working, and then he would make me do things..." He looked at me, his eyes suddenly wide. "Why are you crying?"

His words had filled me with a vague, dark terror. "Because I'm... sorry..."

"I don't care now." His voice was quiet, marble. "I told you of him only so you would understand—that I cannot forget the dark passion, and what it can do to people who can't handle it." He put Isabella down gently on the top of the piano. Her blue childlike eyes seemed to focus on him. "But we will not talk anymore of such things. Sing now, Melody."

I looked at his face, raised towards the painted face of Isabella. "You make puppets because puppets can't be hurt. Because--"

He sighed tiredly. His recollection of the past seemed to have had no effect on him. My heart and mind were heavy with the dark images of his words– but he sat on the piano stool beside me with soulful fire in his eyes and the excited eagerness of a small, unscarred child.

"I can't," I said, trembling. "I can't sing like you can play. I can't..."

"You can," he said. "You can sing better than I can play. You are pure and marked for good, and I am unclean and marked for something else."

Something he had said had snagged my attention– and disappeared. I struggled to grasp the flash of intuition but knew that Jonah would be no help; his eyes stared blankly ahead, and his jaw was set.

"I'll do my best," I said, finally.

"It will be enough." He struck a chord and played the opening aria to "Angel of Music." He played through it again, and then he turned and looked at me.

"Jonah." I paused. "I---"

"Sing."

As the haunting power of music filled the theater, I closed my eyes and sang. When he finished playing I knew my eyes were glistening with tears of gratitude. His face glowed as he turned, and then I saw him hesitate.

"Can I have your hair?"

"What?" My speaking voice sounded harsh.

"For Isabella."

I stood near the piano where he sat; even so, we were at eye level, though he did not look at me. I hesitated, then reached out and turned his face so he had to look at me. His eyes flicked to my hair, lying loose across my shoulders. He picked up a long strand gently between his fingers. Then the haze left his eyes, and he dropped the strand of hair, as if the action had scalded him. He kept his face turned away from me.

"I didn't know that puppets had human hair," I said.

"Melody, I'm sorry—"

I cut him off. "How much do you need? Never mind. Come by tomorrow, Jonah. I'll have my hair cut and ready."

He did not say anything.

"Will you come by the café?" I asked. "I'm not going to cut off my hair if—"

"I'll come." He closed the music score and stood, his figure impressing me again with its skeletal height. "Thank you."

I looked at the piano. I didn't want him to leave me. "Do you ever write music? Your own music?"

"Maybe someday."

"Why not now?"

He paused. "Maybe someday I will compose, when I'm not afraid of what might come out."

What happened in the next few minutes? It was as if I had blinked and Jonah had disappeared back into the shadows of the theater. Suddenly he and Isabella were gone and I was alone. I closed the lid of the piano, and then I left the silent theater.

11.

It took Jonah days... weeks?... to come back to the café. But by early December, the packet of my hair was gone. At first I put the shorn tresses in a freezer bag under the counter, but the sight of it disturbed my coworkers, and so Lucy told me I could use one of the brown paper bags we use for to-go orders. So I put the packet in the paper bag, and I labeled it with a permanent marker:

Jonah– for Isabella

And the bag sat under the counter for days... and days.

Melissa, one of my co-workers, said that Jonah had come in the other day and that she had given him the bag. I asked her if he had read the note I had put in the bag, and she said he had not while in the café. Later, I heard her talking to Karen about the state of the soul and whether or not it can be scarred– so I know that at least she had read the note. I should not have been surprised. Melissa and Karen were interested in Jonah, whom they called "tragic" and "self-exiling" and "Byronic"– and any number of other terms they had picked up in their college literature classes. They tried to read symbolism into everything I said about him. They wanted to know who Isabella was; they wanted to know if cutting my hair had been a symbolic act, and made references to Samson and the IRA and others. I didn't even pretend to understand. I explained that I had simply cut my hair.

"Weren't you afraid to get it cut so very short?" Melissa gawked.

I shrugged. I hadn't known how much Jonah would need, but when I came in and found the bag missing, I didn't miss the hair at all.

Melissa seemed to think for a moment, then said, "Oh. He wanted us to give you something. Karen put it in the back hallway under a bag, because she said it was creepy."

I went to the back hallway and gently removed the plastic bag, and there was Isabella– dressed in white silk, the hems of her dress and sleeves lined with gold brocade. A string of white pearls circled her tiny neck, and a long white ribbon tied back her glistening blond hair.

She was beautiful. I walked back to the front of the café cradling her.

"She looks so much like you, Melody." Melissa smiled. "She could be your child."

"Put her back," Karen said. "She's frightening me. I never could stand those painted eyes. They just stare and stare..."

I looked into Isabella's eyes– a soft, pale blue, like water warmed by the sun. I tucked her into my jacket and put her back on the shelf. I wondered when I would see Jonah next. I wanted to thank him for the precious gift, but there was something else I wanted to tell him, too.

Jonah was the only bright spot in my world, which seemed to be spinning rapidly out of control. Link remained a frequent visitor to the café. I had hoped my changed appearance would curtail his interest in me, but the first time he saw my haircut he would not stop staring at me. He continued to come to the café and refused to be waited on by anyone but me. There was still that look in his eyes– ever increasing in his eyes– and my heart grew more uneasy with each passing day.

12.

Night, and I was lost. Thick, ashy clouds snaked across the moon, and a surrounding haze obscured my vision. Great bolts of lightning and clangs of thunder ripped across the sky, and a fierce rain that stung like needles pelted down to pierce the dead, black earth. My breath puffed out in gray, visible steam before me, and I felt the emptiness of the night upon me like a weight as I wandered aimlessly in the swirling mists. My feet were sore from walking, my eyes raw and red from crying. When the theater appeared I passed through the iron gate. I passed the high arched entrance. I opened the door. My skirt– torn and heavy with wetness and grime–left a trail of sludge behind me as I walked into the interior of the theater.

The empty theater buzzed with human voices, with the deep-throated call of bass and viola, the whisper of violins, the high-pitched siren song of silver flutes. The lobby– the walls and the carpet and the windows– were all stained blood red. I searched for the voices in the auditorium. Inside– darkness and silence. Then a light snapped on over the stage and revealed a little blond-haired girl in a white dress, sitting absolutely still and silent at the piano.

I was filled with the sense of impending danger. I crept towards the little girl. I dared not speak, but she sensed my presence and slowly turned her head. Her cheeks were bloodlessly pale, but her eyes shone a clear, electric blue. She jerked off the stool and came towards me. I stood looking down at her, then I stooped and held out my arms. But she jerked her head– unnaturally, as if someone had caused the motion. The motion showed a thick black string coiled around her hair.

I followed the string with my eyes, into the shadows by the side of the stage's crimson curtains. A form lingered there– a man. I turned my attention back to the child– but she had disappeared. The living blue eyes had glazed over and become flat, painted, lifeless. The puppet's body was swarming with strings that went taut with sudden, violent force. The puppet dismembered– an arm flew to one corner, a lifeless leg to another-- and the golden hair scattered the stage. The man in the shadows dropped the strings and stepped forward, abandoning the broken doll on the theater floor.

He was not anyone I had seen before, yet I knew the cold gray eyes in the lean face. I recognized the long, scraggly locks of raven hair. Dorian-- the puppet brought to life. In his arms Dorian carried a miniature version of Jonah– tied up in controlling strings, a living puppet. Jonah's limbs were absolutely still– only his eyes moved, sweeping the stage of the theater in frenzied arcs, targeting each poor, torn apart limb, each thick coil of hair. Then his eyes centered on me in a wild, voiceless plea.

I felt myself being pulled backwards, back and back, until Jonah and his puppet master were vague, undefinable forms. It was a human arm around my waist that drew me into a closeted room, a human hand that turned the key and locked the door, and when I was released I turned and was confronted by Link's laughing green eyes.

"Not that way," he whispered, stepping closer to me.

At this point I started trying desperately to wake myself up. Link's hand covered my mouth; his other hand twined around my waist-length hair and he jerked my head back. I felt a searing pain deep within me and heard a baby's wail. Then all was encompassed by the image of a pendulum, swinging back and forth, shattering the stillness with its monotonous ticking.

I woke in my room, tangled in my sheets, drenched in sweat and silver moonlight. I looked out into a world of white, watched over by the pale disk of the moon. How I longed to have the cold purity freeze away my hot, feverish thoughts. Yet I dreaded reawakening the illness and so had to confine my restless spirit to my room.

I watched the night bleed into dawn, and I did not sleep.

13.

Finding my way back to the house in the woods was easier than I had thought it would be, though my solitary journey in the darkness set my nerves on edge. I forged my way through the labyrinth of trunks and roots and fallen logs until I came out into the clearing and saw the desolate, moon-drenched house before me. I stood by the dark borderline of trees, watching my shallow breath form weak clouds of vapor in front of me. The front of the house was as I had remembered from when he brought me here during the day... but like the theater, the house was transformed by the night. Away from the trees I became aware of the cold, cutting wind shrieking across the barren land, and I stopped halfway. Yet I could not tell what I was more afraid to do: stay outside in the wild, or proceed into the house, with its single weary light.

I knocked with the one hand I had available. I was here to return Dorian... and I wanted to tell Jonah that he did not have to be alone any more.

The next moments should have been a blur– but my memory remains clear. I went through the creaking hall to the light. I opened the door and Jonah was there, staring out the window with a dazed look on his handsome face. A music score was held forgotten in his hands. The frozen expression on his face– one of stillness and emptiness—stopped me and I stood shivering in the doorway.

I had brought the cold smell of the night with me, and slowly Jonah became aware of my presence. He turned from the window. He did not speak, but our eyes met.

"Merry Christmas," I said.

Silently, he nodded.

I put down the basket and unlatched the clasps. I lifted out the first wrapped bundle and took it to him. "I would have returned him sooner, but since I didn't hear from you..."

His eyes sparked to life as he took the bundle from me. "And Isabella?"

I went back to the basket and unwound the protecting sheet from that puppet. I walked back to him.

"She's yours," he said, refusing to take her.

"Thank you. She's beautiful."

He inspected Dorian carefully.

I spread a blanket over the cold floor. "Are you hungry? I brought a celebration meal, which I thought we could share."

His brow creased, but he came to sit beside me on the floor. He placed Dorian carefully beside him. I arranged what I had brought– grapes, small chunks of cheese, a hunk of bread– and I looked up at him.

"It's not much," I said. "I'm sorry I couldn't..."

"Thank you for coming."

I stopped my apology and nodded. Jonah ate wolfishly, oblivious to the fact that he shocked me.

"I have something to tell you," I said, breaking the silence between us.

He paused in eating, his appetite somewhat sated. "Say it."

My courage failed. "Can you show me how Isabella works?"

He stood so abruptly that he startled me. He snatched up Dorian and strode across the room.

"Come here," he said, almost roughly.

I went to sit beside him on the cot. How long did I spend sitting there, learning how to move the joints of the puppet? It seemed like a moment. And when exactly did the distance decrease between us? Because suddenly I realized that my knees were touching his, that I had leaned in close to catch his instructions and that my face was inches from his, that his keen eyes were fixed intently on mine...

"I love you," I said.

I can't remember anything but his eyes, centered on me in that moment... and how they changed. He drew back, and he looked at me with such coldness that I felt all warmth, all hope, desert me.

"You don't."

I wanted to contradict him. I wanted to explain how I came to this odd conclusion—but more than anything, I wanted him to say something else. *Anything else.*

"I love you," I finally repeated, tears welling in my eyes.

"Don't talk to me of this." He stood and raged back and forth. "You don't know what love is."

I had never seen Jonah angry before– and the furious black rage that contorted his features into a primal sneer of sharp, unforgiving lines frightened me beyond words. Yet still I found the courage– or anger– to speak.

"Do you think I can't love?" I staggered to my feet. "How can you stand here and tell me what I can't *feel*?"

"You think you understand love?" he ranted, his eyes still shooting sparks. "I will show you love."

He grabbed the bottom of his shirt and tore it over his head. Then, once more, he became very still.

I remembered the scars, then. Terrified, I grabbed Isabella, and I fled. Behind me, I heard him start laughing...

I ran to the boundary line of the thick trees. I sat down at the nearest one; I wrapped my arms around the trunk, and I cried. I cried until my face felt frozen with tears; I cried until my breath became ragged and my chest felt hollow. Then I felt quiet inside– and I knew I would be able to return. I had never intended to leave him, though flight had been my initial reaction to the dark energy that I had felt suddenly in the room with us. I turned towards the house and saw the same rectangle of yellow light painted onto the white snow. I gathered my courage and shifted Isabella's position. She was worse for the excursion; one of her tiny hands had been crushed between my body and the tree and had become disjointed. I took a steadying breath and then went back to the house.

I had left the door open and he had not closed it, though a fierce draft was ripping into the house. I went back to the room and everything was as it had been before, except that Jonah had placed Dorian neatly on the shelf opposite the cot so that the puppet was the first thing I saw upon entering the room.

"I'm sorry," I said.

Jonah raised his head. He stared at me. He seemed calmer.

I held out Isabella. "When I ran, I hurt her."

He crossed the room. He hesitated when he got closer to me, then snatched the puppet from my arms.

"She can be easily fixed," he said, retreating.

He had put his shirt back on, but the rolled up sleeves of the blue flannel revealed his strong forearms, and I couldn't keep my eyes from the scars that wound their way along his skin like vines.

"Thank you for bringing her back," he said.

I hesitated. "Can I see the scars again?"

He went rigid. I waited, certain that he would not comply, and then he faced me. He unbuttoned the flannel, button by button. The shirt dropped away.

I kept my distance as I stared at the long, intersecting slashes that laced over his shoulders, across his chest, down his arms. Then I moved closer to him and stopped, trembling. He stood still and looked at me, and seeing the expression on my face, he smiled.

"They cause me no pain, now."

Before I registered that he had moved, he took my hand and laid it on his chest. I traced the lines of what had been a vertical gash on his chest, and then I looked up to see him watching me intently.

"That isn't love," I said. "Maybe someday, I ... I can show you what love really is."

For the briefest of moments, he put his hand against my face. Then all too suddenly he withdrew his touch, as if I had burned him. The hard edge came back into his eyes.

"You don't understand," he said. "Love is not beautiful, Melody. It is not pure. It is about power, and control, and loss."

I shook my head. "If you would let me--"

"No." His voice was flat, and his eyes glittered like ice. "You were very wrong to have come here tonight. Take Isabella and leave."

I stared at his back as he buttoned his shirt, the images of the scars burned into my mind. "Her hand is still broken."

He stopped his movement, but he did not turn around.

"Leave her," he said finally. "I'll repair her and leave her at the café for you." He paused. "Do not come here again."

I sat Isabella against the wall. I smoothed her hair and the white silk of her dress and folded her hands on top of each other. I stood and found that Jonah had still not turned to face me.

"I'm not sorry I came," I said. "I'm not sorry that I told you I..." I paused in the doorway, not knowing what else to say.

"Go," he said.

Is this account what happened in the quiet hours of Christmas evening, or has the memory, pieced together, been distorted by delirium? I do not know. But how can I trust that the reality can be any different from this recounting, which my fevered mind has made me relive over and over in the same precise, clear details... haunting my thoughts even now in my lucid, waking moments?

How much suffering had I inflicted unknowingly on him? The coldness in his voice, the razor edge in his eyes as he looked at me... how I wished I had been born mute rather than to have caused him such pain!

14.

Around this time Vanessa became a frequent visitor to the café. It was clear to me that something was bothering her; though I didn't recognize it then, the first signs of the madness that would later commit her to an asylum were visible in those earliest visits to the café.

On the first of those encounters, Vanessa walked into the café two hours before close, dressed in a furred silver parka. Despite the overcast sky and snow outside, she wore a pair of dark sunglasses, which she pushed to the top of her head as she approached the counter. I hardly recognized her.

"Melanie," she said, deliberately skewering my name. "I thought I'd find you here."

126

The Vanessa Lithstrom I remembered had been a vivacious, charmingly slender woman with a rapier wit visible in her darkly lined eyes; the woman before me now was hugely pregnant, her skin sallow and unhealthy, the area under her eyes pockmarked by dark circles. Her thick hair fell limply around her face in oily clumps. Yet the most frightening change was her eyes, which burned with a wild, infernal light.

"I haven't seen you in *such* a long time, Melanie. I thought I'd stop by and say hello, since you don't seem too busy. Maybe we can have a little *chat*..."

I asked how she was.

"I'm well enough," she responded. She put her hand to her extended stomach and looked at me with those gleaming eyes. "Who made you think I was having complications?"

I would have changed the subject, but Vanessa not seemed intent on pursuing it. She scanned my face quickly and then laughed.

"No, you don't have to tell me, I know it was Gloria," she said, sneering, and put a hand— the nails of which were bitten down to the quick— on the counter. "I dropped out of the production *voluntarily*, Melanie, but didn't Gloria rejoice— all praise and Hallelujah— when I submitted my resignation? I know she's been looking for weeks for... a *kind* way ... to tell me I'm no longer wanted in the troupe. Not with *it* on the way."

The door of the café opened and a group of customers entered, but Vanessa made no move to leave. Her eyes remained locked on my face as she stepped aside to let me take care of orders, and I sensed her watching my every move. When the final transaction had been completed, she stepped back towards me. And smiled.

"I don't want to keep you from your work." Her low whisper was audible only to the two of us. Her brimstone eyes burned into mine. "But I wanted to tell you that I know Link has been coming here to see you. Often. And I wanted to warn you to beware, little song bird, lest he should tear off your wings..."

"You don't need to worry, Vanessa," I said. "I have no--"

She laughed and tossed her scraggly hair away from her face, and then she slid her sunglasses down to cover her frantic eyes.

"I'm not worried," she said. "I *let* Link play his little games. I know he'll always come back to me, because he is *mine*. What are you to him? A passing passion. And what are you to me?" Her eyes narrowed to slits. "A mayfly, born and dead within a day, killed by an autumn breeze." She straightened and smiled. "I carry *his* child. And though you may have some control over the man, the child is *mine*."

She left the café in a burst of frenzied energy. She took the warmth and comfort of the café's atmosphere with her, leaving me feeling cold inside. Perhaps it was my uneasy heart that led me to seek Jonah's company after I closed the café—despite his warning not to go back to the house.

15.

I set out towards the woods and took the path which would lead me to the house in the remote clearing. The cool night calmed my feverish thoughts; the stillness of the trees and the pristine whiteness of the snow energized my tired body and focused my feverish thoughts. Later, much later, I realized I had no idea where I was.

I was completely surrounded by dark, dense foliage. The same landscape confronted me everywhere I turned: trees and snow that seemed to stretch on endlessly without any distinct break in sight. Then—I saw-- a human form a little ways distant– a tall, dark form coming towards me. My overwrought senses and exhaustion could not handle the sudden appearance of this apparition, and without any ability to stop myself, I fainted.

When I regained consciousness several hours later, I found myself lying on the cot in the bare house, placed in front of a fireplace where a fire crackled half-heartedly. My body was stiff and bruised from the fall I had taken when fainting, but my mind was clear. I stood and crossed to the un-curtained window, through which I glimpsed the hopeful blush of early morning and the calming white of the snow. I wondered where Jonah was and how I had come to be in his house. I turned back to the fire and started as I saw him. He sat stiffly in the opposite corner of the room, staring at pile of blank papers spread before him.

"Good morning," I faltered.

"I hope you are well now," he said, when he finally spoke. "I am... sorry... if I gave you a scare last night."

My frenzied brain had not associated the dark form with Jonah. Yet who else could it have been? Who else could have found and carried me back to the house? He had held me in his arms, then...

I blushed at my thoughts. "You saved my life."

"Nonsense."

"If you hadn't found me, I would have frozen."

"If I hadn't frightened you, you wouldn't have fainted."

"But I was ill last night," I argued. "And I had no idea where I was."

He glanced up at me, a look of utter indifference on his face. "You were feet from this house."

"I wasn't. I was lost..."

"You could have followed your footprints in the snow back the way you had come," he said. "There were none but yours, and mine."

"But I wouldn't have thought of that. I--"

"I have never led you out of these woods, yet you have always found your way back to the roads," he said, calmly. "You would have found your way back, if you hadn't seen me and fainted."

"Last night was different. I was exhausted. And I was delirious. If you hadn't found me, I would still be out there," I said. "I'm not sure why you brought me here, but I want to thank you for taking care of--"

"I brought you here because I feared you would die," he said matter-of-factly. Then he paused. "I did not want you to die."

"Thank you," I said, but I wouldn't let myself hope. "I know that you take care of every hurt creature you find in the woods, and I'm glad that you showed me the same kindness you show them."

Jonah looked down at the blank pages in front of him. "I am going to write a song."

I attempted a smile. "You'll have to play it for me."

"Perhaps when it is finished." He looked towards the window. "Now, all the pages are blank slates. Maybe that is how they should remain, but I am going to try..." He looked down at the pages in front of him and became distracted.

"I was very lucky that you decided to go for a walk last night," I said. "And that you helped me."

He looked up. He looked temporarily confused. "Oh," he said finally. "There's nothing odd about that. I walk every night, whether I intend to or not."

I paused. "You could have left me there."

"I thought about it," he replied.

Strangely that response did not sting. "Where were you going?"

His expression remained blank. "I was returning."

"From where?"

"From the shore."

"You went to the shore? So late at night?"

"It was the Eve of the Blank Slate."

"What is the--"

"May I ask you a question, Melody?"

"No, I said, "Not until you tell me what the Eve of the Blank Slate is."

He looked slightly irritated. "I go into the ocean. I try to freeze away the sin— so that, maybe, I can live the rest of my life without being marked. It has never worked, but the pain is good." He sighed. "Now, may I ask?"

"Yes," I said, trying to process this information. "Anything."

His lips turned down in a scowl. "Why were you wandering around in the woods so late at night if you felt you were delirious and exhausted and ready to faint?"

"I wanted to see you."

Jonah looked at me silently. Then, "Come here."

I went to where he was sitting on the floor, and I sat down beside him. For a moment we sat in silence. Then we looked up at each other at the same moment. He reached out and touched my cheek gently.

"I cannot love you," he said. "I cannot love anyone."

I frowned. "Everyone can love."

"No, that is incorrect." He shook his head, talking to himself now. "I meant to say that I do not choose to love."

"Why?"

"I have seen love," he said. "I have seen love, in many of its forms, and I want no part in it. You do not understand, but maybe, someday you will." He paused. "Though I hope you never will."

I looked at him sadly. "Don't you want to fall in love?"

"You have exaggerated romantic ideas," he said. "You are a very great fool to want to fall in love."

"Perhaps," I said, "or maybe I'm curious, never having been in love."

Surprise— maybe something more— flashed into his eyes. "But others have loved you."

"None I've ever cared for in return," I retorted. "And I'd prefer to be alone, rather than with someone I didn't love."

He looked away from me. "You'd do best to make a blank slate of it, then."

"What do you mean?"

"Have you ever thought of renouncing love?"

"No. Love is a very beautiful and empowering emotion, and I can't imagine my life without love."

"Your talk of love reveals, once more, your idealistic notions." He paused. "If you have been alone for so long, it would be a very small step for you. A small step, which would be worth the initial leap of faith--"

"You say I have delusions about love," I interrupted him. "But so do you. You've never known what true love is like, so you can't possibly have renounced it--"

"There is more to life," he said, simply. "If you would renounce your foolish hopes for romance and love, you would see that there is so much more to life." He started pacing the room. "When you think of yourself as being alone... for the next fifteen years... how does that make you feel?"

"I want to be with you."

He paused. "Will you answer my question?"

I did so, reluctantly. "Empty."

"Do you need someone else to make you complete?" He looked at me. "Isn't your work... your music... enough?"

"I like to share my music with others. If there was one person I could..."

"Love invariably involves a narrowing of interests. Better to share your talent with the world," he said, decisively. "But you do not follow me. Love is slavery, Melody. The only price you will pay in renouncing love is being granted freedom. Freedom unlike any you can imagine. Replacing the inconstancy of love with the assertion of your own will--"

"Life would become so empty, Jonah."

"I am failing you." He scowled. "You do not understand. Without preoccupation with love..." He paused. "The world would... open up. Connections with the earth... with music... with life... would become deeper. Everything would become clearer. When you have no hope..."

He paused, his eyes burning. I remained sitting, trying to process his words. But he gave me no time to think.

"Long ago I was marked," he said. "But until the day I die, when my blackened soul will writhe in its eternal Judgment, I will attempt to prove, through my existence, what a wonderful thing it is. To be alive."

His eyes sparked at me. "It would be such a very small step for you."

"I won't live my life without love," I said. "I love the earth, I love the stars at night, I love the kindness I see in random people I pass on the street..." I struggled to stay calm, but the words continued to flow out of me. "I have to love. I have to love everything with my whole being, because soon everything I love will be taken from me."

He looked up suddenly; the look in his eyes chilled my blood.

"Explain yourself," he said.

"My health isn't good, if you haven't noticed," I said. "Each day is a blessing."

Again he started pacing, fury darkening his face like a storm about to break. Yet when he stopped to face me, his voice was calm.

"You can't die yet."

He sounded as if he believed his words could stop the inevitable. I feared he would misinterpret my amusement as a mockery of his earnest words. I spoke to cover my smile.

"I don't have any control over the matter." I paused. "I wish you wouldn't work so hard to push me away."

He did not seem to consider my words; he had resumed his pacing. Though– as usual when I thought him distracted– he had heard me. "Friendship is as elusive as happiness. Though not as ignominious as love."

"Will you come here, please?"

He stopped pacing and turned a blank expression towards me. I picked up one of the blank sheets of paper scattered on the floor.

"Maybe if I sing you a melody, you'll be able to write the notes." I tried to appear completely preoccupied with the blank sheets before me.

He was beside me in a moment, though he kept a careful distance between us as he sat down. After a slight hesitation, he took the sheet of paper from me.

"I will write because you are here," he said. "There can be no evil where you are."

I turned from him, knowing he would be repulsed if he saw the emotion on my face. I began to hum. He stared at the paper without moving; after a moment, he put down the pen.

"Nothing so sad. Let it be a song... of joy."

I turned and looked at him. I saw in his expression the hopeful expectation of a small child who has been promised a gift of great worth. I began to sing softly, without words, without restraint. Jonah went at the blank music score with great energy. The pen flashed across the paper, and this time he did not stop me.

16.

So suddenly had Link dropped all correspondence with me that I had come to forget about him almost completely. Oh world! So many pine for love and would do anything for it... and Link chose me. Why?

I froze as he entered the café. He was like something out of a bad dream; maybe if I closed my eyes, he would disappear...

"Good morning, Melody."

I looked at him silently.

An expression of anger flashed across his features, but vanished as suddenly. He moved up to the counter and smiled.

"Did you know," he said, and suddenly his lips formed into a sneer, "that your friend enters the theater illegally every night through the back alley and then spends the night– until dawn– pounding away on property that doesn't belong to him? And that no one at the opera knows about it, because he comes after the night watchman has closed the premises? Though I have a very good view of it all..." He paused. "But I suppose you *do* know. Since you're there with him."

My heart was pounding. I was full of fear for Jonah. I finally remembered that Gloria had given Jonah the key he used to get into the theater.

"Jonah has full permission to be there," I said. "He has a key so he can practice songs when the actors and actresses aren't there. He has the theater's permission to--"

"But you don't." Link scowled at me. "You have no permission to go and sing for *him*..."

I felt chilled by the thought of Link lurking in the shadows, watching the nightly performances that had become routine between Jonah and me. Sometimes we worked together on Jonah's song, sometimes he played so I could sing. "What I do does not concern you."

"It does concern me," he said, lowering his voice. "Greatly."

"I've already told you--"

"I have my suspicions about you and that madman." His voice dropped to a growl. "But I still know what I want, and I shall have it."

I turned away. "Don't insult me again."

"I also have my suspicions about him," Link continued, as if he had not heard the hostile tone in my voice. "Especially knowing what I do about his childhood history. Which, I am sure, would interest you. Or should." He smiled. "You see, I have something you want, Melody. An exchange thus becomes--"

"I'm sure I know more about Jonah than you do."

"Not what you want to know," he mused. "I'm sure you don't know how he got his scars."

Unfortunately, he had my complete attention.

He smiled. "But that information is only a small part of what I would willingly do in exchange...for one night with you." He traced a line from my cheek to my lips with one finger.

"Such a small thing to ask..."

I jerked away from him and tried to make my voice as cold as Jonah's could become when I missed the pitch of a note. "I don't want to hear any more."

"You might." His voice became hard. "I could give you something Jonah desperately wants."

"I doubt that. Jonah doesn't want anything."

"Jonah might not *ask* for anything. But if he could have his own piano...think about how happy he would be." Link paused. "I know that you meet at the theater because you have nowhere else to go." His lips curled. "Since neither of you could ever afford anything else."

My heart began to beat too fast.

"Maybe you can affirm for me," he continued in the same controlled voice, "that true artists also need a safe place they can go to create, in order to achieve their full artistic potential..."

"Are you implying that the theater is no longer a safe place for us?" I asked. "Or that knowing you're there in the shadows, lurking like some unholy creature, will in any way interfere with our practice?"

"Have you not listened to me?" he said. "I'm trying to help you."

"Damn you," I said, through gritted teeth. "I have had enough of--"

"I could get you a piano." His eyes searched my expression for a reaction before he pressed onward. "For Jonah. I'll have it delivered to where he lives, *as a gift from the theater*. He won't have to know anything... and then I promise I'll leave you alone."

I took too long to respond; he knew I had considered his offer.

He laughed– a cold, dry sound. "Think about it some more, Melody. You'll see it's a very little price to pay—for peace for you, and happiness for him...." He curled my hair around his finger. "*One night.*"

My voice faltered. "You're married. You have a child—"

"Do you love him?" he asked softly.

I stared at him.

His eyes bore into mine and he smiled– the knowing smile of victory. "Don't we have to make sacrifices for the ones we love?"

Still, I said nothing.

"I don't ever go back on my word," he said, watching me carefully. "I have made my offer. You may accept or reject the terms. It is your *choice*."

His last word affected me strangely. Every sense of propriety within me recoiled from the look in his eyes, the implication of his words... but the thought of being able to give Jonah something that might make him happy so blinded me, that my refusal never left my lips.

"Even the caged bird can sing, Melody." He backed away from me, smiling, and left the café.

I realized I had taken for granted the golden evenings with Jonah at the theater... just the two of us with the music. Though my dream had made such a suggestion, I had never suspected that Link had been watching us from some dark corner of the theater. I still could not conceive of him doing something so crazy. Yet how could I doubt the extremes to which love—or lust-- could drive a person? I remembered the sacrifices my parents had made to make my childhood a happier one-- because they loved me.

I knew that Link did not love me, but another part of his offer snagged at me. If I refused him, I didn't know what he would do to me... or what he might try to do to Jonah. And if I did love Jonah, and this piano would make him happy... then Link was right. One night would be such a small price to pay.

17.

Link had invited me to a music store to *look*, but– if I am honest with myself– I agreed to meet him so I could *choose*. I found him by the rows of pianos inside the store, which seemed empty but for the two of us and the employee who had greeted me as I entered the store. I met Link's gaze, and in them burned all the fire of his purpose. He must have read the resolution in my eyes, because he smiled.

There was piano music in the background– the soft notes floating in haunting streams through the quiet store. *I should have known.* I could feel his very soul in the music. But I was so preoccupied with my ugly and tangled thoughts that I didn't realize that Jonah was there. Link once again detailed the terms surrounding the liaison, and I said I understood and put my hand on the piano where we stood... and the music stopped. The sudden silence hung like a grave cerement, like a veil that would forever shroud that moment. The employee remained preoccupied at the other end of the store, but Jonah...

Jonah stepped out from behind a curtain near the pianos. The livid anger on his face distorted his sharp, dark features. I am sure he had heard every word, because his eyes burned only at me. I knew in that instant; I had betrayed him. And I knew—that Link had known Jonah was there. That Link had set me up.

But then...

I saw the look in Jonah's eyes change. His face became as blank as marble, and then the destruction began. With a strength and speed which seemed inhuman, he tipped over the piano where we stood. It crashed to the floor, the hammers inside clanging in horrible dissonance. As if possessed, Jonah continued to destroy the instrument until the white-faced worker hurried over, yelling. Jonah stopped instantly, but not because of the admonishments; he had made his point, and I suppose he saw that in my eyes.

With a black look at me and without another word, he left... followed by a shout from the employee, that the damage would come out of his earnings for the month. I came to understand, later, that he was employed to attract customers with his music, and that he *had* been on good terms with the manager...

I looked after Jonah, my heart breaking, and then I turned back to find Link looking at the wreck in front of our feet with an odd expression on his face. The crazed look had gone from his eyes. He looked at me as if I were a stranger, and then he, too, left without another word. I was left alone with the employee, who seemed to be approaching a state of hyperventilation.

I went from the store to the café. Link was there. He seemed badly shaken, and he stayed only long enough to make eye contact with me.

"I will not bother you again, Melody," he said, and then he was gone.

18.

Vanessa came into the café two weeks later. She thrust out a skeletal hand and there, loosely ringing one of her thin fingers, was a band of gold. She talked to me as openly and enthusiastically as if I had been her closest friend. The business in the café was slow due to the heavy downpour outside– a kind of pelting hail that turned the accumulated snow into thick, frozen slush. She talked of her marriage ceremony and her lack of pleasure on the marriage night– when Link had refused to touch her– and of the long and dreary honeymoon that they had spent mostly apart, since Link had gone off by himself and left her to "contemplate the intricacies of their future together."

Whenever she paused to give me time for a reply, she inevitably put her hands to her mouth and began to chew on the nails, which were already bitten down to the quick. I persuaded her to let me treat her hands with some of the lotion by the sink. I advised her to take better care of herself. She laughed and said she might as well, as no one else would. I told her truthfully how sorry I was to hear of her unhappiness.

"The baby," she said. "When the baby comes, I'll be happy enough. With or without Link. It will be here soon." Her eyes held the crazed, hazy light I had seen in Link's eyes before. "I don't mind that Link thinks he loves you. The ones you trust most are always the ones who hurt you the most. It doesn't matter to me. What matters is *this*." She jabbed her finger at me; the gold ring gleamed in the café's light. "This, and the fact that his *child* will be *mine*..."

Her eyes flicked over me briefly. "He bought it for you," she said cryptically. "Make no mistake about that. Goodnight, dear little Melody." And she left.

Stepping outside the café at the end of my shift cleared my thoughts. The sludge soaked through my shoes and numbed my feet, but the hail had turned into a soft, powdery white snow that fell like magic from the dark sky.

After the scene in the piano store I had resolved never to see Jonah again; I don't know how I had ended up in his woods. The house presented a dark, blank facade to me when I arrived at the clearing. The single path of footprints leading away from the house indicated that Jonah was out wandering through the woods. I hesitated, torn equally to go and to stay. I turned to go and felt that was wrong; I turned back and approached the house. My eyes fell once again on the single track of footprints, leading off into the woods. I knew Jonah needed to be alone... but he had told me, once, that he could stay beside me in his darker times... that I did not seem like I was one of *them*. I feared that my status in his mind would have changed, but my intuitive apprehension was stronger than the fear that he wouldn't want my company. I followed the footprints, stepping in the large gaps his feet had created.

I felt numb with cold by the time I found him– and then he was standing so still and tall that I almost mistook him for another tree in the shadowed woods. The crunching of snow from my steps alerted him to my presence. He turned and saw me. The sliver of moonlight filtering through the trees showed me how pale he was. I could not even guess how long he had been outside standing in that rigid, unmoving manner. As I came towards him our eyes met, and I knew instantly that he wanted me to follow him. I tried to match his long strides, but I soon stumbled and fell. I picked myself up, thinking that he would not be aware that I had started lagging behind... but as I stood I found that he had stopped and turned back– and in a moment, he was by my side. He held out his hand.

Such happiness! Thus linked we continued on, my mind blank as he forged ahead with clear purpose. Suddenly he stopped and let go of my hand. I followed his gaze.

He had led me to a large tree. She was a giant, sprawling her gnarled limbs crookedly to the dark sky. I went to the tree and put my hand against the cool, living bark. I was instantly filled with a sense of peace so deep as to be indescribable. A moment underneath that tree seemed to purify my entire body. I felt tears of gratitude leaking from my eyes and freezing on my cheeks. I turned to Jonah, but his back was to me. He was looking up towards the sky with its sprinkling of stars.

"Follow our footprints to get back," he said.

I hesitated. "You aren't coming with me?"

He said, "Not tonight."

I held out my hand. "Come with me."

He shook his head. I had tried. I turned and went, grateful that he had shared with me this sacred space and its ancient being. I carried the blessing of that night's encounter with me in my heart– a tiny but fierce flame.

19.

Jonah came to the café to find me, and his eyes were troubled and frenzied, his face pale and haggard. He came in, and for the longest time he just looked at me. His gaze was hard and penetrating; he studied me so intensely that I felt as if the apocalypse had come.

"Melody." When he finally spoke– he spoke so sweetly. Yet the haunted look remained in his eyes, and my heart lurched.

"Jonah, what is it?"

He did not look at me. "Can you come with me?"

"Now?"

He paused. "After work."

I don't know if I would have gone with him if I hadn't seen him a few nights before; that scene of destruction at the store, and the look of supreme anger on his face before he had destroyed the piano, had haunted my dreams. But he seemed to have forgiven me; he had held my hand as we walked to the tree, and he had come to the café. I nodded.

He looked at me differently, then– a look of vulnerability that held the same piercing intensity. That look stayed with me as I trudged with a heavy heart through the woods to the clearing, where the house with its single light burned dimly. I saw him, through the window, standing with his back towards me. I saw that the room was no longer bare; the light from outside illuminated a sleek upright piano in the corner. I walked through the bare, drafty rooms until I stood shivering at the threshold of the piano room.

He turned. The look in his eyes stopped me where I stood.

"Come in," he said, very softly.

I stepped into the room. He was standing by the piano, looking down at it with a mix of horror and affection on his face.

"This was a gift," he said. "From the theater."

I remembered the look in Link's eyes after Jonah had destroyed the piano. I realized Link had bought the piano for him. I felt the tears come, inspired by Link's unexpected kindness...

"Did he hurt you?" Jonah demanded.

"No." I looked up, startled. "Jonah, it's not what you think."

Relief... and then those dark eyes flashed. "*What did you do?*"

"Nothing," I told him, truthfully.

His eyes searched my face. "Tell me the truth, Melody."

I didn't say anything else. I wasn't going to try to prove anything to him. He would have to... trust me.

"Fine," he said quietly. "I know what you were going to do."

Jonah kept a shovel in the house, a heavy duty shovel with a metal blade that he used to bury the animals he would sometimes find dead in the woods around the house. He left the room and he came back with the shovel. His face was deathly pale.

"You did this thing for me. I have to accept that. But I *will not accept this.*" He gestured at the piano. "This is the result of the thing that you call love. *You sold your own soul...* in the guise of love." He kept his eyes fixed on me the entire time. "Do you understand now, why love is such a dangerous and ugly thing?"

My eyes remained on his face. I realized he could destroy the piano, if I did not speak—but *I had to trust him.*

Jonah raised the shovel... and then, suddenly, he froze. He turned. He walked towards me, the shovel trailing behind him. He stopped in front of me, and with one cool, pale hand, made me look at him. I met his searching eyes. Time blurred. I remember only that at some point my strength left me and I sank to the ground— and that he dropped the shovel so that he could catch me. And that he held me close to him.

"Why would you have done this?" he asked, taking my face in his hands.

"Maybe now you'll realize that I am not good. Not pure." I turned my face away. "That I am like--"

"You are *not* like them." He did not release me. Then, "Don't cry..."

I sobbed. This reaction, unexpected, threw Jonah into a state of deep agitation. He sprang up and began pacing around the room, pausing frequently to stand still and tear at his hair, or to clasp his hands behind his back. After one bout of agitated pacing– and after I had somewhat regained control of myself, though not to any great degree– he stopped and turned and looked at me.

136

"You have not changed," he said.

"I would have done it." There was no use denying the truth. "If you hadn't--"

He shook his head, picked up the shovel. "I cannot play that piano, knowing what you *would* have done..."

I remembered the cryptic comment that Vanessa had made me in the café... that Link had bought the piano for me. *Because he wanted me to be with Jonah?* I wiped at my eyes. "It was a gift, Jonah. From the theater."

He turned and looked at me. His brow knit; a painful light came into his eyes. I had never seen him so utterly at a loss. Finally he came and stood over me, looking down for only a moment before he stooped, and taking both my hands in his, helped me stand. I raised my eyes and met his.

"I cannot comprehend this thing," he said. Then he let me go and turned away. His hands balled into tight fists. "Get out."

I looked back as I walked away from the lonely house. I saw Jonah standing near the piano– his back towards me, his hands still clenched by his side, his head lowered.

I felt my first flash of anger at him. I had trekked into the woods, this late at night—*for what?*

20.

I thought that was going to be the last time I saw him.

Another period of time passed, prolonged by Jonah's absence... and I was almost driven to desperation by my sense of loss. My heart longed for him and centered on what had been lost, even as I focused on extinguishing every thought I had of him. Still, my undeniable despair took a toll on me. I felt increasingly weak with each day. But sometimes after work I would walk out to the woods, and I would stand among the trees and I would find some sense of peace. I had no regrets for my actions. The shame, the guilt, and the doubt passed away. The trees and the slumbering earth did not judge me. I wasn't going to let my sadness over losing Jonah distort my appreciation for life, and I tried to dispel my thoughts about him when they arose.

Lucy Green's café had once been my refuge from the theater's drama, but now that drama infiltrated even there. I went into work one day and found two notes left for me: one from Vanessa, and one from Link. In so many words, Vanessa told me simply that she was responsible for Jonah's knowledge of the piano's donor. Link wrote to say that Vanessa had gone one night to the house and had seen Jonah and me by the piano. He warned that we should be careful– very careful. Vanessa had started acting strangely, and he thought that the marriage and the approaching arrival of their child had upset her in some serious way...

And then Link came to the café, to make certain that I had received his note. I almost did not recognize him. The forceful confidence was gone from his manner; the manipulative cunning in his eyes was gone. I sensed immediately that he had come to me with a drastically different intent.

He did not even take the time to greet me. "Did you read the note?"

I nodded. "You didn't have to come here to tell us to be careful. I'm probably never going to see Jonah again."

"Good," he said absently. "But that's not why–"

"Why did you come?"

There was a moment of silence between us, and then he spoke.

"The child has been born," he said. "We've named her Caitlin."

"Congratulations. You and Vanessa must be very happy."

His eyes were full of doubt.

I paused. "Is she all right?"

"The child..." He paused. "Or Vanessa?"

"The child."

"She's beautiful," he said. "She's too beautiful for words."

"I'm happy for you."

He paused. His eyes searched my resolute expression, then dropped to the counter. He was silent for a long time. His thoughts seemed to take him very far away. Then he looked up.

"What's wrong?" I asked.

"You'll see." He backed away from the counter. "When it's too late. Goodnight, Melody."

His abrupt exit did not serve to calm my thoughts, but I tried to dismiss him from my mind. I would not trouble myself on his account. So much of life involves waiting; so many mistakes come from acting too quickly. I had determined to quit my job that day– so Vanessa, Link, *and* Jonah would have no idea where to find me– when another visitor stopped those thoughts.

"Little Melody!" Don Juan Fernando came directly to the counter about two hours after Link's appearance. "How changed you look!"

For a moment I was startled, and then I realized he had never seen me after my hair had been cut. But he shook his head when I mentioned this.

"No, little song bird. The color is gone from your cheeks, and the sparkle from your eyes. Sadness is not good for the spirit." He glanced at me. "There are rumors, my dear, rumors at the Opera House, but these you must not let sadden your heart. We know they are not true."

He took the letters I held in my hand. He glanced over them, and then he proceeded to tear them up. "There. And now, let these things be out of your thoughts." He patted my cheek. "Be a happy little bird."

He came back to the café counter after having disposed of the fragmented notes and smiled. I felt a weight slip from me.

"Now," he said, looking through his wallet. "A double espresso for the Signora. I tell her this café will destroy her voice, but she insist she gets old and must enjoy the things in life. I do not disobey the Signora. If I say no to my *prima donna*, I do not enjoy the things in life..."

He winked at me as I handed him the espresso, and he told me that the next time he came in he wanted to see the sparkle back in my eyes. His brief visit cheered considerably. And what he had said about the rumors-- the false and the untrue will always be destroyed, and what is real will find a way to survive.

What did it matter if Jonah did not approve of my actions, if in my own mind I know I was fully justified? Perhaps I hadn't seen the situation clearly, but I had made the best choice I could make at the time. How could I fault my intuition or my judgment, having acted as I thought was right? I began to grow glad that, for so many years, I had escaped loving another person. How quickly my affection for Jonah crumbled my convictions in myself!

Spending the first few nights away from him had been too hard; I had not realized I would feel less content when I was not with him. I thought I had been given back time to focus-- on my music and on myself. This was the offered opportunity that my sense of loss was trying to blind me from seeing. Underneath this loneliness, this emptiness, this exaggerated despair– underneath all of it I knew there was peace, a peace I had not obtained because I had been focusing on Jonah, rather than on my music. For these past few months, I had passed the majority of my time working in a café, and learning how to make an empty doll dance. I had strayed from my purpose, and my focus had wavered...

But those nights I had spent in the theater with Jonah—how beautiful those moments were. And how I missed him still.

21.

I knew the way back to Jonah, but I could not go. I do not know what held me back, but the soul that grows up in solitude becomes something wild and untamable. But I wished. I wished I could let him know that my thoughts followed him gently, that though I did not understand his agony, I witnessed the dark path he was walking and wanted to be beside him always. Maybe I knew that I had to wait until the day Jonah came to forgive me... or I came to forgive myself.

I tried to stay true to my former resolution: to concentrate on my music with my whole heart. Yet my songs, my room, felt empty and bleak. I wondered if my wavering focus and determination were testing my dedication, or if they were an indication that the time had come for new dreams and new passions. My music started to feel like a distraction from what I was supposed to be doing...

I could not remain idle any longer. At one point Link had told me that he had knowledge about Jonah's past-- which meant there was information available. Since I could not see Jonah, I resolved to do everything in my power to learn enough about him to put to satisfy my constant longing.

Tracking Jonah's history wouldn't get me back on track with my music, it wouldn't help me define my course for the future... but what did that matter when the future seemed far away and indeterminate? I decided to let myself take this detour, for my heart was uneasy and my spirit restless.

My search began with Gloria. She listened to my inquiries when I called, but she could tell me only that she had noticed– they had all noticed– Jonah's strange tendencies, and that he had recently disappeared altogether from the theater, to everyone's satisfaction. Despite Gloria's apology for not being able to help me, I did learn a valuable piece of information– Jonah's full name: Jonah Wilkes.

Though he was the most obvious next source, I did not ask Link for information. I was wary to renew that acquaintance, or to be under obligation to him. Oddly, though Jonah had been absent from my life, I felt he was with me in spirit. I believed I would be led where I needed to go if I remained open enough to my thoughts and feelings.

My mama would often tell me that all I would ever need could be found in the library. So to the library I headed. Because I did not know how to use the microform machines, I asked the librarian for help, and told him that I was looking for information about a musician named Jonah Wilkes. He knew of the Wilkes family; he told me of a long acquaintance with an Adrian Wilkes, who had enjoyed an illustrious and singular artistic career before he was committed to a sanatorium in later years. Having known Adrian Wilkes as a boy, this librarian had followed his work and his history throughout the years. He told me what he knew as he searched the library archives; he explained that Adrian Wilkes had contributed magnanimously to various charities during his middle-aged years and that only posthumously had the full darkness of the other side of his history come out. There were rumors while Wilkes was still living, but he had such a humanitarian reputation that the rumors were not widely believed...

The librarian handed me several rolls of microfilm. After showing me how to operate the machines, he informed me that he would be only too happy to help with any other questions I had. For the next few hours I remained absorbed, transported... horrified.

Adrian Wilkes's genius had been recognized by the most renowned critics of his day. His philanthropic gestures had been praised, and, as the librarian had said, the darker side of his history remained largely unrevealed during his lifetime. No questions had been asked when Wilkes moved with his two small sons (unnamed) to a remote location in the middle of the woods following the accidental death of his wife. The world seemed to assume that Wilkes, a world-affirmed man of genius, needed to be away from the stifling nature of society. Later, when asked about his proclivity for solitude, Wilkes stated he could create only in the confines of the pure world he had created for himself, where he could channel the "divine inspiration" he needed for his work through the necessary means.

Jonah had never spoken to any great degree about what he had endured in that barren house at the hands of his father, not in all the amount of time I had known him... yet I was suddenly sure of the pain and torture he must have suffered from Adrian Wilkes's "divine inspiration." Jonah's beliefs about love– about its violence, its power hierarchy, its pain– made sense to me now, considering the only "love" Jonah had known in those early years of seclusion had come from his deranged father.

Adrian's contributions to charities had increased as the years passed, but as he grew older his derangement became apparent in his art– most notably in his exhibition of a number of works involving demonic puppets. His interviews at the time revealed a blatant arrogance previously accounted for as charm. Of the darker turn his work had taken, he told critics that "the knowledge of his imminent death was upon him– he was surrounded and plagued by demons." The locality had continued to support their beloved artist, though mildly troubled by the unexpected turn of his art, until the occurrence that committed him to the insane asylum.

One article in the archive covered the gruesome event at length, while other newspapers enumerated the information that the public had ignored for so long. Now accounts of the almost invisible Wilkes boys proliferated. Adrian Wilkes had kept his sons confined to the house in the woods. No school records existed for Jonah or Michael. He had kept them ignorant and imprisoned, so they had no opportunity to expose him or escape him.

Those articles– about the forgotten boys– were difficult enough to read. But the single article, about the incident that had occurred when Jonah was ten, reduced me to tears.

Adrian Wilkes had counted on the seclusion of the woods to accomplish the executions, but had been discovered by a couple who had ignored the "No Trespassing" signs posted everywhere and taken a stroll into the woods on the warm summer night. The young woman said she had heard crying, and made her husband follow her to the location of the sound-- the *tree*. The tree Jonah had taken me to, that he had looked upon so lovingly and that had filled me with such peace. The body of Jonah's younger brother, Michael, was lying by the tree, decapitated by Wilkes to "release the evil spirits that had infected his dear boy." Adrian had another fate planned for Jonah, who he declared was too "riddled with light" to continue to exist in the world. He told police later that only fire was pure enough to consume the body of his eldest son. Wilkes had tied Jonah to the ancient tree before making him watch his brother die, but he relinquished the boy to the horrified couple without any overt aggression and waited calmly as they called the police. The couple testified that Wilkes had remained controlled and seemingly self-possessed as the police arrived to arrest him. He had paid little heed to anything going on around him; he had kept his sad, tormented eyes intently on Jonah. The woman's testimony concluded the article: "The most disturbing thing of all," she said. "The part of it that still h'ants my dreams to this day was them words he last spoke to that little bairn. 'I failed,' he said. 'I tried, but I could not save you.' And that little boy just stood there, his eyes focused on his father, not makin' a sound. The cryin' we heard... what led us to the spot... was his father, cryin' fit to loose all hell, like t'was somethin' he had to do but what tore him apart to do't. But that little boy, he never made a sound..."

A short article, a few days later, stated that the couple was trying to adopt Jonah, who was undergoing mental and physical therapy and not making the hoped-for progress as he refused to talk about what had happened.

Then the accounts of the Wilkes family stopped. The news held no affinity for the silent, withdrawn orphan. Jonah would not speak; Jonah gave them nothing to talk about.

I asked the librarian about Jonah's life afterwards-- if he had found any happiness in a foster home. The librarian could tell me little about Jonah; his preoccupation had been with the father. The librarian believed that Adrian Wilkes had been done a grievous ill by society in being locked up where he was prohibited to continue his creation-- even in his dying days at the facility. Wilkes had died a year after his admittance-- a death which resulted from the artist's "inability to find an outlet for the vast and powerful energy he channeled." I felt sickened by the librarian's obsession with Adrian Wilkes and started to leave the library, but he kept me there long enough to tell me that the couple who had adopted Jonah-- the Luthertons, that same couple who had found him that night-- still lived in the area.

I thanked the man for his help and left the library. The sun had sunk. With darkness approaching, I had to resolve to start my search for the Luthertons the next day.

22.

In very little time I found an address for David Lutherton.

I was surprised that, having witnessed such an event, the Luthertons had chosen to stay in the area. But the route took me out into farm country, an area that felt as remote from the town as another state would have. I parked in the gravel driveway and got out of my car, and was instantly assailed by a pack of scraggly, barking dogs. I stood absolutely still, petrified, but a shouted command from within the squat building stopped the dogs from circling any closer. A screen door opened and closed, and a stout, red-faced man tromped out into the snow. He seemed startled on seeing me, but the next moment he showed such good manners and consideration that I liked him instantly.

"Dogs, git!" he yelled, and the dogs scattered away from me. He turned to me. "Sorry, Miss, if they frightened ye. Me and Missis ain't used to havin' people out here, so we lets 'em run free. What can I do ye for?"

"Are you Mr. Lutherton?"

"Dave." He squinted against the glare of the sun. "What can I do ye for?"

"I don't mean to impose," I said. "But I would like to ask you some questions."

"Eh?" His eyes narrowed. "Are ye with the government? I done told ye all, I won't sell me land."

"No, sir. I'd like to talk to you about Jonah."

His eyes became slits. He crossed his arms over his chest. "Why?"

"Because I love him," I said calmly. "And I want to help him."

"Ye better come inside," he said, after a moment's pause. "I don't mean to keep ye standin' in the cold, and ye had ruther talk to the Missis."

I followed him into the house, the interior of which was decorated with pictures of roosters and cows on the walls and a large painting that declared "May God Bless This House and Ye Who Enter Here." The man's large boots thumped loudly on the clean wooden floors.

"Cindy!" The man yelled. "There's a girl here, what means to talk to ye."

A fat, florid woman came into the room, drying her hands on a dishtowel and frowning.

"Lord, David, offer the girl a seat," she said.

"I was going to, afore..." he started.

"Dear Lord in Heaven, David," the woman said. "What's she to think of us, if ye go on talkin' to her so rude-like? What with us never havin' any visitors, then ye aim ter frighten her away..."

"Wants to talk to you about Jonah," he mumbled.

"Go and git yerself cleaned up," she said, in a much quieter tone of voice, and he left as if relieved. The woman stood for a moment, then came and sat down across from me. She managed a smile.

"Ye must pardon the state of the house," she said. "It's old enough to be constantly complainin'. Ye see we're tryin' to fix her, but we wasn't expectin' comp'ny. No one comes 'round here, and now what with Jonah gone it's so quiet. Don't ye be frightened off by my great bear of a husband nor that pack o' rat terriers..."

I told her I thought her house was lovely, and she smiled at me warmly.

"Them people from the newspapers came 'round after the fact," she said. "But it's been a long time since we had folks comin' here and askin' aboot Jonah. Ye aren't with the papers, lass?"

I said I was a friend of Jonah's. "I suppose you want to know why I'm not talking to Jonah directly, but..."

The woman shook her head. "Jonah wouldn't talk to ye aboot it, if ye asked him." She settled into her chair. "He never did speak much. He was a quiet, strange child. That's what ye came to ask aboot, isn't it, lass?"

I nodded. She smiled a half smile.

"Lass, I'll tell ye what I can, though it won't be much considerin' he was here for eight years. But whatever ye think, on leavin this house, don't ye doubt..." Her eyes saddened. "That boy, he has a heart unlike any other. He wouldn't talk to me nor David much, but he'd bring any number of animals into this house. He'd find 'em injured on the land– strays and wild ones– and he would care for 'em and talk to 'em. David didn't have the heart to tell him not to, nor did I..." She glanced up at me. "Them animals seemed the only things he loved. Them and them wooden dolls he was allus makin'... he talked to them, too. But maybe you'd like to see them dolls? We kept 'em, David and me, every one."

"Thank you," I said. "I would love to see them."

Cindy Lutherton hefted herself to her feet. I followed her up a set of carpeted stairs and to the middle of the hallway, where she paused and pulled on a chord hanging from the ceiling.

"He wanted to live up there," she said, as a series of stairs dropped down. "We didn't understand it, what with us havin' perfectly good rooms in the hoos. But we let him. Pray excuse me, but I'm goin' ter stay down here. These bones ain't so spry as they used ter be. Ye be careful now on them stairs..."

I started up into the attic. The air was thick and dusty, and the window at the other end was locked and bolted. The ceiling slanted, but the room was large enough to contain a cot, covered by a white sheet, and a small stack of shelves where the puppets sat. Each puppet had been carefully wrapped in a plastic bag before being placed on the shelf. Even so, I could make out the delicate features of each painted face, and I studied each skillful expression before I started down the attic stairs. Cindy Lutherton was waiting for me, and a smile lit her face when she saw me.

"I was startin' ter fear ye choked on the dust," she said.

I smiled at her. "You've taken such good care of his puppets."

"Jonah loved them dolls," she said. "David and me, we didn't pretend ter understand, but we miss Jonah and them dolls are all we have left." She paused, and then we started back downstairs. "Ye said ye were his friend? How is he? What's he doin' with his life?"

I looked into her kind, honest face. "He's become a pianist."

"He still make them dolls?"

I nodded. She sighed but seemed pleased, and her eyes gleamed with pride. "We allus knew he would make somethin' of himself... that he wouldn't end up like his father." She looked away from me. "I suppose he's still livin' in that house."

"The house in the woods?"

She nodded. "Jonah took off when he turned eighteen, and we assumed he went there. We didn't go after him because... well, I 'spect he weren't happy here. We did everything we could think of, but..." She glanced away. "David and me, we knew Jonah's father left him that house when he died. We thought Jonah would be safe there, so we let him go."

"Why do you think he would want to go back? To the house?"

She was silent for some time, her hardy face creased into wrinkled lines of thought. "T'was his childhood home... and Jonah was a queer bairn. So quiet. He never asked for much... except to visit his father. David or me had to drive him ter that place his father was put at least once a week, and t'would be no surprise to me if he walked there on his own. He would disappear for hours sometimes, and bein' as quiet as he were, David and me didn't know when he left and when he coom back. Jonah seemed ter love that man. Like I said, he had the biggest heart of any I've met..." She frowned, wiped at her eye. "But Jonah told us he couldn't love at all. He told us when he were twelve, because he coom upon me arguin' about him with David and cryin' because I felt like we had failed him. I remember that day like it were yester.... standin' in the kitchen an cryin' an turnin' around and there were Jonah, holdin' a wounded sparrow and lookin' at me with them great sorrowful eyes. At first I thoot he were goin' ter simply stand there like that, but he spoke. 'I can't love,' he said, an then, 'Cindy, do you have a box for my bird?' He spoke ever so quaint, even as a bairn. He were so young then but so serious, and we stopt arguin' and jest looked at him. Then David got up ter fetch a cardboard box, and Jonah went after him without sayin' another word." She paused. "I wish I could tell ye more, lass, but I can't. Jonah were a quiet bairn, and the only things what seemed to bring him joy were them animals he nursed to health and them dolls he made." She looked at me hopefully. "But he's happy now?"

"I haven't talked to him recently," I said, after a pause. "The was a misunderstanding between us, and I think I betrayed his trust..."

Her lips drew into a frown, and to my surprise she shook her head. "He's a complex person, lassie. Ye may have read him wrong."

"I was very much in the wrong."

Again, she shook her head. "Ye have a good soul, lass. Tis one of the first things I seen about ye, and David wouldn't have let you in the hoos had he sensed otherwise. And them dogs wouldn't have let ye alone neither. Ye didn't have meant ter betray Jonah, and he'd have seen that in yer eyes..." She stopped speaking and looked at me thoughtfully. "I wouldn't be surprised iffen he loved ye, lassie."

"He doesn't."

"At least, not what yer 'ware of." She smiled and nodded, as if my answer had satisfied her. "Spose ye tell me more boot Jonah."

I told her as much as I could, not realizing how much I had missed him until I started speaking. The kind woman listened to me intently and offered me another smile when I had finished speaking.

"Do ye doubt the affection he feels for ye, lass?" She studied me frankly. "Havin' told me such a story as that?"

"I don't understand Jonah."

"He don't want ye ter understand him," she responded. "Did ye never think he might be afraid of what he might be thinkin'? What he might be feelin'?"

She met my eyes and offered another one of her smiles. "If I were ye, lass, and Jonah had trusted me as much as ye... I wouldn't be so quick ter turn away from him. T'would seem more of a betrayal than whatever else is on yer mind." She paused. "And don't ye let that husband of mine frighten ye away, now, ye hear? It gets lonesome round here with just him and them dogs. Ye tell Jonah we'd like him ter coom round, won't ye?"

I smiled half-heartedly, and the next moment her warm hand was on mine.

"Ye be strong now," she said. "Ye give him some time, and ye have some faith in yer own good heart. Or if ye can't, then have some faith in the music that he and ye love so much. There can't be that kind of music without two, can there be?"

I smiled. "It's difficult."

The screen door opened and the pack of dogs bolted into the house, yelping.

"David," said she, shooting a meaningful look in my direction. "Them dogs fit ter raise hell..."

A scowl crossed his good-humored face as he moved towards the dogs. "Git!" he directed, then followed the dogs out of the room after a curious glance at me. Cindy Lutherton heaved herself to her feet, using the arm of the chair for support.

"Ye come back now," she repeated, smiling at me. As I passed her, she put her hand lightly on my arm. I turned and saw that the kind humor in her face had been replaced by earnest sadness.

Her eyes on me, her face slightly lowered, she said, "I wisht fer many things fer that little boy, after he coom here. But the one I wisht most fervent fer, what I begged the Good Lord in Heaven fer... do ye know?" She nodded to herself. "Ye be silent like he, but yer eyes speak for ye. I wisht most, lass, that Jonah would find someone to love. I wisht he would find a safe place in somethin' alive, not the music nor them dolls or critters." She paused. "When ye see Jonah, tell him we love him."

"I will." I hurried past her, tears in my eyes.

The drive back to my solitary apartment stretched on as dusk painted the sky in dusty shades of burnt orange and moth brown. An ache persisted in my heart. I was again aware of... not a loss, but an absence. The beautiful night– the stars now peeping through the black violet of twilight– would be more beautiful if shared. As the cool air blew in through my partially opened window, I realized that I did not want to walk this part of my life alone. However uncertain the future, I wanted to be beside Jonah.

There is a bird which pushes its breast against a thorn when it wishes to die. The dying song of this bird outrivals the sweetest music. Jonah knew that pain could result in inspiration; he knew about love's darker side. Blood for beauty. But he still wouldn't let me show him the other side of love– that sweetness that comes in trusting, in having faith, in hoping.

The sign of Jonah calls for faith and surrender. I wondered if it would have to all be on my side... especially when the strength of my spirit– the confidence I had found in my own innocence and contentment– had crumbled. But I hoped to find a new strength, to build a new foundation.

I had been love's fool; I would have given up everything to prove my love for Jonah, and I thought I had lost him as a result. And I realized the irony there, because Jonah had never even asked me for a sign.

23.

I knew something was not right. I became profoundly uneasy and on edge. For the first time in my life, there was no outlet, no means of escape. I sang two or three times a week to survive... but I did not feel anything. My voice sounded empty to me, and my exertion in the performances threatened my failing health. I tried to ignore the changes in my body, but I became feverish and cold at alternate intervals and could no longer deny that the passion inside me– whether vented or suppressed– was slowly decaying my strength, that even the constant half-hearted work I did was taking me nearer each day to death...

Such morbid thoughts! Always, before, there was a glimmer of hope– a spark, however small, that let me recognize the wonders of the world. But upon my soul settled the darkness of despair...

Yet memory... memories of music chided me to remember, remember! At one time this emptiness, this hopelessness, was not present. At one point I was content, and so I shall be again. I would not be destroyed by the tides of life; I would not let myself be blinded to beauty. I continued to hope that peace would come again to soothe me, and what remained of me would be true, strong, and ready to embrace the light...

Even as I acknowledged that for that time I had to endure the other sinister sentiments.

Was it death that I so feared? At the time, I thought how much better it would have been for that dark-winged angel to swoop down and claim me, than for white-winged Life to keep me in this perpetual state of uneasiness and interminable waiting!

In retrospect, though, I did not have to wait long.

24.

The early hours of the morning brought to me a visitor who awakened me from the daze into which I had fallen as, unable to sleep, I sat and stared through my window at the falling snow. I approached the door, stupefied from long nights of insomnia, to quiet the loud and persistent knocking. As I stood before my door, thus dazed, the knocking stopped, and I heard a familiar voice in the hallway.

"Melody? Melody, for God's sake open the door..."

I unlatched the bolt; I opened the door, and Link stood before me, panting– his sunken cheeks flushed, his eyes darting madly from side to side, his long hair wet with the melting snow. In his arms, wrapped tightly in a blanket...

"My god, Link," I whispered. "Is that Caitlin?"

"Hush," he said. "You'll wake her."

The babe's face was only just visible, peeping out from under her thick, rich curls and the dark fleece of the blanket. Yet the child's skin was so pallid, and the child herself so deathly still, that for a moment I felt myself grow faint at the possibility that the babe was not sleeping, but dead.

"What have you done?" I cried, instinctively reaching for the babe, whom he relinquished to me immediately. Only holding her in my arms, and seeing her tiny chest rise and fall, convinced me that the child was still alive.

"It's not what you think," he babbled. "Melody, you have to help us. You have to listen to me. Please don't turn us away..."

Growing increasingly alarmed, I tucked the child close to my breast and beckoned him into my apartment.

"I won't assume anything," I said, in an attempt to calm him– or at least, to silence him. "But the child is half-dead with cold..."

"I'll explain," he started, the crazed look still in his eyes as he lingered near the threshold of my apartment's entrance. "By God, give me the chance to..."

"Sit down," I said. "I'll talk to you after I take care of Caitlin."

He came into the apartment and sat down. I left him and went quickly into my bedroom, where I found a warm, dry blanket and undressed Caitlin with the intent of chafing warmth into the child's chilled limbs. I saw the bruises.

"It was Vanessa."

I turned and saw Link standing in the doorway, about to enter the room.

"Stay where you are," I warned.

"I didn't hurt her," Link said. "Melody, that's why I brought her to you, because I was starting to worry that..." He paused, then unbuttoned his shirt and spread open the edges to reveal his chest. There, marring his skin, were purplish-yellow bruises.

"I thought she took out her anger on me." He met my eyes. "I didn't suspect, until recently, that she would... to our child..."

I remained silent, my eyes fixed on him as I rocked the shivering child.

"Vanessa..." He looked at me helplessly. "I can't say it."

"You had better try," I said quietly.

"She..." Once again he paused and did not continue.

I stood and walked past him into the adjoining room, where the lights were brighter and the space was more open. He followed me. I waited a moment before I spoke.

"You didn't hurt this child," I started, hoping desperately that I could trust my intuition. "Therefore you and Caitlin can *both* have shelter here..."

"I thought I could stop her," he said suddenly, making no acknowledgment of my words as he turned his bright eyes on me. "Whenever she got... I let her... to me..."

"Link, you're stronger than she is." I paused. "You could have stopped her from hurting the baby."

"I'm not around her all the time," he said. "She won't let me near Caitlin when I *am*. I thought she was being protective. Then there's this light... that comes into her eyes. Like she's been...possessed..." A shudder wracked through his body.

"A look can't hurt a person," I said.

"She scares me."

I looked at his lowered, pale face, his hunched shoulders, his hands clasped tightly together. I saw an actor who was not acting. Link, who had played the alpha male on and off the stage, would never admit that anyone– especially his wife– had frightened him. But only *two days* had passed since I had last seen Vanessa and Caitlin; then they had both seemed fine, and I still could not grasp the concept of Vanessa beating Link. Yet I realized how quickly and dramatically intense people and relationships can change...

Again he had fallen silent, and I endeavored to prompt him. "When did this start happening?"

"It's why she changed her mind about the child. She wants to get back at me, don't you see?"

"What do you--"

Anger flashed in his eyes. "Don't you *understand?* She knows how much you wanted a child, and she knows how much I want you. She knows she can't own me, but this child, this *child*, Melody..."

Link sprang to his feet and began pacing around the room, his voice rising with his increasing agitation. "This child is under her power, and she's using the abuse to get back at me, because she knows she can't hurt me unless she hurts the child..."

"She's beaten you," I reminded him.

"Because I let her, to prevent her from... but it didn't work." He turned frenzied eyes on me. "Don't you believe me?"

"You bring Caitlin to me half-frozen with cold." I cradled the child to me, worried that she didn't cry. "I have doubts as to whether I should believe you're the good parent..."

"I'm not," he said miserably. "That's why you have to take care of her. I took care of the paperwork. All you have to do is sign..."

I stared at him. "You want me to adopt her?"

He looked at me, his eyes lucid and unflinching. I looked down at the tiny little girl cuddled into the blanket in my arms. "I can't take care of your daughter, Link."

"Melody..." He drew in a rasping breath. "You have to. I'm not giving you the choice."

"She still needs her mother, Link. She's too young..."

"If you don't take her, Vanessa will kill her." There was something ferocious in his stare. "Take her. Take her away. That's all I ask of you."

What madness made me agree? What made me sign those papers and give them to Link?

Link stood by the door and I stood by him with Caitlin tucked in the blanket. He stepped up to me; he looked at the bundle in my arms.

"Goodbye, Caitlin," he said, and stooped to kiss her on the forehead. Then he straightened. "Melody, take good care of her..."

"So this is where you meet her, Link."

He recoiled from the cold voice coming from the hallway. Vanessa strode into the room through the door neither of us had thought to close. Her eyes were bloodshot and gleaming insanely; her teeth were bared in a sneer.

"Give me my child, Melody," she commanded, extending skeletal arms out to me. "Caitlin belongs with her mother."

In that moment, I would have sold my soul to keep the child from Vanessa. The smile contorting Vanessa's lips grew cruel. I looked down at her hands as she clenched them; the nails were extremely long and sharp– like scalpels– and her entire body seemed charged with tense, ungodly energy. Facing her like this– with her face twisted like a fiend's, and that depraved strength radiating from her shaking body– I could understand how she had overpowered Link– how she would be able to overpower someone much stronger than Link. Her lips bared in a snarl, and she rushed towards me. The next moment Link charged at her and wrestled her to the ground, yelling at me to run. Keeping Caitlin tucked tightly to me, I bolted from my apartment and heard an unearthly shriek follow me from the room.

I looked over my shoulder. All I saw before I resumed my flight was my open door and one outstretched arm, the fingers hooked into a claw as they reached towards me. I heard the shrieks and grunts of the continued struggle– a single scream like a gun shot.

I fled to my car in the parking lot and found that two of my tires had been slashed. Caitlin had started wailing. Trying to hush her, I abandoned the car. I stumbled out onto the road; I started down the only route I knew. Fifteen minutes would bring me to the theater, thirty minutes would bring me to the house in the woods... to Jonah. Why, in its darkest moments, does the heart return again and again to that which it has held most dear?

I ignored my heart. I had to get Caitlin to a warm place, and the theater was closer. Full as it was of corridors, ladders, and passageways, the theater would also allow us to hide from Vanessa, should she choose to follow us. But if Caitlin cried... all would be lost.

The child's cries grew fainter as I hurried along the road. Never had I felt such relief as I saw the tall gates of the theater loom into view; never had such despair followed as I realized I had no key. I approached the gates with a sinking heart... but the gate was unlocked, as was the entrance door to the theater itself. I let myself in and quickly moved out of the well-lit lobby to the depths of the theater, and from there up to the opera house balcony. I paused in the shadows to catch my breath, and I found with relief that the warmth of the place was steadily bringing the color back to Caitlin's pale cheeks.

She opened her eyes and looked at me silently, and then she squirmed in my arms as if she wasn't used to being held. I took off my coat and made a makeshift crib for her on one of the theater's chairs. I put her in the folds of my coat and was relieved to see that she became calm immediately. Then I turned my attention to the surrounding environment.

A single light created a spotlight on the piano on the stage, and the dim lights lining the walls of the theater allowed me to scan the rows of seats and reassure myself that Caitlin and I were alone. My thoughts turned suddenly to the unlocked theater doors; if Jonah had entered the theater, he would be on the stage, by the piano... or some trace of him would be, whether it was Dorian sitting on the bench or an opened music score on the piano's ledge. Then I remembered Link's words, that he had watched us from the shadows. He had access to the theater... and so did Vanessa.

I had left the apartment when Vanessa and Link had still been engaged in the struggle, but had she proved victorious and set out after us in a car, she would have reached the theater much sooner than we had. And although she could not have had any certainty of my destination, still she might know about my nightly meetings with Jonah... if Link had told her. Knowing that I was without many friends or family, she would realize, as I had, that my options were limited. I regretted my decision—until I remembered that Link had said that Vanessa had followed me one night to the house in the woods. That place wouldn't have been safe either.

Caitlin started to cry. I cradled her close to me, and knew assuredly that we were not alone in the depths of the theater. What led me to the intuitive knowledge? Was it a higher power, warning me, because of the trust that had been placed in me to protect Caitlin? Was it my own maternal instinct, telling me that the child was in danger? It didn't matter; I knew we were not alone.

Very distinctly, I heard the auditorium door open. A shaft of light filtered in from the lobby and threw a rectangular glow down the dark center aisle. I watched the shadowy outline of another person pass into the theater and pause. Then the door closed, plunging the theater back into semi-darkness.

Caitlin had quieted, and I did not dare move. Even in the dim light I could see the shadowed form making its way to the stage, up the steps, and into the light. Vanessa, distinguishable even at a distance, scanned the rows of the theater from her vantage point on stage.

"Melody." She had learned to project her voice; the whispered word carried to where I was crouching against the wall, holding Caitlin close to me. "Melody, I know you're here. I heard my child. I HEARD MY *CHILD*..."

She scanned the depths of the theater. Her eyes fixed on my location, and she stopped. The way she froze implied that she saw me– or was her gaze a ploy to make me move from a still and invisible state?

Vanessa left the stage.

The only exit from the balcony area was to retrace my steps down one of the staircases on either side. Somehow I knew Vanessa would search the balcony area first; my only hope of avoiding her would be to choose the opposite staircase that she would choose to ascend. I held Caitlin close and prayed for her to be quiet as I started down the left staircase. I saw, as suddenly, the shadow of Vanessa's silhouette moving up that same staircase.

I heard the chord of a melody. A piano chord, struck suddenly and violently...

The silhouette's movement stopped as the lights above the stage flared on. There, sitting in front of the previously vacant piano, was a hunched form. I recognized the breadth of his shoulders and the shaggy dark hair... so dear to me...

"Jonah," Vanessa hissed, as my heart called out that same name. There was silence in the theater. Then, to my horror, Vanessa's silhouette resumed its climb.

I was startled into moving. During that brief pause I should have quickly retraced my steps, retreated, chosen the opposite staircase; yet I had not moved. A second chance was afforded me; another set of chords was struck violently on the piano, and the silhouette shadow paused again. Quickly I made my way up the stairs and across the balcony, fearing every moment that Caitlin would resume her crying. I reached the right staircase and started down to the stage. I reached the bottom of the stairs leading to the balcony when what I feared happened; Caitlin started wailing.

I heard an agonized cry from the balcony above me and a loud thump as, presumably, Vanessa rushed towards the stairs and stumbled in the dark. At the same moment the tormented music stopped. Jonah stood and turned, his arms outstretched as he peered into the darkness.

"Melody!" he yelled. "Melody, come to me!"

For a moment my heart became so heavy that I feared I would not be able to move, and then I rushed towards the stage. Behind me I heard Vanessa tripping down the stairs; before me I saw Jonah, standing in the light of the stage. Somehow I reached him, and as soon as his arms closed around me, I felt a new strength steal through my body and a new clarity come to my mind. He picked me up, holding me to him as I easily as I was holding Caitlin, and bore us off into one of the shadowed wings of the stage. Jonah's face was as pale and blank as marble as Vanessa's shrieks echoed through the theater. I heard her stumble onto the stage, but already Jonah's long strides had taken us deeper into the darkness of the opera house, and Caitlin had stopped her cries. I leaned my head against Jonah's chest and closed my eyes. I hadn't realized how strong he was, or how exhausted I was... or that, at some point, he had forgiven me. This last thought was my final consideration before I passed out for the span of several hours.

25.

Early dawn cracked open the sky. The air was warm, with only the hint of a chill as it streamed in through the open window in the house in the woods. That day we were both the world's fools; certainly, Fate had played a trick on us.

Jonah paced back and forth. He had not spoken to me since we had left the opera house. Caitlin slept quietly in my arms. I didn't want to let Jonah continue his ceaseless pacing, but I could not be the one to break the silence. He had helped me, and I knew he had forgiven me. Yet I could not break the silence.

"You have to leave," he said, suddenly. He stopped pacing and turned a marble face to me. "She knows where I live. She could come here at any time."

"I don't have anywhere else to go." I tucked Caitlin's blanket around her, though she had not stirred. Several days had passed; though the time, for me, was blurred, I had started to hope that we were safe in the abandoned house.

"You have to leave." His pace increased. "You have to leave now."

There was nothing in this town to keep me; there was no reason to protest in the slightest, but I tried.

"Shouldn't we wait for the legal rights for Caitlin to--"

"Now." He came and stood close to me, his eyes cold and resigned. He pulled me unceremoniously to my feet.

My voice broke. "Jonah, will you come with--"

"I can't leave this house. You know that."

"You have to." I paused. "I don't want to go without you. I don't care, I can leave everything... but not you. I can't leave you..."

He stopped and turned. The look of deep sadness etched into his features stopped my words.

"I'll go with you," he said, then jerked. "No, I can't."

I watched him stride frantically across the room. "Jonah. Leave this place. Come with us. Don't you think this is a sign? Permission to finally leave? Caitlin and I need you."

"There are no signs," he said, pacing. "Only choices."

I was silent. He was silent. I looked up and met his eyes, and he recoiled. My heart went out to him.

"Jonah."

He looked at me. He shook his head and turned to face the window. I stood.

"Maybe you can tell me where we can go, then," I started. "My car has enough gas to get me to--"

"I can't leave this house," he said, clenching his hands together behind his back. "I can't, Melody, because..."

I stepped up to him; hesitantly, I put my hand on his shoulder. He turned around; his dark eyes held a naked question I would not answer in words. I took one of his hands and stepped closer to him. I transferred Caitlin to him and put his arms around her. I stepped away. Caitlin did not stir.

Jonah stood looking down at the child. Neither man nor child moved. Then Jonah looked up at me. I met his eyes, and knew then that he had decided to help me.

"Where will we go?" he asked.

"It doesn't matter to me," I said. "As long as we go together."

He looked down at Caitlin, not moving anything except his head– as if afraid that in changing the position of his hands he would drop her. His eyes had become hazy, and his face was pale.

"Take her," he whispered.

I stepped up to him; I took Caitlin from him.

"It is not finished," he said. His eyes were still hazy, and he spoke mechanically. "This place will haunt me still, until it is finished. I will have to come back, some day, but I will leave this place with you tonight."

He left the room without another word. I went back to the chair by the window and sat down. I looked out the window, and I waited for Jonah.

26. *Two years later.*

The sky was painted with the warm twilight when I saw the ugly and familiar building before us. Inside, the stairwells smelled no more of urine and filth than they usually did, and the floors and walls were no more streaked and off-white than usual. A quick investigation revealed that nothing had changed in the apartment. The rooms were dark and the air felt musty and stale, but that was usually how I found the rooms when I came home. I knew that Jonah hadn't come back yet during the day; he would have opened the window. Suddenly the intensity of my feelings came back, as supreme irritation. Suddenly I hated everything. I hated the apartment; I hated the duskiness and dust and emptiness of it. I hated Jonah for facing his demons alone. I hated that he wasn't telling me what was really going on, and I hated that I wouldn't have been able to help him even if he had told me...

I looked up when the door opened. Jonah came in calmly, and there was a ragged gash snaking halfway down his arm. He did not seem to be aware of the bleeding. He did not seem to be aware of anything.

"Jonah," I said loudly.

He walked by me. I followed him. I put my hand on his arm, and because he was facing me I saw him recoil. He drew back as if in horror, his pupils dilating, his mouth forming a thin line. His body became rigid. The Jonah I knew was away; the person before me was sleepwalking. I kept my hand on his arm, and I spoke very slowly.

"Jonah. It's Melody." I watched his unseeing eyes remain fixed on me. "Jonah? It's Melody..."

"Don't hurt me anymore," he said, in a voice that chilled me.

"I won't hurt you. I love you."

"You love me," he said, his voice tinged with scorn and a new understanding. "Yes, you..." Then a flicker of light shot through his empty eyes.

"Melody?" He said my name as a question.

"Melody," I affirmed. I let go of his arm and took a step back.

"Melody..." As the whispered word left his lips, an awareness came into his eyes. He stepped closer to me. The haze had not completely left his eyes, and he still seemed distantly afraid of something. He took my face between his hands. He bent down and his dark eyes raked over my face. For a moment I thought he was going to kiss me, and I felt my heart thumping painfully in my chest. But this was Jonah, my Jonah. His eyes were seeking, searching. I looked back into his eyes. I felt exposed, and I *wanted* to be exposed. I wanted him to see my soul and I wanted him to judge me. But he was more important. I remembered that he was bleeding...

I went to the sink and wet a dishtowel. I sat down beside him on the floor. He looked over at me with a question in his eyes.

"Jonah, you're bleeding," I explained, then slowly raised his injured arm. He sat as docilely as a child as I sponged away the blood, my head lowered in focus over the wound.

"He did it," Jonah said suddenly, in that other voice. "Not me."

His eyes were large and wide and focused on me as if he were seeking my approval. I dropped my eyes back to his wound.

"Who did, Jonah?" The cut was not deep, but I sensed from his tensed muscles that he was trying to keep me from noticing he was in a significant amount of pain.

"It was..." Jonah straightened suddenly, startling me. The haze had left his eyes, which were sharp with conscious awareness and intelligence. "It was me."

"It was you," I said, putting down the towel on the table. "You were reliving that night, and you thought it was him, but it was you."

"It was me." Jonah was looking at the cut. "I did it."

I could not speak. He looked at me, and there was despair in his eyes. He reached out and took my hand in his. His hand was warm and strong; the way his fingers interlaced with mine was more startling than a kiss would have been. The unexpected gesture made me forget that the handsome man across from me possessed a weary and sick soul. His eyes burned at me with the first hint of a deep emotion I had never seen there before, but one I recognized.... and one that I had wanted to see there, for so long.

Jonah did not shy away from the contact with me. His eyes made me dizzy. I could not feel his hand on mine any longer; he seemed a part of me. Jonah raised my hand to his lips and kissed the back of it. I felt that kiss like a burn.

"I have to go," he said. "I have to end this."

He made to drop my hand but I would not let him. He looked at me, his eyes burning in reproach.

"There's nothing I want more than for you to end this," I said. "For you to do whatever you have to do in order to put... to put all of this behind you..."

"Then let me go."

"Jonah, I can't. I don't trust you. Because you aren't... you aren't yourself right now."

"Melody," he said quietly. "You have to let me go, now, or I'll kill myself."

"No, you won't," I said firmly. "I won't let you. You're going to stay here with me."

"If I stay... I'll die slowly. Unconsciously. Like this."

"No," I said.

"There are more," he said. "I wake up. I don't know where I am, and then, there are always more..."

"I know." I had seen the scabs of flesh circling around the old gash wounds, creeping up to hide under his clothes. I felt the tears well up in my eyes. "I'll go with you. We'll do whatever we have to do—but not tonight. There's no one to watch Caitlin, and we can't leave her..."

He looked at me. He looked at me for a long time, and then in a movement that was too quick, he drew his shirt over his head. I had seen the burn marks and the scars before. My eyes had traced the labyrinthine snaking of scars up his arms, across his torso... but the skin had been *scarred*. Now the scars had been cut open, and the pattern on his flesh was open and raw...

"Why don't you leave me?" he asked. "The demons are too strong..."

I did not know that my hands had gone to my mouth until he stepped up to me, took both my hands in his, lowered my arms to my sides.

"I have to end this tonight," he repeated, and then he did kiss me.

I did not feel Jonah's lips on mine. I was aware only of a warmth, penetrating into a space closer than my heart, and then the feeling that I was full of white light that melted me into him. I could feel a pulse, a heartbeat; one was mine and one was his but they beat in time. This was Jonah telling me what he had to do, what we needed to do, since there was nothing separating us anymore...

The air was suddenly cold around me, and I realized Jonah had stepped away. I opened my eyes in time to see him step towards the door.

"Don't go," I pleaded.

The intense pain and fear I felt must have been visible in my eyes. Jonah looked startled. He walked back to me and put a marble hand against my cheek. His eyes questioned me, and then an edge came into them. His voice was flat, but somehow gently soothing. "We'll go tomorrow, then."

I watched him step away from me, thinking some of his confusion and disorientation had remained as he started walking away.

"Jonah, that's..." I paused. "That's my bedroom."

"I know," he said. "Tonight I want to hold you, Melody, and then tomorrow we'll do what needs to be done. Together."

"Let me check on Caitlin," I stammered. I could think of nothing else to say.

Caitlin was sleeping peacefully in the bed Jonah had made for her. I kissed her forehead and turned out the nursery light. When I went into the hall, Jonah was not there.

For a moment I stood as if paralyzed. I felt sure that for the first time Jonah had willfully deceived me; he had used my moment of distraction to leave the apartment, to go out into the night by himself as he had done so many times before. But the door to my bedroom was ajar.

I willed myself to move. I slipped into my room and closed the door behind me. I saw a shape in my bed, under the covers. My feeling of relief was replaced by something else. I hesitated, then slipped out of my clothes and left them lying on the floor. I moved to my dresser and pulled out my nightgown. I paused, torn. Then, I moved to the bed. I pulled aside the covers, and then I slipped under the sheets. I held my breath as Jonah turned and put his arms around me, then I realized that I felt his bare skin against mine. His arms around me were warm and strong. I rested my head on his shoulder, and our feet touched– that, and nothing but the sense of belonging, of right coming into being.

Jonah kept his arms around me, mumbled one word into my hair.

"The blinds," I said. "Let me pull the blinds. I know you don't like the light, and there's so much moonlight tonight..."

"Leave it be," he ordered. "Leave everything exactly as it is."

I let myself relax against him, let the feelings of bliss and peace and contentment wash over me. Though I was afraid to break the comfortable silence, I spoke.

"Jonah?" I felt him shift, ever so slightly, in acknowledgment. "Tomorrow. Let me come with you."

He turned his head toward me, and I steeled myself for his refusal.

"I need you to come," he said.

I remembered, later, the words he had spoken before: *we'll go tomorrow.* In that moment, however, the feeling that I had won a major victory instantly drove out any shard of reason that would have remained to warn me.

"I'll call Rob," I babbled, thinking about the only co-worker I could trust. "Rob will take care of Caitlin until we come back for her..."

"No." Jonah's voice was startlingly cold. "He'll suspect something is wrong."

The sense of the pulse of our hearts, beating together, convoluted my thoughts. I shook my head. "He won't ask questions."

Jonah did not say anything. I struggled to shake off the diseased haze that had congealed my thoughts, dimly aware of the feeling that I needed to ask him something. Before agreeing to whatever crazy plan he had in mind, I needed to be sure of something...

During my silence, Jonah must have been thinking about my proposition to leave Caitlin with Rob, because he spoke.

"We'll leave tomorrow," he said decisively. "Tomorrow night."

And then... I knew what I needed from him.

"I'll only go with you on one condition." My voice was cold. I was too aware that I had begged him to let me go with him only a moment before.

"What?" His sharp intake of breath startled me.

"Promise me we'll come back."

He mumbled something incoherent.

"Jonah. Promise me."

"I promise," he said. His voice was strange.

I accepted his answer. I wonder, now, if the moment felt that much more precious because I was aware that something dark lingered beneath that ephemeral peace, vigilantly waiting for the morrow's night to fall. I calmed my thoughts by listening to Jonah's breathing, and I wished the next day would never come.

27.

Jonah shifted away from me as the first light of dawn cracked open the sky. I pretended to be asleep; I had not slept at all. He stood so gracefully that, had it not been for the cool, empty air that suddenly replaced his warmth, I would not have known he had moved. He left the room silently, only to return a moment later. I watched him from under my eyelids. He left an orange flower on the nightstand, then he gently stooped and brushed his lips against my forehead.

The second he was gone, I threw back the covers and crawled out of bed. I dragged the only chair in my room over to the window, and by the waking light I watched the day be born.

I felt... so many things. Pain, for his memories; admiration, for his strength; apprehension, for what this day would bring.

I realized I would do whatever Jonah asked me to do... because I still loved him more than it is good to love another person.

28.

I stood outside and the air was colder than it should have been for a late evening in early July. The air carried the biting chill of autumn in it. Rob answered the door on my first knock.

"Here she is," he said fondly, taking Caitlin from me with a broad smile.

"Thank you for taking her on such short notice," I said. My teeth chattered.

"No problem," he said. "You'll pick her up early tomorrow?"

When I didn't answer, he still did not look at me. He said, "She won't be a problem." Then it came. "Melody... is everything all right?"

"Yes," I said.

Now his eyes were on me. "I have a feeling. I have this awful feeling."

"I'm sorry you have that feeling," I said.

"You need a break?" He repeated the excuse I had given him.

I nodded. It was a terrible alibi; Rob knew I lived and breathed for the child.

"You know I'm asking for the truth, now, only because I care about you," Rob said, rocking Caitlin in his arms. "And I know how much you value honesty..."

I looked at this kind man who had come along when I needed him. I almost broke down; I almost rejected this crazy notion of Jonah's and almost told Rob everything. But the moment, the feeling, passed. I had agreed to help Jonah, and I could not let myself start to feel again. It would not do for me to think now, when I had already decided.

But even then, I could not lie to Rob.

"Will I see you tomorrow?" Rob asked when I remained silent. His eyes were still deeply troubled. "We missed your singing the other night. You know the deal. I help you with piano and you help me promote the–"

"I know, Rob."

"What can I say?" He stopped rocking Caitlin and stood– as still as Jonah– and looked at me. "What can I say to keep you here, for only a moment longer?"

"Tell me you'll take good care of Caitlin."

"I will," he said, as if I had asked him a question. "Promise me you'll take good care of yourself."

"Rob--"

"Promise me."

"I promise," I said, after a pause.

"That will have to do," Rob said. "Goodnight, dear Melody."

I watched him close the door, separating himself and Caitlin from me. Then I turned. Jonah was waiting for me.

I walked down Rob's driveway, in no hurry to get back to the car waiting in the street, though I wanted this stupid re-enactment to be over as soon as possible. In the moment Jonah had told me what he wanted to do, I had agreed. I had agreed immediately, without doubt or reservation– as if something else had answered for me. Now I was in the car, turning the key in the ignition, and Jonah was beside me, looking out the window. I pulled onto the road, and I thought about how Jonah had looked that morning when I woke, with the sunlight streaming liquid gold on his pale, peaceful face. How the scars and the wounds on his slender, muscular body had too closely resembled the long, thin vines printed on my sheets...

"Turn," Jonah said, and I turned.

We drove in silence. He had made the preparations. I was an accessory. I could have been anyone in the world crazy enough to help him with his scheme, but I sensed that it meant something to him that I was the one who was with him. I parked and turned off the engine. I could see the imposing iron gate of the theater in the distance.

From that point on, a thick veil of unreality covered my thoughts as densely as the thick white mist that crept along the ground.

Jonah did not let me carry anything. He waited while I opened the trunk, and then he took out the rope and slung it over his shoulder. He took out the can of gasoline and waited until I closed the trunk. He did not speak. I tried to find comfort in the silence as we left the streets and lights behind and headed into the dark woods. I remembered the joy I had felt, once, when I had walked this same path– years ago. The empty, still house had frightened me then, but there was always the thought of Jonah and the warm moonlight on the piano keys, and the promise of the harmony of his chords and my voice and this melody we created together, hovering over us like a protective presence, like something larger than either of us and beautiful...

Tonight there was no warmth, no hopeful thoughts. The woods were dead and the silence was flat. I was no longer sure of Jonah's idea, and questioned the evidence that showed re-enacting traumatic events– in a safe form– was supposed to help traumatized individuals overcome their deepest fears. In the oppressive stillness of the woods, the evidence and the theories seemed ridiculous.

If Jonah had shown the slightest uncertainty, I would have insisted that we abandon the idea and turn back. But Jonah's step beside me was steady and resolute. I could feel energy radiating from him and sensed that he would not let either of us turn back. We had passed the point of no return. I was aware of his breathing, of the sound of our steps cracking through twigs and underbrush. There was nothing else– no crickets chirping, not even a lightning bug or star to light our way. Nothing but darkness.

Jonah walked as if we were walking in broad daylight along a well-marked path, and I stumbled to keep up with him. Eventually my eyes adjusted to the darkness, enough so that when the path split, I recognized that we took the fork leading us away from the old house. We went deeper into the woods.

I recognized the tree as it came into view. I knew Jonah had often returned to this site, that he had found a strange comfort in returning. With its wide trunk, spreading canopy, and knotted branches, the ancient tree radiated strength and majesty, and I understood how someone like Jonah– a wanderer, weary and hurt– could find peace in the magical place. But not tonight. As we walked up to the tree, I felt my perception shift; I felt as though I were seeing through Jonah's eyes. The strange sense of being one with him, of sharing one mind and one experience, pervaded my conscious thought, and through this lens the tree did not look beautiful or peaceful. It looked hungry. I knew these were the thoughts that had tormented Jonah and kept him awake at night, and I knew as certainly that tonight would mark the end of these thoughts for him.

Neither of us had spoken a word.

"Tightly," he said then, handing me the rope. "He tied me so I couldn't move."

My hands trembled, but Jonah did not falter. He went to the tree– gladly. He fitted his body against the bark and waited, and was tied to the tree before I knew what I had done.

"Around the tree," Jonah said, nodding at the can of gasoline at my feet. "He did it in a star shape. He said it was to protect me, to guide me into the next world."

"Can we skip this part?" I made myself ask.

"No. I've already traced out the lines, so the star will be symmetrical. Follow the lines, Melody."

"The gasoline will hurt the grass," I said. "I know you don't want to hurt the grass."

"I need to smell the gasoline." His voice was calm, reasonable. "Like I did that night. The fumes were so strong I thought I was going to choke."

Again, it was done before I knew what I was doing. I smelled the gasoline, and I was terrified.

"Come here, Melody," Jonah said, and I went to him. His steady gaze calmed my doubts. "In my pocket."

I reached around the rope. I felt what was there and recoiled. Jonah's eyes followed me, drew me back. I kissed him, without thinking, and it was there again, this access to his thoughts, an understanding deeper than consciousness. When I stepped away, the match book was in my hand.

"Light a match," Jonah said.

"I can't," I whispered.

"Light a match," he repeated.

I shook my head. "It's too dangerous."

"I need to smell the sulfur." There was a tight, excited edge to his voice now.

"I ... I can't." I was shaking. "It would be going farther than you said it went, even then, even back then--"

"Don't be afraid, Melody."

"It's too much." I felt dizzy and sick. "It's going too far..."

Jonah looked at me.

My hand was suddenly steady. I opened the matchbook. I smelled the sulfur as the match scraped across the thin dark strip and there... a tiny blue and orange flame. I was mesmerized. All I had to do was drop this tiny flame and it would spread, and the flame would consume us and the wind would carry our ashes to the sky, and it would be light, all light...

I shook my head, feeling crazy.

"Now," Jonah said. "Finish it."

I stared at him. He cocked his head as if listening to something, and confusion deepened his dark eyes. Then he gritted his teeth and shook his head savagely.

"Take a step back first, Melody." He spoke with difficulty. "You aren't supposed to die tonight."

"Jonah, no." The flame was creeping, slowly, towards my fingers. If I dropped the match, to avoid burning my fingers... we would die.

"DO IT."

His eyes. His eyes were so strange. They consumed me. "Don't you love me, Melody?"

There it was again, that feeling of sharing the same diseased mind, the current of thought commanding me... *that was not my own.* The moment of awareness was enough.

There are no signs. There are only choices.

"Yes," I said. "That's why I won't do this, Jonah."

I blew out the flame before that strange possession had a chance to come back over me. I watched the thin stream of gray smoke from the extinguished match climb towards the sky. So did Jonah. He was silent, until the last trace of smoke had vanished.

"Melody." His voice was hoarse. "Light another match."

The pull on my mind was considerably weaker. I tossed the matchbox away. I kept the burned out match clutched tightly in my hand. He was silent, and then he spoke so softy that I had to step closer to hear him. I heard what he said then, when he repeated himself.

"You've failed me, Melody."

His words cut me, and I was aware only of his disappointment in me and the certainty that I had made a grave and unforgivable mistake. I felt a wave of panic-- it was too dark to find the matchbox I had so carelessly thrown away. But these were Jonah's thoughts; *they weren't mine.* No, they weren't even Jonah's thoughts. They were the demons of a dark time passed, internalized by a scared child as the ultimate judgment. Still, there was that feeling, of sharing one mind... and I realized I could reverse the thought process. I could put an end to his thoughts, by believing in *my* true thoughts. I could make him believe *me.*

"It's all right, Melody," Jonah whispered. "I'll forgive you. I chose you because I knew, in the end, that you *will* help me with this. I told you that I was marked..."

"Marked for good," I said.

"No."

"Yes," I stressed. "Jonah, your father was an evil man. But even he knew you were marked for goo. He said you were 'too riddled with light'..." The force of the sudden dark presence looming over us addled my thoughts. I struggled to piece together the words I knew I must say. "Marked for good. Marked for life. Of course you would be a threat to him, to what he believed and what he was..."

Each word felt forbidden...*forbidden*... and I felt everything slipping away from me as the first roar of thunder sounded in the distance...

"*Riddled with light,*" I mumbled.

"My father was not an evil man." Jonah's voice was cool, but different somehow as he looked at me disapprovingly. "My father excelled in a world of mediocrity, and he did what he thought he needed to do..." He broke off, and his eyes became hazy. "Finish this, Melody. It is what *should be*..."

The voice which finished that thought– was not Jonah's. If Jonah hadn't reproached me I might not have noticed the difference... but the reversion back to that strange voice broke me momentarily from my trance. I looked at Jonah, tied to the tree, and all I saw were his eyes... different now. Imploring me, as they had done in my dream, those eyes were burning with sparks of life...

"No," I said, knowing this was my last chance. "It's *not* what should be. You chose me, you've given me the choice... and I've decided. You weren't supposed to die then, and you're not supposed to die now. You lived then, and I'm here with you to make sure you live through tonight."

A sudden violent shock from the presence... and then it was gone. I hurried to loosen the knots that– I?– had tied at the base of the tree.

"Don't," Jonah said, but the haze was already starting to leave his eyes.

I stopped, and I pulled the loosened rope away from the tree, and I was small enough to slip under the rope, to press my body against his and against the bark of the tree. There was no spare space with me standing beside him; the rope pressed tightly against our skin, holding us in place. I wound my arms around his neck. Jonah looked at me, as if he didn't understand, as if he couldn't...

"You understand," I whispered. "Jonah, you do. *I love you.*"

He sighed. At that moment, I heard it– more rumbles of thunder, and sharp cracks of lightning. My breath caught in my throat.

"We need to move," I said, struggling against the rope.

He seemed not to hear me; his face was tilted upwards, his eyes trained on the nighttime sky. The rope had snagged on my clothing; I could not free myself, and I had to make him understand...

I tried again. "If there's lightning, if the lightning strikes the tree and sets it on fire and the fire spreads..."

"Look up," he responded.

I looked at him, then raised my eyes to the sky. In that moment everything changed. The heaviness left the air, and the tree seemed to support us. Thick clouds were visible through the canopy of the ancient tree's leaves, but the pattern of stars directly above us remained distinct– stars aligned in a pentacle, identical to the size and shape of the pentacle I had traced in gasoline below.

"It's permission," Jonah said. "Permission to live..."

"I thought you didn't believe in signs," I whispered.

He smiled at me as a crack of lightning ripped across the sky. I shivered, and he put a hand to my face to reassure me.

"This tree will never die," he said. "We're safe."

"We can't possibly be safe here," I said. "I want to go back to the car. I want to leave this place..."

"Ye of little faith," he muttered, but he slipped out of the rope and loosened it further, then took me in his arms. He carried me outside the range of the pentacle's lines. Then he went back. He curled the rope into a coil and picked up the can of gasoline. He found the matchbox and put it in his pocket. He moved as if he could see in the dark. I watched him, not moving. He finished cleaning up the area, and then he turned and looked at me.

"Goodbye," he said.

My heart plummeted. Then Jonah came towards me, and I realized he had been addressing the tree. He stopped in front of me, then pulled me close.

"We can go now," he said.

I felt the tears roll down my cheeks. Part of me did not believe him. "*Can* we go, Jonah?"

"Yes," he said, resting his chin on top of my head. "We can go now."

We went– hand in hand. On the way back Jonah threw away the gasoline and the rope. When we went home the apartment was empty, and Jonah followed me into my room, and I fell asleep in his arms again that night. And whatever *it* had been... it was gone.

29.

It is mid-afternoon. I have picked up Caitlin and set Rob at ease and will sing at Scat Cat Alley tonight. Jonah has promised to come; tonight we will share his strange melody for two and see what the world makes of it...

Caitlin is sitting on my knee, behaving for once, as I write these beautiful words. If Jonah could see her now, he would see what an angel she can be. I know that he loves her as much as I do, but that it will take him longer than I thought to be comfortable with loving someone besides me. I have all the faith in the world in him; I will tell him so when he comes back from his walk with Lisa, his new therapist. He agreed to talk to her only as a favor to me, but I am only glad that he is willing to see someone. That was partly what Lisa wanted to talk to him about– about finding someone in the place we're moving who can help him...

Jonah's foster parents are kind, good-hearted people, and we will move closer to them and the country Jonah and I both love so much. I told Rob with my whole heart that I was looking forward to the move– however much I will miss him and Scat Cat Alley.

Tonight will also be a farewell ceremony. I have come to accept that nothing lasts– that nothing is permanent. But Caitlin will grow up knowing her Uncle Rob; Jonah was the one to insist upon visiting Rob, and I refuse to argue with him... on that account. Rob knows we will visit. He also knows he will be with me, even when I am far away. At least– if we must be haunted by ghosts and demons– we are also able to carry the precious moments, and memories of the kind people who love and help us. Having met these people, and made these memories, how can the world ever seem all darkness again? One moment, one person, one love... and we are never the same.

Jonah is playing the piano again. He says he can do so now without fear. He has also started walking at night again. He can leave me alone with Caitlin without worrying he will return to find us gone, and I find I can let him wander without fear of how he'll return.

I would be lying if I said I no longer worry about him. His eyes still burn intensely at times, and sometimes I catch him in the midst of a brooding reverie. But he *has* changed. He is no longer afraid of loving me or being around Caitlin. He says he no longer has to be afraid of hurting us ever again. I think he is still afraid of hurting himself– the cause of those brief moments of darkness– but now he has found some peace. *Peace in the midst of chaos*– not as he thought it would be– but now he knows he is loved and that he is not alone, and he says that as long as I am here beside him he can bear anything.

The article in the paper this morning was short. A forest fire– fifteen miles from here– started by lightning and put out by the rain of the storm that followed. No severe damage was done, and the story would not have made the paper had it not been for the perfect pentacle burned into the ground around a tree left completely untouched by the flames. They– scientists, occultists, meteorologists– will spend fruitless hours wondering how.

But Jonah and I– we do not ask how. We do not even ask why. We say *Thank you*, and we leave it alone.

LUKE

For John

*The only person who believed in me
from the very start*

1.

I think I must have been late to class on the first day of school. The teacher was already onto the Bs when I walked in and scurried to the only open seat. I saw her look at me from behind her glasses, ones with little circular lenses and a shiny string of silver beads falling from each stem, like the ones you picture librarians wearing. She had a pile of honey-covered hair sitting on top of her head like a beehive, and pretty blue eyes that looked like the sky.

"Take a seat," she said to me. "You're late."

"Yes, ma'am," I said. "I'm sorry."

I sat down as quietly as I could and tried to look straight forward so I wouldn't annoy her any more.

"Adam Baker?" she said in a sweet, honied voice. Adam raised his hand. She kept going down the list and I wondered when she'd come to my name. My last name starts with an M. My last name is Miller, which my mom says is a common name, that lots of people have it because in the olden days a lot of people were millers, and before they had a good way of giving people last names they would just call you whatever you did. I wonder if Adam's daddy is a baker, or if he knows how to bake.

"Luke Miller?"

"Here," I said.

The pretty teacher with the honey-colored hair looked up, puzzled.

"Luke?" she repeated.

I obediently raised my hand. "Here."

She bit the tip of her pencil, and her eyes got smaller. I think most people would say they 'narrowed,' but I can't say that because I think that means someone doesn't like you, or someone is suspicious of you, and I very much like Miss Honeydew. So I don't think her eyes narrowed at me. I think they just got smaller, like she was squinting at me because her glasses had slipped onto her nose and she couldn't see me.

"You're a girl."

"Yes, ma'am," I nodded.

"Oh. So, Luc, then."

"No, ma'am." She had pronounced it *loose*, like in Lucy. "No, ma'am. Luke."

Her eyes got even smaller now, and she didn't say anything else to that.

"Jeremy Phlacon?"

Jeremy raised his hand. He is a tall, strong looking boy and I bet he'd make a good friend, if I could ever get up the courage to talk to him. But he wouldn't talk to me, because I'm not a pretty girl. I'm very tall and I'm very thin, what my mom says is scrawny but my dad says is lean, so I don't know, and I have long brown hair that falls about my head like the fur on a drowned rat. It just hangs there in its long flat strands, and I have a smattering of brown freckles all over my face like the chocolate chips in chocolate chip ice cream.

Still you'd like him to think you're pretty, wouldn't you? You'd like to be more than his friend, wouldn't you, you little bitch

Miss Honeydew had written her name on the board in pretty squiggly letters, with curls and big elegant loops and I tried to look at them and see how they all connected together, how they all flowed so smoothly and prettily in that white

167

chalky mixture on the ebony black board. Miss Honeydew kept calling names, going down, down, down, forever, forever and ever, and I watched the honey-colored mop on top of her head as she ticked off the names on her list, her pencil doing a little flourish with everyone.

Phlacon sounds like phallus and you want him to stick it in you, deep down in you. You want him to take off his pants right now and then you want him to . . .

"Stop it," I said, out loud.

Miss Honeydew stopped calling out names and looked at me. Her eyes were very small.

"Excuse me?"

Everyone else was looking at me, too. I know I did something wrong, because people don't all stop and look at you like that, like they've stopped breathing and you're the reason, when you don't do something wrong. I swallowed and looked down at my papers in front of me, because I don't know what I did.

"Lucy, I'm talking to you. Respond."

She said it very nicely, and I looked up but her eyes were still so small and I couldn't speak because now her pretty face was red, like she was blushing, but I don't think she was.

"I'm sorry," I stuttered.

That seemed to make everything all right, and she turned back to her list of names and started calling them out again. Everyone turned around and wasn't staring at me anymore, and I hope I don't do whatever I did again because I don't like having everyone stare at me like that, I don't like having all those eyes on me because they are all thinking things and I can't tell what they are thinking, and their eyes only show that they are thinking but not what they are thinking. I swallowed again and kept my eyes on my paper because then hopefully the white would blot out all the things in my mind.

White like semen white that's going to get into you, when he takes off your clothes and when he's going deep inside you and

I swallowed and concentrated on those big loops, the elegant beautiful curves and sweeps and the untouched beauty of the black behind on the board. Black and beauty. Black beauty. Like the horse, that got out of a fire alive, and that was rescued because it was blindfolded and someone led him out to safety. Mama used to read me that story when I was little and we used to lay in her bed and she'd read to me and act out scenes from the book and if I were very good, then sometimes she'd let me read too.

in bed and all your clothes off gripping you pushing into you it hurts bleeding. . .

"SHUT UP!" I screamed.

Miss Honeydew turned around all the way then and came up to my desk. I watched, but didn't watch for long because she pulled me out of my desk by my elbow and made me stand in front of her, and my face was right there beside hers because I'm very tall for my age my dad says.

"Excuse me," she said again. "But you will not talk that way to me."

"I wasn't talking to you," I said. "I. . ."

"I heard what you said," she said very sweetly, "Get out."

I didn't know where to go, so I just stood there, my mouth hanging open and everyone staring at me like before. I felt my cheeks getting very warm, like they had been kissed by fire, and I felt that I was going to start crying because my eyes got all blurry and I couldn't see very well and I couldn't cry in front of everyone because they would call me a big baby and they would be right and I'm not a baby, anymore, now I'm in middle school and the seventh grade even and my daddy calls me his young woman and his princess and that makes me so happy and if Miss Honeydew would call him and tell him I'm a baby then he wouldn't like me anymore and

"Get out," she said again, clucking at me, and I didn't know what to do so I just grabbed my backpack, purple like periwinkles, and crept to the front of the classroom, making myself as small as possible and trying not to look at anyone because they were all looking at me and their eyes were all very small too. Miss Honeydew looked like she was trembling but maybe that was just because I was trembling, and I left and closed the door as quietly as I could behind me and just stood there because I had nowhere else to go. I stayed there even after all the other students had come out, not even looking at me so that I felt like I was not even there, and then she came out and she started to talk to me and I burst out in tears and then she slapped me.

I won't tell mama that when I go home because teachers are allowed to do that, and Miss Honeydew is a very nice person.

2.

I was sitting in the principal's office. I like being in there, and it's a good thing, too, because I'm there a lot. He has a nice brown desk that shines like someone just polished it, and a golden rectangle of a plaque with his name in huge large letters on it. It always smells just faintly of lemon, like someone just dusted, and that smell reminds me of lemonade and summertime and mama in her big floppy straw-brimmed hat and gardening gloves, and how we used to plant flowers together when she hadn't gone up into the sky. They were lovely red roses, and she would always turn to me and say, with her cheeks red like the roses and her eyes twinkling,

"See, lily dear? See how many layers and how sweetly they smell? And they have so much color to them, so much passion."

Her eyes would become soft at that, and I asked her once if she was sad and she laughed and said no, she wasn't sad, she was very happy, and she gave me a hug. She always called me lily dear and I asked her why once but her eyes grew very distant and far away and she didn't answer me and I got scared and so I didn't ask anymore. I didn't ask daddy why either because she always called me Luke in front of him, maybe because he wanted a son so much though I'm still his princess, and once he heard her call me Lily dear and then his cheeks got all red like the roses and he stomped into the house and slammed the door and scared mama and me so I didn't ask him either. Sometimes when I was littler, though, I'd go and creep into his study and crawl into his lap, and he would show me what he was doing and hold me tight to him and sometimes I would put my hand on top of his head and feel his hair because it was shaggy and brown like a dog and I very much wanted a dog. But I didn't ask daddy why I couldn't get one because daddy is not the kind of person you ask questions to. I found a puppy once and wanted to keep him, but daddy hit him so I took him back into the street and told him to run away, and when he wouldn't then I had to hit him so he wouldn't come back and then I went into my room and cried for a whole two hours, and mama came in and got very pale and then she and daddy took me to the doctor and I just kept crying, crying, crying. I was a baby, then, and I cried a lot.

Mr. Winkelhiemer didn't make me think about puppies, because his head is shiny and bald and looks made out of wax, like his hands. He was looking at me like they all had looked at me, and his hands were yellow and folded in front of him and I could see his gold wedding band curled around his fat index finger, the flesh sticking above it, puffing up like a puffball.

"Luke," he said.

"Yes, sir," I said.

"This isn't the first time this has happened," he said.

I looked down. "No, sir."

"Why do you keep acting up in class, Luke?"

"I don't mean to."

I think that made him angry, because he stood up and his chair fell down and he was right in front of me, staring at me.

"Tell me, why, Luke. I'm not playing games with you."

"I don't try to sir. It's the voice."

"The voice?"

"Yes sir, the voice in my head."

"What?" This seemed to exasperate him.

"The voice in my head, sir. Usually if I tell it to be quiet it goes away. I don't mean any harm, sir."

He put his fat hands in front of his eyes so he couldn't see me, and then on top of his head like he had just completed a marathon race and was trying to catch his breath. I don't think he knew what to do.

"What is the voice saying now, Luke?"

"Nothing, sir," I said truthfully. It was very quiet, it always was when I came here, and I think maybe Mr. Winkelhiemer scared it away. I very much like Mr. Winkelheimer.

"It never seems to say anything when you talk to me."

"That's right, sir," I said. "I don't think it likes you."

His face got all purple when I said that, and he sighed and walked away from me.

"I don't know what to do with you, Luke. Do you want attention? Is that it?"

I looked down, I think, or maybe I looked at his glossy head. He wasn't facing me, and I don't remember where I looked.

"Miss Honeydew is a new teacher, here, Luke. It's her first day on the job. Do you realize how bad you probably made her feel?"

"I'm sorry, sir." I didn't know what else to say.

He turned around and I think apologizing pleased him, because he suddenly seemed to be much more happy with me and I wish I knew what I had done because people so seldom smile at me like he smiled at me and it makes me feel warm and good and like the princess my daddy says I am.

"Luke, I think you're a good kid. I think that you have some problems, but I think you're a good kid, and I think I can help you, if you listen to me and let me..."

let me bash your skull in, you little bitch. Fuck you, making my job so much harder for me, why can't you be normal, why the hell can't you be a normal goddamned kid who follows the rules and doesn't act out and can't stop thinking...

"Are you all right, Luke?"

I put my hands over my ears and nodded at Mr. Winkelhiemer. He seemed concerned.

"Yes, sir," I said.

"All right," he said. *All right enough to fuck where noone can see I can do whatever I want and no one will believe you and I'm going to put my hands all over you . . .*

"Shut up!" I screamed.

He seemed startled, and then he came over and grabbed my arms and pulled them away from my head and then it was not me speaking but the voice, and I wanted it to be quiet because it wasn't my words coming out...

"Get your pig hands off me!"

The door opened and a fat woman wearing a red Christmas sweater and a white string of pearls around her neck peeped in her head. Mr. Winkelheimer let me go and turned away quickly, his face getting very red. The woman looked at me and her eyes got small, and then she clucked, making her chin jobble back and forth, and left the room. Mr. Winkelheimer did not turn around and I don't think he planned on looking at me anymore because he didn't for the rest of the day.

"I'm assigning you to start seeing the school psychiatrist, Miss Clairborne. She is a very nice lady and she's going to talk to you. Starting tomorrow. Come here in the morning before your classes begin, do you understand?"

"Yes, sir," I said. The voice was gone now. "I'm sorry, sir."

That didn't seem to make him happy, like it had before. He seemed ashamed of something, but I can't imagine a man like Mr. Winkelheimer having anything to be ashamed of so I must have just been sad and imagining things.

"Get out," he said.

I nodded, and then I picked up my periwinkle backpack and I skedaddled out of his office.

3.

"Hi, Daddy," I said as I opened the door.

There was Bessy, my kitty, purring and looking to be scratched. She likes it when I scratch her under the chin, and I like to run my hands along her fine, stiff whiskers but she doesn't like that very much. Daddy let me get Bessy after Mama went to the sky, and though I want a dog I still love Bessy very much. I stood up and let Bessy rub against my leg, *miau, miau, miau,* but I had a lot of work to do so she could beg all she wanted. There was a little white slip of paper by the door that I hadn't seen at first, and I went over to it and picked it up, shooing Bessy away because she stepped on it. I opened it up and it crinkled and crackled. There were some words on it, written very neatly in the rich, dark ink of an expensive ballpoint pen, probably one of the ones that my daddy keeps in his office on his desk in a nice little gold stand for when he's doing his important paperwork. I read the note and sighed a little bit, and then I went into the kitchen because I was very hungry.

We have a very nice kitchen. There is a white counter made out of marble and the floor is white tile that shines and a nice refrigerator propped up against the wall that is also white. There are also brown mahogany cabinets, but they don't smell like lemons like in Mr. Winkelheimer's office, they smell like spring rain because that is the cleaner that Missy our maid uses when she comes around and does the housework once a week. She let me help her once and I was very happy to do so, because Missy is very young and very pretty and she smiled at me and it was almost like I had a big sister for once and that would make me very happy, if I could have a big sister. When I was younger and when Mama was still here, I asked her if I could have a sister. She looked at Daddy and they exchanged a grown up look and then mama looked back at me and said softly, "Maybe." I then told her that I'd like my sister to be older than me, though, and she laughed at me and gave me a hug and said that was not how things worked. I wonder why. I asked God. I didn't understand if he could give me a little sister why he couldn't give me a big sister. But now I know why, because I'm in seventh grade now and I've had the talk in gym class and I know all about that now. They showed us a video and the gym teacher, Mrs. Day, gave us pretzels and soda to eat and drink while we watched it and then we burst out laughing when they showed the changes that guys go through while they grow up on the screen, and Mrs. Day said this was very serious and that we needed to act like mature young ladies because that's what we were becoming. Katie Johnston, my friend, she said something to that which I won't repeat but oh, it made Mrs. Day really mad and she threatened to take away Katie's food and then Katie said she was sorry, though she wasn't, and then we all tried not to laugh anymore and sat watching the television with somber expressions on our faces.

I went into our kitchen and got some cookies to eat, because Daddy wasn't there to tell me to eat carrots, which I do not like at all, and cookies taste so much better. He says I act like a two year old sometimes, but I don't see how liking cookies is acting like a two year old: I think everyone likes them, don't they? And then I did a very bad thing. I went upstairs and I went into Daddy's room.

He doesn't like me to do that, he's told me I shouldn't, but I can't help it. It is such a lovely room. He has a large brown desk and a swivel chair that goes all the way around if you sit in it and do circles, and lots of those expensive ball point pens. I never touch anything; I just go in there and sit and look. There is a big dresser stacked on one side of the room and a bookshelf on the other side of the room with lots of old books which I tried to read once but I couldn't. They use lots of big words in them, and there are pictures of gross things in there too. In one there was a picture of a nasty gaping wound on someone's leg and there were all these little white maggots crawling through the broken flesh, and in another one there was a picture of someone who looked all swelled up like a balloon, or like an elephant, because there was a big word, *elephantiasis*, on the page and I wouldn't remember it except it had that word in it that I knew, elephant. And then in another one there was a picture of a naked woman! I know I should not have looked at it, but I couldn't stop. There was a little baby and it was eating, and it was very cute and the mother was very pretty and she looked like she loved the little baby very much, and it made me think of Mama, and that made me cry, and a big tear fell and splotched the paper and I tried to dry it off as fast as I could but that made the letters of the print smear so I just snapped the book closed and put it back and then ran out of the room, and I was very afraid for the next month that Daddy would find out, and that he'd get angry and yell at me, but he either didn't find out or he didn't care because he never said anything at all to me, and I never went back and got that book. But I still remember how that mother looked, and I wonder if my mama used to do that to me and if I was ever that small and it still makes me cry if I think about it too much.

Today I just wanted to go there even though I knew I shouldn't because I was very sad that I had made Miss Honeydew and Mr. Winkelheimer angry, and going and sitting in Daddy's room makes me feel better. I stretch out on the ground so I won't wrinkle his bed sheets or move his chair out so he'll notice, and there is a nice brightly colored rug with all kinds of twisting patterns and textures on the floor that is very comfortable. Today when I flopped down onto it, I could see under the bed, and there was a shoe! I crawled over to it on my belly like a snake, and I looked under the bed. It was very dark under there and dusty too, but there was a shoe. It was bright red and I pulled it out even though I know I shouldn't have because I very much wanted to see it. I held it in my hands and turned it this way and that, just looking over it, because I have never seen a shoe like it except on those very thin women in the magazine ads who have very strange hairstyles and wear very ugly clothes, and I asked Daddy why they looked like that and he said they were models and that was fashionable, but I don't think it is at all. Mama never used to wear shoes like that. She had a pair of red ones only once, because she liked blue or brown or black shoes that she said were 'sensible,' but I liked the red ones and they had pretty little bows on them and there were none of the spikes on the back of the heel like this one had. Then I did something even worse: I put the shoe on. My fingers trembling, I pulled the little red strap out of the silver buckle and I stuck my foot in the shoe and it almost fit, and then I put the little red strap back in through the buckle and I stood up and almost fell down, because I was six inches taller on one side now and I had to hop. But then I got my balance and I stood there, and then I pretended I was one of the strange models and I cat walked around the room, swinging my hips and not looking at anyone, and giving my hair a flick at the end. Then I saw Daddy's car pull up to the window and then I did fall down I was so surprised, and I had to scramble to get the shoe off and gather all of my books together so that he wouldn't see me. I shoved the pretty red shoe back under the bed and stood up very quickly, grasping all of my things to my chest very tightly so none of them would fall away, and then I skedaddled out of the room and closed the heavy door behind me before going over to my own room and jumping on my bed. My door opened a couple of minutes later.

"Hi, Luke."

"Hi, Daddy."

"I'm home."

"Yay!" I said, and jumped off my bed and ran over and gave him a hug. He gave me a little pat on the head and then looked at all of my books, which were scattered all over my bed.

"Do you have a lot of homework tonight, sweetheart?"

I nodded my head.

"Do you need any help?"

"No," I said. "I understand everything, I think."

"You're a very smart girl, Luke," he said, and he seemed a little sad though he made me very happy when he said that. "I'm just going to get a pizza for tonight, okay? I have a big meeting later on and Kara complained in sick for the day."

Kara is our cook. She's thin like a stick and has long silvery hair that is brittle and looks like straw, and blue gray eyes that seem to pierce your flesh when she looks at you.

"Okay, daddy."

He turned to go, with his hand on the doorknob, and then he turned back to me.

"I got a call from your principal today."

"I'm sorry, Daddy," I said. "It was all my fault but I didn't mean to."

He didn't say anything to that at all, but was very quiet and just stood in the doorway looking at me.

"He says you are going to see someone."

"Yes," I nodded again. "Miss Clairborne. He says she is a very nice woman."

"Luke," he said suddenly, and something in his voice scared me but it shouldn't have because my daddy is a very nice person and he loves me very much. "I don't want people thinking my daughter is crazy, do you hear me? Don't tell this woman any crazy shit, do you understand me?"

"Daddy," I said. "Mr. Winkelheimer says that she is a very nice woman and she can help me . . ."

"You don't need to talk to anyone, you're perfectly fine. Do you understand me, Luke? I said, you're not to tell her anything."

"Okay, Daddy."

He closed my door without saying anything else, and it was very loud and caused the wooden frame to shake and quiver and I covered my ears because the sound hurt them. I didn't know what else to do then because I know that I did something wrong again but I don't know what it is and I'm always doing wrong things but I never know what they are so I just didn't think about it and I opened my book. There was a pretty picture of a butterfly on it because we are studying *ecology* and the chain of life in my science course, and I like that very much because I wish sometimes I could be a butterfly, because then I would be beautiful and everyone would like me.

4.

"Luke, if you don't get your ass out of bed, you're going to be late for school," my daddy said.

"Okay, Daddy. I'm up."

I think he grumbled, but I heard my door close and then I did get up. I heard him clop down the stairs in those big shoes he wears, the shiny brown ones that look like they have little tassels made of leather on them. He says they are penny loafers and I ask why he pays so much for them then and he laughed and said that it was so he could look professional because that's very important when you are an important person like my daddy is. He told me that in the real world, not the one I live in, it matters only how you look and that you can do a bad job if you look good and handsome and everyone likes you. Well, I don't believe that, but I didn't say anything to Daddy because Daddy is never wrong.

Well, I heard the car engine start then, and heard the wheels crunching into the gravel of our driveway and I knew that Daddy had left because he needs to leave very early to get to his job on time but he sometimes stays until I am awake to make sure I get to school even though Missy is usually around and she can wake me up just fine, and I have an alarm clock with a pretty unicorn on it that goes beep, beep, beep! To tell me that Luke, you need to get up. I heard the car's horn go honk, honk! like Daddy was saying goodbye to me even though he wasn't there and then I threw back the covers of my very warm bed and hopped out, because I remembered that today I had to go to school again and see Miss Honeydew again and she is very pretty and that made me very, very happy. I even brushed my mousy brown hair extra because maybe if I don't look so ugly she'll like me more. I went to my closet and looked at my things and I didn't know what to wear, but on sudden inspiration I grabbed a knitted sweater which was red and had a big white heart made of yarn sewed into it on the center. That made me think of something else, and I grabbed my backpack and books before Missy could come in and I raced out of my room, closing the door very, very quietly so she wouldn't hear, and then I went into Daddy's room on tiptoe and looked under the bed.

The shoe wasn't there anymore, and I stifled a sigh of disappointment and then flounced around on my hands and knees like a military person, looking for it and pulling up covers but putting everything back in place so daddy wouldn't know that I had been in his room. If he thought I was a snoop he would be very angry and he wouldn't call me his little princess and I would be very sad, and when I heard Missy start coming up the stairs to get me going, as she says, then I jumped up and rushed out of Daddy's room, because Missy tells Daddy everything about me and if she saw me in his room then she would tell him that too and I would have to say nothing when Daddy asked me about it because I can't lie to him and I can't tell him that I want the shoe very much. But I ran out of the room and hopped into bed and pulled the covers over my head right before Missy came in.

"Luke."

"Hmmph," I grumped.

"Luke, you need to get out of bed." She came over and sat on the corner of my bed and tried to pull the covers off of me. I held on tight. She laughed, and then she started tickling my stomach through the sheets and I hate that because I'm very ticklish and she knows it. But it worked and I let go of the covers and she pulled them off and laughed at me as I stuck my tongue out at her.

"Look at you," Missy said. "You're already ready for school! You must be excited."

I was very excited then and told her about Miss Honeydew, and Missy beamed at me and gave me a hug before I could stop her and called me dear and said we would talk later, then said get up out of bed, you lazy bones, before you miss the bus, and so I did because I didn't want to miss the bus and not get to see all of my teachers. Especially Miss Honeydew. Missy followed me downstairs and gave me a brown paper bag that had my name on it, and then I put on my jacket and went outside and just got on the big yellow bus before it pulled away. I love the bus. It is always very crowded, but I usually get my own seat because no one ever sits by me.

I got to school and went to my homeroom, and Miss Honeydew did not make her eyes small at me but just told me that Mr. Winkelheimer wanted to see me and that I should go directly to his office, and all the other kids stared at me and I wondered if I was in trouble, and then I remembered that I was supposed to talk to Miss Clairborne and I told them that but they all stared at me and Miss Honeydew said that we didn't need to know why, that I should just go and keep my information to myself unless she asked for it. I nodded and said yes ma'am and she turned away from me and then I went out the door and down the hall. I never get lost going to Mr. Winkelheimer's office because I go so much.

I said hello to the secretary and she said take a seat and so I did and waited for Mr. Winkelheimer. He came out in about five minutes with his shiny bald head all gleaming and a big smile on his face, and he asked how I was and I said I was fine and asked how he was but he didn't answer me but rather said, follow me, Luke, I am going to take you to meet Miss Clairborne. I asked if I could leave my backpack and jacket in his office and he said that was fine and that I could come back later and get them, so I took them off and followed Mr. Winkelheimer to another part of the main office where there was a big blue door that was closed. He knocked twice on it, his fist making a dull pounding sound, and then he put his ear next to it like he was listening. He knocked again and then knocked again and called Miss Clairborne's name lightly. Then the door swung open and a very badly dressed woman stepped out, pushing a pair of ugly tortoise-shell glasses back onto her nose. Her dark brown hair was all disheveled, piled onto her head and held in place by a black claw barrette, but it did a very bad job because wisps of her hair had escaped and were sticking out from her head in all different spots. She smiled broadly when she saw me and pushed her glasses back onto her nose, and held out her hand.

"You must be Luke," she said, and she said my name *Luke* like the boy's name and did not call me Lucy like Miss Honeydew did.

"It's Luke," I said stonily. *Loose.*

"Oh." She smiled at me even more broadly and I started to think she was a very stupid woman. "That's lovely. How are you today, Lucy? I'm very happy to be working with you."

I didn't say anything and Mr. Winkelheimer cleared his throat because Miss Clairborne was talking to me and ignoring him and he doesn't like to be ignored because Mr. Winkelheimer is a very important person and I am just a kid and she shouldn't have talked to me first. I told her so and told her she was silly and she laughed and said I was silly, of course I was important, and then Mr. Winkelheimer got very red in the face and cleared his throat and said that Miss Clairborne was to talk to me just until class began and then send me to class and that was to be all, thank you, goodbye. I watched him go, and Miss Clairborne smiled and told me to follow her and I went into her office.

There were piles of loose paper everywhere and it was very messy, like my room, and I asked her what kind of an office was it, why were there papers everywhere and why didn't she keep it clean like all the other grown-ups. She sat down in a wooden chair across from her desk and told me to have a seat anywhere I liked, would I like to sit in the chair or would I rather we sit on the floor and talk like the Indians did when they had powwows and such, and I said what kind of a stupid idea is that and noone sits on the floor. She smiled and said, okay, I could sit in the chair, then. She pulled a pile of papers towards her and I saw my name on the top one, not Luke or Luc but Lucilia Amoretta Miller, which is my full name, and she said that she had never heard of anyone with a name like that. I told her that it wasn't my real name– which was Luke Orange because I liked the color Orange so I just changed it. She said I couldn't do that. I said 'Yes, ma'am.' Then she nodded and looked at the papers in front of her, then folded her hands on top of them and stared at me from behind her thick glasses.

"So how are you today, Lucy?"

"I'm fine," I said shortly. "Thank you."

"That's great. Is anything interesting happening in your life right now?"

"Excuse me," I said. "But Mr. Winkelheimer said you were supposed to be talking to me about my behavior in class."

She kind of just stared at me, then said softly, "I don't care what Mr. Winkelheimer said, Lucy."

"Well you should," I said quickly. "Mr. Winkelheimer is very important."

She got up and went to stand by a big bookcase crammed full of books stacked on top of each other, and her back was turned to me for a moment and then she came back and sat down and folded her hands on top of each other again.

"What would you like to talk about today, Lucy? We have," she checked her watch, a big plastic thing that looked like she had bought it at the nearest convenience store. "About twenty minutes left."

I was silent and I just looked at her. She smiled at me and just sat there smiling as if she thought that would make me talk, like we were two friends about to share secrets with each other even though we were not. She just waited and waited and I counted as the hand on the clock went by and followed it with my eyes, tick, tick, tick. Finally, her smile faded just a little bit and then she said quietly,

"Do you have any pets, Lucy?"

I hesitated, because I remember that Daddy told me not to say anything to her, but I thought this was probably okay.

"Bessy."

Her eyes seemed to light up then, and she smiled. "What kind of an animal is Bessy, Lucy?"

"A cat."

She nodded her head and tucked some of those loose strands of hair behind her ears. "What is Bessy like?"

"She's a cat."

Miss Clairborne looked down, then smiled at me again. "I had a cat too, when I was your age. Her name was Marmalade, and she was an adorable little orange tabby."

"Marmalade is a dumb name for a cat."

Miss Clairborne nodded. "Yes, I suppose it is, but that's what my mom wanted to name her, and I was just happy to have a cat so I didn't even care, but I called her Lady instead because she was very beautiful and regal. But she was also very mischievous. She would climb all over everything and make my parents very mad, and she liked to sneak up on my father and bat his hair when he wasn't looking."

I wanted to tell her that I didn't care about her stupid cat, thank you, but I wanted to hear more about Lady.

"She sounds like a nice cat," I said.

Miss Clairborne nodded. "Lady and I were very close. She would sleep on my bed, all curled up in a large ball of fluffy orange fur, and she would lick my face in the morning so I would get up and go to school on time. If her raspy pink tongue on my cheek didn't wake me up, she would sit on top of my face until I got up. Does your cat do that?"

"No," I said.

Bessy isn't allowed in my room. Daddy says that cats don't belong in people's beds. I tried to imagine Bessy swiping at Daddy's hair and I couldn't. Miss Clairborne kept on talking.

"She was a wonderful cat though. I think I must have annoyed her, because I didn't have any brothers or sisters at the time and so she became like my sister. I dressed her up in my Mama's jewelry once, in this big strand of pearls, and she strutted around the house with those pearls dangling from her neck like she was queen of the world."

"What did your Mama say?" I asked, astounded. I couldn't ever imagine doing something like that to Bessy. "Was she mad when she found out?"

Miss Clairborne smiled at me. "Oh no. She thought it was very funny, and she took a picture of us dressed up before she took the pearls away and said that I shouldn't do that, because Marmalade might choke on them and get hurt. So I didn't do it anymore, but I remember that. I'm sure you love Bessy very much, don't you?"

"Yes," I said, and that was true because I do. "But I want a dog."

"Oh?"

"Cats are stupid. Not Bessy. Bessy is nice. But cats are stupid."

"I see," Miss Clairborne said, and the bell rang. "Well, Lucy, it was lovely to talk to you, but you need to get to class now."

I got up right away and Miss Clairborne opened the door for me. "I'm sorry I called you by the wrong name, Lucy."

"Good bye, Miss Clairborne," I said without looking at her and went out of the door, and started to leave the office. Mr. Winkelheimer passed me as I left the office, but he didn't look at me. I left the office but then remembered that I had left my bag and my jacket there, and I needed them for class, so I rushed back because I didn't want to be late for Miss Honeydew's class. I opened the door very quietly and bent down to get my books, and I saw Mr. Winkelheimer's shiny shoes in front of the big blue door and I heard Mr. Winkelheimer's deep scratchy voice say,

"How was the first session with the little devil?"

I can't be sure of what happened next because I couldn't really see, but I did hear. Miss Clairborne slammed the door in his face, just like that.

I tiptoed out of the office and let the door close softly behind me.

5.

I raised my hand all throughout class, but Miss Honeydew must not have seen my hand, even though I am the tallest kid in the class and so my hand was the highest. But I was a little bit late because I had forgotten my backpack and had to sit in the very back of the classroom and so that probably explains it. But maybe it was a good thing, because none of the other kids looked at me like they had before, except maybe two. One of them I know, because he hates me very much. His name is Xavier. I don't know his last name, just his first because it's long and I've never heard of anything like it before. I beat him in the fifth grade spelling bee and he hasn't liked me ever since, but it wasn't even my fault because he got an easy word like 'pyramid' and he missed it, and he said that it wasn't fair because I got an easy word like 'specify' and he could have spelled that if he had gotten it. I told him to spell it and he said that he didn't have to because he didn't have to prove anything to me, and then the teacher came in and asked what was wrong and he called me a bitch under his breath but the teacher didn't hear so I said that Xavier was just saying what a good job I had done in the spelling bee. Our teacher had smiled at him and said wasn't that nice that he was such a good sport and his face got very red and he didn't look at me until the teacher had turned her back to teach us a lesson in history, and then he poked me. Not very hard, just a little poke, but right in my side with his pencil, and his pencil was sharp and left a little pinprick of black lead in my skin which swelled up a bit after I had got home to look at it. Xavier always looks at me but I don't know what he is thinking at all.

The other boy I have not seen before and I think he might be new, but I don't think he likes me either and I don't know what to think about him. His eyes are gray and kind of watery and he has really thin blond hair which is plastered against his head, and his skin is very pale and his face is very thin and he looks a little bit like the skeleton model that was in the room where Mrs. Day took us when we had the 'talk.' He is also very tall, maybe even taller than me, though I am not anywhere near as thin as he is. I don't know his name because he raises his hand a lot too but Miss Honeydew never calls on him either, but I know that Xavier doesn't like him either because he's always doing mean things to him, like dropping his book on his hands or stealing his papers and then crumpling them up or tearing them up. At least Xavier doesn't do those things to me, but I feel bad for the new boy, even if he doesn't like me and always stares at me.

I went to my locker after class, which is blue like Miss Clairborne's door except it's dull and metallic, and very narrow. I was putting my books away when someone tugged on my hair. Hard.

"Ouch," I said.

"Well, if it isn't little Miss Luke," Xavier said, grinning.

"Leave me alone," I said.

Xavier shook his head and wrapped my hair around his hand tighter. I wished my hair wasn't so long because then he wouldn't be able to grab it like that. He yanked on it hard again.

"Ouch," I said. "Quit it."

"Or what?" He leered. He looked like a hyena. I told him that, and he got angry and let go of my hair.

"Watch yourself, Luke," he said, and then he turned around and left me alone. I closed my locker and walked away. I didn't like Xavier, so I wasn't going to think any more about him.

I saw the new boy watching me too, because his locker is right down the hall from mine, and as I passed him I stopped and we just stared at each other, our eyes kind of locked like we were trying to read each other's thoughts. I realized he was taller than me, but not by much.

"Hi," I said.

He didn't say anything but dropped his eyes to his feet and then closed his locker and I walked past him and didn't say anything more.

I guess that's when we became friends.

6.

I followed the new boy home after school the next day because Daddy was scheduled to work and so wouldn't miss me. It just kind of happened that I ended up beside the new boy. He slouched and kept his head down the entire time that I walked beside him, but he didn't tell me to go home and he didn't say I shouldn't follow him. I asked him what his name was.

179

"Peter Gray," he said.

"I'm Luke," I said. "Luke Orange."

He didn't say anything to that but kicked at a stone on the other side of the road. I kept talking to him and he didn't say anything at first, but I could tell he was listening.

"You shouldn't let Xavier pick on you," I said. "Just because you're new around here and he's popular. You're bigger than he is."

"So are you," was all he said.

"Yeah, but I'm a girl."

He stopped. "So?"

I rolled my eyes. "So I couldn't fight him, that's all."

He studied the cracks in the sidewalk and then said quietly, "Someday I think you should just punch him."

I acted like I didn't hear that. "So where are you from?" I asked him.

"New Jersey."

"That must be nice."

He shrugged. He didn't ask me why I was following him either. But when we got to his house, which is big and white and has black shutters and was built in a colonial style, I stopped, because I thought it was probably wrong just to go into a stranger's house without even being invited. There was also a fence made of tall wooden pikes, fencing the house in so I could just see the very top of it. I just stood there, looking up and trying to see his house.

"I have a dog," he said.

"I like dogs," I said.

He put his ear up to the fence and listened, then nodded satisfactorily to himself, and then he pushed open the gate part of the fence and I followed him. Inside of the fence there was a pretty green lawn, and a huge oak which spread its branches in a canopy over the front of the house, and from one of these outstretched branches there were two long, thick ropes that trailed down and attached to a swing. It was not a lovely swing, like the ones that people at the high school sit on when they have their senior pictures taken, but it was simple and rough-looking, like someone had made it himself. There was a small round ball underneath the swing, and on the other side of the yard there was a pentagonal shaped doghouse with red paint and black tiles and a white sign nailed onto it.

"Fox is my dog," is what I thought I heard him say.

"Fox is a silly name for a dog, isn't it?"

"I don't give a damn about what you think, Luke Orange," is what he said to me.

"Well I think it's dumb to name an animal after another animal," I replied. "I mean, you wouldn't call a peacock 'Armadillo' or a kangaroo 'Leopard' so why would you name a dog Fox?"

He burst out laughing then and I thought he was going to fall over and choke on all the hilarity bubbling out of his mouth. He actually grabbed his sides as if he would split open if he didn't, and I think some tears might have squeezed out of his eyes.

I put my hands on my hips. "Well what's so funny?"

He laughed harder when he saw I was angry, and then he straightened up and controlled himself long enough to speak.

"Fawkes," he said. "F-A-W-K-E-S. Not fox like the animal. Haven't you ever heard of Guy Fawkes?"

"Who?" I said.

"Guy Fawkes. He led a conspiracy in England called the Gunpowder plot in which he tried to blow up King James and his Parliament. But it didn't work out."

"Oh," I said. "How am I supposed to know about that? How do you know about that? Why would you name your dog after some psycho?"

Peter Gray looked at the ground and started to dig a hole in the soft grass with his foot. I watched him. Scrape, scrape, scrape. The top layer of the light green skinned off like a scalp, exposing the dark soil underneath.

"I lived in England for awhile," Peter Gray said. "And Fawkes is a bad dog. He tears everything up, like Guy Fawkes wanted to do."

"Well I guess that makes sense," I said.

"And I want to set the world on fire," Peter Gray said. He started to smile slightly.

I stared at him.

"Literally?" I asked, because I was curious, and Mama used to tell me that curiosity killed the cat but we weren't talking about cats, we were talking about Peter Gray's dog and setting the world on fire and blowing things up. So I guess it was okay.

"No," he said. "But I like to start fires."

"Oh come on," I said. "You don't."

"I do so," he whined, nodding his head up and down and complaining like a four-year-old who thinks life is unfair. "I do so, just watch me."

Then he went around to the other side of the house and just left me standing there, staring into the empty dog house, and I went over and sat on the swing and rocked back and forth, back and forth. I was afraid it might break at first, but it was a very good swing, and it held me very nicely and I had a very good time on it before Peter Gray came back and scuffled over to me.

"Well are you coming?" he asked me.

I stopped propelling myself forward on the swing, my feet scraping to a stop and the dusty soil covering the tops of the black shiny shoes I was wearing. The swing creaked against the ropes.

"Where?"

"Oh just come on," he said, and he grabbed my hand and pulled me off the swing. I didn't protest but let him lead me to the back of the house, and then he dropped my hand and bent down by a pile of sticks that were standing up like a triangle in the middle of a big stone patio. There was some newspaper crumpled up under all those sticks, and a little box of matches with bright red sulfur heads laying open nearby. Peter Gray bent down by the pile of sticks and he picked up the matchbox and tore out a match, and then put the match's head against the little brown strip on the back.

"I want to light it," I said.

"No." He shook his head. "It's my fire, I'm going to light it. You don't know how to do it."

"Fine," I said. He was right, I didn't know how to do it. Daddy doesn't let me play with matches, he says I'll burn myself. But it would have been more fun if he would have let me try.

But Peter Gray ignored me and he struck the match's head hard against the strip, and there was a fizz and then an orange-blue flame spurted out, glowing brightly and flickering in the air. Peter Gray watched its dance for a second and then shielded the flame with his hand like it was something precious that only he should see, and he bent down and put the flaming head against that paper and *poof!* The flame started eating the paper hungrily, charring the words and the creamy white of the newspaper and making it crackle and blacken and turn in on itself. Then gray smoke started billowing out of the sticks, puffing and spilling over the patio.

"That smoke looks like dry ice," I said.

"What?" he said, but he didn't sound very interested at all.

"Dry ice," I repeated. I know about dry ice because Daddy gets it at his office sometimes, because it's packaged with some of his medicines which need to be kept really cold so that they work.

"It's a teepee fire," he said as he watched the flames start licking greedily at the newspaper. Crackle, crackle, crackle. "I'm the best at making teepee fires."

I watched the flames burning higher and higher and higher. Flames are very fun to watch. They twist and turn and hop all over each other like children playing leap frog, and now I know why they were used in so many ritualistic dances and prayer services among different types of people. I remember reading about that in my cultures textbook. Especially the Native Americans and the Africans, they used to use fire all the time for purification and asking their gods for good hunts and things like that. Fire is very greedy, though. It consumes everything it touches, and draws in the attention of the people watching it as well.

"Why do you yell in class?" Peter Gray asked me suddenly.

"I do not," I said, my eyes on the flames.

"You do so. You told Miss Honeydew to shut up."

I didn't look at him, and I didn't say anything. He was silent, and then he looked directly at me and I could see there was gloating in his eyes.

"I'm glad you did," he said. "I don't like her."

I stomped the fire out then, just took one shiny black shoe and crushed the life out of it. Embers and orange sparks danced around my foot and I could feel the sole of my shoe getting warmer, so I was careful that I didn't catch on fire by picking my foot back up and stomping, again and again.

"I didn't mean to," I said. Stomp. "It was the voice in my head. And I like Miss Honeydew." Stomp, stomp. "She is a very nice person."

Peter Gray was quiet and he didn't say anything, but just watched me stomp out his precious little fire, and when I was done stomping and my leg was covered in thick, dark ash up to my ankle and in speckles up to my knee, he said so softly that I had to strain to hear him,

"No she isn't. She never calls on me."

"Maybe she doesn't see you. She doesn't call on me either."

"I know," was all he said. Then, "She's mean. I hate her."

"Well you're stupid," I said. "Miss Honeydew is a new teacher and she has it very hard and you should be ashamed of yourself for hating her."

"Yeah, well I don't have voices in my head," he said.

"Peter Gray, you can go to hell," I said. "And you can build fires there all day long, for all I care."

I started to leave, but he grabbed my arm.

"Aren't you going to help me clean up the ashes?" he asked.

"No," I said, and then I waited as he went into his garage and brought out a trashcan and a shovel.

"We have to make sure they are all picked up," he said, handing me the shovel. "My Mom will be really mad if she comes home and sees them. She doesn't like that I build fires."

"Well I should think not," I said as I attacked the ashes with the shovel, then dumped them into the trashcan. I thought it was pretty cool that he built fires, but then I thought about my mama and me gardening and planting tiny helpless seeds in the warm ground, and then I knew that she would probably not like me building fires either. Peter Gray just stood holding the garbage can in place and watching me shovel away. I scraped up the last little bit of black and then scuffed at the blackened patio with my shoe. The stone of the patio was light like the house, and I could still see where the fire had burned a small black circle onto the surface. I wiped my hands on my jeans and then thrust the shovel back at him.

"Thank you," he said simply. "Will you come again tomorrow?"

"I guess so," I said, and then I left.

7.

he'll fuck you in the morning, fuck you in the evening, fuck you in the bright sunshine. . .

"I love you in the morning, love you in the evening," I sang, swinging my hands back and forth though I was on the bus and everyone was staring at me. I bit down on my lip, hard. I wanted to cry. But I bit my lip and tasted blood and kept everything under control, because I was on the way to school, where everything would be fine.

on the road to insanity, all roads lead to insanity you bitch. Don't you know you'll never get there on time if I don't

"How much farther are we from the school?" I asked the bus driver.

"Fifteen minutes," he said shortly, but I don't think he was trying to be mean. "Sit up and look straightforward and stop your goddamned singing."

His name is Bud and he is very thin and has brown hair and a brown beard and little watery eyes that are always squinting from behind his glasses. His voice is always very irritated and very short but I like him because there is a picture of a beautiful girl about my age taped up into the corner of the mirror on the bus. The girl has long blond hair and is in a white dress and there are daisies laced together in a crown around her head in a circle and she is smiling and she looks like she's looking at me and smiling and saying it's going to be okay. Bud must love her very much, because I think she is his daughter and she is very beautiful.

"Yes, sir," I say, and I clamp down on my singing and bite my lip harder and now I can see the blood and not just taste it but I need to bite my lip because I need to feel the pain and if I don't I might have to scream. I do not hear people sniggering behind me, not at all, it's my imagination because no one would laugh at me, not when I'm hearing the things in my head and biting my lip so it bleeds and having tears creep up into my eyes. I blink and I watch Bud, and he shifts the stick beside him which tells the bus how fast to go.

Push down baby all night and all day keep driving away

"Fifteen minutes," I say aloud.

That's when, if things couldn't get worse, Xavier comes over to me from the back of the bus. He's wearing his jacket with the letter on it, because he is in eighth grade even though he's in my homeroom. Eighth graders can compete on sports teams and he does and that's what the letter is from. He comes over to me and he sits down beside me in my empty seat and spreads his legs very wide so that he's touching me, and I squeeze over to the other side of the seat so that I'm pressed up against the window and far away from him.

"Good morning, Luke," he says to me, and I wonder what trick he is trying to pull. He sounds so polite, not like Xavier at all.

"Good morning," I say in a voice I hope sounds like cold water, and I wish I had some so I could pour it over his head.

"Look, Luke," he says, and he leans in very close to me so that he's whispering and I don't think that Bud can hear him at all, but if he can he's ignoring it because his eyes are on the road or sometimes on the girl taped to the mirror.

I scootch as far away from Xavier as I can, because he smells funny. Not bad, like he hasn't washed for a week or more, but just really funny, like nothing I've ever smelled before. I don't want to hear what he has to say at all, but he doesn't care because he says it anyway and I have nowhere to go because I am pressed up against the window and unless I jump out of the bus or crawl under Xavier I'm not going to be able to get away.

"What do you want?" I say shortly. I might have to listen to him, but I don't have to do it nicely.

His breath is hot and he's very close to me and I look at Bud but he's looking at the road.

"Come sit in the back of the bus tomorrow," Xavier says. "With me."

"No," I say. I've heard that stuff goes on in the back of the bus, and I don't know what it is but I don't want any part of it, especially not if Xavier does it.

"Aw, come on," he says, and then he grabs my hair and pulls it really hard, but I don't let him know it hurts because he would like that and besides, it didn't even hurt that much and I'm not a baby and noone is going to know that it did hurt a little if I don't let them see it. He pulls on my hair and then he gets up a little bit shakily. "I have something for you. Something you'll like."

That sparks my interest and I think about asking him about it further but then Bud looks up.

"Sit down when the bus is moving!" he says. "You rotten kid."

Xavier is swaying back and forth and I wonder if maybe he was sick but he sticks up his middle finger and then wanders back to the back of the bus and Bud's face gets very red and Xavier is laughing and everyone else is laughing but it's not the same laughter as when they were laughing at me. I know it, even though it sounds the same.

"Rotten kid," Bud mumbles under his breath and I don't know whether he's talking to me or Xavier or even the little girl in the picture. Sometimes things are just so confusing and I just don't know.

Everything is all of a sudden very quiet in my head and I see that I did make it to the school, that maybe something about the funny smell on Xavier made it go away but I don't know, I'm just really happy to be at the school even though now I have to go see Mr. Winkelheimer and Miss Clairborne, and I like him but I don't like her. Mr. Winkelheimer is a very smart man, and if he thinks she can help me then maybe she can but she doesn't like him and I can't tell her anything because Daddy said not to and I can't do what Daddy says not to do, and besides, Miss Clairborne isn't very good at her job. She's supposed to be a counselor, but I always have to tell her what to do and such. She is very sloppy and wears weird clothes and talks all the time about stupid cats and asks if I want to sit on the floor. Doesn't she know that isn't how things are done?

8.

"Hello, Luke," Miss Clairborne said. "How are you today?"

I didn't even correct her, because I'm so used to going by Luke that I didn't even think about it at the time, didn't even remember to tell her to call me Lucy like Miss Honeydew had the first day.

"I'm fine," I said. "How are you, Miss Clairborne?"

"I'm doing well," she said with a slight nod of her head, and then she was silent, as if she expected me to say something.

"You look almost like a counselor today," I said.

She laughed, but it wasn't my fault that I had said that, because she did look different. It looked like she had actually brushed her hair and it was very pretty and even gleaming a bit, and tucked up against her head with a dark blue barrette. She was wearing a very pretty baby blue sweater, too, with little white pearl buttons that looked real.

She smiled at me. "What would you like to talk about today?"

I just stared at her stonily. She just kept on smiling at me, her smile didn't even sag the slightest bit, but I knew what she was thinking.

You stupid little bitch, what's the problem? Too stupid to say anything aren't you. . . .

Miss Clairborne smiled at me and it looked like a conspiratorial smile, like she was going to say something secret to me, like I was her confidant or something.

"Do you want to talk about boys?" she said in a lower voice with that smile of hers, and then she stopped looking like a counselor and instead looked like a little girl playing make-up at a slumber party, where everyone gathers around and tells about their crushes.

"No," I said. "I don't like boys and they don't like me."

"Oh." She looked taken aback, like she had made a mistake or something. "But you're a very pretty girl, Luke. I'm sure boys like you."

"No they don't," I said. "I look like a mouse."

She laughed at that and shook her head, and I don't think I could live like that, to laugh and smile all the time and never be sad about anything at all. Then she paused again as if she wanted me to say something.

"How about school? Is everything going well for you?"

"Yes," I said. "This is stupid. Can I go now?"

Miss Clairborne just looked at me and was quiet for a minute, and then she asked slowly, like she was hesitating for some reason or like she was thinking, "Do you want to talk about your behavior in school?"

"I don't know what you mean," I said, even though I knew exactly what she meant. Part of me was relieved though, I think. I didn't understand why she wanted to talk about cats and boys and all of that stuff because that's not what Mr. Winkelheimer had told her to talk to me about at all, and she wasn't even doing her job when she talked to me about stuff like that.

"You said the first day that we should talk about your behavior in class. Would you still like to do that?"

"No," I said.

She tucked a strand of her dark hair behind her ear, because it had popped out of her head like Medusa's did in all those pictures about Greek mythology in one of my textbooks when I was in the sixth grade.

"Why not?" she said.

"My daddy says I can't tell you anything."

"Oh," she said lightly, without anything in her voice. "Well, I'm very sorry to hear that, Luke."

A sudden bolt of fear shot through me. "You're not going to tell him I said that, are you, Miss Clairborne?" I suddenly felt very shy around her.

She shook her head, like she couldn't even believe I said that and I almost liked her in that moment. "Of course not, Luke. Everything that you tell me stays between you and me. It's the same for everyone I talk to. It's called confidentiality, and it exists so that you can be sure that you can tell me whatever you want to. You don't have to be afraid. Okay? Don't think of me as your counselor. Think of me more as a friend who you can really tell anything you want to, because I'll never tell anyone your secrets and I can give you advice as well if you want me to. Okay?"

"Okay," I said, but she was lying through her teeth as Daddy would say. He wouldn't have told me to stay quiet if it hadn't been for my own good. I didn't trust Miss Clairborne one bit, and I wasn't going to let her be my friend.

"Mr. Winkelheimer says you hear voices in your head."

She just came out and said it, blunt, just like that. I just stared at her, because now she was looking at me very seriously like I was an adult or something. No more talk about cats and sitting on the floor or dress up and her mama's pearls and her cat named Marmalade which she called Lady. Miss Clairborne looked very serious all of a sudden.

"Let's talk about boys," I said.

She looked torn for a minute, like she was considering it, and then she shook her head and said quietly,

"No, Luke. We need to talk about this."

"There's a boy named Xavier," I said, not listening to her. "He wants me to sit in the back of the bus with him tomorrow but I'm not going to because he's a very bad boy and I think that he's going to pull a trick on me . . ."

"Luke."

I didn't want to listen, because I didn't want to hear what Miss Clairborne had to say, but I didn't have any more boys to talk about except Peter, and I didn't want Miss Clairborne to know about Peter. Peter was mine, he was my secret, he was my friend, and I didn't want her to know about him so I just stopped talking and glared at her and said "What?" very meanly so hopefully she would understand that I didn't want to talk about it. But like I said she's stupid and she didn't understand at all.

"Luke, is it true? Do you hear a voice in your head at times?"

When I was quiet she looked down in front of her, then offered me a little smile. "I mean, it's okay if you do. Many wonderful people have had thoughts pop into their heads from unknown sources. William Blake. I don't think you know who he is, you probably won't read him until you're a bit older. He thought that he heard God talking to him and had visions of all kinds of celestial beings which gave him advice, and. . ."

"That's weird," I said. "He must have been crazy."

She shook her head. "He wrote a lot of very good poetry, and he was also an artist. You can see his works in lots of famous places, like the Tate Britain and . . ."

She broke off and didn't say any more because I was looking at her blankly because I had no idea what she was talking about.

"Oh," she said softly. "I can see I'm not getting through to you at all."

The bell rang then and I breathed a heavy sigh of relief and lumbered out of the chair, grabbing my purple backpack and shifting it onto my shoulder in a hurry. I started towards the door.

"Luke . . ."

"Humph," I said.

"Here," she said, and I looked towards her. "I want you to have this."

I started back towards her and took what she was holding. It was a book, with a shiny cover and a picture of a young boy on it holding a lantern and on the front of it beside the little boy were two beautiful dogs that looked very solemn, with the firelight from the boy's lantern glinting off of their shiny fur. In the background there were dark woods and in big white letters was the title of the book, <u>Where the Red Fern Grows.</u>

"Thank you," I said, looking at the dogs.

Miss Clairborne nodded her head. "You're welcome," she said. "I remember you said you like dogs. I think you will really like this story. It's about a boy and his two dogs, as you can assirtayne from the cover."

She said that big word like she thought I knew what it meant and I just nodded my head because I figured that it didn't matter. People just use big words to sound smart, like they have something to prove, because big words don't mean any more than do smaller words that everyone knows. I tried to look it up later– and it wasn't even in the dictionary! But I nodded my head and I said thank you and she smiled.

"Do you like to read?" She asked, and her eyes followed mine to the door that I wanted to run out because I was going to be late for class and then Miss Honeydew wouldn't call on me.

"Yes," I said. "A lot."

I know I should have left but I couldn't help it. I wanted to stay then, just because I like to read a whole lot and I like to talk to people about reading but I don't do it because no one else likes to read and it's just one more thing that shows I'm a weirdo. But Miss Clairborne didn't seem to think that it was weird that I read and she just smiled bigger at me and I liked that picture, of that boy and his two dogs, and I wanted to talk to her more about it and I think she could tell.

"Well, you have to get to class," she said. "But read what you can if you have some free time after your schoolwork is done, and then if you want, we can talk about the story when you come in. Would you like that?"

"Yes," I said. "I would like that very much."

I couldn't help myself from saying that, and I meant it, and Miss Clairborne just smiled and nodded and I picked up my backpack and I put the book in it, with its shiny cover and all, and I made sure that it wouldn't get crinkled in my backpack, and then I zipped up my backpack.

"Here," I said on my way out, and I handed her something.

She looked puzzled. "What is it?"

"That's a picture of Bessy," I said. "You can have it."

Then I left.

9.

"Come here, Lukey," Xavier said the next day, and he grabbed my arm and pulled me out of my seat and started to drag me to the back of the bus. I shouldn't have gone with him, but I did, because I was curious. Xavier's never nice to me and I wanted to see what he wanted, so I let him hold my arm and drag me back there. I thought he was going to trick me, like take me there and then there wouldn't be a seat for me, but there was an empty seat and he slid into it and patted the brown, ripped leather beside him.

"Sit down," he said.

I sat down and he pulled out a little brown bag and he pulled out a little mirror and a little razor blade and then he poured out a white fine powder onto the mirror and started to chop it up with the blade. The bus was bouncing over all the bumps in the road but Xavier kept his hand steady and he didn't lose any of it, and he told me to watch the damn bus driver so that if he started looking back at us, I could tell him and then we wouldn't get in trouble. I asked him what he was doing.

"Drugs," he said. "You want some?"

"I'm not going to smoke pot," I announced to him. "It's bad."

He started laughing and he sounded like that hyena he used to look like, but I can't really say he laughed because he more like choked on his laughter because he didn't want anyone to hear him.

"It's not pot, stupid," is what he said. "It's coke. And you don't smoke it, you snort it. Like this."

Then he took out a dollar bill from his wallet and he rolled it into a little tube and he put the tube by the white stuff and then into his nostril and he breathed in really deeply. He closed his eyes for a moment and then looked at me and smiled and handed me the dollar bill.

"Here," he said. "Your turn. It'll make you feel good."

"I'm not putting that thing in my nose," I said to him. And I didn't, either.

He got kind of angry then.

"Come on, Luke," he said. "I've been mean to you before and I'm trying to make up for it. Can't you let a guy do a good thing for a lady?"

He called me a lady. I was so shocked that Xavier had called me a lady that I just sat there and stared at him. Finally, I broke out of my surprise for long enough to say something.

"I'm not doing any drugs," I said. "They're bad for you."

He smiled, and I knew that he had never expected me to, that maybe that had been the trick all along. He smiled and then he tugged on my hair.

"Luke," he said. "Always the same Luke. You're so boring."

I just stood up then and got away from him, because, 'lady' or not, he was still Xavier and I didn't want to be with him. Bud must have been in a really bad mood because he was swerving everywhere and driving really fast and going over all of the bumps really fast, and I lost my balance and fell into one of the seats. I heard Xavier laughing at me from behind

the wheels on the bus go round and round his dick goes down his dick goes down

and I felt myself blushing because I was embarrassed even if it was Xavier and even if it wasn't my fault that I had fallen down but there was nothing I could do

round and round

and so I just stood up and tried to act dignified as I walked back to my seat and the bus lurched this way and that and Bud yelled,

"Sit down when the bus is moving!"

down and down

I was trying to but I didn't tell Bud that because he might ask me why I was all the way in the back of the bus when I never sat there and then I might have had to tell him about Xavier and I can't do that because even though it's really bad what Xavier is doing still it's his choice and I'm not a tattletale and besides, I never talk to Bud anyway and he never talks to me.

I started to like Xavier a little more after that but that ended soon enough because when we got to the school he was as mean as anything to me. He knocked my books out of my hands and then he tripped me, and I wouldn't have cared as much if he hadn't done it in front of Peter. But he did it in front of Peter and I fell down and I looked like a fool and that made me want to cry because even though Peter is just my friend still I looked silly. Peter didn't say anything to me at all, didn't act like I was an embarrassment but didn't exactly stop Xavier either. But he didn't have to.

Later that day I smelled something and everyone else did, and then there was an alarm and we all went out of the building really fast like we had practiced. Then there was a bell that said it was okay, and we went back to class and then there was an announcement that made everyone go to the auditorium and then Mr. Winkelheimer told everyone that someone had set a fire in Xavier's locker.

Mr. Winkelheimer didn't say it was Xavier's locker but I knew. Xavier looked really upset, really angry like he wanted to kill someone or kick something. And I saw his locker later, all smudged with black. Mr. Winkelheimer said they would catch whoever did it. He told us that if anyone had any information as to the perpetrator they should let him know immediately.

But I'm no tattletale.

10.

"Why'd you do it?" I asked Peter Gray later that day when I went over to his house after school. "Why'd you set the fire in Xavier's locker?"

Peter Gray scuffed the dirt with his shoe and didn't look at me. "I don't like that he's so mean to you," he said so softly I could barely hear him.

"Well you shouldn't have set a fire in his locker."

He looked at me then. "Do you really think that?"

I nodded my head. "It was a nasty, rotten thing to do."

"Oh," he said and he hung his head and looked at the dirt he was scraping away. I think I hurt his feelings.

"Let's go inside," I said, wanting to change the subject because now I realized he had set the fire for me, that he had done it all for me.

"Okay," he said, and we went in.

The inside of Peter Gray's house is like the outside: blank. The walls are all white, and even though there are pictures they are all rectangular in neat little black frames and are boring, like pictures of flowers or fruit in a basket on the table. I told Peter Gray I wanted to go to his room, and he led me up a flight of stairs to the second floor of his house and then to the middle of the hallway where there was a cord hanging down from the ceiling which he pulled and steps came down. They just came down from how they had been folded up like an accordion and I couldn't help but stare.

"You live in the attic?" I said to him, awe-struck.

"No. But I like it up here. Come on."

Peter Gray started up the attic steps without even turning back to look at me, but I just stood at the bottom of them and watched him because I wasn't going up there. Attics are dusty and dirty and stuffy and there is never much light and they are usually packed full of cartons of really scary things that the people don't want, like dolls whose heads have come off or musty old photographs that are half eaten with fuzzy green mold that smells bad. I don't like attics, and those accordion stairs looked really flimsy, like I would break them if I tried to go up them. He must have turned back at some point though because all of a sudden I heard him from above me somewhere, his voice all muffled.

"Come on, Luke," he said impatiently. "Hurry."

I just swallowed and put my first foot on that step and hoped that it wouldn't break and I wouldn't fall through, because there was no one to complain to and no one to tell me it was okay. I just had to go up the steps and so I did. And I like Peter Gray's attic. It's unlike any I have ever seen before.

"Wow," I said. "This is amazing."

He smiled proudly. "I've worked on it a lot. My parents don't even know I come up here all the time."

There was light streaming in from one end where there was a double window pane that had an arched top and looked Gothic, and there was a crack in the bottom of one of the panes but it wasn't very noticeable. There was also a little easel set up and a big dusty-looking rug set up on the floor in front of it. It was a pretty tight fit, with the top of the easel scraping against the ceiling, and I saw it was uneven too because the legs had been sawed off slightly to make room for it. There were boxes but they were stacked up in the corner far away from the window and the easel and they were all closed really tightly with thick mailing tape so that none of the scary contents could be seen.

"I come up here all the time," Peter Gray repeated fondly. "And I paint."

"What do you paint?" I asked with curiosity, and Peter Gray smiled.

"I'll show you," he said, and he went over to one stack of boxes and he moved them aside and he pulled out this old leather carrying case that looked really worn but still had that leather smell to it. It was full, bulging out in places, and Peter Gray came back lugging it along and sat down on the red woven rug and I sat down beside him and he opened the old carrying case ceremoniously.

"Here," he said, and he handed me a painting.

"Wow," is all I said.

He handed me another one, and another one, and another one. The creaking boards of the floor of the attic were soon filled with all of his paintings.

"Where'd you get the ideas for all these paintings?" I said, because they weren't like anything I had ever seen before. Some of them were pictures of bloody red sunsets that I could make out even though the sun doesn't look like that here, and some were of really grand buildings I had never seen, but some of them were weird. Some of them had weird shapes that didn't come together to make a picture and were painted in clashing colors that were really ugly, and I looked at these more than I looked at the other ones because there was just something about them that I really liked, ugly colors and all.

"Some of them are from England," he said. "The other ones I made up. Sit down. I want to paint you."

"What?" I said.

He was already in another corner of the attic and he came back holding a slate in one hand and a bunch of white tubes of paint, and a paintbrush with long, camel-colored bristles in his mouth.

"Sit down," he said.

"What if I don't want to?"

"I don't care. Sit down, it takes awhile, it'll be easier for you not to move if you're sitting."

"You're not very nice, Peter Gray," I said as I sat down on the rug. "You can't just go ordering people around like that."

He snorted and arranged the paints around him in a semicircle, then picked up a tube and squirted a splotch of color onto the white slate.

"Go sit behind the easel in the light," he said.

I grumped and stood up and went and sat where he told me to, acting angry and irritated though I was really excited to have him paint my picture, even though I knew I wasn't going to like it at all because I'm not pretty and you can't make something pretty that's ugly to begin with.

But I sat as still as I possibly could, and listened obediently when Peter Gray said things like, 'tilt your head this way' or 'raise your chin a bit.' I sat and I sat and I sat and it seemed like forever that I sat. Peter Gray had this very thoughtful look on his face the entire time, and he kind of bit his lip and looked very much like an artist and not at all like the Peter Gray in school, not even the Peter Gray who built fires. After a really long amount of time had passed, he smiled at me.

"It's done," he said.

I scrambled up. "Can I see it?"

He nodded solemnly and wiped the paint off the brush he had been using with a paper towel. I noticed the paint was black and that confused me since I wasn't wearing black and the only thing black about me are the pupils in my eyes. But I was really confused when I saw what Peter Gray had painted.

"That doesn't look like me," I would have said, but I just stared at the canvas that had been white and was now black. So black, every inch of it was completely covered in black, except for the areas where there were red streaks of paint slashed across in jagged lines. Then there was a bit of gray shading, something that might have resembled a face in a very abstract kind of way. It was chilling.

"Well, what do you think?" he said finally. I saw he was watching me very closely.

I swallowed. "What is it?"

"It's you," he said. "I told you I wanted to paint you."

"That looks nothing like me," I said, unable to take my eyes away from the painting.

"Well it's you," he said shortly, and I could tell he had expected me to praise it just like I had all of the other ones. But this one didn't look like the other ones. It didn't look like *any* of the other ones. I swallowed again and didn't say anything.

"It has to be you, because that's what I felt when I looked at you," he continued stubbornly.

"It's scary, Peter," I said.

"But you like it."

"I like it." I stood up, ready to go. I had homework to do. "But it's not me."

He looked at me from his artist eyes and just inclined his head slightly, as if he were thinking.

"I'm going home now," I said.

"Bye," he said.

11.

I'm going to make you bash your fucking head against the wall so hard that your skull cracks open and your brains ooze out through shards of bone, dripping onto the floor in pulpy clumps. You'd like that, wouldn't you? You said you didn't want to live in this world, and that's all it takes. All it takes is a couple of slits. You could even do it with that compass you're holding right now. Jam it through your wrist, right here, right now, and watch it. Watch the blood spurt out in crimson jets... maybe you'll get lucky and you'll hit an artery and then you can watch it spurt out of your body like the baking soda in that idiotic science fair project you made in second grade. . .

I was sitting in math class and we were drawing angles and circles and I was gripping the desk in front of me so hard that my knuckles were white and my hands hurt. I was trying not to cry but I couldn't help it, I couldn't help it because that compass point was so sharp and it's not my fault that I saw Angel Donohue using one on herself in the bathroom last week and that's how the idea got put in my mind...

"No, no, no, no, no," I whispered, bowing my head so that no one would see that I had lost it and I was crying now. I could feel the tears splotching down my cheeks and dripping off of my nose, landing in hot, salty puddles on the desk in front of me. I tried to say it quietly but it was loud and Miss Honeydew heard me. It's always Miss Honeydew who hears me, I hate it, why can't it be with Miss Clairborne or even with Mr. Winkelheimer because they know what to do to make it go away, they know what to do to make it stop.

"There is no 'no' on how to draw a circle, Luke," Miss Honeydew said. "Unless maybe you think we should do it freehand and have the angles work themselves out."

Someone sniggered but I didn't care. I had to get out of the room. I had to get out of the room and I had to get to the bathroom right away.

"Miss Honeydew," I said, and my voice was very tight and very controlled and I was very proud of myself. "I need to go to the bathroom. Right now. Ma'am."

"No," she said. "The period ends in five minutes. You will stay till the end of the lesson, and then you may go. Now class. . ."

"Miss Honeydew, I need to leave now."

My voice was cool and calm and it cut through the classroom like a melted knife cuts through butter when I make my toast in the morning. Miss Honeydew looked at me, holding up this white piece of chalk and she started talking, but my eyes were on the chalk . . .

Shoved up or down white choke on it . . .did it feel good, bitch?

I covered my mouth with my hands. I was going to vomit. I knew it. I closed my eyes too so I wouldn't see everyone staring at me, but then I opened them because I needed to get out. I didn't even pick up my book bag, I just pushed my desk over and went to the door. No, I ran to the door, and I pushed it open so hard that it slammed into the wall outside the classroom and then I heard my shoes slapping off of the floor in the hallway and I could hear Miss Honeydew yelling at me from behind but I couldn't stop, I couldn't stop until I reached the bathroom and pushed open one of the stalls and bent over the white porcelain toilet and threw up everything I had eaten from the day. I wiped away tears from my eyes with some toilet paper, I always cry when I throw up, I don't know why, and then I cleared away my mouth and blew my nose. There was blood on the toilet paper when I pulled it away, and I didn't know where it was coming from until I got out of the stall and looked at myself in the mirror. It was just a nosebleed, but I had thought it had come from my stomach and that had made me very scared.

It was very quiet when the voice started again.

Luke.

I looked at my reflection in the mirror and it wasn't me. I mean, it was me but it wasn't me. Those weren't my eyes, staring back at me that wide, that wasn't my mouth curled into a smirk. I wasn't that pale. It wasn't me.

You're right, you bitch. It's me.

I started to run the water over my hands which were shaking, trembling back and forth in little spastic jerks.

It's me, Luke. It's me. Peter Gray saw. Look at me, Luke.

I looked down into the basin and I splashed water on the mirror without even looking at it.

Luke.

Now I couldn't help it and I had to look up, and even through the water droplets on the mirror, I could see. It was smiling.

Peek-a-boo.

I don't know what happened then, I really don't, except that I screamed and I broke the mirror because the nurse had to wrap my hand in thick white gauze and I had broken a knuckle and I was running a fever. The doctor told me all this later when I woke up, after someone had found me and carried me to the nurse because the world had become black for me. My daddy came and picked me up when he was done working, but that wasn't until later in the night and I got to talk and talk with a very nice woman in the hospital who seemed very concerned about me and had beautiful blue eyes and who said her name was Judy. She put her hand on my head and she felt to see if I had a fever, and she didn't even wear those bad-smelling tight gloves that doctors like daddy wear when they are doing surgery on people. But then Judy left and Daddy came in and he brought me a lollipop from his office and led me out to the car and he asked if I was all right but he didn't look at me. He told me to get in the car and then we went to our house and he didn't say anything at all to me except how many people had seen and I told him none because I was in the bathroom and then he sighed and put one of his hands on his face. The other one was on the steering wheel so he could drive, but he wasn't looking at the road anymore and he suddenly looked very old and very tired and not like Daddy at all.

"Daddy, keep your eyes on the road," I said.

"Right," he said, and he smiled a little and sat up then but it was not a happy smile at all and it made me want to cry again, but I just bit my lip and looked out the window and watched the grass and the buildings go by in a blur. I hate myself.

I found out later that Peter Gray was the one who had found me. He left the classroom before class ended too without even telling Miss Honeydew where he was going, and he went into the girls bathroom and found me and took me to the nurse. And for all of this, Miss Honeydew only gave him a week's worth of detention. I don't care what Peter Gray says. He's lucky Miss Honeydew is such a nice person. He could have been expelled.

12.

I went over to Kerri's house after school, and she grabbed me by the hand and pulled me into her room. She had on dark blue eye shadow that went all the way up to her eyebrows, and hot pink lipstick on and crimson blush that covered half of her face.

"You look pretty," I said.

"Thanks, Luke," she said. "Now it's your turn. Hurry, hurry, come on, come on!"

Kerri is my best friend in the whole world because we do stupid things like this, like playing dress up even though we're too old, or like getting a movie from the Blockbuster right down the road from Kerri's house when her parents are out of town and then we just come up to her room and watch it and eat popcorn and cry at the sad parts and laugh at the funny parts. Today, though, was much more serious.

I plopped down besides Kerri on her pink star rug on the floor of her room as she handed me a TeenGirl magazine and then went over to a corner of her room and brought back a whole stack of them. Kerri's room is perfect. It is painted a peachy pink and there is a mobile of little gold stars hanging down from the ceiling and lights that go all the way around the room and which are in a tube, and she has an old antique dresser with a big mirror where she keeps all of her makeup and brushes and such lined up so it looks like a beauty salon.

"Which one do you want?" she asked me. "Pick carefully because, Luke, this is really important."

I looked at all of the beautiful girls staring up at me from the pages of the magazine, with their glossy lips and their glossy hair and their dark, come-get-me eyes and their boobs sticking out of their shirts and I just stared at Kerri.

"Maybe I won't go to the dance," I said.

She pouted and stuck her hands on her hips. "Don't be silly. Of course you're going to the dance. We always go to the dances together."

"But this time it's different," I said. "This time we're supposed to go with boys."

"So?" Kerri was twirling one strand of her long, blond hair.

"So," I tried not to make it sound mean. "So, has anyone asked you?"

Kerri stopped twirling her hair. "Well," she said slowly. "Not yet. But I think the boys are just shy. They try to act so cool and heroic, but they're cowards. They can't even talk to us. But I'm sure when the pressure is on and they realize that they don't have dates, then they'll all rush around trying to find people at the last moment."

"Humph," I said. "Well I don't want to go."

Kerri looked at me from her all-wise eyes. "Luke, are you afraid someone won't ask you?"

"No," I lied. "That's not it at all."

Kerri nodded. "Good. Because we're both going to have dates, and we're both going to tell them soon, and I'll tell you why. . . ."

"But you just said that the boys aren't going to ask us until the last possible moment," I said stubbornly. "And I'm not going to wait around and then be treated like a sack."

She laughed, then suddenly became very solemn, and she looked like a fortune teller in all that make up. Her eyes looked huge.

"You won't," she said mysteriously. "Because we're going to ask them."

"What?" I said, and my mouth dropped open. "Kerri, what if they say no?"

She smiled at me. "They won't. We'll ask them in front of their friends and they won't be able to. They'll have to do it to protect their macho image. It's in *TeenGirl*."

That's another reason I like Kerri. She knows everything. I don't even know what a *macho image* is.

"If you say so," I said.

She himmed and hawed for a moment and then she saw I had stopped looking through the magazine and she picked it up.

"Is this the one you want?" she said. "It's pretty."

"Yes," I said, not even knowing which page the magazine was open to, but knowing I didn't understand these things and so was glad to have come to some kind of decision. "Or you can pick."

Kerri shook her head expertly. "No, this is great for you. Here, wait a minute."

She went over to her dresser and she picked up a bunch of tubes and vials and cases and then came back and plopped back down next to me.

"Hold still," she said, and I closed my eyes and pushed out my lips and just waited while she put all kinds of gunk on my face. She was very close to me and I could feel her breath on my face and the intensity of the concentration with which she was making me beautiful. I don't like not seeing what's going on though and I wished she would hurry up so I could open my eyes, and I was also very eager to see how I looked. Maybe I did want to go to the dance, though just a little bit.

"Do you know who you're going to ask?" Kerri the cosmetician said. "I think I'm going to ask Jacob. He's really hot."

"I don't know him. . ." I started to say, but she hit me over the head.

"Stop, you'll smear it!" she said and I closed my lips again because she was trying to put lipstick on.

"Sorry," I mumbled.

I heard her sigh, and then she said, "Maybe you should ask Xavier."

"What?" My eyes flew open with my lips, and she jerked back so she wouldn't stick the eye shadow brush in my eye. "Kerri, are you crazy?"

"Luke, I told you not to move," she said, and I reluctantly closed my eyes again. "And no. You should go with him. He's cute."

I didn't say anything because she had told me not to but I knew that when she was done, then, whoo boy, I was going to have a whole lot of stuff to say to her then. Thankfully that wasn't too long.

"Done," she said, and I heard a final case snap shut in satisfaction. "There, Luke, what do you think?"

"I think it's ridiculous," I said. "Of all the boys, Xavier?"

"No silly, I mean about your makeup." She thrust a mirror at me.

"Xavier?" I repeated, ignoring her.

She sighed, realizing I wasn't going to look in the mirror until we had resolved talking about this. "Well why not? He's cute and he's not going with anyone yet."

"I can't go with Xavier," I said. "He hates me."

"No, he doesn't," she said. "He likes you. A lot."

"How can you say that?" I almost yelled at her. "He pulls on my hair and trips me and . . ."

She sighed again, one of her infinite-knowledge Kerri sighs. "Luke, that's what boys do when they like a girl at our age. It's in TeenGirl."

"Where?" I said. "That's so stupid. Why would someone be mean to you if they like you?"

She ruffled through the stack of magazines, then exclaimed when she had found the right one, and opened it in a hurry and rifled through the pages and then thrust it under my nose.

"There, read it if you don't believe me," she said.

I skimmed the little article and saw she was right. Kerri is always right about things like boys.

"Fine, I believe you," I said. "But I am *not* going with Xavier."

She wouldn't let the subject die. "Well, *why* not, Luke?"

I avoided the question. "He wouldn't even go with me, that's why."

I don't think she knew what to say to that, because she just handed me the mirror and told me to look and tell her if I liked it because I was going to the dance, and I was going to the dance whether it was with Xavier or not, and I simply had to, and that was that, so what did I think? I took the mirror, a really pretty one that was silver and had a lot of detail carved into it and that looked like the magic mirror Belle uses in "Beauty and the Beast" and I looked at myself.

"Wow," I said, then frowned. "Kerri, you did such a great job."

"But?" she was looking at me eagerly.

"But I don't know if this is me."

She took the mirror away from me. "Luke, you silly, of course it's you. You look beautiful."

The only problem was that she was right and that I did and I didn't think I liked it, knowing I could look like that. What would Xavier say if he saw me with all this green eye shadow up to my eyebrows and this red, red lipstick covering my lips like a bleeding rose, and were those really my eyes shining so brightly and my hair that looked glossy like those girls in TeenGirl...

"You think Xavier would go with me?" I asked suddenly. "You really think he would?"

She had started to put away her things into a pretty little sky-blue purse with rainbow beads sewn all over it, but she paused and nodded her head.

"Yes, I think he will," she said. "And then, when he sees you at the dance like this. . ."

"Okay," I said. "I'll do it."

Kerri nodded her head and then I knew that I would ask Xavier and he would say yes, because Kerri is never wrong about things like this.

13.

The dance was on Thursday and it was a Tuesday when I asked Xavier. But it was the Tuesday before the Tuesday before the dance, so there was over a week left when I could have put it off until the very last moment like Kerri did with the guy she asked. Kerri's guy told her no. Xavier told me yes.

I didn't even believe it and I still don't. It was the most embarrassing thing I've ever done in my entire life and I'm sure I looked like such a fool but then why did he say yes? I still think it's a joke, I really do. I went up to him when he was standing by his locker and I mumbled a hello. I think he looked surprised because he didn't respond right away, but then he slammed his locker shut with a huge metallic clang and grinned at me.

"Well, hello there, Lukey," he said, and he reached out and tugged on my hair.

"Ouch," I said. "Do you want to go to the dance with me?"

No one I knew was around us, and it was very quiet and empty in the hall, with only a few students changing books at their lockers and only a few pieces of scrapped paper lying around in abandon on the shiny white ground. Xavier stopped tugging on my hair and his stupid grin froze on his face, and he actually started shaking a little bit.

"Is this a joke, Luke?" he asked me, and I hated Kerri in that moment because she was wrong, and this was such a stupid idea, and I should never, ever have asked him even though I trust Kerri.

"No," I said.

"You've got to be kidding me," he said very meanly, shifting the books he was holding in one hand and trying to look important. "You've got to be kidding me."

"No," I said again.

Xavier was staring at me, his eyes very large, and he looked like he was thinking, thinking very hard, and he just kept his eyes on me but there was nothing mean in his eyes. His eyes weren't mean like his voice was. His eyes were. . . strange. I don't think a guy has ever looked at me like that before and I started to get uncomfortable because I don't even know what exactly that means anyway, to have a guy stare at you like that.

"Yes," he said.

"What?" I said.

"Yes," he said. "I'll go with you to the dance."

Then my mouth dropped open and he saw I was surprised and then he stopped acting strange and became Xavier again. He patted me on top of my head like I was a kid and he smirked and then he tweaked my nose.

"That took guts, Lukey," he said. "I like a girl with some spunk. I'll have my dad pick you up. Later, babe."

Then he left and I went back to my locker though I didn't need anything and I just stood there looking into my locker because I didn't know what to do because I just felt so happy all of a sudden and didn't understand any of it. Then I looked around and no one was there, and so I burst out laughing and laughed until I was crying but the happy feeling didn't go away and I was smiling so much when I got home from school that Missy took one look at me and asked who the boy was and I said don't be ridiculous there's no boy, and she smiled in her smart Missy-way and told me I'd tell her in time, don't you know, because I would have to, don't you know, and that she'd find out sooner or later. I said, pshaw, no you won't, because I won't tell you, and she said ha! That proves you like a boy and I just blushed and ran up into my room and slammed the door so she would think I'm mad at her even though I'm not. I'm just too happy to be mad at her.

I went over to see Peter Gray but he wasn't there, just his mom who said that he was out but that he'd be back soon, and would I like to wait for him. I said that yes I would, if he wasn't going to be too long, and she asked me if I wanted a lemon drop cookie, and I said yes, that would be very nice. Mrs. Gray is very nice. She came back with a plate of cookies and a tall glass of lemonade, and they looked very pretty, the cookies just sitting there with the pale dough sprinkled with sugar that looked like crystals, and the ice cubes clinking around in that tall glass. I thanked her and said the cookies were delicious because they were, and she smiled and nodded her head and said she was glad Peter had such a polite friend, and if I wanted I could go out and play with Fawkes while I waited, and I said didn't he bite? And she said no, that was just what Peter told people so that no one would play with Fawkes, but that Fawkes was actually a very gentle dog and I should go play with him. I left my plate and the glass there and then I went outside to where I had seen the dog house before and now Fawkes was there! He must have been sleeping when I came in because I didn't see him, but now he came out with his big pink tongue lolling out of his mouth and his tail whipping from side to side and I laughed out loud. He looked like a big ball of fluff, with all that white and gray hair, and he looked so funny just running towards me like I was his best friend. He was very well behaved though and stopped just in front of me, falling over himself in his excitement almost, and I couldn't understand why Peter Gray would name him Fawkes or say that he was vicious when he wasn't. He was just a big, awkward ball of fluff who licked me with his warm pink tongue and wagged his tail, and then jumped up and ran into his doghouse.

Then I went inside to tell Mrs. Gray I would talk to Peter Gray later but before I did I asked her what kind of a dog Fawkes was and she said a Shetland sheepdog and I said I had never seen one of those before, and then Peter walked in and he saw me.

"Hello, Luke," he said. "Let's go up to my room."

I should have gone because that was why I had come over, to see Peter Gray, but suddenly I found I didn't want to anymore. I couldn't look him in the eyes for some reason.

"I'm sorry, Peter Gray," I said. "I have to go home and do some work."

"Oh," he said, and he looked sad, and then he perked up. "Well can't you stay anyway? I'll paint a picture of you and I'll make sure it looks like you."

"No," I said. "I really need to get home."

His smile faded. "Okay. Well, some other time."

"Right," I said. "Goodbye."

14.

Daddy came home very angry and tired and his face was very white and he just acted tired but he was shaking so I could tell he was angry as well.

"Come here, Luke," he said.

I put away my book and went to him, because when Daddy uses that voice it is very important that I listen to him so that he doesn't hit me.

"How are your appointments going with Miss Claymore?" he asked in a deathly quiet voice. I swallowed and didn't tell him that her name was Miss Clairborne.

"I don't tell her anything, Daddy," I said truthfully. "We talk about Bessy and about cats and she gave me this really good book about this boy and his two dogs and it made me cry and cry . . ."

"Luke," he said, in that calm voice. "Be quiet and listen to me."

I shut my mouth and looked at him so he knew I was listening and I didn't say anything.

"Luke, I want you to tell Miss Claymore about . . ."

He stopped and was quiet like he couldn't speak at all or like he didn't know what to say.

"What, Daddy?"

"Nothing," he said, and then he left the room without looking at me and without saying anything more. I didn't know what to do, so I just stood there. Tell Miss Clairborne about what?

15.

Xavier came up to me the next day with a group of his guy friends. I looked up quickly from my locker and then looked down. There was something in his eyes I didn't like, and his friends were all chuckling and snorting down laughter. Xavier leaned against the locker beside me, slouching, his hands in his pockets.

"Hey, babe," he said. "How's it going?"

Before I could even answer he stopped leaning against my locker and he stood up, and came over to me and leaned against my locker so I was trapped between it and him, with his arms out to either side of me like a cage. I just stared at him.

"I'm fine," I stuttered. I could not for the life of me think of anything else to say. He was looking at me very strangely and his guy friends had stopped chuckling and now were watching us with very solemn, serious eyes.

"One more week till the dance," Xavier whispered.

"I know." I nodded my head, trying to figure out what he was trying to imply. I looked away from him because I couldn't meet his eyes.

Then he did it. I wasn't expecting it but he just leaned in and put his lips on mine and then he. . .he. . . I can't even say it. His arms were around me and I couldn't even move, but somehow I disentangled my hand and I brought it into his stomach in a fist and that made him stop so I could breathe again. He put his hands around his stomach and wheezed a bit, and now his friends were laughing and Xavier's face was very red as he stumbled backwards from me.

"Geez, Luke," he said. "Why can't you be a normal girl and slap me?"

This made his friends laugh even harder, and one slapped him on the back while looking at me. Still, something about how Xavier was looking at me scared me. He looked . . .hurt. And not just because I had punched him. But he stood up and looked at me very civilly as I shrank back against my locker.

"Come on," one of his guy friends said. "We can all see just how much you're getting, Xav."

I looked at him then and maybe I looked like I was the one who was hurt, because suddenly he wouldn't look at me. I should have said something. I should have called him out on it, I should have made him look like a fool in front of all of his friends because that's what he deserved, and besides, it was Xavier, and I didn't like him whether I was going to the dance with him or not. I should have done anything except just standing there and looking at him. But I didn't. I couldn't.

"Let's go," he mumbled to his guy friends. "Bye, Luke."

They sauntered off and I couldn't hear what they were saying but I could tell they were making fun of Xavier and that made me feel bad even though it shouldn't have. I didn't have too much time to think about it, though, because Peter Gray came up to me.

"Hi," he said simply.

I turned around. "Hello."

"Was that Xavier?" he said.

"Yes," I said.

"What did he want?"

"He was just being Xavier."

"Oh." Peter Gray was quiet for a moment, then he said, "It looked like he kissed you."

"I punched him," I said. "So don't go doing anything that would make us sit through another assembly..."

Peter Gray was smiling, and he even laughed, which is the first time I ever heard Peter Gray laugh. He even wiped a tear away from his eye.

"I saw," he said. "That's great, Luke."

Suddenly I had to tell Peter Gray the other thing that Xavier had done. I just had to.

"Peter Gray," I said.

"What?" He looked at me, the happiness still brimming in his eyes.

"When Xavier kissed me. . . ."

"Yeah?"

This was the critical moment. This was when I had to tell him, but I was very embarrassed.

"Well, when he did. . ."

"What, Luke? Tell me."

I looked at Peter Gray and he was looking at me with very solemn, mature eyes and I felt that I could tell him. The dirty words came out of my mouth, but I didn't feel regret that I had spoken them. Instead I felt relieved, like by saying what had happened it had erased what actually had happened.

"He put his tongue in my mouth."

Peter Gray seemed extremely disturbed by this fact. He was quiet for a moment, and then he said softly,

"No wonder you punched him."

I looked down. "Yeah."

"That must have been . . .gross," Peter Gray said quietly, and I could tell he was thinking other things.

Maybe like. . .

"Yeah," I said quickly. "It was."

I said it but I was thinking something else, and maybe this was why the voice shut up when I told it to and didn't say anything else, like maybe what Peter Gray had really been thinking. Because while I was agreeing with Peter, I wasn't thinking about how gross Xavier's kiss had been.

I was thinking how nice.

16.

I had cried out several times more in class and Miss Honeydew was starting to become very angry with me. She did not even look at me anymore. I stopped raising my hand. Nothing I had to say was very good anyway. But I still think Miss Honeydew is a nice woman, and she is a great teacher. She knows so much. Peter Gray doesn't think so, though. He keeps telling me that Miss Honeydew won't call on him, or me, because we know more and that she's afraid we'd ask her a question she wouldn't know how to answer. Peter Gray does not think Miss Honeydew is a nice person either. He is still mad about how she gave him detention that time when he came to see me in the girls bathroom.

But my yelling more often is why Miss Clairborne was looking at me so solemnly. She didn't look like she was going to talk about dressup or when she was little; not anymore. Now she just looked at me like I was a puzzle she needed to put together. She looked at me with her face all thoughtful, and she looked at me very kindly but I didn't like her look anyway. I had seen her once a week since that day when Mr. Winkelheimer first told me I was going to, and now it was almost the end of the year. That's why there's a dance coming up. It's for all the people who graduate and go on to the high school. Xavier is graduating. I don't know if I'm happy or sad about that any more.

But Miss Clairborne just kept looking at me as all these things raced around my head like the greyhounds at the racing tracks, except with the greyhounds once they get old then their owners don't want them anymore and they get killed if they don't get adopted. But Miss Clairborne just looked at me today, and then she said very softly,

"Luke, I want you to tell me about the voice in your head."

"Okay," I said. "There isn't one."

She looked at me very intensely then. "Really, Luke? Is that the truth?"

I looked down. I mean, I believe in being honest and all, but I wasn't sure that I wanted to talk about this. I mean, it's just not something that I talk to people about, unless it's people like Peter Gray, who I know won't tell anyone at all even if it makes them paint weird pictures with black paint and red slashes. And Daddy had told me specifically NOT to talk to Miss Clairborne about the voice in my head because he said she would say I was crazy and that would make him look bad and it would make me look bad too so I shouldn't do it, I shouldn't say anything at all about it. But I wish I could tell Miss Clairborne about my voice. Sometimes it scares me very badly. It is starting to more now, now that I'm thinking so much about Xavier and going to the dance and I'm glad Kerri said I should ask him because now I am very excited to go and Kerri always knows about things like this. She always, always knows.

"Yes," I said, and I looked down again because Daddy told me that even if it is there, it doesn't mean that I'm crazy and that Miss Clairborne is supposed to talk to crazy people. Daddy called her a shrink. I wonder if they are called that because they shrink your problems so you can think about other things. But Daddy was very upset when I said I liked Miss Clairborne and that I was supposed to keep seeing her until I graduated or until the voice went away and I don't think it's going to because like Peter Gray said it is a part of me but I want to know why it is there because I hate it, I hate it I hate it I hate it and it makes me cry and. . .

"Luke," Miss Clairborne said again very softly. "I thought we were friends now. You can tell me."

I swallowed. "No, Miss Clairborne," I said, "I can't."

She was very nice and offered me candy and another book about a dog that she said I would like called Old Yeller but I said no, I could not tell her about the voice, because the voice didn't exist. She then asked me why I talked out in class so much if there was no voice and I was just quiet and sat there shaking my head. I was thinking about telling her I didn't know what she was talking about, but that would be a lie and I hate lies and I especially won't tell them to nice people like Miss Clairborne. I remember when I used to hate Miss Clairborne because I thought she was disorganized, but she is very pretty now. She let me do her hair one day back when we didn't talk about things going on in my life, like my grades and even about Xavier. I told her about Xavier, I did, about how he's taking me to the dance but not about any of the mean stuff he's done to me before I asked him to the dance, and she says he sounds like a nice boy and that she is very glad I have found someone who makes me happy. I didn't tell her about Peter Gray, though, but he makes me happy too. But not like Xavier. And besides, I don't want to talk to Miss Clairborne about Peter Gray, because then I might tell her that he started the fire in Xavier's locker. Not because I would mean to, but because Miss Clairborne is a very smart woman, and sometimes I tell her things I don't mean to. That's how she found out about Xavier anyway, and I can't even remember how she did it but suddenly I wasn't talking to her about dogs and adventures anymore, but I was telling her about Xavier and how I was starting to feel funny around him now, and she explained everything to me and that's probably when I started to really like Miss Clairborne, because I've never been able to talk to anyone like I talked to her before, especially about boys.

But she looked very different right now when she realized that I wasn't going to tell her about the voice. Her eyes were glowering at me and her lips were pulled into a tight line of a scowl. She stood up and was very tall, and I couldn't even believe what she said to me. Her voice was rough and scratchy and very, very angry.

Look you little bitch. . .

"Look you little bitch," she said.

I'm going to tell you a story, you bitch. I'm gonna tell you how they stick me in this goddamned fucking janitor's closet and give me fuck ups like you, and I have to sit here for hours and listen to your goddamned

"I'm going to tell you a story, you bitch," she said. "I'm gonna tell you how they stick me in this . . ."

bullshit about boys and grades and how your insignificant life is so goddamned terrible, which you shouldn't even worry your piddly little brain about because you don't matter. You aren't important. . .

". . . aren't important. Did you hear me, Luke?" She was glowering at me, glaring and glaring and glaring and I felt like crying but I also felt very, very angry as well.

Did you hear me, Luke? You're not worth the fucking time I'm even taking to talk to you. You godforsaken ass of a child, just like Mr. Winkelheimer said you were. . .

"You're nothing, Luke. Do you understand me? YOU ARE NOTHING. YOU'RE NOT WORTH THE FUCKING TIME I'M EVEN TAKING TO TALK TO YOU. . ."

Miss Clairborne was now standing very close to me and she was so, so angry except for her eyes. Now that she was close to me I could tell that her eyes were not angry and then I realized what she was doing. She was trying to make me mad so the voice would come out so she could see it, so I would have to acknowledge that it existed, but I couldn't, not even before I realized what she was doing. I was very angry before I realized what she was doing, but I still could not do it, I couldn't, because even then, I was too surprised that the voice knew, that it knew exactly what she was going to say.

Miss Clairborne had stopped yelling and swearing at me now. She had actually started to sweat and her hair was sticking out again like it did before I had fixed it for her and then showed her how to do it. And now she looked scared. Now that she realized it hadn't worked, she looked scared.

"It's okay, Miss Clairborne," I said. "I'm not offended at all. I know what you're doing."

Then she stopped looking scared and just looked surprised. And maybe she looked relieved as well. But the one thing I was glad, really glad for, was that she believed me. She believed every single word I said, because her next words weren't more swear words or even more trying to get me to talk about the voice. The only thing she said was a question, and that question was,

"How?"

That's what she said, that's exactly what she said, and I still could not say anything because I was just too surprised. I didn't have to though because then the bell rang and I had to leave and I left in a hurry because I didn't want to be there anymore. I picked up my backpack and I left and I didn't even say goodbye.

17.

Peter Gray came up to me at my locker that day after school, but Peter Gray always comes up to me before our bus leaves because I always go to Peter Gray's when school is over. He does not like my house, he says it is too big and too fancy and says he likes his house better. He says he couldn't build fires in my driveway, and my attic is dusty and filled with boxes full of junk and the floorboards creak and are weak and Daddy tells me never to go up there because I might fall through the roof. I thought to tell him I might fall through the floor but didn't because that would be correcting Daddy and that always makes him really, really mad. And Peter Gray's attic is very nice and cozy, and almost like a scene out of a fairy tale book, because there is that big window at the one end that lets in all of the beautiful golden sunshine and there are little motes of dust floating around in the air like specks of gold, and then there is the easel which Peter Gray always paints on. He never made me another picture of me, not like he said he would. He says he likes the black paint.

Peter Gray was acting strange today when he came up to my locker and I knew he had something on his mind, because he kept shuffling around and he wouldn't look at me, not directly, and that's how he acted in the beginning days before we became really good friends.

"Hi, Peter Gray," I said. "What's wrong?"

"Nothing's wrong," he said. "Why would you think something is wrong?"

I knew something was wrong, but I never figured out what it was because then he left my locker all of a sudden and he didn't sit with me on the bus and then when his stop came he got up really fast and raced off, like he didn't want me to follow him, so I stayed where I was until my stop came and then I got off the bus and called him but his mother said that he wasn't feeling well and that he would talk to me in school tomorrow.

I hope he isn't too sick. The dance is only two days away now and I don't want him to miss it. I wonder who Peter Gray asked?

18.

Well now I know that Peter Gray didn't ask anyone to the dance because today he asked me.

He came over to my locker again acting all strange, but this time before I could say anything at all he looked down at his feet and mumbled. I told him I couldn't understand what he said, would he please repeat it, and then his face got pink and he said in a slightly louder voice,

"Luke will you go to the dance with me."

I told him that I was going to the dance and that I would see him there because I didn't want to tell him that I was going with Xavier. But he was very stubborn and he said he wanted to take me as his date and did I want to go, he and his parents could come pick me up and drop us off as the school. I stumbled a bit and just told him that I was very sorry, but that someone else had asked me and that I was going to go with him. I guess that was a lie because I had asked Xavier, but I didn't tell Peter Gray that. I just said someone else had asked me and I didn't really think about it until the words were out of my mouth. Peter Gray just said oh and then he looked at me, and then he asked me who it was and I said that it was just someone from school and that he would see later that night. I don't know why I didn't want Peter Gray to know that I was going with Xavier, and I knew he would figure it out when Xavier and I came in, but I just didn't want to tell him because I was afraid that he would laugh and I am also still afraid that this is one big joke that Xavier is playing on me and I know Peter Gray is smart and that he would tell me so and Peter Gray is like Kerri, he is never wrong except when he says that black painting is me, and thinking about that made me think of something else.

"Peter Gray," I said. "You can go with my friend Kerri if you don't have a date. She wants to go and she doesn't have anyone to go with."

He didn't like that idea at all and he told me so. He said, "I want to go with you." He said, "You're my best friend here." He said, "We should go together." I said I was sorry.

I thought he would back off but he didn't. He said, "Luke, tell me who you're going with." I said, "Peter Gray why do you care." He ignored that and asked me who I was going with again but I shut my mouth tight and I just didn't say anything at all to him. But Peter Gray is smart. He figured it out. Suddenly his face got very red.

"You're going with Xavier, aren't you?" he said very loudly, and if there had been people in the hall they would have stared.

"Peter Gray, we're going to miss the bus," I said. "Come on, let's go."

He grabbed my arm. "I don't care about the goddamned bus, Luke. I don't want you to go with Xavier."

That made me angry, having him grab my arm like that. "Who said I was going with Xavier?" I said as I shook off his hand.

"Well you are."

"So what?"

"So I don't want you to," he said.

I slammed my locker door shut. "Peter Gray, give me one good reason why I shouldn't go with Xavier."

He just stood there and glared at me and I waited, my hands on my hips and part of me actually hoping that Peter Gray would say something because I guess a part of me was still scared about going with Xavier though I don't know why.

"He's an asshole," is what Peter Gray said, but I knew there was more to it. He wasn't looking at me anymore and I knew that he knew something I didn't know.

"Not anymore," I said. "Now he's nice to me. Really, really nice."

Peter Gray kind of mumbled at that and looked at the ground and just kept repeating don't go with him Luke, don't go with him, don't, and at one point he even said please don't go with him Luke and I said what do you know that I don't and he said nothing and then I said he was lying and he said he didn't care just please don't go with him. I wasn't going to stand there anymore and I told him so and then I marched out of the school and he didn't sit with me on the bus that day either and I didn't go to his house that day either. Because I'm going to the dance with Xavier. Kerri is coming over beforehand and she's doing makeup that will make me look pretty and it's going to be really fun and I'm really excited. Nothing can go wrong, because Kerri will be there even if she doesn't have a date and just because this is the first time that I'm going to the dance with a boy doesn't mean anything bad will happen.

19.

Kerri came over to my house right after school and helped me get ready for the dance. I showed her what outfit I was going to wear and she shook her head and I asked what was wrong with it. It was my favorite outfit, a long jean skirt and a pretty pink top with blue flowers on it. Kerri said it looked very middle-schoolish. I said we were in middle school, what was the problem. Kerri sighed and said that Xavier is *graduating* soon, that he's going to the *high school*, and that I should look like a high school girl if I wanted to get maximal results out of the night. I asked her what she meant. She said she had read about it in TeenGirl. I didn't ask Kerri any more questions.

"Close your eyes," she said, and I did, thinking she was going to start putting on my eye shadow, but then she said "Open" and when I did she was holding out an outfit for me that I had never seen before. My mouth dropped open. I didn't even know what to say. Kerri laughed and threw the outfit at me.

"Here," she said. "I got this for you."

I bent over and picked it up off of the floor because I hadn't caught it when she threw it.

"I can't wear this," I said.

"Yes, you can," she said. "I bought it for you. It's a gift."

I swallowed. "No," I said, "I mean, Kerri, I haven't ever worn a dress like this before. It's so tiny."

And it was. I didn't even see how I was going to fit into it, or even how all the straps worked. The dress was black and there were sequins and there was a ruffled skirt but it was very short. Very, very short.

"Oh, shush," Kerri said. "Let me do your makeup, then you can put it on, and then if you don't like it then you don't have to wear it. Okay?"

"Okay," I said. What else was I supposed to say, when Kerri put it like that?

"Close your eyes," she ordered, and I did so and I felt the cool makeup going on my eyes and I smelled that chalky, powdery smell.

"Purse," Kerri ordered, and then the lipstick was gliding smoothly across my lips, coating them in its bright red color. I heard the same snap of the cosmetic bag that I had heard before.

"Now," Kerri said. "Go put on your dress."

I took the dress from her and I went in the bathroom and I closed the door. Then I locked it. Then I got undressed and put the dress on. Then I stared. I didn't even look like me.

There was no way I'd be able to wear this to the dance, ever, ever, ever, ever. I mean, even if I could, there was no way that my daddy would let me out of the house looking like I did. He would say I looked too old for my age, which is what he says about the girls in TeenGirl when Kerri lets me borrow one of hers.

"Let me see," I heard Kerri say.

"No," I said.

Then I didn't have a choice because she opened the door and saw me, and stopped moving and just stared.

"Luke," she said. "You look beautiful. You have to wear that to the dance."

"I can't," I said.

Kerri paused. "I dare you."

I've never turned down a dare in my entire life, not even when I was little and I had to eat a worm or when I was older and I had to steal Mr. Winkelheimer's wig, though I put it back the next day. That dare was harder than this one, because he only took it off once a day and I had to skip class and everything so I could take it. For this dare I just had to wear a little dress; I could always change at the dance. I just had to wear it there. I told Kerri about this.

"Okay," she said.

"And I'll have to wear a coat so my daddy doesn't see."

She nodded her head in agreement, but I didn't really think this was a problem because Missy was here to make sure I was all right and Daddy was in his study doing his work. And Xavier's parents were going to take me to the dance.

I went in my room and Kerri helped me pick out a coat, and then I put it on and then the doorbell rang and it was Kerri's parents to pick her up and take her to the dance. She fluffed my hair out a bit and then she nodded her head in satisfaction and then she was gone. And I was left waiting for the doorbell to ring again, all the while still thinking it was a joke until I heard it go off, and then I finally realized that it wasn't. I was going to the dance with Xavier. I took a deep breath and then I walked down the stairs.

20.

Xavier was standing with his hands in his pockets and slouching when I opened the door, and I took one look at him and stared because he looked really handsome, and he took one look at me and he stared, and we just stood there staring and staring and staring. Finally he said something. He said,

"Hello, beautiful."

I think I probably blushed. Probably, though I hope I didn't. I was so embarrassed I couldn't even say anything at all, and then I looked and saw that his parents were waiting in their car and I said to Xavier they'd probably be mad if we didn't get going, and then he took my arm and, he actually took my arm like they do in the fairytale books, and then he escorted me over to the car and opened the door and I got in and then he got in. It smelled good in the car, like it had just been cleaned.

"Hello," Xavier's mother said. "You must be Luke. I've heard so much about you."

Xavier's mom was a very pretty lady with long brown hair that was very straight and I blushed more when she said it.

"You're embarrassing me," Xavier said to his mom.

"It's nice to meet you," I said to his mom.

"What a charming lady you've picked out, Xav," Xavier's dad said.

"It's very nice to meet you, sir," I said to Xavier's dad.

Xavier just scrunched up into a corner of the seat and I could tell he was very, very embarrassed by his parents, but I liked his parents and besides, it was less awkward talking to them than to Xavier so I talked to them on the whole ride up and it was fun. Xavier kept sneaking glances at me and I kept sneaking glances at him and thinking, wait until he sees the dress and then I was glad that I was wearing it because it made me feel . . .sexy. I thought that because I was having bad thoughts the voice would be very loud and then Xavier's parents wouldn't like me anymore, but the voice was not even there. I was glad.

Xavier hurried out of the car the very second we got to the school, and I thought how weird it was to be going to school this late at night when the sky was so black because there were no stars and only the bright yellow lights on in the building, and there were no bells to tell us when to change classes and no teachers dressed really nicely but it was only us and the gym that was decorated and the loud music blaring and the cookies that were a quarter each to buy. I shook Xavier's parents' hands and then I followed him outside, and it was a very nice night. The air smelled sweet and there was a bit of a breeze and it was so clear even if there weren't stars and then I heard Xavier's parents driving away and he took me by the hand and led me into the school. It was bad when he took my hand, because suddenly I started to feel very, very hot.

We got into the school and the gym and suddenly I wanted to take off my coat and I wanted Xavier to see me in the dress. So I did. He sucked in his breath and just stared and stared and stared, and I just stood there and let him. Then he said, really low,

"You wanna dance?"

I said, "Yes."

Xavier didn't even look around for his friends, and when they came up to him he brushed right by them. He had his eyes locked on my face and I liked it, I liked it so much that I didn't think about anyone but him. The music was very loud and he put his hand on my hip, not on my waist but on my hip, and I put my arms around his neck and we were so close our bodies were almost touching, and I put my chin on his shoulder and just let him hold me like that. I closed my eyes. He said I smelled good.

We didn't even stop touching like that when the slow song stopped and a fast one began, we just danced the exact same way. We were in a corner of the gym and no one bothered us except one teacher who came by and told Xavier to watch his hands and then said we were being inappropriate. Xavier acted all angry and suddenly I wasn't very sure of myself.

"What's wrong, Luke?" he said. I told him I didn't know, and then he said he couldn't hear me and could we go outside of the gym and I said yes and so we went somewhere where it was quiet enough that I could hear him and he could hear me. Then he asked me what was wrong again because he said I looked sad and what was it. I told him I didn't know we were being inappropriate, I told him that I was sorry and were we really being inappropriate? Xavier looked at me and said fuck the teacher, screw him. Then he saw I didn't like that word though he didn't know it was because I hear it in my head so much and so he said, kind of gently, in that really low voice, Luke, don't let that teacher bother you. We weren't doing anything wrong. And I said, weren't we? Then why did the teacher say and he put his hand on my shoulder and looked in my eyes.

"We didn't do anything wrong," he said again.

"But," I said.

"Did you feel like we did anything wrong?"

"No."

I didn't even pause, I just said it because he was looking in my eyes and his hand was on my shoulder and it hadn't felt wrong, being that close to Xavier, it had felt good and I wanted to be closer to him.

"Then don't worry about it," he said. "Stay here, I need a fix."

"A fix of what?" I said.

"A fix of what," he said and laughed. He laughed and walked away. I waited and just stood there and watched him go into the boy's bathroom which was right near where we had been talking. I waited and then he came back, and his eyes were all glazed and far away looking.

"You shouldn't do drugs," I said to Xavier, because I had figured it out.

"I know," Xavier nodded his head, his lazy eyes falling on me. "They're bad. They're really bad for you."

I just stared at him.

"You want a fix, Luke?" he asked me. "I got enough if you want one. It'll help you relax."

"No," I said.

"Relax, babe," he said. "I won't make you."

Then I started to realize that Xavier was going to the high school and he suddenly felt very much older than me because he knew about all these things like drugs and he called me 'babe' like the men on the television did to really pretty women and it made me feel pretty, to have him call me babe, but it also made me feel uncomfortable because I suddenly felt like a little girl, even with my makeup and the pretty dress Kerri bought me, and when I felt like that then I wanted to prove to Xavier I wasn't a little girl, I wanted to make him realize I was a grown up girl even if I wasn't going to the high school.

"Xavier. . ." I started.

He held up his hands. "It's cool, doll. You just look so hot tonight, I thought I'd ask."

Then I know I blushed and he saw it and I know he saw it but he didn't say anything. But he did something. He took my chin in his hand and he made me look at him and I started to feel all hot again and I know that he saw that too. But he didn't say anything about that either. All he said was,

"You wanna go outside, Luke?"

I thought about all the people back in the gym and the loud music and how that teacher was there and when I thought about that teacher I just felt even more embarrassed and blushed even harder and didn't say anything.

"Come on," he said. "Let's go for a walk."

He took my arm and I let him. I let him. I let him, I let him, I let him. He took my arm and we went outside and then he took me back behind the school where there are woods, and then he took off my dress which he liked so much and he stuck his thing in me and it hurt, it hurt, it hurt so bad, and even though I was crying he said shut up, shut up, you want it and I just screamed but he put his hand over my mouth so no one could hear me and then when he was done he said don't tell anyone because they'll call you a slut and you were good and I had fun and I said you're an asshole and I was crying, crying, and then I put on my dress but it was torn and I ran away from him and I ran all the way home and locked myself in my room so no one would know, and no one will know.

I hate Xavier. I hate him, I hate him, I hate him. I hate him.

21.

Sometime I fell asleep because the next thing I knew I was waking up because something was crashing into my window. I got up and went over to my window and I looked out and Peter Gray was there beneath my window, with his face very pale in the moonlight and a handful of stones in his hand, and I opened the window and screamed for him to go away and he tried to say something but I slammed the window and then I just sat on my bed, too stunned even to cry. Maybe Peter Gray knew, maybe that's why he told me not to go with Xavier. He'd say I told you so. If that was why he came then I didn't even want to hear him.

I did hear the stones on my window again and then I went over to the window and looked down and he was still there looking up at me but now he looked sad and I knew he wouldn't tell me I told you so, Peter Gray wouldn't, and I opened the window up just a little bit.

"Luke I need to talk to you," he said. No, he shouted it, like he didn't know that if my Daddy heard him he would be really mad and would probably come out and yell at Peter Gray and chase him off our lawn. He didn't know this so I told him and he said I don't care and I said Come up. Then I closed my window and I wiped the tears off my face and I went into the bathroom and I washed off all of my makeup and I went back in my room and took off the dress and bunched it into a ball and threw it in the corner and then I put on my pajamas and sat on my bed and waited for Peter Gray to come up.

My door opened and then he was there, but when I saw him I didn't cry like I was afraid I was going to. Peter Gray's face was very white and he looked very sad and very scared, and he looked very thin, like he was a ghost. He said are you okay. I said, Peter Gray, I need you to build me a fire. He came over to me and took my hand and he didn't say anything and we crept out of my house very quietly so no one would hear us and we went over to his house and he took me back behind the white building to the patio and then he built the biggest fire I've ever seen and I watched the black dress burn and Peter Gray held my hand and didn't say anything.

22.

Summer's beginning now and I'm going away to camp for the whole time, so I won't get to see Peter Gray at all. I said goodbye to him and he looked awkward and said goodbye and then I said I'd write letters to him if that was okay and he said it was, and that he'd be thinking of me and that he'd show me all his new paintings when I got back from camp. I said okay. Then he went to his house and I went to mine and the next day Daddy drove me to my camp and dropped me off. I didn't give Daddy a hug and I just watched him go away. Something about me just feels different. So different. Everything. Is. Different.

I just watched him go away like I watched Peter Gray go away and I just have all these thoughts in my head and everything is changing. Changing, changing, like the seasons, like the leaves on the trees change color. Now the leaves are all green, at the camp where I am. And when the leaves change colors, I'll be back in school.

I'll be in eighth grade this year.

23.

Peter Gray was very mad at me. As soon as I got back I raced over to his house and when he came out I threw my arms around his neck and hugged him hard. He looked like a tomato, his face got so red. He spluttered and then turned away from me and asked me if I had gotten his letters. I said I had.

"Then why didn't you write to me," he said.

I told him that I didn't have time, because at camp there were all kinds of things to do and I was tired at the end of the day and that's what I told him, because I was too ashamed to tell him I had forgot and that I hadn't thought about it. He seemed to know though, because I don't think he was really that upset that I hadn't written to him. I didn't want to hurt his feelings, so I tried to change the topic.

"How was your summer?" I asked him.

"What do you care?" he said. "If you cared you would have written."

"Peter Gray," I said angrily. "Don't you even want to know about my summer?"

"No," he said. "I wanted you to write to me."

Then he turned around and walked inside, like that would have finished it. I marched in right after him. He was in the kitchen, and he looked at me surprised. I just ignored that look and acted like he had invited me in, because I've been over to Peter Gray's house so much that it feels like a second home to me.

"Well it was lovely," I said. "I had a lovely time and I met lovely people and I met a boy as well, but you probably don't want to hear about him."

Peter Gray dropped his glass when he heard I had met a boy, and then his face got red again and he turned away from me again.

"No," he said. "I don't."

That's when I wanted to kill him. *To bash his head against the counter, to take that knife he was buttering his bread with and slice it across his goddamn grinning face, to fuck him so hard he had to listen to me . . .*

"Well I'll tell you anyway," I said, and when he looked at me he started frowning. Maybe he saw something in my face. "I had a good time. We went rock-climbing and kayaking and I got to do arts and crafts stuff as well . . ."

Stop looking at me like that you goddamn freak. Why the fuck are you so mad anyway Peter Gray? What the hell is your problem, you haven't seen me for the whole summer and now you gonna pull shit like this on me, give me the cold shoulder you motherfucking dickhead.

"And the guy I met," I said. "His name was Jack. He taught me how to get through the obstacle course as fast as . . ."

"I don't care!" Peter Gray screamed suddenly, slamming his orange juice glass down on the table so hard that all of the pulpy stuff sloshed over the top. "I don't care, Luke! Can't you see I don't care?"

His face was purple now and he was very angry but he also looked like he was going to cry, and then he picked up the glass and he threw it at me. I ducked and it slammed against the back wall and shattered into a million pieces, shards of glass raining down onto the ground. Some of the anger left Peter Gray's face as he looked at me, and then he just turned around and ran up the stairs and I could hear his door slam. I just stood there in the kitchen with the sunlight streaming in through the windows in golden streams and hitting me, and everything around me was neat and put in place and clean except for the glass that had been broken.

I could have followed Peter Gray up to his room and tried to patch things up, but I was too fucking angry. I crossed the kitchen to the storage closet. I got out a broom and a dustpan and I cleaned up the glass and I put all the little shards in a plastic bag and tied it up so that Peter Gray's nice mother wouldn't cut herself if she went and reached in the garbage can for some reason. Then I put the plastic bag in the garbage can, then thought that if Peter Gray's mother did go in the garbage can then she might wonder what it was and if she wondered then maybe she'd open the bag and if she opened the bag then Peter Gray might be in trouble. So I took the plastic bag out of the garbage can and I decided to take it with me to my house because even if Daddy finds it he won't ask me about it. Daddy is strange these days. We don't talk anymore, even though we didn't talk before. He won't even look at me much if he thinks I'm looking, but if he thinks I'm not looking then I always find him watching me with this hypnotized look on his face, like he's thinking but he's very far away. Then I go to my room because that look scares me and I always hear the door to his study slam after that.

I finished cleaning up the glass and then I stood in the sun streamed kitchen and I just looked at the stairs where Peter Gray had run up.

"Fuck you, Peter Gray," I said.

I didn't yell. I whispered. He didn't hear me. I don't think I wanted him to. But I wanted to say it nonetheless. So I did. Then I went home.

I wonder if Mrs. Gray realizes that there's a glass missing from her cupboard. And if she does, I wonder if she wonders why.

24.

I still get up at the same time because I'm still at the middle school, which is lovely. I still ride the same yellow bus to school. So does Peter Gray. I still sit in the same seat, I still have the same homeroom. I still see Miss Honeydew every day in homeroom. I still see Miss Clairborne every week behind her big blue door. Everything is the same. Everything is different.

Peter Gray's stop is before mine on the bus route, and he was already sitting there when I got on the bus. I went straight to him even though I was still angry with him. But when I got there he didn't even look at me, and then my anger was gone and I was actually afraid. Afraid he wouldn't let me sit with him. I even started trembling a little bit. I just stood there trembling and looking at him and was afraid he wouldn't let me sit with him and I almost went by him to sit with someone else but then he looked at me for the briefest second before he pressed his forehead against the window again, and so I took that as a sign that at least he didn't hate me and I sat down but I didn't say anything to him. I looked out the window to see what he was staring at, but I don't think he was staring at anything. Peter Gray looks even more pale now, even though he's sunburned from being outside so much. He looks older and his face is longer and he looks different. When the bus got to the school I stood up.

"Have a nice day, Peter Gray," I said, and my voice was all wavering and cracked and I rushed off the bus before he could say anything to me, but I saw him turn his head and look at me and I felt like he was watching me until I got off the bus. I went to homeroom, then I went to my new locker. Eighth graders don't have partners. I get the whole locker to myself this year. Miss Honeydew seemed different as well. She seemed more disorganized. She seemed meaner.

"Good morning, Lucy," she said when I walked into the room. She wouldn't have said anything, except I went directly up to her desk and said Good Morning.

"It's Luke," I said.

Miss Honeydew wrinkled up her nose when I said that. "Sit down," she said.

I sat down. This year, though, I sat down in the first row and I stared at her, without blinking. She hated it, I could tell. But she seemed so different. She did not seem like the person I had known at all. And she knew I knew it. Something about me must have seemed different, as well, because before she had never looked at me, and now she kept sending me little brief glances like she was afraid of me. Peter Gray knew something was up as well. When he came in he took one look at me, staring at Miss Honeydew, and his face got all pensive, and then he sat down beside me and started staring at Miss Honeydew as well. She took one look at us just sitting there, staring, and she knew that something would happen, though she knew as little as we did what that something would be. Peter Gray and I felt it, and it kind of reconciled us, whatever it was, because when the bell rang he turned and looked at me.

"Hey, Luke Orange," he said.

"Hello, Peter Gray," I said.

He didn't apologize, but he didn't need to.

25.

    I eventually told Miss Clairborne about the voice that I still hear in my head. I didn't originally intend to; it just sort of happened. It happened because I was angry at my dad, and because I was angry at him I wanted to do something that would make him angry. I didn't know what to do. He's never around so I couldn't do something annoying like make buzzing bee noises or sing really loudly. And I didn't have the guts to do something like steal stuff out of his medical bag or slit the tire of his car so he couldn't get to work. That's what the voice said to do. But I didn't listen.

    One day though I just couldn't help it. I felt so strange. Nothing seems like it used to be before, everyone is so different and I wonder if it's because they all changed while I was at camp or if it's because they were always that way and now I just see them more clearly. But my dad came in and took one look at me and I just got angry because I had cooked dinner and he said it was bad and I almost threw the plate at him. But I stopped, and I didn't do it, and it's a really good thing because if I had I would have been in a heap load of trouble. I just took ten deep breaths, which is what they told us to do in the guidance class we have to take if we want to graduate and go to the high school, and when he closed the door to go to his study I stopped myself from hurling the plates at the closed door, but only by a little bit. The voice was really bad after that and I was angry, so when I went to school the next day and Miss Clairborne looked at me and asked very nonchalantly if everything was all right, I just started crying and I told her everything. She patted me on the back, but she didn't tell me it would all be all right. I don't think I would ever have trusted her again if she had. I mean, psychologists can't know everything will be all right, and if they don't know, then why would they tell someone that it will be? I thought the reason that principals like Mr. Winkelheimer assign people like me to people like Miss Clairborne is to help us figure everything out, not to tell us lies that will make everything even more muddled.

    She didn't tell me it would be all right, but she asked me what the voice had been saying to me and how it had made me feel, and did I ever do what the voice told me to. I blew my nose into the Kleenex she had given me.

    "No," I said. "I don't do what the voice tells me to."

    She looked at me and her eyes were very dark and very big and very serious. "Why not, Luke?"

    "Because it scares me," I said.

    Miss Clairborne looked very pensive and then she said, "Have you *ever* done anything the voice told you to do?"

    I thought and shook my head, then paused. "Well, once I did."

    "And what did you do, Luke?"

    I hesitated even more then because I couldn't tell her what I did if I didn't tell her anything else about the person I did it to.

    "I said 'fuck you,'" I whispered. "Because the voice wanted me to do more but that's all I could do."

    "Who did you say that to, Luke?"

    So then I had to explain to her about Peter Gray, and she wanted to know all about him, and the bell rang long before I was even able to tell her all that much.

That was okay, though, because I didn't want to tell her more. Miss Clairborne still seemed like she was listening to me, but now she also seemed troubled as well. She asked if my dad knew about the voice, then looked even more troubled when I had told her that I wasn't supposed to talk to her about it at all. She said it was unhealthy. Then she asked how I felt about taking medicine.

"How do you feel about taking medication, Luke?" she said.

"I'm not crazy," I said. "Only crazy people take medication when they come talk to people. I'm not crazy, Miss Clairborne."

"I know, Luke," she said very kindly. "I still think it would be a good idea, though. I'm going to talk to your father about it, but don't worry, I won't get you in trouble."

She talked to my father and I guess he agreed to it because I started taking the medication. I didn't understand it at first, because I have gotten so much better about not talking out. I haven't at all since last year, not one single time. Then I realized it was probably because I told her that when I had stopped responding to the voice out loud, then I had wanted to start hurting myself. I guess that's what they mean when they say hatred turned inward.

26.

Peter Gray was very upset when he found out I was on medication for hearing the voice.

"What the hell are you on that shit for?" he asked me.

"They told me I needed it," I said. "Don't swear."

"I'll fucking swear if I want to," he said. "You're too smart to be on shit like that, Luke. It's going to dumb you down and that's all."

"It's just supposed to help the voice go away, Peter," I said. "It's not going to make me dumb at all."

"Do you know that?" he said. "Fuck them, Luke. You don't need it."

"I need the voice to go away," I said.

"Why?" he said.

"Because it's scary," I said. "It tells me all kind of things I don't want to do or even want to know about."

"Well maybe it's something you need to hear," Peter said. "Maybe you need to hear it for a reason." He paused for a moment. "Maybe, Luke," he said, and his voice was very quiet. "Maybe you shouldn't try to hide from it. Maybe..."

His voice got even quieter. "Maybe you should listen to it."

I sat up straighter. "Listen to it, Peter? Are you crazy?"

He looked at me and his eyes were burning into mine. I felt myself go warm and felt my mouth go dry.

I don't know when I stopped taking the medication, but it wasn't too long after that.

LUKE 2:5.

I was scared at first, to listen to the voice. At first, I even fought it. But one day I snapped.

I was sitting in Miss Honeydew's class. I have her for my English class now and we were going over creative writing. I don't know when I decided that someday I want to be a writer, but sometime between seventh and eighth grade I started writing and I started to realize how good I could write if I actually tried. Peter told me to drop out of school and write, but I didn't think I was *that* good and I wanted to see what high school was like...

I turned in my first creative story and I got a C. I asked Miss Honeydew about it, but she turned up her nose at me and told me to try harder, and maybe I would improve. I got a B on the next paper, and I knew I deserved an A. But Miss Honeydew said I could do better. So I pushed myself harder, and the last paper I turned in, I wrote when I was in a trance. I let the voice write it. I let everything I had out onto the paper, and I didn't even realize I wrote it. I remember sitting at my desk, and then I remember picking up my head and the pencil was clamped in my hand and there were ten sheets of paper in front of me, crammed with this spiky cursive handwriting I didn't even recognize. But I had written it. I turned it in and waited for Miss Honeydew to turn it back.

The day came and I watched. I watched as she walked down every single row with a prissy little pout on her lips, and I watched as she praised the top student. But she didn't give me back my paper. She didn't look at me. She walked by me, her lime green high-heeled shoes clicking on the floor as she sashayed by me. At the end of class I went up to her desk.

"Miss Honeydew," I said, putting my hand on her desk and leaning against it. "You didn't give me back my paper."

She hesitated, then took off her horn-rimmed glasses with one hand and rubbed her temples. "I need to talk to you about your paper, Luke."

"What about it?" I said, and my voice was defensive... and angry.

She looked at me, and she no longer looked like the beautiful teacher I remembered from seventh grade. Now she looked fat, ugly, like a fish blown up with air.

"Are you still seeing Miss Clairborne, Luke?"

"What does that have to do with my paper?" I asked.

"You should not even know about what you wrote about," Miss Honeydew said. "You are a seriously disturbed girl, and I am very worried about you. Such graphic and grotesque violence at your age . . ."

"Miss Honeydew," I said, and my voice was very quiet. "You told us to write a story about whatever we wanted. You said to make our readers feel what we were writing about, to see if we could bring out emotion with just our paper, our pencils, and our ideas. You told us to be daring. You challenged us to push ourselves. That is exactly what I did."

"No, Luke," she said, and she sounded extremely angry. "Your writing does not aim to make people feel. . . it aims to make them go insane. Your speaker manipulates the reader in a way that is not even ethical. I'm going to have to ask you to rewrite the paper, with a more appropriate topic and writing style for a girl your age."

"That's the most asinine thing I have ever heard," I said, and the voice didn't sound like mine but it was mine. It was mine, and it was cool, calm, and completely under control. "I refuse to rewrite the story, Miss Honeydew. If it made you feel that strongly, then it did exactly what it was supposed to do."

"Then I have to fail you, Luke," she said.

I stared at her. "I wouldn't," I said. "I really, really wouldn't do that, Miss Honeydew."

She positively glared at me. "What will you do about it, Luke? You are a student. I might not have been here for a long time, but I have connections, and nothing you ever say will damage my reputation. . ."

"My story is good," I said. Calmly. "I wouldn't fail me."

"But you aren't me," she said, and her voice was slightly hysterical. "And your story is not good. . . it . . . is . . . garbage."

She seized my paper with one hand, her long red nails striking against the black ink and the white background, strangely devoid of red correction marks, and she rent my paper in two. Then she clawed at the halves, ripping, shredding, destroying.

"It is garbage," she said, her voice rising as her hands ripped the paper. "You will rewrite it. I will not accept this. I will not. I will not. . ."

I watched her panting and ripping and speaking to herself. My eyes fell on every violated scrap of paper that fluttered like a broken winged bird to the ground, and my story lay at my feet– destroyed, ruined, meaningless fragments of words that my voice had written. Then I looked at her. When I looked at her, I wanted to hit her. I wanted to bash her skull in against the blackboard, have her blood streak the dark slate surface in gory streaks of darker ebony. Maybe I would have listened to the voice. Maybe I would have attacked her. But she was so damned weak. I looked at her and she shrunk away from me.

"Stay away from me, Luke," she said, and she backed up.

I stood, staring at her, and then I made my face go blank. I stooped and scooped up the little fragments of paper tenderly: they were still my words, they were still my work, and even if they were torn apart, they could be put back together again. I held them together, and then I stepped closer to her.

"Listen to me, you fucker," I said. "I don't know who the hell you think you are. I don't give a damn if you don't like me. I don't give a damn if you turn up your prissy little nose at me every single goddamned day I have to sit in this stuffy hell hole of a classroom. But don't you ever destroy my writing again. You're a teacher. Get over whatever fucking problems you have and at least be fair. What I wrote was good, and you know it. Grow up, Miss Honeydew."

She glared at me, but she also got very, very pale. Maybe that's why I went further.

"I'm not rewriting my paper," I said. "What grade did I get?"

She didn't answer me. Her eyes were trained on my hands, and I suddenly realized she was afraid I was going to hit her.

"I don't appreciate your attitude, Lucilla," she said quietly, but her voice trembled. "You are a rotten student and a rotten child and. . ."

"What is my grade, Miss Honeydew?" I said. The words were mine. The voice was not.

"A," she said. "A. It was excellent. Get the hell out of here."

I left. We moved on to Shakespeare the next class period, even though the creative writing unit was supposed to last for another week.

That was the first time I listened to what the voice told me to do. And as I did what it told me to do, it got softer. Life became easier for a while, but that was only because I still restrained the voice. A bit.

27.

Peter Gray asked me to be his girlfriend in March of that year and I said no. I told him he was my best friend, and he blushed and said that was a good thing, because it wouldn't be awkward. He said he liked talking to me and I was the only girl he could talk to, and that he really liked me and felt comfortable around me. He said that his mom had said friendship was important in a relationship and it was better to be friends first. I asked him if asking me out was his idea or his mom's. He blushed beet red and told me not to be an ass, it was his idea and did that change things. I told him no again. He asked if I would come over to his house after school so he could paint my portrait. He said he remembered I had always wanted it painted. I said yes.

I hadn't been to Peter Gray's house much since seventh grade ended, and maybe it was because I learned he liked me *that* way the summer I got back from camp. But I went with him and we sat together on the bus ride there, and he stayed towards the window-seat side and made sure that not one part of his body was touching mine. I thought that was very funny, and several times had to choke back the laughter that threatened to burst forth from my lips. As we stood up to get off the bus, I deliberately turned back and bumped into him.

"Oops," I said. "I'm sorry. I forgot my backpack, Peter."

He blushed like I knew he would and handed it to me, careful our fingers didn't brush. I turned away quickly, suddenly feeling very playful, and breezed out of the bus, shaking my hips slightly as I had seen the models Daddy doesn't like do on the catwalk. I heard Peter Gray walking behind me, and his feet sounded like those of a prisoner on his way to execution. Clump, clump, clump. I jumped off the bus and ran to his house in exuberance, elevated by the chilly spring air and gently warm rays of sunlight. I heard his footsteps quicken as he chased after me, but he didn't catch up until I stopped at his house, and then he was puffing like a steam engine as he put a restraining hand on my arm.

"L-luke," he puffed. "What the h-hell do you t-think . . ."

I smiled at him and his breath caught, and I turned and went into his house. Knowing smiling had done that to Peter made me feel beautiful, like a princess, and maybe that's why I did what I did later. I was feeling out of control.

"In your studio?" I asked.

He nodded. "Yeah."

We had started calling the room in the attic Peter's studio, because that was what it had become. There were canvases, some of them sporting masterpieces, some of them half-finished, some of them presenting blank white faces to the world, but canvases stacked all over the room. Peter confided to me his parents never went up into the attic, and he had thrown away all of the junk in boxes by degrees. He said he needed more room for his work, and that the stuff in the boxes impeded his creativity. That's what he said, but I think the truth is just that the junk scared him, and I didn't blame him at all for doing it. Those dusty boxes were creepy.

I pulled over an empty box and sat down as I heard Peter coming up the attic stairs, then struck a ridiculous pose. He did not laugh.

"Luke, be serious," he said. As he went about picking out his brushes and paints and canvas, I saw he was in artist mode. His eyes were dark and pensive and he moved rigidly, like an automaton going about a routine. It chilled me and made me feel helpless, the way his eyes looked at me so coldly. I smiled flippantly, trying to stay in control, and the box I was sitting on caved in and I fell, sprawling comically on the ground.

"Oops," I said.

He threw his paintbrush at me, and his voice was very, very angry. "Do you want me to paint you or not?"

"Yes," I said in a small voice as I got up and uprighted the crushed brown box. "I'm sorry."

He sighed, stooped and retrieved the abandoned paintbrush, and then gestured with it at the rug in front of the easel.

"You can sit there," he said.

I brushed off the dust from my skirt and then went to sit on the rug, folding my legs under me, not feeling playful or seductive any more. He looked at me with a critical eye, then squeezed some of the acrylic paint onto his pallette. It landed with a plop as it squeezed smoothly out of the tube. I couldn't see the color; the easel blocked everything except Peter Gray's eyes, the eyes that appraised me. I hoped he hadn't chosen black.

The attic room was so quiet, his eyes so cold, and I looked around the room as he painted, trying to divert my own attention. I watched the dust motes floating lazily in the sun that streamed in, I looked at the blank canvases and wondered what they would hold, and I thought about Peter Gray and how he wanted me to be his girlfriend and wondered where we would be when we went to the high school next year, if we would stay friends, what else would change between this year and the next. That made me feel even more helpless and sad and scared, and suddenly I couldn't stand being alone in the room with another person who was devoid of any emotion or feeling. I wanted to put the light back in Peter Gray's eyes, I wanted to see him feeling something. I wanted to scream at him that his cold eyes were killing me, because I couldn't understand his world and I wasn't any more a part of it except as something he wanted to paint. I stood up.

His eyes flickered and darkened immediately, but something about my face made him stay silent, even though he stood up angrily and looked like he was going to hurl not just his paintbrush but the entire canvas at me. I didn't lose any time and I didn't think about what I was doing. Just as smoothly as he transferred paint to that canvas, that's how smoothly I slipped out of my clothes.

I turned my back to Peter and stood in the center of the room and then, very slowly, I unzipped my skirt. It fell with a soft rustle to the ground, letting the cool bare air of the attic lick my naked thighs. Then, I slowly bent and unbuckled my shoes, let them fall from my feet with heavy clunks to the ground, then slowly peeled off my socks so I was standing barefoot on the rug. My breath came short and quick, my heart pounding, and I trained my eyes on the sunlight streaming in through the window. I would not look at Peter Gray until I was done. Behind me he was deadly silent, and I could hear the ticking second hand of my watch. I took it off, and it joined the pile by my feet.

I drew my t-shirt off over my head, and then I paused. I still didn't hear anything, so I continued. My hands were shaking as they gripped my pale white underwear and I stepped out of them, adding them to the pile. I had to take a deep breath, then, as I straightened.

There was only one thing left. I reached behind my back and my hands fumbled for the clasps of my bra, searching, but not finding them. Then I felt Peter Gray behind me. He had moved up to me as silently as a cat, and I stood still, trembling, as his fingers latched onto the clasps and undid them. I felt my bra straps sliding off my shoulders, felt my bra sliding down my stomach and dropping to the ground. I turned around, my face inches from his.

Peter Gray never touched me. I stood stripped before him, shaking and trembling. My eyes locked on his in naked vulnerability, and his eyes never left my face.

"There," he said. "There, on the couch."

I turned away from him and I went over to the second-hand couch behind the rug, the one that Peter Gray had found in someone's trash and hauled up to the attic with the help of a garbage man when his parents weren't home because I had complained there was nowhere to sit in the attic when I came over to talk with him. I laid down, stretched out, and closed my eyes.

"Don't move," he said.

I didn't. I heard Peter Gray shuffle back to the easel, and then I did not hear another sound from him. I suppose he started painting, continued painting, and finished painting. My heart rate gradually slowed, and I fell asleep. When I woke later, I was curled up on the couch in a different position, and I wondered if Peter Gray had moved me or if he had been angry that I moved in my sleep. I couldn't ask him; he was no longer in the room. The sky had darkened considerably and the attic was dark. There was one light sheet covering me, tucked in at the corners so that I was enclosed underneath it like I was in a cocoon. I looked around the attic and then pushed back the sheet, and saw my clothes where I had left them on the floor. I went and picked them up but did not put them on, and walked over to where Peter's easel stood. The painting was still there, and I wanted to see it, so I went over and looked.

There was not even a single figure on the canvas, only a shape. It was a red heart, drawn as shakily and with as rudimentary a form as that of a second-grader's clumsy sketches on Valentine's day. A single red heart.

I put my clothes on and then I left, the attic stairs creaking as I went down them and the door of Peter Gray's house banging shut behind me. I was crying.

28.

He acted like nothing had happened the next day when I went into home room. I slid into my seat beside him in the front row and looked down at the desk in front of me. He was the one who turned to me first.

"Hey," he said.

I said, "I finally got my story back from Miss Honeydew."

"Oh?" he said. "How did you do?"

"I got an A."

"Great!" He grinned. "I said you were good. Good enough to make that bitch give you an A, even."

"Yeah," I said. "I guess so."

"I got a B-," he said. "I can't write worth crap."

"But you can paint," I said. "If you could express yourself in words like you can through your paintings. . . ."

"I guess," he said. "Are you still in love with Miss Honeydew, Luke?"

That was as close as we came to discussing what had happened the day before in the attic. Peter Gray did not seem like he wanted to discuss it, and he didn't bring up asking me to be his girlfriend again, either. I was embarrassed so I let it slide by. I don't think I was ever ashamed, but I was embarrassed. I don't know why I did it, but I don't think I regret doing it, and it was all so complicated and incomprehensible that it was easier to take Peter Gray's escape route, to take the lifeline he had thrown out to me.

"I hate her," I said. "I can't believe I didn't see what she's really like. . . "

Peter Gray snorted as the honey-topped power-hungry semblance of a teacher waltzed into the room and set down a stack of papers with a thud.

"Standardized tests!" she announced with a sickeningly sweet grin. "I hope you all brought your number two pencils, but for those of you who forgot, I have some here. Now let's all get excited for these wonderful assessments which so clearly describe just how much you all don't know, which is why you are in need of professionals like me. Now," she said severely. "Make sure that you do your absolute best on these exams. They will determine whether you can take honors classes in high school which will increase your chances for getting into a good university. No pressure, of course, children. These tests are a very... accurate. . . method of categorizing you to the place where you belong. If you fail, it's your own fault and you will get the remedial work that you need."

Peter Gray rolled his eyes at me as Miss Honeydew briskly handed him an exam booklet. He started to slit open the white adhesive keeping it closed, and she hit him sharply over the head with the remaining stack of papers.

"Do NOT," she said, turning to the class, "do NOT start until I, the designated proctor, tell you that you may."

Peter Gray closed the booklet immediately and folded his hands across it. I took the test exam booklet that Miss Honeydew gave me as if it were the diseased skin of a leper. I hate standardized tests. I never know how to answer the questions and I never have enough time, and I never try because what can a test tell anyway? So when Miss Honeydew told us we could begin, I opened my booklet just like everyone else and obediently set about filling in all of those identical little blue bubbles, but I didn't even care that I skipped most of the math questions and barely finished the verbal section. I turned in my exam booklet just like all the other kids, but I didn't feel any anxiety or guilt. Then I had to go back to my seat because there was still a lot of time left for the people who were actually trying and going over their work. I looked over at Peter Gray and his face was an inch above his paper and his face was dark in thought, his pencil filling in those maddening bubbles at a frantic pace. I pulled out the book I was reading and read for the rest of the class period. Miss Honeydew shot me some nasty looks but there was nothing she could do. I had already turned in my paper so she couldn't accuse me of cheating, and there was nothing in the rules that said reading was prohibited if the test was finished early. So I read and she glared and Peter Gray kept on scribbling in bubbles, until the very end of the exam when Miss Honeydew called "Time!" Then he put his pencil down reluctantly because she snatched the paper away from him. I jumped out of my seat and was out the door in an instant, but I waited for him there until he had packed up his things and come out, looking drained of all energy.

"Hey," he said. "I don't think I did so well on that."

"Whatever," I said. "It's not like it counts for anything."

Peter Gray dropped his head and was quiet for a moment, then looked at me in utter defeat. "I guess you did well. You got done so fast."

"Yeah," I snorted. "Because I didn't try. Peter, they don't mean anything at all."

"HOW CAN YOU SAY THAT?" he yelled, and slammed his notebook against the locker nearest us. I looked at him in surprise.

"Of course they matter, Luke, don't you know that?" Peter Gray said in a slightly calmer, but still hysterical, voice. "These ones in particular matter. The high school is going to look at them to see which classes we should take next year."

"So?" I said, the realization that had hit Peter Gray before the exams began not yet dawning on me. "I don't see what the big deal is."

Peter Gray drew in a deep breath. "Well, Luke, let me tell you this. There are honors courses at the high school. Honors English courses. Ones that will help you be a better writer... and those tests we just took are going to determine who gets in from the beginning. That's why they matter."

He walked by me dejectedly, and I turned back to the classroom in horror. The classroom door was closed and the lights turned off. I felt as if Peter Gray's words had smacked me in the stomach.

29.

The rest of the days of eighth grade flew by, and soon it was April and the birds were back in the trees singing and the flowers blooming and emitting their sweet fragrances. The grass was green and the sun was shining, and it was that much harder to sit inside of a classroom and concentrate on learning math or grammar or French. Around mid-May, a student from the high school came to talk about what one could expect at the high school, and to answer any questions about high school life. I listened, and I realized I was nervous. I never thought about how easy it is to go from grade to grade in the junior high. Suddenly, there is this huge gap between eighth grade and ninth grade. In eighth grade you know everyone and everyone respects you: in ninth grade, you are the freshman everyone picks on and tries to trick, you don't know anyone, and you go through your first year of teen angst.

I got into the honors English course, even though my grades on the standardized tests did not merit it, because I petitioned and sent writing samples and got them back with marks saying they were impressive. So Peter Gray and I are going to be in at least one course together, and that comes as a huge relief. At least I will know someone. But at the same time, I'm starting to become more wary of Peter. He's stopped asking me to be his girlfriend, but I can tell by the way he looks at me that he still thinks about it a lot. It seems like now more than ever all we do when we're together is yell. Peter Gray gets upset over the most trivial things. Yesterday I said he looked like a ghost– being so pale with his silver-blond hair– and he blushed bright red and wouldn't talk to me. I told him he needs to go exercise more, to get outdoors and away from his painting and reading all the time and he yelled at me and told me to stop worrying so much about his fucking life.

But I yell at him too. Sometimes I have a reason, and sometimes I just do it to be mean to him. Yesterday he was reading one of my short stories, sitting there without saying anything with his eyes pensive and dark as he pored over the pages. He was quiet and wasn't doing anything, but I suddenly wanted to hurt him.

"Peter Gray," I said. "Why are you such a bastard?"

He looked up from the page he was reading and he looked dazed. "What?"

"Why the hell are you so weird? You light fires and stay inside all day..." I should have stopped, but I didn't. "And you look at dirty magazines and talk about girls to seem more like a man but you have no guts whatsoever and you wouldn't even know what to do if a girl offered herself to you."

He looked at me, clearly stunned and hurt, which is what I had wanted. I don't think he knew that I knew about the magazines, but one day when he was painting me I looked under the couch I was sitting on and I found one. I hadn't mentioned it because I was embarrassed and if I was then he had to be, but I hadn't expected that of Peter Gray and so I started paying more attention to him, and that was when I heard him talking to some other males of our class about girls and what girls liked and what they would do to girls if they could. Hearing them talk about girls like that made me wonder if that's what Peter Gray thinks about me, when he looks at me the way he does, and it made me more curious than anything. But it made me angry too, especially when those guys started talking about me and Peter Gray didn't say anything in my defense, and maybe that's why I wanted to hurt him so much.

"I would too," he said lamely.

"Oh yeah?" I said. "Why don't you show me?"

"Fuck off, Luke," he said, and looked down at my story again. "I don't need your sarcasm. I'm trying to read, and it's hard enough as it is. Why do you always write about fucking and romance? This is so boring I can hardly keep my eyes on it."

"Well you're only bored because you don't know anything about romance," I yelled at him. "And I'm not kidding. Kiss me if you're such a man."

"What?" He looked up at me.

"How come you didn't deny what those guys were saying about me?" I said in what I hoped was an angry voice. "I heard them talking, and they said I was your sex toy and you didn't say anything."

The paper fell out of his hand then. "When did you hear them say that?"

"Oh, why does it matter?" I said. "You're such a bastard, Peter Gray. You wouldn't even know what to do if I asked you..."

"I would," he said quietly.

"You're not normal!" I shouted. "I was fucking naked and you didn't do anything! What kind of a . . ."

Peter Gray stood up and came over to me, and then he took my head in between his hands and I felt my heart flutter. Then he shook me.

"Shut up, Luke," he said. "Shut up."

I stumbled over a chair and fell onto the floor, and then sat there glaring at him. He was glowering at me, and fire shot between our eyes as I picked myself up. He shifted.

"Are you all right?" he asked gruffly.

"Don't you fucking come near me!" I screamed at him. "How dare you! How *dare* you!"

He came over to me, the anger gone from his face, and put a hand on my shoulder. "Luke, I'm . . ."

I punched him, hard, in the stomach, and he doubled over, his face white with pain and surprise. I stood staring at him, my hands on my hips, as he straightened.

"What the hell did you do that for?" he asked me. "I barely even touched you. . . ."

"I don't care," I said. "I felt like it. Don't you ever treat me that way again, you hear me, Peter Gray? Besides, I'm a girl, that shouldn't even have hurt you."

"Some girl," he said, and he turned away from me so I couldn't see his face. He bent down and picked up my story, then sat back down on the chair he had been sitting on and started reading again. I strode over to him and ripped the story out of his hands.

"Don't bother," I said. "If all you're going to do is say it's stupid romance, then don't even waste your fucking time."

I turned to leave and got halfway to the door.

"Luke."

"What?" I spun around angrily.

Peter Gray's face was a mask. "It was just starting to get good."

I flung the story back at him, watching as the stapled pages fluttered like the wings of a white butterfly, then stormed out of his house.

30.

I started going by Lucillia, my actual name, when I got to the ninth grade. I thought it would make me sound more elegant and mature, and in so doing would make me less of a target for the older students. But I was wrong. So wrong.

I walked into the building on the first day of class, and instantly felt as if someone had sliced away the carcass of my skin, leaving my nerves naked and open to every jangling bell, every raucous scream of people laughing and going by. Crowds of people in the *couloirs*, pushing by me with the deriding smirks on their faces announcing they knew I was a freshman, and that I was something to be walked over and ignored or cozened and taken advantage of. I don't remember much of that first week. Everything went by in a blur. But I do remember the first person who talked to me. He came up to me, stood by my locker, waited by quietly until I closed the locker door and saw him.

"Hello, Lucy," he said. "How was your summer?"

The person I was looking at was tall, lean and muscular. His eyes burned intensely into mine, and his bronze tan lit the rest of his face. His hair flashed in a golden, disheveled sweep away from his high forehead, and I felt my heart lurch into my throat.

It was Peter Gray. I stood looking at him, speechless and not able to say anything. He helped me.

"Would you like to come over to my house after school?" he asked, as if nothing had changed.

I unlocked my mouth. I said yes.

31.

Not much had changed about Peter Gray except his appearance. He was still quirky, crazy, sensitive, moody. Still as frustrating as hell. But now instead of getting angry, I found that I was feeling something very different, if not as intense and incomprehensible. Because now that Peter Gray was attractive, so were his qualities. I thought about how shallow I was.

The sun was smiling down at us as we walked the block from the high school to his house, the sky azure blue and the clouds bounding across the sky like fleecy sheep. He was humming a little bit as he walked, and I asked him why.

"Camp," he said.

"Camp?"

"Yes," he said, nodding his head and sending the sun's beams glinting off his hair like molten gold. "I remember how much fun you said you had at camp last year, so I convinced my parents to let me go. And my little sister was coming, so my parents were glad enough to get me out of the house."

"You have a little sister now, Peter?" I asked, trying not to keep staring at him.

He nodded, scuffed the pavement with one toe of his new shoes. White shoes. "Yeah. Her name is Magdalena. Magdalena Gray. Isn't that pretty?"

I agreed that it was, then asked him about camp. What had happened at camp that had put him into such a good mood? His eyes lit up though they were centered on the cracks in the cement of the sidewalk, the ones where obdurate snatches of weeds stick up. Peter kept his eyes on the ground and sent a huge boulder of a stone skidding away from us.

"Ashley," he said.

"Ashley," I said, and heard the bitter contempt dripping like acid from my voice. "Who the hell is Ashley, Peter?"

"Ashley is a girl I met at camp," he said. "She's amazing, and I'm in love with her."

I tried to control my emotions. I tried, but I did not succeed.

"What do you mean, you're in love with her, Peter? How do you even know what love is?" I said angrily.

He looked at me and his eyes were hurt. "Don't you even want to hear about her, Luc?" He said it *loose*, like Miss Honeydew had before. I swallowed and turned my eyes away from his as they searched mine. Something about the way he called me Lucy, or Luc, before he even realized that I didn't want to be called Luke anymore because Luke is a boy name. . . something about the way he called me Lucy set something like wildfire racing across my heart.

"Fine," I said, my voice hard and closed. "Tell me about her."

"No. Not if you don't want me to," he said quietly. Now neither of us was looking at the other.

"Fine," I said, my voice more gentle. "Tell me about her, Peter. Please."

I put my hand on his arm and he stopped walking, his eyes lingering on my hand before he raised his eyes and met mine.

"I'm serious, Peter," I said, seeing myself reflected in his eyes that swam like the steely gray sky before a thunderstorm. "I want to know about her. I want to know what kind of girls you like."

He hesitated for a moment, and I removed my hand from his arm. We started walking again, an awkward silence between us for the first time in all the years that I had known Peter Gray. Then he cleared his throat and he started talking to me.

"Her name is Ashley. I don't know her last name." He looked at me defensively. "We never said them at camp."

I didn't remember if I ever knew the boy's last name that I met at camp, but I didn't remember it while Peter Gray was talking to me, and I found to my dismay I could not remember his first name either. I didn't say anything to Peter Gray. He didn't seem like he was even talking to me so much as trying to remember and think things through for himself.

"I met her in a nature class," he said to me or to himself. "And she was so beautiful. She has long blonde hair, and it was let loose and tumbling over her shoulders, like, like. . ." he struggled to find words. I glanced at him.

"Like molten gold," I said softly, and stopped to tear the head off of a dandelion growing by the side of the path.

He nodded. "That's good, Luke. Like molten gold."

I didn't comment on his lapse back to my childish name. I felt like I was going to cry or explode as soon as my mind decided which one it wanted to do.

"And she was so quiet," he said. "She was sitting between two other girls who were her friends, and she was looking at the grass in front of her, this peaceful look on her face as the sun spilled over her. She looked like an angel."

"Uh-huh," I said. "So what happened?"

Peter Gray took a deep breath, and a smile lit up his face. "All of a sudden, her face scrunched up like a rabbit, and she stumbled backwards. She was wearing a skirt so I . . .I . . ." he looked at me solemnly. "I saw her underwear. They were pink."

I threw the dandelion head at him, or what was left of it as I had been shredding it as we walked. "Just tell me what happened..."

He laughed and dodged the dandelion head, and I could tell he was enjoying keeping me in suspense more than I was enjoying being kept in suspense.

"Well," he said, "her face scrunched up and then she yelled, 'a bug!'"

"A bug?" I said. "Did no one tell Ashley there are insects in nature?"

"She said it in a very cute voice." He frowned. "If you're going to be such a sarcastic bitch about it, I won't tell you anymore."

His words should have stung me, but I felt a small glimmer of triumph.

"I'm sure you don't speak to your precious Ashley like that," I said.

His face fell a little when I said that, and his eyes were full of a hurt that was somehow steel hard at the same time. "She's not mine, Luke." He scuffed the ground again. "She belongs only to . . . to herself," he finished lamely.

There was more behind what Peter Gray was telling me. I had written too many stories and described too many scenes just like the one we were having to know that he was not telling me the pure, unadulterated truth. I decided to let him off the hook, this once.

"What did you do after she saw the bug?" I asked Peter Gray.

"I . . . got it away from her," he said. "She told me thank you. Then she asked if there were more bugs where we were going and the camp counselor teaching nature said there were and she grabbed my arm and told me to protect her."

"What a hero," I said sarcastically.

Peter scuffed the ground. "Yeah," he said quietly. "What a hero."

We had gotten to his house, the familiar fence and white block of a house looming quickly into view. Peter unlatched the plank on the outside, held the gate open so I could pass before him.

"Thank you," I said, suddenly wanting to patch things up with Peter Gray. The Peter Gray that I had known hadn't held doors open for girls... or maybe he had and I just didn't notice it. I started up towards the attic, but when Peter didn't follow me I turned around and looked at him quizzically.

"I don't go up there anymore, Luke," he said quietly. "I closed it off."

"Where do you paint, then?"

He did not look at me. "I don't paint anymore."

"What?" I said, genuinely shocked. "But Peter, you love to paint..."

"Not anymore," he said firmly. "Painting is for girls...."

"What the hell are you talking about?" I said incredulously. "What about Da Vinci, Rembrandt, Van Gaugh... in fact, any really famous painter?"

"They are exceptions."

"Like hell they are," I said. "There would be too many exceptions, and you know too much about art and the great artists to say that..."

"Just drop it, Luke."

"Don't be a misogynist, it's not you," I said, feeling like I was talking to a complete stranger. "What the hell is with this new attitude anyway?"

"Let's just go talk in the kitchen like normal people," Peter said, not looking at me.

"Are you all right?"

He looked at me quickly. "Of course, why wouldn't I--"

"Then why are you acting so fucked up?"

The back of his neck reddened, announcing his embarrassment, and he said shortly,

"I am not." He paused. "That sounded childish. But I am not fucked up, Luke."

"Like making it into a complete sentence makes it any less puerile," I said.

"Just shut up with the grammar, Luke."

"Don't tell me to shut up," I said.

"I don't understand why you always have to be like this."

"Like what?" I practically screamed.

"Like this," Peter swept his hand at the air in front of me, as if that would explain anything. "I say one thing and you start screaming. . ."

"If you weren't acting so fucking different...."

"People change," he said, his skin color back to its Apollonian bronze. "I've changed. Please don't shout."

"I'll do whatever the hell I want to."

Peter paused, then looked at me from those steely gray eyes. His tan face might as well have been covered with a thicket of thorns and shadows.

"Luke."

I froze. Something about the way he said my name paralyzed me, and I stared at him with the wide-eyed stare of a child.

"Luke." His eyes, like the pure silver of a newly minted coin, glinted. "Let's go in the kitchen. I want to talk to you. I don't want to shout at you."

I paused for a moment, my temporary anger fading as quickly as it had flared up. I started to follow him.

"Okay," I said as we passed through the hallway by the door. "I can tell you about my summer..."

"I need some advice," was his reply. "About Ashley."

I stopped, frozen, and stared at Peter's back in front of me.

"She's a really pretty girl and I don't want to make a mistake with..."

I didn't say anything. I bit back the angry words before they cracked from my mouth like violent fire sirens, and then because I was in danger of choking on them, I turned to leave the house even as Peter Gray turned around and stared at me.

"Luke? Where are you going?"

"I'm going home," I said. "Have a nice day, Peter."

As I left by way of the main door, I could have sworn I heard Peter laugh.

32.

I woke up twenty minutes late for school the next day, and swearing as I hopped out of bed, threw on the only clothes that I could find, meaning a short gray sweatskirt and a gray tube top, over which I threw a bright yellow coverup. I wound my hair onto my head in a ponytail and bolted out of the door. I had missed Peter Gray, who came each morning to walk with me to the bus stop, and I had missed the bus. I would be walking to school.

At Cedar Creek High, there is an obligatory hour before classes begin called 'homeroom,' where students are supposed to go to see their teachers for extra help or finish their homework from the night before. As I trudged along the streets, I decided I would probably miss homeroom, but not much else if I kept going at the rate I was going. I had an excuse; I could be late. I veered off from the main roads and headed off into the woods that bordered the one side. If I did not get lost, I would still be able to get to the school before the end of the school day, and so would not miss classes.

I cut through the woods and came out at the back of the school about forty-five minutes after I had started out. I went up to the silver guard rail that marks the boundary between where the woods stop and the high school property begins, and clambered over that so I could get to the school. Three guys were leaning against the wall of the building and smoking as I was walking up. They were not allowed to do that. They hadn't seen me, and I altered my path and went a different way before they had a chance to. I smelled what they were smoking, and it wasn't cigarette smoke.

I walked into the school and was instantly pounced on by a teacher and conducted to the late to school office. They actually created an office for such things. That says a lot about the school system I was supposed to be a proud member of. I don't care and I don't like to think about it, I just wanted to fill out the necessary paperwork and get the hell out of the office. It was later than I had thought and I didn't want to miss my first period, which was English. If I missed English there wouldn't even have been a point in me going to school that day at all.

I filled out the stupid form and went down the hall right when the bell rang to let the other students out of the dreaded homeroom. There were so many students in the hall that I didn't even see the signs that were posted up everywhere. I didn't even see them afterwards, when I was walking through the halls alone and there was no real reason I should have missed them. I guess my subconscious blocked them out because I didn't think they would ever apply to me. I didn't notice when people started talking probably for the same reason; it didn't concern me and I didn't have any female friends at the high school who would have definitely brought it to my attention. I probably wouldn't have noticed it even as it came and passed unless it was brought to my attention by Peter Gray.

"Would you go to the dance with me?" he asked later on that week, and in my surprise, I slammed my locker door on my hand and didn't even feel it.

"What about Ashley?" I stuttered.

Peter shrugged. "Ashley's in Georgia."

I stared at him.

"So will you or won't you, Lucy?" he said.

I just stared and stared at him. My face must have been as red as the planet Mars. If there were gods that same one would be in my heart, where it felt like the battle of the century was going on.

"I didn't know there was a dance," I said.

"How could you not?" Peter leaned against my locker, the tinny slate blue metal making his gray eyes that much darker and more mysterious. "There are signs all over the fucking... sorry. All over the school."

That was something about the new Peter Gray. He didn't swear, he said, around the *ladies*. I figured I must be half-lady, half something else, because he still swore around me. When he didn't catch himself.

"I don't know," I said. "Are you going to talk about Ashley the whole fucking night?"

He grinned at me. "Probably."

"You're an asshole, Peter," I said and turned away from him. I felt like I wanted to go into the girls bathroom and cry my eyes out. "Yes, I'll go with you."

He didn't say anything immediately, and when I turned back to him he was looking at me in silence.

"You'll go with me," he repeated. "With... me."

"Of course with you," I said, irritated. "You asked me, didn't you?"

"Gee. Wow." A smile broke across Peter's face. It looked like Phaeton driving Apollo's chariot across the sky right when he lost control, and the sun had escaped and was now dancing across Peter's face. "I mean, I didn't actually think you would."

"You should just be glad I don't have any morals," I grumped. "Considering you have a girlfriend."

Peter Gray just kept grinning and didn't even look like he had heard what I said. He grabbed my hand and crushed it in his, pumping it up and down.

"Gee. Thanks, Luke." He looked and was acting so much like a little boy that it was ridiculous. I mean, we were in *ninth* grade already. I realized I was blushing fiercely.

"So, what, do you want my dad to drive us or something?" I said, turning scarlet.

"No. I'll get us there," Peter grinned at me. "Just you wait and see... everything is going to be so perfect."

He kept grinning at me and then he went away, disappearing down the hall on the way to his next class. I closed my locker and put my forehead against it to cool the burning lump of my blushing forehead, then turned away. Directly across from my locker on the opposite wall was a huge pink sign written on with glittery pen. "Fall Formal" it announced.

Fall Formal
Formal Fall
Fall
Formal
I'm going
with
Peter
Peter Gray
Peter
Peter
Peter...

There were actual leaves plastered onto the poster and someone had drawn in and colored stenciled pumpkins. I went over to the poster, and before I even realized what I was doing, I tore off one of the yellow leaves. It was a really fancy sign, all things considered. Whoever had made it had really gone all out for the dance. I realized right then that so would I.

I went back to my locker and opened it, then stuck the leaf on the inside with one of the magnets that was there before I closed it again. Yellow for hope and sunshine and happiness. I didn't take the red leaf; red is for love, and that was not something I wanted to think about.

33.

The days until the formal literally crawled by. I thought high school was going to be much more exciting, but it wasn't. Freshmen get treated like shit, juniors are too worried about SATS, and then seniors are divided into those who don't care enough and those who care too much about their future. Only the sophomores seem like they get cut a bit of a break, but then there are still classes to deal with and everyone is still in cliques and self-absorbed and complicated. I guess that never really changes with time, though, so maybe it's just something I should get used to.

But then there was the FORMAL. For some reason, my heart always pounded when I thought about it, as if there were a little elf inside my body knocking on the walls of my heart and trying to get out. I didn't know how to approach this dance. I don't know when I fell in love with Peter Gray, or maybe I just thought I was in love with him because he wasn't showing any interest in me besides the fact that I was his best friend. That's usually how it seems to work with me, that I want something, but as soon as I get it, I don't want it any more. There is nothing shallow in that; it's simply being human and being interested by what I don't understand.

I didn't know if I should try to look my best for the formal, and try to get Peter Gray to fall in love with me that way. I pictured the girls in the prom dress books I looked through, just for fun because I could never afford any of the dresses. Those girls were all tan and had their hair piled up in ringlets and curls on their head, and some wore jewels in their hair as well or tiaras. They all had long dangly earrings and silky wraps that matched their dresses and trailed around their arms and down to the floor, all were smiling from behind lip-glossed lips, all were so beautiful. I would see one and think that she was the most beautiful person I had ever seen, then I would turn the glossy page and there would be another one.

It was depressing. I know that some people think I'm really pretty, but I don't see what they do. My hair is still long and straight and lanky. Maybe it's more curly than it used to be, and more glossy as well, and it is definitely longer, but it is still mouse brown and I still have a layer of caramel colored freckles under my hazel eyes. I'm thin because I have a high metabolism, but it is a boyish thinness. I know I'm only in ninth grade, but I still have the body of a little girl. I actually wish for love handles because then I might actually have a little curve to my hips. But I can't change how I was made! It's just that there is no way in Heaven or Hell that I would be able to wear one of those dresses and look good in it. No way at all. I couldn't even hope to seduce Peter with looking beautiful. Besides, he knows me too well. He would think, if I dressed up and looked like one of those Prom models herself, that I looked ridiculous.

But I could also take revenge on Peter at this dance, and it was something I seriously considered doing. I could always show up in the dress I had seen at the thrift store. It was bright orange except for the one place it was stained brown with coffee and the big pink bow on the left hip. There were yards and yards of orange taffeta sticking out at the waist of the dress, making it look like an obscene tutu, and I imagined twirling around on the dance floor in it, hearing the swish of all that taffeta as Peter's face turned as pink as the bow. Get back at him for talking to me about damn Ashley. Sometimes I think I would kill her if I could, but then I hope that I'm not really that messed up as a person. Besides, I don't want Peter to take any pride in a criminal record I might incur. That would be too much like saying I cared about him, too much like a victory for him. I don't know if that approach would bother him, though. Peter isn't like other guys my age. I don't think I've embarrassed him once on all the occasions he should have been embarrassed, and he can't expect me to look pretty anyway. I mean, has he seen me lately, with my freckles and boy body and lanky hair? So maybe trying to show up ugly wouldn't have the effect that I think it will. I mean, if Peter wanted a pretty date, he could definitely have gotten one. He has his own little fan club, and I'm sure that any one of the glitzy girls in our school would have said yes to him. I really don't know why he asked me.

The question of my dress, though, flopped out of my hands, and I let it. My father came home one day from whatever he does at work and called me over to his study, and I went over to him. He had fired the woman who used to take care of me, I can't even remember her name, but he hadn't talked to me any more since she left. There was a dry erase board on our refrigerator and he told me when he fired her that if I ever needed anything– food, clothes, money– I was to write it on the dry erase board and I would get it, but don't you fucking abuse the privilege or I'll get rid of the board. I only wrote on the board three times; once to announce that I had become a vegetarian and needed more fruits and vegetables, once for a hair brush, and once for some money for a little Beta fish I bought at the pet store and named Bruce. Three times, that was all, but each time he had come to my door and asked how much I needed and then given it to me and gone away without any other questions. The dry erase board wasn't there because my father didn't love me; it was there because he was busy and if he was home he was either working or taking a break from working by drinking, and in either case he didn't want to be bothered by me. I didn't really mind, I was happy living on my own, but I did miss whoever that woman was and I almost asked for her on the board once.

But I was in ninth grade, after all, and I shouldn't have needed someone looking after me. But wouldn't it be wonderful if there was another kind of dry erase board, like the one on my refrigerator but magic? And whatever you wrote on it you would get. Love... zap! and a soul mate is in front of you who will never make you hurt and never make you cry. Happiness. zap! No more tears, no more worries, sunny days and blue skies. Peace... zap! I don't even know what peace would be like. Maybe the board would send a white dove that would take you off to a better place. I wouldn't have to ask for friendship. I had Peter, after all.

"Luke," my father said. I was in the kitchen, pouring myself a glass of orange juice from the carton in the fridge. "Come here. I want to talk to you."

I followed him down one of the dim hallways in our house– after our maid left, my father insisted on keeping the lights off or low, to save money and because he says there doesn't need to be a lot of light in the house anyway, just in my room and his study. So I followed him down the hall to his study, which has just a big desk overflowing with papers on it and a bunch of shelves overflowing with encyclopedias and medical journals and pamphlets on bizarre case scenarios. He sat down in the chair behind the desk and I stood because there was no place else to sit unless I wanted to sit on the ground.

"I hear that there is going to be a Fall Formal at your high school," he said without looking at me, propping his head up with his hands. My father looked very old, very tired, all of a sudden.

"Yes, sir," I said.

"Let me tell you something, Luke." He leaned back in his chair, staring me down. "The person who is catering to this dance was my best, and only, friend in college."

This was getting good. My father never talked about when he was young. I didn't think he had the time, or maybe he had just forgotten, but if he said he had a friend then he meant he had a friend who had done him a favor at some time or another. I was curious in spite of myself.

"Who is he?" I pried. "What was he like?"

My father dismissed my questions with a negation of his head. "That is not important. What is important is that his son is going. You will also be going. That is not debatable. I won't be caught looking bad because my daughter is not at this dance." He paused as if he expected me to argue with him. He was ordering me to go to a dance, where there would be cute boys, where there would be music and dancing, where there would be *Peter*. He wasn't an understanding man and I realized that now, because he was looking at me like he actually thought I was going to protest to this command more than I would if ordered to do the dishes or vacuum the living room. When he realized I was not going to protest, he pulled out his wallet. "Now, I understand that dances in high school are a lot different from dances in middle school, more fancy, that the girls get dressed up in expensive gear. While I think this is frivolous, this friend means quite a lot to me and I want to make sure you appear... as beautiful as you can. I'm assuming you don't have anything you can wear to this dance. How much does one of these outrageously priced dresses cost?"

I thought back to the TeenGirls I had been looking through. Colors, styles, glossy smiles and shiny hair flitted through my mind, but I could not remember a single price value. I hadn't been looking. I had thought it would be better to keep

The Dress as an elusive impossibility. I didn't want to know how much out of my reach those dresses were.

"I- I don't know," I mumbled.

He looked at me coolly for a moment, then pulled out a wad of money. "Then I will give you one-hundred and fifty dollars. Make good use of it."

My breath exploded from me in a gust of air. "One hundred and fifty dollars??!!"

That seemed to please him for some reason, because he smiled, the first time I've seen him smile since I remember.

"Your old man is made of money," he said, then turned his face away from me. "It's nothing."

"Thank you," I mumbled.

"You're welcome," he said. "Now, the person's name who you will be going with is Vincent Lombardi. He will be picking you up at eight o'clock on the night of the Formal, and taking you to the high school. He will drop you off here when the dance ends."

My newfound happiness died instantly. I frowned. "How do you know I'm not already going with someone?"

My father scoffed, and when I say scoffed, I mean that he laughed at me. "Because, Luke, the formal is three days away. If you were going, you would have needed money for a dress, and if you needed money, I assume you would have written it on the dry erase board. Furthermore, Vincent does not have a date, and he is set on going to this dance. It is the least I can do to repay my friend for his former kindness and help. You will go to the dance with Vincent, and that is final."

I wanted to cry. I suddenly related much more with Juliet in the play we were reading in English class, I felt how she must have felt when her father demanded she marry Paris or else he would disown her, but when Juliet was already married to Romeo. Maybe Shakespeare actually did know what he was talking about, with the condition of the human heart and all. I opened my mouth to say I was going with Peter, *Peter*, but my father had just given me one hundred and fifty dollars for a dress and he had just smiled at me for the first time in *years* and I was never that good at standing up to him anyway.

"He's driving?" I asked.

"Yes," my father said. "He's going to be a junior and he has his license, so he will be driving you to and from the dance. At first Mr. Lombardi was concerned about the age difference, but I told him that you were a very mature girl for your age and that there should not be a problem."

I swallowed, choking on my uncried tears. "What's Vincent like?"

My father looked at me oddly. "Vincent is a gentleman. I am sure that he will treat you like a lady." Suddenly, with a rare flash of insight, my father actually seemed to see me for a moment. "You don't look happy, Luke. Is something wrong?"

"No," I said.

"Then you will go to the dance with Vincent."

"Yes, sir. If you want me to."

He didn't ask me if *I* wanted to; that would have been beyond his limited power to perceive. But he did still seem puzzled, maybe even mildly concerned. His voice was gentler when he spoke to me, though it was still gruff.

"Luke... you are not to do anything with this boy that you are uncomfortable doing. Is that clear? He doesn't expect you to, and I forbid it. Mr. Lombardi has assured me he is a perfect gentleman. You can always... call, if something is wrong."

"Oh, I'm not worried," I said truthfully. "I can take care of myself."

My father stared at me in the dim light of his study, as if evaluating what I said and who I was for the first time in my fourteen year old life. That's what I felt more than anything else in that moment. My despair over not going with Peter, my anxiety over who Vincent really was, and my gratitude for the money in my hand and my father's permission to go to the formal, all faded in comparison with that one feeling. The feeling of being judged, and for once in my life, not found lacking.

"Very well," my father said with a dismissive nod of his head. "I have work to do. If you need anything else, I expect that I shall see it on the board."

"Y-Yes," I mumbled.

I was already opening the door to his study and on my way out when he stopped me by repeating my name. I turned around hesitantly, my face blank, my mind racing as to what I had done wrong. I suppose that, maybe, I was terrified of my father.

"You're a good girl, Luke," he said, and then his face was buried in his paper work and I was going out of his study and closing the door behind me, and then all of a sudden I started to cry as I went up to my room and closed my door and flopped onto my bed and buried my head in my pillow and started to smother my tears with it, each teardrop falling from my face like a small flame that burned into the pillow's fabric.

There was no way in Heaven or Hell that I could back out, not when my father had called me a good girl and I had his money in my hand. My other question, about how to approach the Formal, was also solved.

I was going to the dance, and I was going to be pretty.

34.

I felt terrible the night my father told me I would be going to the dance with Vincent, but that feeling of bitter anguish and despair was nothing compared to how I felt the day I told Peter Gray I couldn't go to the dance with him. I told him right away, though, so he could get another date for the formal. So when I told him, there were only two days left. When I told him, I kept it simple. I just told him that I couldn't go with him.

He was standing at his locker, getting his books, and he looked up at me. "Is something wrong, Luke?"

"No," I said. "It's just that I'm... I'm going to go with someone else."

Peter froze for a moment and just stared at me, his cold eyes penetrating my face. He stepped back from his locker, then closed it with infinite gentleness. When he saw I wouldn't meet his eyes, he turned his face away from mine and said very softly,

"I see."

I looked at him quickly. "Peter, I just have to go with this other guy."

"I said I see, Luke," he said, softly. "And I do. See."

"No you don't," I said, exasperated. "My father is making me go with this other guy. . ."

Peter could have fed me some line about doing what I wanted, that no one could make me do anything I didn't want to do, but he didn't. Maybe he figured I had already beat myself up, maybe he didn't think about it, or maybe he just didn't care.

"All right," he finally said. "Thank you for telling me, Luke."

Need I say that he had fallen back to calling me by my childhood name, Luke, all the time? Maybe it was just because our friendship was too strong. But right then it was making me feel like he was treating me with a child, a child compared to the cool, tall young man standing beside me and acting with such restraint. If Peter would have broken off a date with me two days before the formal, I would have thrown something or screamed or at least made him feel bad. But I twisted it around, used the two day gap to my advantage.

"You know, Peter, you still have two days," I began hurriedly. "Two days to find someone else. It won't be hard, I think half the girls in our class are already in love with you."

Peter turned and faced me, his tanned face solemn. I pleaded with my eyes for him to believe me, and it shouldn't have been hard because I wasn't lying, most girls in our class really did like Peter. He was mysterious, handsome, and he was a gentleman: there was nothing not to like about him. Sure, he had still remained a little bizarre, but I already *knew* that about him. And I *liked* it about him. Fuck, I *loved* it about him, and it wasn't making it any easier for me to keep standing and staring and having him look at me like that....

"Luke," he said, very quietly. "If I can't go with you, then I'm not going to go with anyone."

He started to turn away but I grabbed his arm. I was afraid he would pull away, but he didn't.

"Peter," I said. "Don't be like that. It sounds all noble and brave, but I don't want you to miss out because of me. I really want you to go, and I really want you to go with a beautiful girl, a really beautiful girl. Please go to the dance with someone. Please."

Only then did a look of disgust cross his face. He shook my hand off.

"I'm not going to ask another girl out, Luke," he said. "But it has nothing to do with you. I'm thinking about Ashley. I mean, I love the girl, and I never should have asked you to the dance anyway, not when she is constantly on my mind. I just thought I would ask you because you are my friend and you understand I'm crazy about Ashley. That's why I can't ask another girl. I thought you, of all people, would understand that."

DAMN Ashley! I wanted to burst into tears, partly because he liked her more than me and partly because I was a fool to think that he actually liked me. Hadn't I wondered since he asked me why he asked me? It wasn't because I was pretty or because he secretly liked me, it was because I was his *friend*, his girl*friend*, and his going with me to a dance would not jeopardize his relationship with the beautiful *Ashley*.

"Oh," I said, shaking. "Oh, right. Well, I'm sorry, Peter."

"You aren't angry, are you?" he asked me, an intriguing look on his face. He seemed to be watching me from a distance, evaluating me. This new side of me, the one who wanted to cry instead of throw things and scream, was as new to him as it was to me. I guess it is my hormones or whatever, that's what the nurses would say at least, but I didn't like it and I knew he didn't know how to handle it. I wished I could be the old me, not the Lucillia or the Lucy but the good ol' Luke, the one who got angry and screamed and yelled and had the heart of a wildcat. But maybe that part of me had died when the voice, the mean voice, had gotten quieter and then gone away. The person who now stood before Peter Gray was a little girl on the verge of tears. I did not feel angry, just weak and shaky and sad. And empty. The only thing seeming to fill the cavity of my heart was regret. Regret, regret, regret.

"No," I said. "No, I'm not angry. I am sorry though, Peter."

He watched me for a moment to make sure, then gave me a reassuring smile. "Well, have a good time at the dance, Luke. Feel free to tell me how it goes, what it's like. What *he's* like."

Everything about what he said was so formal, so cold and professional, so calm and devoid of emotion, that I just wanted to cry harder. I didn't even know what to say to him, I just stood in front of him, my breath coming in and out in little ragged bursts. Peter paused, then looked at me from the corner of his eye.

"We are still friends, Luke," he said, smiling quietly at me.

I latched onto his words and felt a ray of hope lighten my laboring heart. But that small glimmer of hope made me want to cry even harder.

"I know," I said.

"Good," he said. "I'll talk to you later, Luke."

He started walking down the hall and I started staring at him. He cut a handsome silhouette, his tall and lanky frame sidling down the empty corridor lined by dull blue lockers on either side. I felt like I was in a movie, watching the love of my life walk away from me and not doing anything about it, watching him be swept away with the wind and not being able to snatch him back in time. I don't know when I lost him to Ashley, but it was the biggest damn mistake in my life, and maybe if I hadn't been such a stupid little girl back then... maybe I would have seen it.

35.

The dress I ended up buying is red, and it is beautiful. But I wasn't excited about the dance anymore. Even when I put the dress on and twirled around, so that the sequins flashed and the multiple layer skirt flew away from me in swirling waves of expensive cloth, even when I should have felt like a sexy Spanish senorita or an alluring cocktail hostess... even then, the only thing I felt was empty. Empty and alone, and fake.

I don't know why I picked red. I actually wasn't thinking about it, just went into the shoe store first to see if they had anything I liked, and then I saw the shoe sitting there on one of the plastic display mounts that all shoe stores seem to carry. The red shoe was sitting there, proudly displayed like a fire goddess, haughty and seductive in its blazing color and elegant in its simplicity. It had a good four inch heel which presented a problem, not only because I was afraid I would trip over myself and break my neck, but also because I was afraid it would make me tower over Vincent. I'm tall as it is. But my father had said Vincent was a junior, so that means he would be taller than the boys I went to class with, and besides, the appeal of the shoe was compelling. Overpowering.

I went over to it and picked it up, turning it around in my hand. It had a single red strap going across the front of the foot, and then a crisscross back that held the foot in. There were no diamonds, now bows, no flourishes: the shoe was frankly and simply red, and it screamed confidence. It was a shoe that did not need to adorn itself with fancy accessories. I looked at the price and the price was right. The shoes came with me out of the store, and I still had 135 dollars to spend on my dress.

So I ended up matching my dress to my shoes, and not the other way around, but I was new at this and didn't really know how these things worked. I just saw the shoe and had to have it. It reminded me of something. I left with the shoes snug in their box and banging against my thigh as I went into the department store with all of The Dresses, and they had one red dress and I tried it on and it fit and that was all I cared about. I just wasn't as excited as I would otherwise have been. If Peter hadn't asked me, then maybe I would still have been excited; maybe if he hadn't asked me I would be more excited, especially when my father ordered me to go with a mysterious man who was a *junior* and a *gentleman*. But the excitement was not there because Peter HAD asked me and I HAD said yes and I HAD gotten excited about going with him. I had made my father proud, but I would have made Juliet weep.

The night of the formal came and I got ready, which entailed me putting on the dress and shoes and twisting my hair into a chignon on the back of my head and then forcing myself to put on a little makeup as well. I still had to look good even if I didn't care, and I *didn't* care. I just wanted the stupid dance to be over. I mean, who even goes to a formal when they're in ninth grade? I didn't have the body for the dress I was wearing, and I definitely didn't have the attitude to be going to the dance, so why the hell was I even going? Peter wouldn't even be there. Because of *Ashley.*

Despite my lack of care I must still have looked good, because when Vincent showed up on my doorstep he looked pleased. My father came out, frowning, and told Vincent that he expected me home directly after the dance and that he would be waiting up so don't worry about waking him when we came back. Vincent didn't even seem embarrassed by this, just nodded and said he definitely would bring me back right away, and that it was very good of my father to trust him.

"I don't trust you," my father said gruffly. I think Vincent had charmed him, though, because the rough quality in his voice that he used with me wasn't there. My father wasn't being mean to Vincent, he was simply being a father.

"Well then I look forward to gaining your trust, sir," Vincent said.

"Hmph," my father said and turned and went inside. He closed the door. That's when Vincent turned to me and smiled. He handed me a bunch of red roses that he had kept hidden from sight.

"These are for you," he said, and he said it sweetly and it made me blush even though I didn't want to. Who the hell gives a ninth grader flowers like that? I didn't know what to do, so I mumbled a thank you and didn't look at him until he followed giving me the flowers by extending his hand.

"I'm Vincent," he said.

That at least I knew how to handle. I stuck out my hand and said without thinking, "I'm Luke."

"Luke? Luke.. oh, Lucy?" He paused. "My father said your name was Lucy."

"Oh," I said, embarrassed. We were now at his car, which was a sleek midnight blue something or other, and I paused as he opened the door for me. The truth was that Vincent was actually very handsome, and I wasn't thinking the best around him. I worried that if my face didn't return to its normal color soon, he would think I had some kind of disease and wouldn't want to be around me at all. I slid into the car, thankful for the darkness, then listened as he closed my door and went around to his side and opened it and got in.

"Well, it is Lucy," I said after a moment. "But when I was little I liked the name Luke and that's just what it's been for such a long time that sometimes it still slips out."

"Do you prefer Luke?" he mused, snapping on his seatbelt.

"Lucy is fine," I said.

"So Lucy," Vincent said, turning the key in the ignition and setting the car engine humming. He turned and grinned at me, full of charisma. "What do you think of this crazy idea our parents threw together?"

I blushed fiercely. "I'm just glad I bought the right color of dress for the ... the flowers."

He laughed. "So you like them."

"Yes," I said. "They're beautiful."

Vincent nodded as if this pleased him, then glanced at me quickly. "You look beautiful."

"Um," I said, then sat there wringing my hands in my lap.

Vincent laughed. "Look, Lucy, I know this isn't the most normal situation in the world. I'd really like to just have a fun evening. I don't really want to go to this dance, but my father insisted I should."

"Mine too," I blurted out. "I mean, you seem nice, but I don't... I don't really want to go tonight either."

Vincent shook his head as he started to drive. "Kind of like Romeo and Juliet in reverse, eh?"

"More than you know," I said.

Vincent laughed again, his eyes on the road, and I started to relax, then listened spellbound as he started to speak.

"Truth is, Luc," He said it *loose* and his voice was somber. "I actually have my eye on another girl, a girl my own age. She's wonderful. I met her when I was a sophomore. She's smart and she's beautiful and she wants to be a singer. She has the prettiest voice in the world, like silver bells or a nightingale's song. I'd seen her around school and I wanted to talk to her so badly, so one day I waited around until after her choir practice and she always walks home rather than take the bus so I started following her. Not like a stalker, but just long enough until I could catch up to her and get her attention, and then I walked with her for a ways. But before I got her attention, I heard her singing, singing a song without words, to herself. She is always singing, always singing. So that, of course, was the first thing I asked her once I caught up to her. Why she was always singing."

He paused, smiled at me. "Maybe I should have said who I was first, because the poor girl had no idea. She didn't seem scared though. She said that she had seen me around school but she didn't know my name. I asked her if she wanted to. Smooth, eh? I know, I sounded just like a bunch of other love-struck fools. But it was enough, because she said that yes, she had actually wanted to talk to me, but that she was rather shy... and she looked away from me when she said this, as if to prove her point... but that she was glad that I had come to talk to her and would I like to walk with her for a bit? So of course I said yes and we walked, and then I told her she had a beautiful voice and I asked her why she liked to sing so much. She said she just liked to. She didn't tell me she used it as a way to hold onto what was beautiful in the world, didn't tell me it was a way to get away from her life. Her father is an alcoholic and he doesn't treat her very well. Treats her like shit, in fact. It makes me angry, so damn angry, to see her going through the hell he puts her through. Makes me wonder what kind of a world we live in, you know? She's so sweet, so patient, so beautiful... and then she has all that to deal with when she goes home. It just makes me angry."

I had absolutely no idea what to say to that but Vincent saved me.

"Sorry," he said, glancing over at me. "I'm sane, really, I promise. It's just that when you care about someone you want them to be happy, you know? You don't want anything to hurt them or make them cry."

"What's her name?" I finally said. "It isn't Ashley, is it?"

"No," and he smiled. "No, it's Veronica. Who's Ashley?"

"Um," I said, then didn't know how to continue. Vincent waited though until I found the right words. "Um, Ashley is this girl. I mean, she's a girl that a guy that I like likes, and..."

I sounded so juvenile compared to the long, eloquent speech that Vincent had just given, and I stopped speaking in embarrassment. He had declared his true passion and emotion for a girl who was fighting for her life by singing, and I had presented him with a garbled version of a clichéd teenage soap opera. So much for being 'mature.' But Vincent only nodded his head understandingly.

"Who is the guy you like?" he asked.

"His name is Peter," I said, finally admitting it openly to myself as well as to him.

"How did you meet him?" Vincent said, then, "Mind if I smoke?"

"No," I said, and he lit a cigarette and started blowing out smoke. Cruising down a dark highway alone with a boy at least two years older than me was exciting enough, but the smoke took my excitement to a higher level. I realized all of a sudden that I *was* having fun, just sitting and talking to Vincent and it was okay to talk to Vincent because he was a gentleman and he liked a different girl and he was older than me and he *understood*, understood what I didn't and he was a guy and maybe he could give me some advice about Peter. "But we met..." Then I had to stop, because I didn't remember how we met.

"I don't remember how we met," I said lamely, more and more and more embarrassed.

Vincent didn't even pause, didn't treat me like a child. "You two must be really good friends then."

"Yeah," I said, warming to him. "Yeah, we are."

"What kind of things do you like to do together?"

"Um," I said. "Well, we just talk a lot, and sometimes he paints me and sometimes we build fires. . ."

Then I broke off because I realized what I was saying and I also realized how it would sound to someone who didn't know me and who *heard* what I was saying. One thing was certain, though, I had finally ended up breaking Vincent's cool facade.

"You build fires?" he asked, his eyes glittering.

"Um," I said.

"That's cool," he said. "You sound like an interesting person, Luke."

I smiled, feeling comfortable and safe and older than I actually was in the dark with Vincent and his cigarette and him being old enough to *drive*.

"Why can't you go to the dance with Veronica?" I asked him. "It sounds like she likes you."

His eyes darkened. "You think so?"

"Yes," I said. "Yes, as a girl, I know so."

"Oh," he said. "Well, I asked her, but she said she didn't want to go with me."

"Did she really?" I didn't mean to rub it in; I had a point to make. "Or did she just say she didn't want to go?"

He seemed to think, but maybe he was just trying to make me feel smarter than I had been acting. "Well, I think she said that she didn't want to go."

"Well that's completely different," I said. "Maybe she just didn't have the money or she had to work or her father wouldn't let her or something. But you should ask her again."

"Maybe I will, Lucy," he said, sounding far off. "I'd really like that, I really would. She's a very special girl, but she doesn't take care of herself. Doesn't value herself, what she has. I'd like to be the person who helps her see that. But you're right, maybe I gave up too easily. Sometimes the most valuable things have to be sought after a little harder, right?"

"Right," I agreed, thankful that he was asking me questions that necessitated only short answers. "Definitely."

"So is Peter going to the dance with Ashley?" he asked.

"Ashley is in Georgia," I said.

"So why aren't you going with him?"

I hesitated, not wanting to say anything and dreading when I would actually have to. But Vincent caught on, and glanced at me again.

"Because you're going with me. I'm sorry, Lucy."

"Don't be," I said, and I meant it. "I'm glad... I'm glad we had a chance to talk. Really."

"Me too," he said, and laughed. "Really."

Then we were at the school and I was quiet as Vincent concentrated on finding a spot and parking his car without banging into the cars on either side of it. He held me in a kind of awe, being able to maneuver something as big as a car into that tiny little space. But the thing about Vincent was that he didn't make me feel young, or even stupid. He made me feel special. Veronica was a very lucky girl for having caught his eye. I found myself liking Vincent immensely as he crossed over and opened my door. I even found myself looking forward to the dance. Just a little, though.

He held out his arm and I took it. I had to, wobbling around on those four inch heels of mine that still kept me shorter than him. But somehow, Vincent understood that, too.

Our school had been transformed. Even though the dance took place in the school's gymnasium, the decorations looked amazing. There were brightly colored streamers everywhere, and along the edges of the gym the decorators had put clumps of pumpkins and dried leaves. In one corner of the gym there was even a straw filled scarecrow with a big painted on grin who smiled at all the students who passed.

And all the people! I felt like I was in New York city watching models on the runway. All of the girls looked so beautiful, but I was relieved to find more than one wobbling around on heels that were even smaller than the ones I was wearing. In spite of all the glitz and glamor, though, there were a few girls who simply had not dressed for the occasion. I saw one girl I didn't know walking around in lace up black boots and a dress as dark as night, with bolts of crinkly purple fabric sticking out at the bottom and a purple tie lacing up her bodice. Her lips were black, and she had a pile of black hair stuck up on her head that looked like some sort of furry creature. Then there was another girl who was wearing the dress I had seen in the thrift store! It actually fit her nicely, but the colors clashed so terribly that I don't think anyone could have saved it. I didn't see the coffee stain though, so at least she took time to remove it.

Then there was the other group of people. There were probably about ten of them in all, which makes sense: five boys, five girls. Five couples. Apparently they hadn't been thrilled about the 'formal' idea and so they dropped it and came dressed in Halloween costumes. And why not? Halloween was just around the corner. The girls were dressed as a mummy, a witch, a flapper girl, a kitchen table, and a prostitute, and the guys had dressed up as a cowboy, a ghost, Indiana Jones, a green sea monster, and an ape. I had no idea who was with who because they apparently hadn't thought to coordinate their costumes, but the ten of them stayed together for the evening, laughing and having fun, so maybe they were just a group of really good friends.

I asked Vincent what he thought about them. He shrugged.

"They're having fun, they're seizing life and making it more interesting for all of us. I don't see the harm in it." He paused. "Would you like some punch, Lucy?"

"Sure," I said, my eyes on the Big Ten and thinking about what Vincent had just said. "Thank you."

Vincent started off towards the punch table, threading through the crowd, and for a moment I wanted to follow him. I felt very awkward, standing alone. I knew people at the dance, but I didn't really have any friends at the high school and the acquaintances that I did know had come to the dance with boys and so weren't likely to pay me much attention. A couple of my closer girl acquaintances commented on my dress (all good) when they passed me and smiled, but that was it. Music was already playing and a few people were dancing, particularly the Big Ten when the Monster Mash came on. I started tapping my foot to the tune, which is one of my favorite songs of all time but then the song ended and the DJ started playing a slow song. Couples moved closer together accordingly, clinging to each other as the thick music drenched the gymnasium. I shifted on my high heels nervously: would Vincent want to dance like that? I didn't have any problem with physical contact, but it wouldn't seem right after what he had told me about Veronica. But Vincent did not even have a chance to ask me to dance, because at that moment, the crowd in front of me parted and I had a full view of the Big Ten. The ape took off his mask, and there stood Peter Gray. He turned exactly at that moment, and saw me. A current like a lightning bolt shot across the space between us. He didn't move, just stood there staring in his furry brown ape costume with the ape head mask dangling from one hand, and then he raised one fur covered hand in a small wave. I was paralyzed. I could not move. The hand quivered in the air for a moment, then dropped back down to his side. He turned away.

Vincent came back with a drink and saw me staring and frozen. He handed me the drink and I took it mechanically.

"Are you alright?" he asked.

"Peter," I said.

Through this verbose explanation Vincent understood me. He followed my eyes, then laughed.

"Ape man?" he said, then chuckled when I nodded. "I should have known, Lucy. Only someone interesting for you."

I finally looked away, turned my attention to Vincent, saw the merry twinkling in his eyes.

"Go on, kid," he said. "Have fun."

"What?" I said. "But Vincent. . ."

"Do you have a ride home from the dance?" He cut my protestation off, and that's when I realized he was really serious, that he would not keep me from doing the thing I wanted most because of what our parents had told us.

"I'm sure Peter can take me home," I said, thinking that even walking back to my house through the woods would work. It might take me awhile, and it might be a little scary, but I had a way home no matter what.

"Then go," he said.

I thought about my father, who was up waiting for me. Would he be suspicious if I came home walking? As long as I kept track of the time and left with enough time to get back at a reasonable hour, he wouldn't ask me questions– I hoped. But my reason was flawed, and the compulsion to go to Peter was too strong. I pushed my punch glass back at Vincent hurriedly and started off before I turned around.

"What will you do?" I asked, pausing.

He smiled at me. "I'll just hang around here, I guess. Talk to some people I know. . ."

"Go to Veronica," I said. "Vincent, go to her."

"What?"

"Why not?" I still felt younger than him, but suddenly I also felt wiser. I *was* a girl after all; I knew how they worked. Somewhat. "You have a car. She's probably at home right now wishing she were here. Go get her and bring her here."

"Vera isn't really into dances," he said, but I heard in his voice that he liked the idea. "And besides, she said no."

"Then make her say yes to something else. Trust me, no girl in this high school wants to be alone tonight. If she doesn't like dances, then suggest doing something that she wants to do, that you both want to do."

"I don't know," he said, but his reasons were crumbling. "Do you really think she would agree to something like that?"

"Yes," I said simply.

"All right," he said. "All right, I will."

After he decided to go see Veronica, a smile broke across his face and he threw the glass of punch into the air. The liquid sprayed up in a stream of liquid red, red like the leaves, red the color of love. Luckily it didn't land on anyone, or else they would have been mad. Vincent was too happy to be embarrassed about it. He stepped across the floor to me and pressed my hand warmly.

"Thank you, Lucy," he said. "Thank you."

Then he bent down and kissed me on the cheek. I started blushing furiously.

"No problem," I mumbled, then held out the bouquet of roses I still held. "Here, you should probably take these to her..."

"No, those are for you. I'll pick up some sunflowers for Vera on my way..." He smiled at me again and pressed my hand, then turned and walked across the room, towards the exit, a new energy in his step.

I turned and saw Peter watching me, a scowl on his face. I smiled, and started towards him.

36.

He tried to look like he had not seen me as I came towards him, but we both knew that he had. He looked like he wanted to move away, but there was nowhere he could go. The Big Nine weren't moving, and I now sensed that they were staying together for a reason. Maybe they were afraid to go out into that colorful sea of prom dresses and black tuxes. But Peter Gray was embarrassed. He started to put the ape mask back on, then paused when it was halfway to his head and lowered it again. And I kept walking towards him.

"Peter," I said. "You decided to come."

"Hey," he said, "Hey, Luke."

I glanced around at the people he was standing with, who were still dancing and cavorting and unaware of my presence. Four of the Big Ten were actually dancing together, but of the three girls who were not, none was looking at Peter expectantly. I wondered if he had come with someone or not.

"So why did you decide to dress up?" I shouted as the music kicked up into a hard rock song. "It's a great idea, but how did you . . ."

"Luke, I can't hear you," he said and I could barely hear him. He touched my shoulder briefly. "You want to go somewhere else?"

I nodded, then followed him out of the gymnasium. So he definitely wasn't here with someone else. Or maybe he was just giving me preference, since I was his *friend*. We left the gymnasium and I was surprised to find how hot it had been inside, and that I was steaming with sweat. My ears were numb from the music, and the quiet outside the gym felt abnormal. We walked down a flight of steps to the ground floor and then Peter sat down on the steps and stared out the door near us, into the darkness of the night outside. I sat down beside him. The red sequined fabric on my knee touched the plain black fabric of his pants.

"Now what were you saying?" Peter asked me hollowly.

I moved my knee away from his. "I just wanted to know why you decided to dress up. Why you decided to come. Are you here with anyone?"

Peter was not looking at me. "I decided I wanted to come to this dance. I thought it might be fun. But like I said, I didn't want to come with someone I might like because of Ashley. Or someone who would like me, because that wouldn't be fair. But I didn't want to come alone to a formal, and I knew some other people who didn't want to come alone and who didn't like the idea of a Halloween Formal . . ."

"Fall," I said. "Fall Formal."

"Whatever, Luke," he said, angry. He was already starting to scowl. "So we got together and just decided to ditch the whole thing. Do you like my costume?"

I smarted at his arrogance. "It fits you."

He bristled. "Yeah, whatever. At least I was having fun. So if you'll excuse me, I'm going to go back."

He stood up and waited for me, but I didn't get up. His ape head was still lying on the ground at the bottom of the steps, and he stooped to pick it up and grabbed my arm simultaneously. He tried to pull me up. I sat like a dead weight, refusing.

"Come on, Luke," he sneered. "Your date will be missing you. You seem pretty comfortable with each other, for having just met."

I shook my arm away from him, hurt. Was he thinking about Vincent's good-bye kiss? Well, let him. Why not play it up. If he was going to dangle Ashley over my head when he knew it bothered me then why couldn't I do the same with him?

"Vincent is a very nice man," I said. "I enjoyed my time with him immensely."

"I'm sure you did," Peter said. He tucked the ape head under his arm. "I don't want to miss a moment of this dance. I told Ashley I'd write to her about every detail of it."

Now he was smiling again, that faint curl of his lips lighting up his face. I snapped.

"Damn you, Peter Gray," I whispered.

He hesitated on the steps, the ape head still under his arm, one hand on the stair's railing for balance. "What?"

"Damn you," I said. "Damn you, and damn Ashley."

He stopped, scowling, and turned to face me. "Take that back, Luke."

"I will not," I said, my voice rising. "I hate her, Peter. I don't even know her and I hate her."

"You wouldn't if you knew her," he said. "She's a very sweet girl, and you're just jealous."

"I am!" The words erupted from my mouth. I stood up on the stairs and turned to face him, shaking. "Is that what you want to hear from me, Peter? Then I'll say it! I am! I am jealous of your damn little girlfriend, and I hate her."

"Luke," he said, his voice cold. "I started seeing Ashley because you didn't want me. If you could have me, you still wouldn't want me. We both know you too well. I have Ashley and I'm happy. Just leave me alone."

He might as well have slapped me. I stood staring at him staring back at me, my mouth open and tears threatening to spill down my face. I could have yelled at him, I could have screamed, but the new part of me that liked to cry was taking over the old, angry part of me, and it won. I sat down on the steps and I put my head on my lap and I started to cry.

I heard his footsteps coming down the stairs, felt his warmth as he sat down and put his arm around me.

"Luke," he said, and his voice was completely baffled. "What's wrong?"

I wanted to put my head on his shoulder and cry. But there was Ashley. There was always that stupid fucking ugly Ashley of his. I pushed myself away from him and wiped the tears away from my eyes.

I glared at him. "I'm not going back to the dance."

Peter Gray seemed uncertain of what to do. He sat with his hands in his lap, his tan face anxious. "But what about Vincent?"

"He left," I said. I had never lied to Peter and I didn't want to start now. I didn't feel the need to. I felt hollow, empty, sad. I didn't care if it was his victory. "I came with him because my father told me to, and he came because his father told him to, but we both really like someone else and so I told him to go get the girl he loves. It would have been stupid for us to stay together at the dance when our thoughts were obviously miles apart, so he went to her and I stayed here." I slumped against the wall farthest from Peter.

"He kissed you," Peter accused me. "I saw him."

I shrugged. "So what? He kissed me and I liked it. Did you see that too?"

"Yes," he said tersely.

"Why do you even care?" I said, but my voice was tired and not angry. "Will you at least answer me that?"

"Because you're my friend," he said, on cue.

I sighed. "It still shouldn't matter to you. You have Ashley. Congratulations, Peter. You win. I'm going home."

"Luke."

I turned around. My voice was desperate. "What do you want, Peter?"

"This isn't a game," he said. He still sounded angry. "I'm not trying to beat you. I just have Ashley and I'm happy, and I've only been telling you about her because you are my friend and I thought you would want to hear about what makes me happy. I listened to you talk about Jack when you came back from camp."

Jack? So that was his name.

I was still out of control, still shaking, still crying. "I'm sorry if I'm a bad friend. But I can't listen to you talk about Ashley all the time. I can't. I'm sorry."

"Why?"

Peter Gray was standing on the steps, I was standing by the door, and though there was distance between us I felt like he understood me perfectly. What would be the use in telling him? What, except to get it out of my system, and then be so embarrassed that I would have to stop seeing him, stop thinking about him?

"Because I like you, Peter," I said. "And I did want to go to this dance, but I wanted to go with you. Even when I was with Vincent, I wanted to be with you. That's why he let me go. Because he knew."

Peter looked stunned. "You only like me because you can't have me, Luke."

"Do you honestly think that's true?" I said. "Peter, we've been good friends for such a long time and you've helped me through so much. You were there when the darkest part of me was there, you've seen how crazy I can get, you know who I really am."

"Yes," he said.

I was tired. I wanted to go home. "I wish I could be happy that you have Ashley, but I can't. So I'm going home. Good night."

I was halfway to the door when he said Luke. I turned around but didn't say anything. Peter Gray had moved away from the steps, and his face was ashen. His gray eyes were burning darkly. The ape mask lay forgotten on the steps, sitting there in its fur like a decapitated head with blank, empty eyes.

"Luke, is what you said true?"

"Yes," I said without hesitating.

He looked away. "There is no Ashley, Luke."

"What?"

"There is no Ashley," he repeated. "I just made her up because I was tired of how you were treating me and I was tired of you talking about boys and I've wanted you so much for so long and you never seemed to notice. So I made up Ash. . ."

I slapped him, hard. He stopped speaking and staggered backwards, one hand clapped to his face where my handprint was starting to become visible in angry red against the tan.

"Don't you ever say her name again," I spat. "How dare you, Peter Gray..."

He lowered his hand. He was grinning. It was a grin that said he understood, that he knew we both understood. He stepped towards me and grabbed my arm, knowing I would not protest.

"Let's get out of here, Luke," he said.

I glared at him, wrenched my arm free, and then fell into him as I tripped over my shoes. He caught me and put his arm around my waist. I set myself upright and grumped, but I let his arm stay where it was.

"Fine," I said. "But I'm not done with you, Peter Gray."

He smiled. "I know," he said, and then he swept me up into his arms, easily. "But you can't walk in those things."

I struggled but he didn't put me down until we were outside, and then he put me down gently, effortlessly, and I took off the shoes and let them dangle from my hand.

"Where should we go?" I asked, but we both knew the answer, so I switched my question. "How will we get there?"

He looked around him, at all of the shiny cars glittering in the moonlight. He turned back to me and shrugged. "Walk?"

"All right."

"Here." He took off his shoes, gave them to me. "There might be glass. I don't want you to get hurt. I have socks."

I took off my shoes and took his shoes and put them on. They were far too big for me and my feet slipped inside of them, but they belonged to him and I was glad to be wearing them. He saw I was shivering, and then took off the top part of the ape costume, revealing the thin white undershirt he was wearing underneath.

"Here," he said, draping it around my shoulders. The moonlight dripped off his tanned skin, his body muscular under the flimsy shirt that clung to it.

"I must look ridiculous," I said out loud, nestling into the thick fake fur.

"You look beautiful," Peter Gray said.

He hesitated, then reached out his hand for mine. I slipped mine in, felt as our hands matched, felt the warmth flow from his body into mine. We started walking.

I thought about the drive up, about how sexy and mature I had felt in Vincent's car with Vincent's smoke surrounding us and all of his elegant talk. Then I thought about the road back, walking beside half of an ape man and dressed in a cocktail dress, half an ape costume, and fuzzy fur stockings. I thought of my skin on Peter's, of my hand in his. The road back was different.

The way back was better.

37.

I was lying in bed next to Peter Gray in his attic, my head nestled against his bare shoulder, his arm around my bare waist. His eyes were closed and facing the ceiling and one arm was angled behind his head, but I knew he was awake. I cuddled into him, closer, felt his arm tighten around my waist and breathed in the smell of his skin, a mix of strong Dial soap and the static, stale smell of the fur of the ape costume.

"Peter," I said.

"Hmm," he mumbled, not opening his eyes. "What is it, Luke?"

I didn't want to break the sweet silence, didn't want to leave the warmth of his body. Everything had happened so fast, but I didn't regret it and I knew he didn't either. When he told me his parents were out for the night and no one came to the attic, when I slipped out of my one hundred and thirty-five dollar dress and let it crumple to the ground like an unwanted rag, and when we mutually agreed without words, it had not felt dangerous, risky, wrong. It had felt necessary, right. Long overdue.

"I have to get home, Peter," I said. "My father said he would be waiting up for me, and if I come home later than. . . than is reasonable, I'm going to get in trouble. I'll have so much explaining to do, and I'm too happy now and I don't want anything to spoil this feeling."

He was silent for a moment and I wished I hadn't spoken, was going to let it slide by and hell to my father, and then he nodded, his eyes still closed.

"All right," he said.

He opened his eyes and looked at me from their gray depths, then leaned over and kissed me. His breath was sweet, like honey. I stood up, let the covers slide off my naked body like liquid and smiled at him, and he turned away.

"If you keep doing stuff like that," he said. "I'm never going to let you out of here."

I smiled at his turned back and looked around the attic, feeling like I was in a fairy tale. The light lit up the canvases, lit up his seascapes and country sides and abstracts, creating a display of worlds and far off places that only existed in his mind. My eyes lit on the sofa where I had once posed for him nude, where he had covered me with a blanket and gently kissed my closed eyelashes. I walked around the room, studying the paintings one by one, some of them new, most of them old favorites. I came across my own portrait, the one that he had painted that was all black, and my eyes lingered on it even as I felt his eyes lingering on me. I picked it up and turned to him, clutching it to my stomach.

"Do you remember this one?" I asked him.

Peter leaned back on the bed, propped up by his one elbow.

"That's the first one I ever did of you," he said. "I remember how mad you were."

I held the painting out from me, revealing my nakedness once more, and glanced over it uneasily. "I still don't know why you painted it all black."

"That's what I saw." Peter shrugged. "I was just starting then, Luke. I didn't understand what I saw, what I felt. I still don't. But don't worry. Whatever I saw then, I don't see now. It's gone, whatever it was."

"Really?" I said in a small voice. A voice of hope. "It's really gone?"

Peter Gray looked at me, long and hard, his eyes no longer those of my friend but those of an artist evaluating his subject. "Yes."

"I'm glad," I said, and I was. I put the painting back with a shiver. "I never liked that one."

"Do you want to torch it?" he asked me. "I have gasoline in the basement."

The idea was enticing. I imagined that square of black charring and burning in the flames that licked it, purifying it, demolishing it. "But it's your work, Peter."

He shrugged. "If you don't like it, we can destroy it. Besides, art is supposed to reflect truth. And what was true in that painting no longer is. Do you want to, Luke?"

I hesitated. "But even because it's not true now doesn't mean that at one point it wasn't, Peter. It was a part of me, and it is a part of you. Of your work, I mean. You shouldn't. Besides, I have to get home. It's really late."

"All right," he said. "Put your clothes on. I'll walk you back."

I went over to the sofa, picked up my dress and slipped it over my head. I retrieved my panties from where they were lying, crumpled, under the bed, and saw one of my shoes under there as well. Seeing that red shoe under the bed sparked a memory, but I couldn't think of what it was, couldn't remember how it connected to my life. I stood up and started looking for my other shoe, found it across the room by the window. I had no idea how it got there, or why my clothes were so spread apart. I knew it had been an explosion on both of our parts, but did not realize we had been so vicious and wild until I saw the state of the clothes and their locations.

I slipped the spiked shoes onto my feet and stood on wobbly ankles, then turned to face Peter. He was buttoning up a white dress shirt and had put on a pair of black pants, opting to leave the ape costume discarded where he had dropped it. He looked up when he felt my eyes on him, smiled at me.

"Are you ready?" he asked.

"No," I said. "Not now. Not ever."

He smiled, his face lighting, and then he stepped across the room and took my hand and pulled me close. He was so warm, so strong, and I felt my excitement begin to build again as he buried his face against my shoulder, his mouth on my neck.

"Peter," I said weakly. "I have to get home."

He paused and I could feel his breath, warming my neck with its hot air. His grip on me was like a vice, firm and strong, but not painful. Then he nodded and straightened, letting me go except for his hand in mine.

"You're right," he said. "I don't want you to get in trouble. And this place is a mess. I'll have to have some time to clean it up before my parents get home."

"Right," I said, patting my mousy hair down into place as best I could. He looked so handsome, standing in the bright light of the attic, his hair gleaming gold and his face tan, the white of his shirt making him look angelic, Apollonian. I felt his smile light me like a fire. He let go of my hand long enough to let down the trap door to the attic, then went first because he knew I was going to hobble down after him along with my heels. After I descended the first step, he held out his hand and I fell into his arms. He caught me with one arm, held me, and closed the trap door with the other, then gently put me down.

"Let's go," he said, and took my hand again.

I walked beside him silently, the night licking my skin with its coolness and the alive smell of autumn leaves surrounding us. There was a three quarter moon in the sky and it shone down on us, drenching everything in its silvery light. Stars twinkled in the sky, but a hazy fog had also climbed into the sky and was threatening to smother the stars, one by one. We reached the driveway of my house and Peter made as if to continue, but I stopped him.

"My father won't be expecting you," I said. "You should probably stay here."

He looked reluctant, then nodded his head. "Okay, Luke."

He let go of me and I looked at him, and then he stepped forward and encircled me with his strong arms, and I was drowning in the scent of Dial soap and freshly starched white cotton. I felt my knees go weak and slumped into him, closing my eyes.

"Luke," he said. "Luke, I want to thank you for giving me the best night of my life. I will never forget this night, I will never forget you. I love you."

I opened my eyes and looked up at him, not understanding the sadness in his voice. His dark eyes were pensive, and he did not seem aware of my consternation.

"Never has my heart known such open bounds, never my imagination such freedom and craving. Craving for the aesthetic, the beautiful, the pure, the sublime." He had lost me. "You have opened a door for me tonight, Luke. You are a beautiful creature. I love you. I love you."

He kissed my cheek, erasing the kiss Vincent had planted there. I stared at him, too happy to contemplate what he was saying, or what he was thinking. I pulled his head down towards me, kissed him on the lips.

"I love you, Peter." I said. "Peter Gray. I always will."

He brought the hand he was holding up to his chest and our hands stayed there, locked against our hearts. The moonlight reflected in his eyes, eyes that were murky and enchanting.

"Farewell," he said, then kissed my hand and let it go. I stood watching him as he sauntered back towards his house in the darkness and almost went to him three times. My cheeks and my heart were burning already with longing for him, and I wished for nothing else but to be back in his arms in his bed in his attic, my smooth cheek against the firm muscle of his chest. To fall asleep in his arms, to wake up in the morning and have him beside me, the sun drenching us with its light and its warmth. I loved Peter. Peter loved me. I repeated it to myself as I turned and walked back to my house.

Peter Gray loved me.

38.

I didn't actually think my father would be waiting up for me when I got home, thought it had just been an excuse to warn Vincent, but I smoothed my dress and my hair again before I went in the door. There he was reading a newspaper and sitting in his chair.

"Do you know what time it is?" He said, looking up from behind his reading glasses as I came in.

"Well," I said. "The dance ended at eleven and then most everyone wanted it to last longer so we stayed at the school until about eleven-thirty, and then the chaperones complained but couldn't kick us out until eleven-forty five, and then it's a fifteen minute drive back here." I paused, hoping I sounded convincing. "So it's probably about midnight."

My father was not a man easily convinced, but he could not argue with my logic. "It is exactly midnight, Luke. Your answer sounds calculated."

It was. Peter and I had left the dance around 10:30, the walk would have taken us till about 11 because I knew a shortcut, and the walk over to my house had taken about ten minutes. That left us fifty minutes to do what we did, and considering how we acted, I thought that was pushing it. I didn't say anything: saying anything else would subtract from my original story. Better to stay firm, and keep it simple.

My father relented. "So you had fun?"

"Yes," I said, taking off my heels. "Vincent is a gentleman, just like you said. We talked about a lot of really interesting stuff. He is very smart."

"And you behaved like a lady," he said, as if doubting my intentions.

I froze. "Of course."

"Vincent enjoyed himself as well?"

"Yes," I said, then paused. "At least, he seemed very happy."

"Then my debt is repaid." My father folded up his newspaper and took off his reading glasses, then stood. "Thank you, Luke. Get some sleep. You do have school tomorrow."

He actually sounded kind, pleased with me. I didn't argue, but crept passed him and went up to my room, the shoes dangling from my hands. I didn't start humming until I got into my room. I didn't want him to be suspicious. Then I took off my dress and hung it neatly on a hanger and stuck it in my closet. I put on my pajamas, then stacked my red shoes with their stabbing heels in my closet beneath the dress. I went over to my mirror and brushed my hair, straightening the tangled curls into frizzy waves. Done, I put the brush back on my dresser and stared at my reflection. I looked more like me now that I was out of the dress, out of the glamor, but I didn't looked like me. I looked different. Older. Prettier. More at peace.

The way I looked made what Peter Gray said apparent to me. Whatever had been there was gone. I smiled at my reflection and for once didn't mind my thin lips or large teeth. They were part of me, the me that Peter Gray loved.

I turned off the light and crawled into bed. My covers accepted me warmly, and I snuggled into the fluffy depths that smelled of too much laundry detergent because I didn't know how to wash fabric the right way. I smiled up at my ceiling, feeling warm and alive and awakened, but I couldn't sleep for a very long time.

39.

When I woke the next morning, I no longer felt beautiful. I felt fragile, like something inside of me was getting ready to break into a million pieces, and I felt weak. I crept over to my mirror and looked at my reflection, and I still looked beautiful, older, happy. I turned away from my mirror and realized that what was making me uneasy was the feeling of apprehension lodged in my stomach, like the stones that the children made the wolf eat in that tale. That Grimm tale.

I was shaking when I went back to my bed and straightened the covers, pulling them tight and then trying to make my room look presentable. It was a routine I had, to clean up my room a little bit every morning. It helped me get out of bed, made the acknowledgment of a whole new day's potential a little less frightening and overwhelming, and gave me some time to think. I brushed my hair and put on my clothes and got ready for school, and then looked at the clock and saw that I had gotten up really early, and that I had an extra hour to spare.

I left the house anyway, and I walked over to Peter Gray's house. He was probably asleep but I would wake him up and see if he wanted to walk to the school instead of taking the bus and talk. We hadn't walked to school together since middle school and the walk to the high school was a lot longer, but I didn't think he would mind. I could at least ask him. I hadn't asked him because of Ashley, but she had disappeared and so had my reason for staying away from Peter Gray. And I didn't like the feeling in my stomach.

The morning was somber and dreary, and the dew that always accompanies early morning was wet on the ground, clinging to the sharp blades of glass like crystalline blood on green scalpels. I was wearing flip flop sandals though we aren't allowed to, and the dew splattered onto my feet and made each step I took squeak. I got to Peter Gray's house and stood there staring at it, at the tall oak tree and the flat board tied onto the ropes that was the swing, at the derelict dog house of the defunct Fawkes, at the fence that surrounded the property and cut off the sulking white house from view. I paused then looked up to the highest window in the house, that domed arched window that was unlike the normal, rectangular ones of the lower levels, and hoped that Peter would be there, staring back out at me. But the window was empty.

I shivered and pulled my sweatshirt around me more tightly, but it didn't help because the coldness was coming from inside. I went through the gate, listening to it clatter shut behind me, and crept up to the front porch. I didn't know if anyone would be awake in Peter's house. It was five thirty in the morning. If they weren't and the door was locked, I would turn around and go home and that would be the end of my worrying. I would see Peter in school and we could talk then, but everything would be resolved.

The doorknob turned smoothly under my fingers, the door opening with an inoffensive squeak. I stood on the threshold of the house, one foot on the welcome mat and the other foot inside, the half-open door cutting my view off at a forty-five degree angle.

"Peter?" I said softly, knowing he would not answer me. I stepped inside and closed the door behind me, praying that the Grays were not yet awake because if they came down I was going to have some explaining to do and I have never been good at thinking on my feet. My feet knew the way, as did my heart, and without another word I moved as silently as I could to the staircase behind the main foyer of the house, willed my feet to move up the steps one by one. Very few of my dreams ever stay with me after waking, but now I felt caught in the one where I'm always trying to climb up a set of steps whose number continually grows, and the harder I try to reach the top, the slower my motion and the farther away the door at the top becomes. But the number of steps in Peter Gray's house stayed constant, and inevitably I reached the top and stood underneath the entrance to the attic, the little cord hanging down which would open the trap door and let down the folded stairs.

I stared at the motionless cord and listened to the silence of the house, knowing that the steps would unfold with a shudder that could not be prevented and alert the sleeping Grays that there was an intruder in the house. I needed to see Peter alone. I couldn't take that risk. But Peter would be in the attic. It was his refuge, his asylum, his sanctuary. It was where I needed to be. I held my breath, then pulled the cord and cringed as the noise exploded through the silence, deafening to my ears. I did not hesitate to see if someone would come see what was going on. I didn't have the time. I climbed up the stairs as quickly as I could, then turned and pulled them up after me before even looking at the attic space. When I turned around, there was Peter, sitting by the window and looking at me.

"I had hoped you would come," he said, a sad smile on his face. "Before."

I stepped into the attic, into the morning light beginning to shine through the one window. I wanted to ask him what he meant but the words were choked in my mouth behind my sealed lips. I felt tears starting into my eyes.

"What are you going to do, Peter?" I said, my arms hanging limply at my sides and my feet as cemented to the floor as if someone had taken iron spikes and nailed them in place. I couldn't go to him, and that was what he needed.

He looked away from me, looked out the window. "I wanted to say goodbye, Lucy."

"But where are you going?" I wailed.

He stood up and went to a corner of the attic, where he picked up a canvas and held it to him so that I couldn't see it, hugging it to him as if it were a child or a precious belonging. He came over to me, put his finger on my lips and pressed the canvas against my chest so that it was sandwiched between us.

"I have to," he said. "Lucy, I have to. You know I have to. I know you understand. Can you really stand here and tell me that you don't?"

I looked into his gray eyes, not understanding but not being able to tell him. My arms crisscrossed over the canvas, locking it in place against my chest, and he stepped back and simply looked back at me. I didn't know if I would be able to speak, and didn't know what I would say until the words were out of my mouth.

"I love you, Peter Gray," I said.

He seemed to consider this for a moment. Then he stepped up to me, took one of my hands away from the canvas, and kissed it.

"And I love you, Lucy." He smiled at me, then looked away.

"Then do something for me."

He turned his steel eyes back onto mine. "Don't ask me to do something I can't."

I swallowed. "Peter. Peter..."

"What?" He watched me warily. "What is it?"

"Will you... will you call me Luke? Like when we were younger. When things weren't so complicated, when hurting you was fun, when we never dreamed it would come to this..."

"Luke," he said, and smiled. "I love you, Luke Orange."

I felt the tears burning in my eyes. "Do you remember everything, Peter? Miss Honeydew and my voice and the fires and. . ."

251

"I remember everything," he said. "How could I forget, Luke? Those were the days I lived for. You were the only thing that kept me alive. I would have ended it long before if you hadn't come."

He was holding my hand that he had kissed, holding it tightly. His hand was warm, mine was ice cold. He was looking at me again, searching my face for something, something I hoped desperately was there. Then his eyes met mine, and I was calm.

"What will I do, Peter, once you're gone?" I said softly. "What kind of life will I live?"

"Any kind you want, Luke," he said. "You have a whole world of possibility open to you, and what's more important, you're open to the world. That's all it really takes. That and a little bit of bravery, a little courage to push the limits."

"Will you tell me why?" I said. "Why you're going to do this?"

"Last night," he said. His grip tightened on my hand. "Last night I experienced the sublime. Do you know what happens when that happens to an artist, Luke? Maybe you don't but I've read about it. Once an ideal is achieved once, earthly happiness is impossible, like being at Heaven's gate and being told it was a mistake and then being sent back. It's not the same any more. Nothing is the same anymore."

"But it's still real, Peter," I said.

"Yes," he said, "It was real. And it would continue to be real. With you, every day would be real."

"Then why can't you stay? With me?"

He looked away. "That kind of happiness drives men insane, Luke. I've read about that too."

"Did no one ever tell you that books lie?"

"Don't let yours," he said, his voice grim. "Luke, when you write your books... don't lie. Always portray the truth."

"Of course," I said, angry. "But I can't write if you aren't here. Peter, you're more to me than a friend. You're everything."

"You'll find someone else."

I glared. "Peter Gray, don't you dare say that. I'm not standing here and telling you that you mean everything to me as a cliché or to be... why the hell are you laughing?"

"I can't help it," he said, wiping away a tear that trickled down his cheek. "Luke, I always loved when you threw temper tantrums at me. That above all else."

"I don't find it funny," I said. My voice broke. "Peter, how can you do this to me?"

He stopped laughing.

"Luke," he said, very quietly. "You're going to go out in the world and you are going to find someone, and you will write and change the world and I will not get in your way."

I felt myself on the verge of tears again but I fought them back. "Peter, I don't understand any of this."

He shrugged. "You're young."

"And you? What are you?"

"I'm an artist," he said, glancing around the studio as if for the last time. His eyes lingered on the canvases, on the couch, on the rug, on the window, and then they came to rest and lingered on me.

"Peter," I said. "Are you coming to school today?"

"Yes," he said. "It's the last day."

"Before break," I said. "Just before winter break."

"Yes."

He went over to stand by the window, looking out across his yard. I looked at his hunched shoulders, at his hands thrust deeply into the pockets of his pants, at his golden hair that still caught the few stray streams of light from the sun. I felt the canvas jutting into my chest and remembered it, realized for the first time it was wrapped in green crepe paper.

"Can I look at this, Peter?"

"Not now," he said. "But later. Later, yes, you can."

"When?"

"Tonight," he said, and turned around to look at me. His eyes were dry, his voice firm. "It's my gift to you, Luke, for all you've given me."

"Thank you," I said, instinctively clutching the covered canvas. "I'll go now."

He smiled, and turned back to the window. "Okay."

I was at the entrance to the attic and had lowered the steps once again, more quietly this time, when I heard him speak. I paused, not knowing if he was speaking to me because the words were so quiet, and then he turned and looked at me.

"Luke."

I hesitated. "What?"

"After today," he said, and turned back to the window. "After today, never come here again."

I stood in the dim light of the attic, the canvas in my hand, a chill spreading through my body like frost. I couldn't speak. Peter did not turn around but stood staring out the window, his body lit by the light, his forehead pressed against the pane, his eyes staring out vacantly through the glass. I turned and went down the steps, heard him draw them up behind me as soon as my feet touched the floor. I heard his echoing footsteps going back across the attic room, and then I heard something crash and I started running. I heard him throwing things against the walls as I bolted down the steps and out the door and I knew, I knew, that he was tearing his world apart, tearing apart the work he had done and destroying everything. As I ran out the door and out across the lawn, I heard the glass crack, turned back and saw his easel falling like a dead body out of the attic amongst a shower of broken glass. I heard him scream and that set the fear inside me loose, and I turned and sprinted away from that house, not looking back, never looking back, because Peter, oh *Peter*. . .

I woke up and I was in my bed, in a heap of heaving sobs. The salty tears stained my pillow and sheets, but I laid my cheek against the wetness and drew in deep breaths, in and out and in and out and in and out . . .

40.

I don't know if Peter Gray went to school that day. I didn't. I stayed home. When my father came in he said I looked ill, why the hell was I so pale. I turned away from him and he slammed my door and went away muttering something about adolescent girl drama. At some point, I fell asleep again.

When I woke up it was already late afternoon, and by the time I got away from my house and went over to Peter Gray's it was early evening. There was a fine layer of frost on the ground, enough just to coat the ground white, and I crunched through it and went up to the house. I stood and I looked but I could not bring myself past the fence, could not force myself to open the gate. I stood and I looked and the wind bit me with its coldness, and then I turned around and went back home.

I sat in my room and thought, and then I saw something in the corner. A canvas covered in green paper. I went over to it and brought it back to my bed and sat with it on my knees, my hand smoothing out the wrinkles in the green paper that had torn away in places. It was like Christmas, except the anticipation was greater, because this had been Peter's last . . . this was Peter's masterpiece. It would contain his essence, everything he had, and I knew it. And that scared me. For what it was, and because he had given it to me. That he had chosen me.

I turned the canvas over and used my hand to slit the three pieces of tape he had used to close the ragged edges together. Slowly, very slowly, I pushed the pieces apart, then turned the canvas over and stared at what Peter had done. I stared at the painting for a long time up close, and then I went across my room and propped it up on my wall and went back to my bed and stared at it from far away.

I did not cry, could not cry. Peter had given me. . .

Peter had given me the Truth.

41.

I think maybe I will go to Africa. When I graduate from high school I will go to Africa and learn about the people there, or if I need a degree then I will go to college and then join the Peace Corps and then go to Africa. Or maybe I will write for *National Geographic* and be able to go right after high school. I don't know why, but it has to be Africa. They understand the heart there, they understand magic and danger and heat and Death. . .

It's been a month since the new owners of the Gray house moved in. They are nice people, a Mom and a Dad and their twin sons, Caleb and Jake, aged two. They stopped in to see us once but only I was home and the mother, whose name is April, told me that I would have to come over sometime for dinner, and I could even take care of Caleb and Jake if I wanted to because she needed help and she would pay me well because they were 'rambunctious little tykes.' I smiled and said that was very nice of her and I would love to, if I could watch them in my house, and April laughed and said that was fine, but she expected me to come over and help her bake cookies someday all the same. I smiled but didn't say anything, and as they left I heard her mumble to her husband something about 'little girls too old for their age' and 'a girl needs a mother.' Maybe I shouldn't have told them my mother died and that my father was always working. I didn't mean to. It just came up. But clearly any one can see I'm growing up just fine.

I got my first story published in a literary magazine called The Crab Apple Review. It is a story about an artist who encounters the sublime. And lives. And lives. My English teacher saw me scribbling away at it when we were supposed to be writing a persuasive argument from Romeo or Juliet to their parents, and at first she was angry that I wasn't doing my work. She took it away from me and yelled at me in front of the class and gave me a new piece of paper and told me to do what I told her. I took the paper and started writing obediently, but I couldn't help but see she was reading *The Attic Room* during the rest of the period. When I went up to her after everyone else had left after class with what I had written in hand, she sat up very straight and asked if I had really written *The Attic Room* and I said yes. She told me she wanted to help me find an agent and that I should just continue letting my own spirit out, and then she grabbed the paper in my hand and threw it into the trash can and said I was to write whatever I wanted and she would work around it. I said, thank you, but can I get my paper from the trash. She laughed and said she would work around the curriculum, that I could forget about the persuasive argument from Romeo and Juliet. I said that was very kind, but that she had thrown away more of *The Attic Room* because I hadn't been writing about Romeo and Juliet at all. She looked surprised, then said of course, and I fished the paper out of the trash.

I will write. I will write and see the world and make my dreams come true. I will follow my life through its course and I will live it as fully as I can, and I will be open to ideas and experiences and wonder. I will wonder, and I will remember.

I saw Miss Clairborne the other day, but now she is named Mrs. Donald, which is an ugly name, but she is much prettier and seems much happier. Her hair falls past her shoulders now and she is pregnant with her second child, a little boy she and Mr. Donald want to name Michael Gabriel. I said that was a good name, that I was a writer and I knew a good name when I heard one. She smiled and said, really, so I was a writer now? And I said yes and told her about *The Attic Room* and the new idea for a novel I had and she looked a little worried and said I was awfully young to be tackling such things, but she knew I could do it and she would look for my name on the shelves. I told her not to bother. Oh? She said, why is that? Do you have a pen name picked out?

And I said, yes, yes I do.

Breinigsville, PA USA
25 March 2011
258451BV00002B/6/P